To JON,
MERRY XMAS '96
   CHEERS.!!
♡ TONI & AMANDA

P.S. We thought
this might be
appropriate - enjoy!!

EDITED BY
Matthew Condon and Richard Lawson

SmaSHeD
AuSTRaLiaN DRiNKiNG SToRiES

RaNDom HouSE

Random House Australia Pty Ltd
20 Alfred Street, Milsons Point, NSW 2061

Sydney   New York   Toronto
London   Auckland   Johannesburg
and agencies throughout the world

First published in 1996
Copyright © Richard Lawson and Matthew Condon
© in individual articles retained by individual contributors

National Library of Australia
Cataloguing-in-Publication Data

Condon, Matthew, 1962– .
Smashed : Australia drinking stories.

ISBN 0 09 1832527.

1. Drinking of alcoholic beverages–Australia–Fiction.
I. Lawson, Richard, 1960– . II. Title.

A823.308355

Design by Yolande Gray
Illustrations by Jeff Raglus
Typeset by Midland Typesetters, Maryborough
Printed by Griffin Paperbacks, Adelaide

CoNTentS

INTroduCTioN

I t would never have happened without the zebra. The
stuffed zebra mounted on the wall of the Safari Bar
in the Exchange Hotel, Balmain, Sydney. The zebra
we call Ralph.

It's not all of Ralph, of course. Not even Hemingway
mounted the whole hide and hooves. Just the head of Ralph.
And what a head. Tipped at a jaunty little angle, like he's
sitting at a bar, his felt hat next to a pack of Lucky Strikes.

1

The Frank Sinatra of Zebras. Cool ears. A trace of insect-nibbling around the mouth. A faint sheen of nicotine to his white stripes.

But if there was ever the perfect motif for drinking, it is Ralph. It's all in the eyes. The amber marbles of Ralph that gaze down on the patrons of the Safari Bar. The faraway look that makes you wonder. What is Ralph thinking? Is he contemplating the great questions of life? Or is he wondering what happened to his torso, legs and tail?

Not far from Ralph, in the Safari Bar, is a settee. It is covered in zebra skin. The zebra skin couch is just out of Ralph's vision so he doesn't have to worry if it's *his* skin or not. Then again, he may catch the occasional reflection of it in the beer fridge doors. Still, if it is Ralph's hide, it presents an interesting dynamic. Where else could you sit on the back of a zebra and admire its head across the other side of a room?

—Can you cut this waffle and get on with it? And I'll have a schoonie of VB while you're there.

—This isn't waffle. It's how this whole thing came about. *Smashed*. You know. The collection.

—You shouldn't bring Ralph into it. It may embarrass him. Ralph has feelings too. Look at the cigarette burns in his coat.

—You should never smoke on a zebra.

—Get on with it.

We met at the Safari Bar. It was summer. We played pool. As a team we find we perform best with Phil Collins playing in the background. We hear Phil and we think of those clean, bald balls. We have been unable to figure out the connection.

—You really can never get enough of Phil Collins, can you?

We drank a number of schooners of beer and then

shifted onto the next plain. Bourbon. The great wide open plain of bourbon for great, wide open drinkers. The sort of plain Ralph would have galloped freely across in his pre-stuffed days. How could he have known, his hoofs clipping across the baked earth of an African plain, that his head would end up in a small bar in Sydney, Australia?

—Leave Ralph out of it.

We discussed great drinking stories, as drinkers who drink too much do. It is a way of getting into the saddle of bourbon. We were well and truly mounted after a few shots and our spurs were glinting. So many stories. Believable yet unbelievable, like the one that became 'On Jungle Juice'. How could they have drunk formaldehyde?

—Don't give too much away.

—Sorry.

And it comes to us, out of the blue. Why not a collection of great Australian drinking stories from great Australian writers? Not just your average tales from braggarts, your volume-of-alcohol yarns—the sort that Ralph hears all the time. But something more. Something about the plains that we all ride across after a few too many. The different landscapes we visit whilst drunk. The ones we pass through whilst getting drunk. The ones we find ourselves stuck in when we can't take another drop. Now that would be something.

—So would another bourbon. Easy on the ice. I always like to say that. 'Easy on the ice'. It sounds sophisticated. Depending on the sort of drink I take, I can be almost anywhere and anything. I can time travel. I can sip on a Sidecar and be back in New York. In a tuxedo. At my favourite table at the Stork Club, with a dame. Yes. Easy on the ice.

—I like 'twist of lemon'.

—Why doesn't that surprise me?

—T-w-i-s-t o-f l-e-m-o-n.

—Get on with it.

Not only the strange plains—the other-worlds of drinking—but the psychological states. Doing things you would never dream of doing if you weren't drunk. The things you say that you would never say otherwise. The words you throw around, having never uttered those words before. The courage you develop, or the cowardice. The aggression that rises in you. The affection you hand out to strangers. The entanglements you initiate. The faraway looks you end up with.

—Like Ralph.

—I thought you wanted to keep him out of it?

—He's looking more attractive by the minute. No more ice, thank you. I have elegant sufficiency in the ice department.

—I'm surprised you can even say elegant sufficiency with such elegant sufficiency.

—It's the way I am. I am a Pygmalion drinker. I get more refined the more I consume.

The response to the idea was, in short, remarkable. Either there are a lot of writers out there who drink a lot, or a lot of drinkers who write a lot. Perhaps it's best to return to the master chronicler of the Australian drinking ethos, Henry Lawson, who wrote in a letter to the *Bulletin* magazine, circa 1903. To paraphrase Henry: 'I get drunk because I'm in trouble, and I get drunk because I've got out of it. I got drunk because I was rejected; and I got awfully drunk the night I was accepted. I get drunk because I had a row last night and made a fool of myself and it worries me, and when things are fixed up I get drunk to celebrate it.'

—Now there was a drinker. Have you seen his grave?

—No, I haven't.

—Very long and narrow, for a grave. The drink'll do it to you.

—It killed him, the drink.

—It made him.

—Pardon?

—He had to write to earn the shillings to buy the drink, didn't he?

—I guess.

—Keep Ralph out of this.

—I didn't mention Ralph.

—Oh.

So who do you pick for the collection without offending their sensibilities? By merely asking them to come to the club of the anthology, to pull up a chair and order their favourite snifter, are you branding them potential drunks? Hey, I hear you can put it away pretty well, how about being in *Smashed*? They certainly rushed the doors. Look at Carmel Bird. Hardly touches the stuff, yet presents to the bar an eloquent tale about cider, life, death, the works.

—You can always trust a cider drinker.

Frank Moorhouse. His prose as delicious as the olive in the martini, as the shape of the martini glass itself. Barry Dickins. The Keith Richards of Australian letters.

—And better looking.

—Cheers to that.

Peta Spear on imaginative uses for an empty beer bottle. John Birmingham and the Tasmanian Babes. Phew. Gretel

Killeen. You'd like to have *her* representing you in court on a drink driving charge. Any day. Luke Davies. Definitely a sting-in-the-tail beer chaser sort of guy. Venero Armanno. You'd like a crate of what *that* guy drinks. Nick Earls. Who hasn't pulled up a bar stool with Nick at some stage in their lives?

—You got that right. I remember I was in a similar position behind the Vic Walsh Memorial Oval in 1974.

—I think Ralph just yawned. May I continue?

Max Cullen. An actor who drinks too much and writes or a writer who acts too much and drinks? Margaret McClusky. Tough drinking boots there. Christopher Cyrill, a poet awash in liquor. Tim Baker. Anyone who drinks absinthe *and* sees Salvador Dali in the foggy aftermath must be fairly serious about his craft. Of drinking *and* writing. We could go on.

—Please do. While I wait for the ice bucket.

—We've finished half the bottle already?

—There will always be other bottles. By the way, I have a theory.

—Please proceed.

—Bourbon is an interesting drink. If you take wine, for example, a good bottle may change on the palate two or three times in the course of drinking.

—Granted.

—But bourbon. Bourbon changes *you* several times in the course of an evening, while it remains constant.

—That's the dumbest theory I ever heard.

—I'd expect that, from a 'twist of lemon' man.

Leonie Stevens. Ben Widdicombe. Robbie Lappan.

Introduction

Anyone who can write successfully about brandy can write about anything.

—I'll drink to that.

—And you will.

—I just have.

Mandy Sayer. Terry Serio. Jose Borghino. Emma Tom. Rosie Scott. Christos Tsiolkas. Candace Sutton. David Ireland. Tim Moltmann. Jean Bedford. Rosemary Creswell. Susan Errington. Barbara Wels. Need I go on?

—We started all this? Here? Under Ralph in the Safari Bar?

—You bet.

—It is a veritable liquor cabinet of delights.

—You feel dizzy just reading them. I like to think of each story as a single shot in a nice, thick and heavy shot glass.

—That's very nice.

—I like to think that the reader, on approaching this anthology, is the same as a person walking into a bar on a Friday night. The working week is over. You're dressed up in your finest. The bar is crowded and it's smoky and the shelves behind the bar are lined with bottles, their contents glittering like jewels.

—I firmly believe you should be banned from speaking after a half-bottle of bourbon.

—Thank you so much.

—It's a pleasure.

—Did you say ssspleasure?

—I said no such thing, as Ralph is my witness.

And just as there are many people who visit this bar, the anthology, *Smashed*, so too have the writers presented a multitude of responses to the question of alcohol and overindulgence. The stories on our top shelf will attest to this. There is love and violence. There is alcohol as a saviour and alcohol as a sinner. There is tragedy and triumph. There are hangovers and cures.

—When you've finished your philosophising, may I speak?

—Go ahead.

—Is it distinctly Australian, this bar of a book, as you like to call it?

—Did you say Shhtraylian?

—Ansher the question. And quickly. The bottle is almost empty.

It is and it isn't. It seems we are not the beer-swilling yobs we like to picture ourselves as. Certainly there are drinking forums in Australian backyards, loungerooms and pubs. But some of our characters find themselves stonkered in restaurants in India, behind the wheel of BMWs in central London, eye to eye with bulls in Spain. If anything, *Smashed* reveals a very cosmopolitan drinkership.

—Drinkership?

—I just made that up.

—It is your right, as we approach the end of the bottle.

It seems the alcohol question is, too, far more complex than we initially presumed. It can open windows to the heart, to the mind, to the soul. It can bring on romance or destroy it. It can make you happy or sad. It can end in a kiss, or a knife in the chest. Anything can, from the Fluffy Duck to the whisky sour to the bottle of Pale Dinner Ale.

—You shouldn't have mentioned Fluffy Duck.

—I'm sorry.

—Mentioning Fluffy Duck has almost ruined my evening.

You have tarnished the spirit of the bottle. Here, finish it off.

—Much appreciated.

—Ssspleasure.

—Shall we have another?

—Can I get back to you on that? I just realised I actually did say ssssspleasure.

—Sssssokay.

—Sssankyou.

Ralph the Zebra continues to look down, this patron saint of the drinkers in the Safari Bar. And as we contemplate ordering another bottle, staring ahead into the jewels behind the bar, the ruby and emerald and amber and gold contents of those beautiful bottles, we cannot see it, but we look exactly like the animal's head mounted on the wall.

—Here's to the glass eyes in all of us.

—Cheers.

—Barman? Another, if you please.

Matthew Condon & Richard Lawson
June, 1996

Henry Lawson

FoReWoRd

Dear Bulletin,

I'm awfully surprised to find myself sober. And, being sober, I take up my pen to write a few lines, hoping they will find you as well as I am at present. I want to know a few things. In the first place: Why does a man get drunk? There seems to be no excuse for it. I get drunk because I'm in trouble, and I get drunk because I've got out of it. I get drunk because I am sick, or have corns, or the toothache: and I get drunk because I'm feeling well and grand. I got drunk because I was rejected; and I got awfully drunk the night I was accepted. And, mind you, I don't like to get drunk at all, because I don't enjoy it much, and suffer hell afterwards. I'm always far better and happier when I'm sober, and tea tastes better than beer. But I get drunk. I get drunk when I feel that I want a drink, and I get drunk when I don't. I get drunk because I had a row last night and made a fool of myself and it worries me, and when things are fixed up I get drunk to celebrate it. And, mind you, I've got no craving for drink. I get drunk because I'm frightened about things, and because I don't care a damn. Because I'm hard up and because I'm flush. And, somehow, I seem to have better luck when I'm drunk. I don't think the mystery of drunkenness will ever be explained—until all things are explained, and that will be never. A friend says that we don't drink to feel happier, but to feel less miserable. But *I* don't feel miserable when I'm straight. Perhaps I'm not perfectly sober right now, after all. I'll go and get a drink, and write again later.

Letter to the Bulletin (1903)

Frank Moorhouse

MaRTiNi

He mixed the martini in the jug, stirring with studied performance. 'Always stirred never shaken,' he told her.

'I've never drunk a martini in my life.' She made it sound as if she were now fifty and had astoundingly missed the martini. Instead, she was seventeen and with no reason to have tasted a martini. 'We can pretend we are in New York.'

'Paris. It was actually invented by a Frenchman.'

'All right. If you like you can be in Paris and I'll be in New York. I really want to be in New York.'

'That'd be no fun.'

'We could call each other from those night-club table telephones.'

'I like to know the vermouth is there,' he said, scholastically, sniffing the jug for the vermouth, 'many don't. The great martini drinkers just want the gin mixed with mystique. Let the beam of light pass through the vermouth bottle and strike the gin—that was sufficient, sayeth Luis Buñuel.'

'Who is Luis Buñuel again? I know you told me once.'

'Buñuel is a Spanish film director. When we are in Spain we'll go ...'

'... *Belle de Jour*! Right?'

'Correct. I took you to see it in some town in Victoria.'

'What I remember is you at the motel afterwards.' She giggled.

'When we go to Spain we'll go to Buñuel's birthplace.'

'You made me take money from you.'

'Aragon.'

'You showed me how a whore does it. And why do we have to go to people's birthplaces?'

He hadn't answered that question before. 'You're too questioning. You go to see where the magic started. You go to see if you can be touched by the magic. To see if there is any left.'

He carefully carried the brimful martinis to her on the balcony of the beach house.

'You're incredible,' she said, taking her martini, 'you've even brought along the proper glasses. I know they're martini glasses, that much I do know.'

'The glass is half the drink.'

'As you always say.'

Was he beginning to repeat himself?

He looked out at the sea in which he'd swum as a boy. 'I've never made love to anyone here in my home town—you are the first. That's unbelievable in a way, given that I lived here until I was seventeen, your age ...'

'I'm eighteen now—you keep forgetting.'

'Sorry. But it took me to this age, well, getting towards forty, to have sex in the place where I was born. Says something.' He tried to muse on this but nothing occurred to him.

'What does it say?'

'I don't know yet.'

'Was it different?'

He kissed her fingers, one still slightly pen-calloused from her schooling. 'It's always different with you.'

'No slimy answers,' she said, 'tell me how it was different. I want to know.'

'Did the earth move?'

'Don't make fun of me. Tell me.'

'Different because of "formative circuits",' he teased. 'Do you want me to say things like that?'

'Whatever screwing circuits. Tell me!'

'I think you seek poetry.' He couldn't tell her now. 'I'll tell you when I've worked it out. I'll write a sonnet.'

It was different because he was getting emotional cross-tunings. He was making the cross-tunings.

'Another thing,' he said, 'is that it's my parents' home. Or at least their beach house. Which will do.'

'Will do what?'

She bridled when she sensed he was using the conversation to talk to himself.

'Well there is always, you know, the mother, always the mother, if it's not the bed where I was conceived, it's near enough.'

'Yuck,' she moved swiftly away from that. 'It's a beautiful drink. I could become really hooked on martinis. But what do you do with the olive, do you eat it at the beginning or the end of the drink or is it just a ... garnish or what?'

Garnish, nice word.

'That's a personal preference. It's useful to play with during conversation. You can prick it with the toothpick and the olive oil seeps out.' He did it. 'See, the olive oil comes into the drink.'

'The olive on the toothpick gives the drink an axis.'

Yes, she was right.

She pricked her olive.

But regardless of the cross-tunings he was getting, seeking, he wanted also to imprint at the very same time a uniqueness onto their experience. To mark her off from his crowded personal history. He had used up so much—she couldn't be his first, well, first anything just about, not first love, first wife, nor first adultery, not even his first seventeen-year-old—and he couldn't give her any of the body's six or seven significant virginities, although at seventeen—eighteen—she seemed also to have exhausted most of these herself. Well, not all. And some she had given him. And they did share one or two sensual firsts of the minor scale. He supposed he was trying to consecrate their experience by bringing her to his home territory, the aura of kin if not kin. Into the family beach home—almost home—if not a bride then as someone in her own significant category. He wanted to rank her equal with love if not *as love*. He couldn't tell her this yet.

'The olive is like leaking radioactivity,' she said. She was preoccupied with nuclear war but not as an issue—more as a macabre firework or as a sort of video game.

'I'll give you a twist of lemon next,' he said, 'that's the other classic garnish.'

She moved against him, began to arouse him, but he was in another mood, and said, 'I thought this was the cocktail hour.'

'I want to get rid of that sad look you have.'

'I'm not sad.'

But cross-tunings were coming in across the sea from his youthful marriage to a girl from his home town (although they'd never had sex in their home town—except for some vaguely recalled, fumbled caressing on a river rock in bushland, a 'fully dressed rehearsal', which he chose not to count). And a crude, bizarre ejaculation in a classroom late one afternoon—but no entry. The cross-tunings were entries of ill-handled love, their artless fumbled living ...

In the sedate lounge of the Windsor he called the waiter. 'This martini is too warm, we asked for it very cold and very dry. It is neither.'

He was relieved that at twenty he had got the complaint out, slowly, and with some force.

'Yes sir.' The waiter went to take their drinks away.

'Leave mine,' Robyn said. 'Mine's all right.' She put her hand out over the drink.

'Yes madam.' The waiter took only his drink. 'I'll bring a fresh martini, sir.'

The waiter moved away.

'You are a pain in the arse sometimes,' his wife said.

'I thought you were big on consumer rights. Waiter!'

The waiter turned and came back to the table. 'Take my wife's martini also—we'll both have a fresh one.'

'Yes sir.'

She let the waiter take the drink this time.

'You give me the shits,' she said.

'So much for our second anniversary.'

'Fighting with waiters isn't my idea of a good time. It's alcohol, isn't it? I thought that was all you cared about.'

He knew he'd complained as a way of getting at her. He didn't really care about the martini.

He wanted to be in New York drinking martinis in Costello's bar with Thurber. With the sophisticated Louise.

'I wish I was in New York. In Costello's, only the Americans know how to mix a martini.'

'What would you know about Costello's or New York?'

'Travel isn't the only way of knowing.'

'The martini was invented by a Frenchman, anyhow.'

'Crap.'

'Have it your own way, I read it in *Origin of Everything*.'

'Crap.'

'And stop big-noting yourself,' she went on, 'you're just a country boy—you've drunk only one martini before in your whole life. You get it all from Scott Fitzgerald and you get it wrong.'

He remained silent, stung, taking balm from a private relishing of a secret score against her—that on the day before they'd left on their anniversary trip to Melbourne he'd drunk martinis in bed with Louise.

He reached across to take her hand, reversing the mood to place her at a disadvantage, gaining himself virtue for making the move to heal the mood while at the same time continuing to relish Louise.

'I'm sorry,' she said, taking the blame onto herself.

'We don't have to stay the country boy and girl all our lives.'

'I'm quite happy to be the country girl,' she said, quietly . . .

'Stirred never shaken,' Louise said, putting a finger on his nose to emphasise her point, stopping him with her other hand.

He'd been doing an American bartender act with the cocktail shaker, Louise being the first person he'd known to own a cocktail shaker.

'That's how I've seen it done in American movies.'

Louise laughed. 'You have been going to the wrong movies. There are some cocktails we do that way, my love, but not the martini, never the martini.'

'That's how we do them in my home town,' he said, trying to joke over his naivety.

'I'd believe that.'

He put the shaker down and removed the top and looked into it, 'They seem all right, they haven't exploded.'

'They'll be bruised,' she laughed, 'or at least that's what an aficionado would say.'

'Should I throw them away and start again?'

'No—I'm sure we can drink them with impunity—and I have an idea.'

He stopped himself asking who the aficionados were.

He began to pour them but Louise again stopped him. 'Tch, tch,' taking away the wine glasses he'd taken out and bringing back martini glasses, 'a classic drink demands a classic glass. And my idea is that we take the martinis to the bedroom and watch the sun set over the city.'

She led him to her bedroom, he slightly trembling with desire, the martini slightly spilling.

Looking out on the city at dusk from her bed he felt regret that he should need to be doing this against his young wife, felt the abrasion of his spirit. But it was numbed away with the lust for Louise, Louise who had the skills of living and such completeness.

'What's wrong, love—guilt?' Louise asked.

'No,' he lied ...

'What's the matter?' he turned over in bed to face the question from his seventeen-year-old—eighteen-year-old—girlfriend.

'Memories spooking about,' he said.

'But you said you hadn't brought anyone else here.'

'That's true,' he said, putting a hand to her face, 'but the heart is a hotel.'

He reached over and took his martini from beside the bed and finished it.

Where had his young wife learned about the origins of the martini back then? He had looked in the book *The Origins of Everything*, she hadn't got it from there.

'I don't want you thinking of other women while you are sexing on with me.'

He smiled. 'They have their rights.'

She rolled on to him and began to arouse him again.

'Mix another drink,' he said, 'first.'

She left the bed and went into the bar, her naked, youthful grace tightened his heart. She looked into the cocktail jug.

'There's some left,' she said.

'It'll be mainly melted ice.'

He was taking from her the flavours of young, first love. She was trying out her own explorations.

'I'll make a new lot, tell me how,' she called.

He was collecting pleasures not taken when he'd been seventeen. He was taking also perhaps the last taste of pure youth.

The first martini, though, had honoured his ex-wife and Louise. This next one would be theirs.

'One part vermouth, five parts gin,' he called back to her, 'some would argue—but that's my mix now.'

Carmel Bird

Why Breezy McCarthy Drank the Cider

Y ou'd have to say Breezy McCarthy was a slut—well,
a bit of a slut anyhow. Good-time girl, fast. Breezy
was fast.

This is the story of how Breezy came to drink the cider
that Maris Joyce and I were making in a cupboard at the
back of the locker room at school.

French was taught by Sister Apollonia, a little old nun
with shaky hands, enormous teeth and a few white whiskers,

whose accent was flat and Australian, but whose love for all things French was a great inspiration. It was the chapter on Normandy, on the manufacture of cider, that gave me and Maris the idea. We consulted an encyclopaedia for the finer details: 'In small fermentations it is usual to start things off with a little brewer's yeast ... A tub can be placed underneath to collect the yeasty froth which works out of the bunghole, and the cask must be topped up to keep it full and to allow the scum to overflow.' I rather admired the phrase 'allow the scum to overflow'. And another: 'If the fermentation is tumultuous ... ' There was a recipe for cider cup, and we longed for the day when we could combine our cider with sherry and mint leaves and sugar and cucumber and soda water. Cider cup. Sophisticated. If the fermentation is tumultuous ... Allow the scum to overflow.

The making of cider is done in three processes. The apples are ground into a pulp, called the pomace; the juice is squeezed out by a press; then the juice is fermented. You can pound a few apples at a time, using a heavy hardwood bruiser. (We had a mallet.) The pulp is spread eight centimetres deep on a cloth which is then folded over the pulp. More cloth is placed on top and the process is repeated several times until a 'cheese' is made. This cheese is then pressed, standing in a tub which catches the juice. The juice is then run into a wooden cask where it ferments with the aid of brewer's yeast and honey and flour suspended in a little bag. When fermentation ceases and the liquid shows signs of clearing, the cider is run into a clean cask and stored in a cool place.

Our cider never showed any signs of clearing. It was

stuck in the first wooden cask (which was in fact a wooden money-box) complete with brewer's yeast and flour and honey in a little bag, and it turned to poison.

Over the weeks the cider grew thick and black, and was streaked with fine threads like a sort of furry cotton. It bubbled quietly on the surface, developing a particular type of silvery scum, a dark, purple and sinister experiment. A witch's brew. You could detect the smell of apples and decay and something else as soon as you walked into the locker room. We would have just thrown it out in the end, but one day Breezy came and asked me if she could taste it. She had heard we were making cider in the cupboard, she said, and she was a fairly experienced drinker. She would taste it for us and tell us what she thought. I imagined she was joking. From her blazer pocket she took a small silver tumbler, big enough for a shot of whisky.

Maris and I just stood there like idiots while Breezy filled her tumbler about six times and tossed down the cider, fast. She didn't make a face, didn't turn a hair.

'You girls,' she said, 'you don't know the first thing about making cider, do you? You ought to talk to Mex. He makes gin. He'd put you right on your piss-ant cider.' She laughed. She put her tumbler back in her pocket and flounced out of the locker room. I dipped my finger in the cider and tasted it. Maris did the same. It was revolting beyond belief. We stared at each other, stared after Breezy. What a girl!

Breezy McCarthy, good-time girl, fast girl, slut, was a sort of widgie, if that word from the fifties still has any meaning. This was a time when there were gangs of bodgies and widgies that hung out on street corners and struck a kind of fascinated terror into the hearts of decent people. Breezy went around on the weekend in full-circle skirts that reached just below the knee, and that were puffed out with yards and yards of white rope petticoats mixed up with scarlet taffeta. So you got this nifty little redhead with long skinny legs, mesh stockings, black suede flatties (very down-at-heel), full black skirt with the red and white rope and stuff underneath, bare midriff, little pink top and a very great deal of make-up. Of course she looked different in school uniform, but even then you could tell she was a bit of a slut. She hitched her tunic up to show off her legs. Such as they were. Her ears, of course, were pierced and she wore little silver rings. In those days such ornaments were seen only on Italian girls. Or girls like Breezy McCarthy. She would get, people said, her comeuppance. It was a small town. Big country. Australia in the fifties.

The main boyfriend was Mex—baby-faced Mex with the high wave of black hair, gleaming with oil, Brylcream I suppose, sweeping up off his forehead. Maybe his name was really Max, but he was called Mex, rhymed with sex. Breezy's name was Bridget, but even the nuns called her Breezy. Mex worked for a car mechanic, always smelt of oil and grease, and he rode a loud black motor bike, a BSA, on the back of which you would often find Breezy. (Never mind that her sister Madeleine was killed on the back of a motor bike in 1957.) They chewed gum and drank hospital brandy. They smoked. And Breezy's voice was highly over-cultured by her strict attention to the elocution lessons we got from the nuns.

Once I had a dance with Mex and I nearly fainted from excitement when he pressed himself hard up against me so I could feel his cock. Breezy noticed all this and came and took him out of my grasp. Came spinning across the dance floor with all her rope petticoats frothing away under her skirt. She stood behind Mex and put her hands over his eyes and he let me go, dropped me like a hot potato, and went off with Breezy. Then to the beat of Bill Haley and his Comets he threw Breezy between his legs and then over his head and carried her out the door. We believed she never wore underpants. Breezy had been doing it with boys for years and years.

So it was no surprise to anybody when Breezy and Mex had a shotgun wedding. It was quite a fancy affair, a nuptial mass in the little weatherboard church on the corner. The McCarthys had tickets on themselves, and knew how to throw a party and hold their heads up. But in fact Breezy wasn't as sure of herself as she pretended to be. She was very young to be getting married, and she was scared— scared of having a baby, scared of being stuck with Mex for the rest of her life, stuck in the old home town.

Six weeks before the wedding, she was rushed to hospital with violent stomach cramps and vomiting and diarrhoea. That was when the pregnancy was discovered. But of course Breezy knew about it already. They asked her what she had eaten, what she'd drunk, and she dobbed on me and Maris Joyce. She told Sister she had swigged the cider we were making in the cupboard in the locker room. Forget about Breezy and her problems—I thought *we* were going to be expelled. Sister told us that Breezy's life hung in the balance, and that the new life she was carrying (this was the first we had heard of it) was in terrible danger from our evil mischief. I remember the way she said that, with a kind of slow pleasure. Evil Mischief. And where had we got the recipe? And, Mother of God, *where* had we got the *idea*?

Dear little old Sister Apollonia was dragged in to give an account of the chapter in the French text book dealing with the manufacture of cider in Normandy, and thereafter that section of the book was banned. Never mind that this was the chapter where the use of the demonstrative adjective is consolidated; never mind that students would no longer have the opportunity to write a composition on the subject of the contrast between the character of the Provençal shepherd and that of the Norman peasant. Gone, the chance to translate into French: 'Let's go to the farm and see how they make the cider. Look at the ancient stone vat where the millstone turns, pulled round by Biquette, the old donkey. The great heap of apples rolls about in the vat as the millstone begins to turn slowly, crushing the beautiful apples under its weight, crushing them and reducing them to a thick brown paste.' (Let the paste ferment for twelve hours. Then into the oak press in the cellar where it gets squeezed, and squeezed and squeezed until the juice flows, 'sweet and thick', pure juice. The flavour of apples ripened in the summer sun is stored in the juice which is left to mature.) All this information became, because of our misdemeanour, our evil mischief, unavailable to the future students of Sister Apollonia.

Maris and I were marched to the locker room where the cupboard was opened, and we had to pull out all our paraphernalia and put it on the table. Sister stood silently while we did this, while we sobbed and shook with fear and shame. What if Breezy died? What if the baby died? The baby? Breezy was going to have a baby. This was perhaps the most terrifying part of all, for me anyhow. I felt I somehow participated in Breezy's sin and shame and ultimate disgrace. Supervised by Sister, Maris and I took everything out to the great incinerator at the bottom of the garden. It took three trips to carry it all, and the hellish symbolism of the incinerator was not lost on us. Afterwards Sister said she was going to speak to our parents, and she reminded us, with no apparent irony, that it takes only one rotten apple to ruin the crop. And we were that apple.

It was a while before I really worked out what all this was about: Breezy McCarthy figured that if she drank our powerful poisonous cider she would either lose the baby or else die. When I realised this, I wondered which she would have preferred. Really. Did Breezy want to die? Or just get rid of the baby? In any case, she gave up alcohol altogether after baby Colette was born. Took the pledge. People said that along with her teetotalism she went frigid. The marriage didn't last. And all the zing went out of Breezy until she took up serious drinking in her thirties and from then on it was downhill all the way.

Breezy McCarthy, good-time girl and slut, fizzed and sparkled for a moment some time between being a child and being an adult. And then, with one thing and another, life being what it is, she went flat. The episode with the cider was somehow a turning point. The rest was life in a small town in Australia in the fifties. Routine. And then some.

The memory of the little brown bag of flour and brewer's yeast and honey lingers. Tied up with string, dripping, slimy, grotesque, it lay on the table in the locker room as its juice seeped out of it.

The great heap of apples rolls about in the vat as the millstone begins to turn slowly, crushing the beautiful apples under its weight, crushing them and reducing them to a thick brown paste.

RoSCo

I t was Saturday mornin when the coppas rang bout me mum. Saturday or maybe Tuesday, cos I remember Jan's pension was just about due in so then again maybe it was a Friday.

Me an Jan was still in bed when the phone went off an I rumbled me way out to the lounge all limpy from the night before an picked up an said piss off we don't want none of ya shit.

An this chick with a real deep voice says what?

An I says is this anuvva one of them telemarketin pricks?

An this chick says nah mate, it's the coppas we bin tryin to call youse since 6.

That woke me up good an smart I can tell ya so I just laughed an said me an Jan we sleep as heavy as a-bombs, cos I dealt with blueys long enough to know just how to talk with em, and then this lady coppa says we got some bad news for ya Mr Davidson.

After that I reckon I was in shock or somethin cos I don't know how long I sat there next to the phone not watchin the telly not starin at nuthin. And after a bit Janny got up to go to the pisser an on the way back she saw me an said shit Rosco what's up.

Mum's bin messed up, some bastard messed me mum I said, me voice all quiet an rocky like the sides of the road before they seal it off against the elements.

An I told Janny what the lady coppa told me bout how me mum was lyin all messed up at the Base Hospital cos some bastards in combat gear an knitted heads'd cracked her one over the permanent wave while they was doin an armed robby on the values unna her bed.

Cracked her head open Janny I said, voice all roady again. Fuckin poofta bastards cracked open me mum's head.

An Janny she lit me up a Benny an wiped some shit off the side of me face an said settle Rosco, just youse settle, we'll go straight up the Base an pay your mum a visit.

But I was all black an dismal at the thought of it. I swear I coulda wept like a woman thinkin back over the number of times I told me mum not to leave her fuckin values unna the bed.

They just walked in an took it like they was takin cash outta a wall, I was sayin to Jan. What's the world comin to. What's the fucking world comin to.

Buck up Rosco, Jan was sayin. Buck up an we'll go straight up the Base. Youse can get inna ya good shirt, you know the one with the pockets it's clean I reckon an I'll get inna me church dress and we'll go straight up the Base and say hooray to ya mum.

An I looked up an looked over at Jan drinkin her first black instant of the day an smokin on her Benny with her hair all messy from the bed an I said you're a good egg Jan, you know that, you're a good egg.

Sunnyside up or no, Jan said an we both laughed an then Jan then said keep ya hands to yaself ya randy so an so, how youse can think about that at a time like this with me old enough to be ya mother meself.

But I just laughed again cos even though she was talkin serious the sides of her eyes was curvin upwards an the wrinkles on each side of her mouth were stretchin out sideways so she was smilin with the sides of her face an not just her lips.

Jan found her church dress but my blue shirt weren't nowhere either of us could see so it was a singlet or go streakin. You'd lose ya head if I didn't keep it screwed on for ya, Jan said as we went out the front door and started walkin down the bus stop.

But we didn't get more an halfway there before Janny stopped still an spun back round to face the house with a shit, fucking shit.

What, I says.

The lectric bed, she says. I've left the lectric bed on.

Well that's fucking great Janny, I says. That's just fucking great.

But by then I wasn't talkin to no-one cos Janny had gone racin back to the house with her thongs goin slap slap slap against the road like some kid coppin it.

All the good feelings I'd had about Janny back at the house went just then because I was thinkin how Janny'd bin crazy over that fuckin blanket ever since I won us all them lectrical goods in the raffle down the super.

The stupid thing was I won me an Janny more lectrical items than we knew what to do with—all still in the cardboard boxes an all. Big colour telly for the bedroom. Heap of kitchen shit with handles an spinnin blades. Even a lectric knife.

But all Janny was keen on was that fuckin blanket. Soon as I brought home the bacon she ripped the belly out of the bed, whacked it on and switched it on four which was the highest it'd go. Middle of summer. Middle of the fuckin arvo.

Novelty valued, that's all it is, novelty valued, I was tellin meself out in the loungeroom watching the old black an white telly in a sulk. I tried to concentrate on the box but all the while me head was sayin Rosco Davidson, that Janny'd rather lie with a lectrical bed than lie with you ya good for nothing old stink.

When me an Janny finally got ourselves up to the bus stop an up onto a 731 inna town Janny took off her sunnies to draw the usual black nightmares round her eyes so I says you feelin alright Janny.

An she says yeah fine.

That's orright then I says deliberately lookin out the window an actin cooler than cruises.

How come, Janny says after a minute.

How come what, I say.

How come ya said that?

Said what, I said.

Why'd you ask was I feelin orright, Janny says muckin up one of her eyes in her big quest to get to the bottom of Rosco Davidson.

So I say ohh, ohh I dunno Jan. You just look a bit sick is all. Bit tired maybe.

An that kept her shut up til town. Cos she knew I didn't mean tired. She knew I meant old.

Weren't no buses goin direct from our place to the Base so we got out outside Maccas in Rally Street an started walkin up the hill towards the Base an Christ I'm tellin you it was so fuckin hot each one of me legs felt like it was fulla boilin water an even Janny was sweatin so much that all the black shit unna her eyes was runnin ran down her cheeks makin her look older than ever.

So when we reached the Diggers Janny looked over at me with her eyes slippin down her cheeks like they were tryin to escape an she says just one drink hun, whattya reckon we go in for just one drink.

I was still huffy over the blanket so I pretended like I was doin her a huge favour, sayin well I really gotta get up this hill an see me mum Janny, specially since you've already run us late on account of the blanket.

But Janny she was starin into the dark an the cool of the pub sayin carn Rosco, carn.

So I said ok Janny, but no more than one schooner an it's straight up that hill.

Here's trouble, says Rachel from behind the silver tops when me and Janny walked in. An she winked at me cos me an Rach we used to have a thing a long while back before Janny an me. An Janny she saw the wink an says you feeling ok today Rach, you sure you're feelin ok cos you're not lookin well you know, Rach. But Rachel she's not as thick as some and she just looked straight at Janny and smiled big an wide with lips not wrinkles an said never been better luv, what'll it be then.

Me an Janny we ordered two schooners of brown when Rach said five dollars forty thanks an Janny goes for her purse an smacks her palm into her head an says shit Rosco, shit, we got no money, me pension aint in yet remember.

An I give Rach anuvva wink over the silver tops an pull the notes outta me back pocket an says lucky some of us know how to budget ay Rach.

Me an Janny weren't even halfway through the second schooners when Rach brought out the two plates of eggs an bacon. What's this, I said, starin at them eggs like I never seen eggs before in me life. What's all this then Rach.

New promotion Rach said. Everyone what orders a drink before eleven gets a free brekky.

An what's that then, Jan said pointin to a pile of green pubic mongrels on the side of the plates.

That'll be alfalfa, Rach said all high an mighty.

Alfullavit, more like Jan said when Rach went back behind the bar.

Waste of good bloody food, Rach said when she came back for the plates still full, but I couldn't say a thing because I was still pissin meself over the alfullavit.

After a while I dipped into me pocket to pay for anuvva round an all I found was a heap of white flakes that might've bin paper or a dole form, who could say? But they definitely weren't drinkin money that was for sure.

Carn Rach, I said. Pay youse back tomorrow I promise.

Piss off Rosco, Rach said. You illitrate as well as alcho? Sign says no fucking credit.

Town bike, I said to Jan outside when we were out in the sun again walking up the hill towards the Base an me mum. Town fucking bike.

Wish I had any fucking bike, Jan said startin to sweat again. This hill's as steep as a bastard.

We'd only walked about fifteen minutes at the most

when we passed the Canbra an this time it was me who said how about stoppin for just one more drink, just onna account of the heat and ya nerves an me mum.

We ain't got no money, Janny said. But I knew she wanted it as much as me.

Canbra's got efpos, I said. We can use ya cards an get some cash out of efpos.

An what's gunna happen when the government cashes the cheque for the rent an it bounces, Janny said. But I knew, I knew Janny wanted it as much as me.

Fuckin technology, I said to the bloke behind the bar at the Canbra. Where'd we be without it, ay. But he was a dismal cunt, all dressed up inna white shirt with a black tie in the middle of the day if you can believe that, so I decided he could talk to the taps for all I cared.

Janny an I drank for while without sayin much after that. That was one of the good things about Janny. You could sit with her over a couple of browns an not feel the need to make some smartarse conversation about this or that just to fill up the gaps.

We just sat in the dark corner next to the jukey, her twistin a piece of hair round her finger an me thinkin about me mum.

Guess we should get goin again soon ay, I said after a bit.

Guess we should said Jan.

An then a few beers later. You ready to make a move hun.

Course hun, Jan said wipin her mouth with the back of

her hand. I'll just go to the little ladies room an put me face on so I look nice for ya mum.

Right you are then Janny, I said. I'll just go get us two last beers for the road.

An then a bit more time went by an Janny still hadn't come outta the little ladies so I polished off me beer an polished off hers as well so by the time she finally came back I'd bought us anuvva two browns just to pass the time.

An by then I don't mind tellin ya I was startin to feel real good, real good within meself. The young pup behind the bar looked like a real good bloke and the other drinkers all looked like good blokes an even the sheilas looked like good blokes, an then when Janny walked outta the door of the little ladies with her face on I just had to stop an stare.

Youse look like somethin off the telly, I said to Janny. And it was true. She'd done herself up so nice an right you could of taken her anywhere. All her hair was packed up on the top of her head with stringing bits hanging down round her eyes just like somethin off the box.

I whistled under me breath as Janny sat down back at the table an then I said what's a nice young thing like youse doin round a shit heap like this.

Youse mind ya mouth, Janny said back, playin hard to guess.

Why don't youse sit down here with me little girl, I said, playin along with her game. I won't do nothin you don't want me to.

An so Janny sat right down hard on me with one leg

this way an one leg that way so I could feel meself gettin up beneath her good church dress.

An I ran me hand up an down the inside of her legs where her thighs sat nice an wide an soft an meltin all over me, skin smellin warm like a cat that's bin lyin out in the sun.

Don't youse start anythin ya can't finish. Janny said, lookin down at me through all the black an blue of her eyes.

Oh I can finish it alright, I said runnin me hand up even further an gettin the shock of me life when it runs straight into her bush.

What's this then, I said, gettin more an more worked up. What's all this then little girl.

Youse know what it is, Jan said rollin her hips over me busy fingers.

Yeah but I want youse to tell me, I said real quiet into her ear the way chicks are always after. I want youse to tell me.

That's me cunt Rosco, she said back, real quiet. That's me cunt you got there Rosco.

I want youse to tell me what I'm doing with this cunt of yours Janny.

You know what ya doin ya perve.

But I want youse to say it, I wanna hear youse say it Janny.

As it turned out I didn't get to hear Janny say nothin cos that's when I felt someone grabbin me arms real hard from behind.

Janny jumped back fast an I just got to see a flash of

her frenchie before the poofta behind the bar span me round an asked what the fuck we thought we was doin.

Janny was still between me knees but squashed backward into the wall an that poofta from the bar had one hand up round me neck so I was completely mobilised.

What the fuck didja think youse were doin, the poofta said. An that's when I realised he wasn't just a poof he was a wog poof cos the stink of garlic was about to make me bring up me browns all over his white shirt.

Tell me what the fuck youse sick cunts thought youse were doin, he said, real nasty. I wanna hear youse say it.

Youse were thinkin of stickin ya filthy old cock inta this weren't ya sonny, the poofta said liftin up the front of Janny's good church dress so youse could see her bush an the mole next to her bush an even the thin blue vein that ran down the inside of her leg like a missed piss.

You're a filthy old cradle snatcha you are, the poofta said to Jan grabbin the front of her bush between his fingers like you'd grab someone's chin to force em to listen to ya.

An you're a fuckin mutha fucker he said to me. A filthy stinkin mutha fucker.

Me an Janny didn't say too much walkin up the hill after that one. Her face real hard like it was in all the photos of her married before she met me.

Youse got lipstick on ya teeth luv, I said, but when I stuck me hand over to wipe it off she pushed me away, all hard an steely an fuck off Rosco.

Not far to go now Janny, I said, an I wasn't even lyin to

make her feel better. Youse could see the big palm trees out the front of the hospital in the distance an the sun was settin behind it so the sky was all fulla colours.

Weather turned out orright after all, Janny, I said. Think there's bin a souverly change I reckon. Might even get chilly enough for the blanket tonight, what do ya reckon Janny.

But when I looked over at her there was two big tears drippin down her face.

Carn Jan don't youse cry on me now. Janny youse know how much I hate to see ya cry lovie. If youse can't stop for me then stop for me mum. We're almost there ya know luv an she's not gonna wanna see youse bin cryin.

But that just made her cry even more and I thought jees, fuckin women.

We was about to reach the start of the long driveway up to the Base when I suggested we stop off at the back bar of the Servos at the foot of the hospital drive, just until Janny got her shit together.

But we aint got no money Rosco, Janny said cryin harder an harder by the minute.

That's where you're wrong Janny, I said smilin an laughin like the total prick I was. An that's when I pulled out the Canbra poofta's brown leather wallet outta me back pocket.

Your pockets are fulla surprises today Rosco, Janny said kind of cold, but I could see she couldn't get enough of the sight of those notes fannin backwards an forwards in the sunset.

Servos was more crowded than the other two bars cos the day was gettin on and a heap of Daves an Stewies from round the town were finishin up their day jobs an droppin off for a creamin brown an a chew of the fat with the other bastards.

An even though me an Janny had more than enuf money to keep us in browns for the rest of the night it made me feel kinda dismal watchin all those bastards slappin each other over the shoulders an sayin gotta get back to that missus soon or I'll know about it.

Me an Janny didn't say nothin at all. She just stared inna her brown while I stared up at the footy on the box.

Fuckin idiot I said after a bit. Fuckin lazy bastard just dropped the fuckin ball for the second time in a row can youse believe that Janny.

But Janny didn't say nothin.

Janny, I said louder than before, I said can youse fuckin believe that.

What? she said. What was that Rosco?

Oh nuthin. Nuthin at all. I should've known better than to think you'd have the time of day for my interests Janny. Should've known much fuckin better.

More an more people were packin inna the Servos an it was gettin harder an harder to push ya way through to get a drink.

So I was right on top of Bretty Smythes an the girl in the white dress before I knew what'd hit me.

I tried to pretend I didn't see him but I could barely move for all the Daves an Stewies pressurin me from every direction an next thing I knew it was hands shakin an Rosco old boy how are ya have ya met Michelle we're engaged ya know an how ya bin keepin Rosco old boy haven't seen that much of ya since school, where ya bin hiding yaself Rosco boy, how come youse don't come out with the rest of us no more Rosco youse still playin footy Rosco an did I tell ya Michelle she's a teacher Rosco fancy that would ya Rosco fancy me gettin hitched an straightened out by a good woman Rosco old boy.

For the life of me I can't remember what I said back to Bretty Smythes but when I think back I can still see the look in Michelle's face as she reached out to shake me hand an how when she got hers back she wiped it on her little white dress so it left a streak of grease right down the side.

Michelle she wants a white weddin, Bretty was sayin, an I don't think there's anythin wrong with tradition you know Rosco, an Michelle was smilin up at him with her little white teeth all in neat little rows an I was thinkin I gotta go I gotta get outta here an that's when Janny crabbed her way through the crowd and leaned up against me sayin aren't ya gunna introduce me to ya friends Rosco an I could see Michelle watchin the way she was swingin backwards an forwards like there was a great big wind blowing through the Servos an Janny was the only one what could feel it.

Love to stay an all, but we really gotta go I was sayin to Bretty all the time pullin at Janny who was sayin nah Rosco, let fuckin go of me Rosco I wann anuvva drink Rosco, youse promised me anuvva fuckin drink. An outside the Servos I whacked her one across the face on account of her bad language an on account of her embarrassin me in front of me friends an on account of her showin no interest in me footy interests an why the fuck carnt ya shave unna ya arms when ya wear that dress ya ugly old bitch.

Janny started runnin off down the hill away from the Base an I yelled fuck ya Janny, fuck ya, but she kept walkin an runnin an stumblin back towards our joint with me walkin an runnin an swearin after her until eventually we're back on the front porch openin up the front door.

Jees I need a fuckin drink, Janny said like there was nuthin weird about the two of us runnin home through the dark like that.

An Janny she started tearin the place up, pullin out the casks proppin up the lounge an the casks proppin up the table an even the casks proppin up the telly.

What the fuck you up to? I said. Youse know they're all empties.

Yeah well your pockets aren't the only ones with surprises, Janny said all slurry. An after pullin out an shakin up 20 maybe 30 of our old empties she finally stood there holdin up a box of mossy in both hands an I could tell by the way the muscles were poppin out on each of her arms that they weren't empties at all.

Janny turned on the telly an sat down on the couch dippin in all directions cos all the casks had been moved an started in on her rainy day mossy, drinkin it outta her I Love Trouble mug without the handle.

I knew better than to think she'd offer me anythin after what'd gone down at the pub an I knew if I moved too fast she might get the shits all over again so I started up a conversation about some television bastard or anuvva while I picked up the closest mug I could find.

I could tell by lookin out the corner of me eyes that the mug was the same one Janny'd been drinkin her black instant out of that mornin an I could tell from the feel that there was still some of the black stuff inside but I was so dirt keen to get a bit of that mossy without Janny chuckin a wobbly that I went right on ahead an poured me a mugful anyhow.

Taste good Rosco? Jan said, that's a real class drink you got there.

Just fine, I said, an drank the lot down in one go then poured me anuvva just to show her.

After a while I realised I wasn't feelin too hot, not too hot at all. Then all of a sudden on comes that advert for the black instant where the mum an the son share a cuppa together an all of a sudden the sickness wasn't just down in me belly it was up in me chest too.

Shit I said.

What said Jan.

Oh shit Janny.

What.

I didn't go see me mum Janny.

Yeah well what's done is done an it's too late now Rosco.

But Janny I said (an now I was feelin so sick I had to hold a hand round me gut when I spoke), but Janny; she's lyin up in the Base with her head all crushed in waitin for her only son.

46

Listen Rosco, Janny said, an I could tell she wasn't really payin me that much attention cos she was changing channels as she was talkin. Youse just settle an we'll go up to the Base inna morning. We'll find ya blue shirt an I'll hang me church dress up tonight an we'll go up in the mornin.

Hold on, I said, forgettin what the hell I was sayin thanks to Janny changin the channels back an forth. Go back two. I wanna watch the footy.

Yeah well I wanna watch the movie, Janny said.

Well I'm afraid that's just too fuckin bad, I said pushin her outta the way. Some girls have a bit of respect for their blokes' interests Janny. A bit of fuckin respect.

Have it your way then, Janny said, picken up the second full cask of mossy. I'll watch the telly in the bedroom then.

That really pissed me off I can tell ya. It wasn't that I'd forgotten about the new bedroom telly. Sometimes it just slipped me mind that's all.

I heard her turn the light on in that bedroom then I heard her trip over somethin an swear an then I heard her settlin back with the new black remote in front of that great big square while I sat all alone on the tilty couch watchin the old black an white.

I didn't go in straight off. I finished off the cask an tried to watch the footy. But all I felt was sicker an sicker an darker an darker about Jan, about the telly, about Bretty Smythes an all the little white Michelles, an especially about the fact that if it wasn't for Janny I'd be up the Base with me old mum givin her creature comforts an makin her feel better after what those bastards did to her.

Janny was propped up against the pillows like it was her an not me mum that was the sick bitch an she had the remote in one hand an the lectric bed controls in the other an she had her movie on nice an big an would ya fuckin believe it was in black an white.

Jan, I said real slow an careful.

What.

You're gunna have to watch ya movie in the lounge.

Silence.

Cos I'm gonna watch me footy in here.

Nothin again.

Jan.

What.

Go out to the fuckin lounge.

I couldn't say for sure what happened first. Me switchin over the channels. Janny pullin on the back of me hair. Me whackin her one in the face. Her cacklin like the old hag she was. Me whackin her again. Her turnin the channels back. Me kickin her at the back of her legs. Her throwin I Love Trouble at me an missin an splatterin mug an mossy all over the floor. Me turnin the volume up all high an mighty for some fuckin reason. Then her screamin an cacklin an screaming an cacklin an me runnin outta the bedroom to escape an her followin an throwin whatever she could lay her hands on an screamin stuff at me that don't bear repeatin. Bad shit, I'm tellin ya. Stuff about me an about me mum an pretty soon before ya know it I was screamin back an turnin the volume right up on the telly in the lounge an all I could think of was me mum an meself an wantin to chuck all of the sick outta me. The sick of me mum an the sick of Jan an the sick of Bretty Smythes an the little white teeth an the sick of it all.

When I woke up the next day I was feelin real sorry for meself I can tell you. I was havin one of them nightmares, dreamin I was bein sat on by somethin large an hot an crushin the livin daylights outta me an so I woke up gaspin an swearin but you can guess what it turned out to be can't ya. That's right Janny's electric blanket was still on full bore an both tellies still screamin away. One in the lounge an one in the bedroom both screamin out mornin cartoons an it was all I could do to pull meself up and turn em off.

I smoked one of Janny's Bennys to get me head together but I was seein double and triple and hazy all round like I was still pissy so I went in to look at Jan an she was still sleepin.

I dug the poofta's wallet outta the smashed shit on the floor and told Jan how I was gonna go buy us some milk cos drinkin black instant all the time just weren't no good for ya gut linin.

Youse want the telly on or no, I said to Janny but she didn't say nothin so I switched it onto her favourite mornin aerobics made sure the bed was on nice an high just like she liked it an out I went to get us some milk to have with our black instant.

Youse got milk, I asked Rach down at the Diggers. Youse

got any of that pink milk with the flavourin? Janny's sleepin in an I wanna surprise her when she gets up for her black instant.

How many times do I gotta tell ya, Rach said. I bin tellin ya all day we don't sell no fuckin milk.

So I just stopped over for a couple more browns an a few more an next thing I know I looked into the poofta's wallet and would ya believe it no more fuckin money left.

Carn Rach honey I said, just one beer, just for old times sake.

What old times sake, Rach said then. What fucking old times sake.

You remember Rach, I said, leanin good an close to her ear. You remember how it was with you an me.

I don't remember nuthin of the sort, Rach said. All I remember is you grabbin me arse one night an me tellin ya to fuck off that's all I remember bout you an me.

An as I was walkin back home under the sun an the sky I was feelin low I can tell ya. I guess I shoulda been feelin sorry for Jan cos she was the one who was gunna miss out on the pink milk. But it was me, it was me I was feelin sorry for as my thongs did the slap slap slap up the road.

Once I got back up the house an opened the door I knew straight off that somethin weren't right.

There was a bad smell, a real bad smell, an I caught the first gob of it as soon as I opened the door. So I called out Janny, Janny. I called out her name like you wouldn't believe an still no answer an when I got to the bedroom door an opened it that's when I knew that the bastards had gotten at her too.

Janny was lyin right where I left her on her side with the telly still goin an she had a terrible look to her face. An when I walked round with me sleeve over me mouth to pull down the blankets that's when I saw it, that's when I saw our big new lectric kitchen knife stickin right out of her chest. I tried to pull it out, I swear it. But the second I got close I spewed an I spewed an I spewed until there was nothin left inside me but empty space.

Ever since that bad Saturday or Tuesday or Friday, they've kept me down here while things get sorted out. Sometimes it's not so rough. Sometimes when Maxo an Wogga an The Dick (they call him that after the dictionary he's such a smart prick) an me get together of a lunch time an mix up home brews out the back of the kitchen when the blueys an screwies are off havin their arvo smokos, sometimes then it's not too rough at all.

But other times it cuts me up, cuts me up real bad inside that they won't let me out to go visit mum an Janny up at the Base. Cos now I've got the two of em up there, the two of em done in an jacked out of their minds with waiting for old Rosco Davidson to make it out of here and up that hill.

And I don't feel no shame to say that them times, them times when I'm full of the wantin to get out and have a sit with me mum or a brown with Janny down the Diggers, them times are as rough as they come.

U^m   Hellooo,   bonjourno...... ciao.

My nom is,

nO

wait a minute,

here . it   tis

(on my amex,)

my nom is,

                         oh!

                                   its not here,

                    but my expiry date is August 97.

Hello.

I'm thirty-three, thirty-six, twenty-four, thirty-six, five foot seven.............but not necessarily in that order.

I have three sistes, they're all married and two of them wear upturned collars, blue jeans, white sandshoos and pearls whenevre they go to a bring a plate, dress casual function.............and the only sex either of them gets is when the horny family labrador trys to root thier legs.

My other sister is the President of the Lets Help Those Less Fortunat than Ourselvs Club,
and last yer they sent rollerblades to Ethiopia.

We're very prod of her, (despite her huge hips)
Id like to help people, just like she dos,
         cause she's in the solcial pages nearly all the time.
I'm going to start with very very old people...because that's not a really bog commitment.

um yes, anyway, we are a very caring family, what else, i put all my paper out for recycling. I even steal from other peopl's piles just to make mine bigger.............and my mother, after extensive plastic surgery, has recycled herself so many times her knees are her breasts and her breasts are her shoulder pads

Fabulous. we're very enviroemtnally aware you know,
we could never live in the west,
for example.

oh and this is the natural colour of my hair and its just a

coincidece that it matches the interior of this car and if you want proof I can show you down pubic there which is neatly trimed in the shap of a littel hart. Sorry I don't know whay i said that, here would you like a drink?

no?

cheese, cracker?—oh thats good,

because I haven't got any.

But enough about moi, you're very attroctive, hi.

i like men. My father is an extremely nice man and he knows lots of judges and very important people and his name is John, I don't know if you know him, lots of people do, um, his friends know him of course, and so do.......other pepople as well, which is good, and anyway, we call him papa, with an accent on the last pa, paPA, though we're not french, we're from Burgoyne Street, which is a bot of a cul de sac, if thats any help.

And we had a ballet bar in our basement, because we're all very close, and just madly in love with each other, and haven't you got gorgeous teeth. What's your name, Gunther, Dwayne, Everley? Everley means 'a place where wild boars fight and dig up tubors' I read that somehwere, at the har-idreser i think, are you

Mr spunky buns?

They say

they say

they say choosing names for a baby is like buying y-fronts
for a stranger,

cause you jst don't know if they'll fit,
until the little thing pops out.

Bom bom.

I think i'm going to be sick. Actually I've got three children,
they're all temebdously gorgeous, and extremely brilliant
and I named evrey one of them a aftrer something signifivant
to the conception,
the first is called Midnight,
the second is called Bolly
and the third is called Oops.

Cheers.
cest la vie, tout suit et cet era
and this is Pamela Anderson, my POODLE, she wants to
drive the car, isnt that cute, SOMETIMES I LET HER
CHANGE GEARS, ITS VERY EASY IN THIS CAR,
THAEY MAKE THEM THAT WAY SO YOU DON'T
DAMAGE YOUR NAILS
My poodle and I are VERY CLOSE,
SOME PEOPLE SAY WE EVEN LOOK ALIKE
but I think it's just the hair.

but I was just making more of a comment on something,
before I was ruddely interrupted   by myself,
and what was that,

oh yes life,
and then there you go, and what do you know, and I'm
between husbands you know and this is my best friend,
um
....
..............sounds like....

oh shit....

I remeber Ita Buttrose saying that if you're not good at reme-
bering peole's names you should think of something distinctive about them, for example the ample bulge in their
trousrs, and then remeber for example Gunther *ample bulge
in his trousers*, Smith, and then I don't rem,ebr how that
actually helps, but anyway, this is my friend fat arse.
(now isn't that hilarious),
lucky she's unconcsious,. Doesn't she lok hilarious when she's
unconscious   with her mouth wide open,
and her legs wide apart,.
Actually that's exactly what she always looks like, but she's
more interesting to talk to when she's passed out.

We havne't been best friends all that long, I met here when
she was having an affair with my husband, but we've only
been *best* friendssince she married him
and then found out he awas having an affiar,
its amazing how bonding that can be.

She should never have married him of course,

she should have just done the fling -a-ling -ling with him,
cause when you've got a man by the dick, you've got him
by the balls.
Anyway her tits aren't real, and neither are mine, And we
both can't go flying in the Concorde,
in case our breasts explode.............and its amazing how
bonding that can be...too.
Sometimes I think I should be a lesbian, but they dress very
badly.

yuss.

So anyway wee went to lunch, she et moi, and we drank
lots of champagne because that says 'NE CELLULITE BE
GONE!' and we stayed their for five hours, because you
have to drink quite a lot of it, and we had spagetti al pesto
which gave me a rash beause Italian is so passe, which is
why I fired my gardner. but anyway we were there, in the
restaurant for hours, with my sunnies on, cause its one thing
to be passe, its quite another to be seen to be, and anyway
we were there for hourse
because if you chew every mouthful 47 times,
you actually lose weight.......while you're eating!

And then, when we'd finished, we got in the car,
which was parked right outside,
And
I think the car belonged to the waiter,
but I'm sure he won't mind,
because we left him a huge tip,

and spent alot of time over lunch suggesting we'd give him
a blowie if he'd get us more garlic bread,

so
anyway,
we're in the car,
and then we said (amongst ourselves),
where to now we said,
and the car said, to that bitch fag hag tart other woman's place
and literally drove itself d over to the other woman tart liposuction desperado's place and rammeditself into her car and
then drove off, and I yelled 'bitch, tart, slag, saggy bum,'
cause it just seemed like one of those social occasions when
you really
should say soemthing,
you know,
and then we drove away,
and stole her cat which just died I don't know why.

And then we went back,
feeling terrible,
and burnt all her clothes,
except for the slinky little back chanel jump suit,
which I am wearing now, gorgeous, thankyou yes,
lucky really, that I saved it,
before the whole house went,
lucky we got the cat out,
before it died in the fire,
so it could   die here
(I don't know why)

excuse me,

so nladylike!
my fourth husband could burp the whole alphabet,
backwards,
he was very smart.
You look smart,
especially round the chestal and biceptual areas.
Yes,
and where was I, um........do you like that song Bette
Midler...did you know...If I could fly. like an eagele.
those are the notes,
but they might actually be in a different order,
(I used to be a dancer you know we had a ballet bar in our
basement) anyway that song was about two very dear
friends, and the one with the excess collagen implant lips
died, which I think is a lesson for us all, but do you think
m ine friend's dead, not that she's got big lips, she's got very
thin, sort of reverse lips, and huge pores, shocking
it i'd be good of she was dead,
she could sue for a packet,
although just between you and me I wouldn't wan tot be
seen dead in an outfit like that.

Sh'es probably just out of it. We had a few anti depressants
in the car, they don't really do anything unless you take a
whole lot,

so we tok a whole lot,
Tthey're not easy to get but I borrowed them from my
grandmother who shouldn't be taking them anyway,
because you should be making the absolutel most of reality
when youve only got a couple of minutes left, but sh'es
addicted, and unfortunately reacted badly to my request
and finally we had to dismantle her form the life support
system jst to shut her up, I think sh'ell be right...short
cicuited the whole place.......most excitement they've had
in years,
nodoubt tthe old Restez Vous Retirement Village will be
inviting US back for the CHRISTMAS PRARTY.
I wonder what I'll wear.

Anyway, after the fire we
and the cat died,
which is a coniceidence becasue my frist husband died. Not
that anyone could tell the difference for God's sake..

Oh those times were very tough, single, young, beautiful,
alone with a child called Midnight, but its is amazing what
one can do where theyres awill, and fortunatley there was a
will.....and that was good, not that much, but anyways i met
my next husband at the fineral so I was only between husbands for a very short time. That time.
Although I did wear black to my weddig.
which was a coincidence
because my third husband was into recycling, and his name
was.

his name wsa,

...

his name was

it should be on my licence

cause I never changed my nom on it, but what was the point I said, they wouldn't let me drive anyway, because of my eyesight, but I siad to them well for god's sake, theres no point in driving a convertible if half youf face is going to be covered up by a pair of orthopaedic bifocals is there, I think not, so anywhere whre the hells that licence, Oh I know I left it in the house, after we broke in to the mole's hole, through the door, I guess I could ring his secretary on the mobe and check what his name is, but

anyway, its coming to me now,

'shut up, you stupid,

shut up you stupid, I'm going to take you for all you've, you're the biggest,

mistake, that was his name.

god I tell you what that marriage taught me,

never stand in the middle of the street and yell 'hey you arse hole come her', cause every man in Australia will start walking toward you

But anyway, we were leaving Restez Vous, and I was under extreme pressure, because I'd suddenly realised I'd put the wrong lip liner on and I panicked, you know the way you do,

and I thought I saw a silly old man, walk in front of the car, wearing pyjamas with his fly undone,

and the car lurched forwad, and i thought oh my god i've hit **somebody**, and I got out of the car, and I had a look, but oh thank godmoh oh thank heavesn,
ut was just a nobody,

and then we just drove, backwards up that one way street because we dodn't want anyone to follow us and then we stopped by the side of the road because chicken face here wanted to pee, but she couldn't get her body suit undone, adn then she passed out.
so I took some yellw pills, shich asre sort of like prozac but WHIITH A LOT MORE SYLLABLES,
which I take evry day, but you can't take it if you're driving, so..........I always take it bfore I get inot the car.......and then I drive.
so there we are, where were we oh yes, she was still out to it, and we were parked outside the very exclusive Marcos brasserie, and sushi bar and so I said here have a snort,
of coke you know, which I've really only just dicovered sicne my fifth divorce, an dits a great drug and there are no side effects, except for the molto epensivo nose jobbo caving inno, but you can always get that re done, and it's certainly cheaper than six monthes at Jenny Craig and cer-tainly more titillating than doing aerobics with no bra and a g-string.
but not as fabulous as my pearly boy multi armed, mutli direcitonal rotating vibrator whichI got in a divorce settlement, when my husband got the kids.

Anyway, well I
oy yes, so I shoved some up her nose and she started to take

her clothes off and cry I love you Barry Jones, which is not the sort of thing you say in blue ribbon liberall district, and she pulled out a gun, and so I shot her.

And then all these men started runing our of Marco's because they all thought their creditors had come to get them, and my ex husband came running out too and when he saw that it was just me, and that I'd shot his thin lipped fat arsed wife, he said darling I love you, and got into the car, and thats where he is now, sitting here, on the floor, with his face between my legs,

But enuf about me, lets talk about you, are you gay, you look gay, all good looking men are gay, I'm thinking of having the op, just so I can become a gay man snd sleep with all those gorge queens.
and you look gorgeous,
you look exactlylike one of the village people.
that uniform really suits you.

You should meet my ex husband.

Ex husband, policeman
Policeman, ex husband.

Say hello to the policeman darling,

You'll have to speak up darling, the officer can't hear you, talk clearly,
and get your head out!

Its rude not to look at someone when y're addressing them,
and besides,
........it tickles when you talk down there.

The End

Barry Dickins

A Pot of Air-Conditioning Fluid

The Albion Hotel was a SOB, a pot of air-conditioning fluid, a crowd of Christmas schoolgirls singing carols to their fathers with the horrors on Christmas Day: on any day of the Albion Hotel—true chronicler of Life's distended liver. The Albion Hotel on the corner of Faraday and Lygon Street, Carlton, the old vomiting streetcorner of shame. The old streetcorner with something in its eye. What can it be but boredom in the alcoholic dust-motes, boredom in the respiratory-problem broom cupboard. Drunks with names that all started with Captain. Captain Cunt ran the ship at full-throttle to nowhere. Captain Arsehole did the ashtrays and stood corpses upright after lights out. Like putting mops away.

Captain Nowhere did the red plastic buckets full of chuck. If a girl sicked on your back you got a root. Probably a good one if she was drinking Ouzo. A prick named Luke did the bar. He enjoyed flattening old mums when they weren't looking. He once hit a hippie so hard the chap never spoke again in his hippie life. Had to have his jaw wired up at PANCH Hospital; but the wire corroded in his mouth and he went funny from septicaemia. I drank with a man named Nuclear Frank who drank air-conditioning fluid from his car out the front when he ran out of pot money. A pot was sixty-eight cents. No one ever had sixty-eight cents: Except some of the lawyers; but they only shouted sluts. You could dance with a moll there and put your cock in her cappuccino: there was a certain liberty at The Albion Hotel. Most of the drunks were surgeons, eye ones; who drank Murine eye-drops when they ran out of pot money—which was all the time. It was a Shout and Fuck Bar. You shouted a pot and got a fuck or sulked and went down like a bag of shit. A lot of men looked pretty good at 8 p.m. at the front bar but left pretty flat after 11 p.m. for some reason. I don't know now why we went there—The Albion. I suppose to die—but I'm still alive to tell the chronic tale of Spud Green and why in particular he wanted to walk over the ICI Building.

Girls in 1970 at The Albion either looked like op shop Jane Fondas or Tequila Tinker Bells hanging out for a palmful of salt and a squeeze of lemon. On Friday evenings The Albion smelt like a fist fight, like shit Indian takeaway, like your father's shorts, like oxen during a heatwave. The band might be on. The light might be on. The musicians dressed in what was appropriate. Donkey stockings. Purple violent footwear with foot-thick pumps of cork. Their waist-hairs were violet or white due to barbiturates or listening to remote planets. Their chests were caved in due to 100 Marlboro a day. They wore black cowboy hats and laughed all the time or fell into sulks because their systems had run out of Mandrax or Moselle gulped straight down in ten-ounce hits of instantaneous hangover. They played shit, ate shit. They were all Graeme or Joff. They'd bludged on their parents since birth. They wouldn't work in an iron lung. They slept in all day and put on black leather pants for a living. They thought they were The Grand Funk and they were The Grand Funk.

The played The Albion and were lonely and no good, which is worse than anything, even having no one to love you. Which is even worse than having hardly anyone to hate you.

At four in the afternoon which was when I got there each day, often it was as flat as a teetotaller's funeral. You might have a good game of pool with Nuclear Frank, who mumbled 'Woomera' all day, sputtered space program equations all day through his foul bush of a beard that had bits of pie snagged through it, it smoked on its incredibly dead own, the beard did; Frank could hide things in it with the shakes like a cake bag—rats might roost in it for all he knew or cared. Frank stank something shocking—like the end of the world with a mildewed corduroy jacket over it. Still he wore the illusion of scholarliness, for he could quote rocket-fuel data and mutter stanzas from 'The Wasteland' at Luke the barman who hit Frank till he stopped quoting. Fair enough.

Frank had a very fat wife who was English and always pissed, who sang similar to a squall. Her voice was sweeter than cider with which she pissed herself like bees need oxygen. She sang 'Joe Hill' to us one night, near the Gents it was, and everyone cried because Joe Hill's a beautiful story about rebellion. I bought Mrs Frank a jug of claret for that. Stanley Leasingham, $6. Waterfront intellectuals got there about 5.30 p.m. for a fight and sometimes it was so crowded at the front bar you'd hear a blow—a good punch—because so many times men who are pissed fight like birdies—use claws and scratch instead of fighting like a man—it was often so crowded in the front bar you'd hear a punch, loud punch, and the man who got hit couldn't fall over: he just stood there drinking himself stupid. There were lots of pseudo-intellectuals in the front bar. One guy used to sprinkle sawdust on his hairy shoulders in the men's to look as if he'd toiled all day at a woodyard. He rolled Drum with incredible sensitivity. Like a blowfly with a real feeler for it. He wore a dark blue work singlet but never worked. He never washed. Men who couldn't get a root never washed, for some reason. He rubbed himself with a dry old rag and sprinkled baby powder all over himself. He told me he was fucking Janis Joplin **before anyone had heard of him,** let alone her.

He could really depress the girls, Randy.

He sipped shit white in the corner later, when the band had packed up or got a hiding. I didn't drink with Randy. Nobody did. I drank with Spud Green who once had an art exhibition at The Albion. One of his works was supposed to be Marilyn Monroe's underpants. It sold for $8 and Spud was so rapt he turned up next day on roller skates and drank pots on the run, laughing all the time, slapping Nuclear Frank on the back and perving down Eilene and Aileen's fronts.

Eilene and Aileen assumed they were Joan Baez but they weren't really that much like her on concert-night, which was what they called Saturday night, when various freaks got up drunk and impersonated famous people like Bob Dylan, The Grand Funk or Johnny Cash. Eilene was lovely and sweet actually and everyone was a bit gone on her including me. She seemed to represent the only decent woman in captivity in Australia. She wore old-fashioned ballroom dresses and danced alone in a beam of moonlight near the smoke machine. I saw her once—she looked like the daughter of charms. I couldn't stop looking at her.

Danny Kramer once shat on the bar, leaving an elephant amount. I examined his crude deposit and saw screwdriver handles in it, bits of wire and broken stubbie glass and cig-arette butts probably still smokable, only I wasn't going that bad. Beautiful South Yarra girls used to pull into The Albion, looking so different because beauty is always supe-rior to bullshit. It was The Albion that was pretentious; not the excellently perfumed Irish-Catholic Beauties of the night from South Yarra, who had wit in abundance and statuesque beauty—in profile they were magnificent—they were literate and some of them could sing better than Joan Baez, even if they later laughed at the communist words of 'Joe Hill' sung by the daughters of The Albion. They always drank whisky in a sharp expressive snort and satirised the bullshit-artists in the front bar.

'What time's the Revolution, Shit-For-Brains?'

'I don't know, M'am . . .'

'Two quadruple Irish whiskies, my man.'

And the shitkickers in the front bar ate their hearts out at the tireless sight of true aristocrats laughing at them.

'You're a pisspot as much as me, ma'm,' giggled Nuclear Frank, and the whole bar laughed. He was right.

If you had no dough at least you had The Albion. Mates lent each other enough for a round of pots or wine in pot glasses. Smokes were always shared.

'You got a smoke, mate.'

'Here y'are.'

'Oh, beauty. Winfield Red. My boat's come in.'

'Get fucked. Just smoke it.'

Spud and I were drinking with some good-time girls opposite where Pedro used to cook the Indian food one night, and I noticed the guy rolling all the joints was a copper with a wig on. We were all dead drunk and still I noticed. I turn into Sherlock Holmes after 100 wines.

'You still got a room in Carlton, man?' he asked.

'Are you still a copper? I replied.

He left so quick the big bag of dope fell on the ground. The girls seized it. They rolled preposterous joints the equal of lamp-posts.

Girls were different to femininity then. If they fancied a man they had him.

'Hello my love. Sick of yourself?'

Off they went, to their own quiet little gentle Revolution, light some incense and listen to the wind go crook up the lane. Snivel.

Women went up to lonely men and befriended them.

'You look like Robert Redford.'

'I feel like Robert Menzies.'

The Albion went weak at the knees.

There was one good-time girl named Julia who carried a stiletto knife in her boot and I saw her slash a girl's throat one night. They had a slapping-fight on the floor. I don't know why I drank so much then. I could always make people laugh, they paid me back in kind drink. I was pretty worried about the Hanoi thing. The war in Vietnam. I was taking the strongest form of sedation to forget Cambodia. My doctor said to me:

'Take ten Valium a day
And Vietnam'll go away.'

I suppose it did. Everything did. Even Julia.

Sometimes old diggers turned up on Saturday nights for the Dinner-Dance: they did their own intro's and got up in front of the mike and sang Bing Cosby songs and spoke of the Kokoda Trail and Japs and Spud and me used to weep at the hopelessness of it all. The soggy old carpets! God, if they could only speak! The pretty young noses broken into them. The old pugs who lied they knew someone. Pulverised by someone who couldn't take the bullshit. The vomit and promises ground in. The lovely nouns. The elegant adverbs. The come-on lines and genuine shyness.

'Gee, you're pretty. Can I sit with you?'
 'I'd like that. You're not bad yourself.'
 'Two pots of shit Red, thanks.'
 'And where do you come from?'
 'Preston.'
 'I'm from near there. Sydney.'
 'Can I see you again?'
 'Why don't we just sit here tonight together?'
 'Please don't speak. Sometimes it's important not to.'

The Albion blushed scarlet. It could go shy suddenly.

Through the hungover nauseous thump of amplified lust and red-eyed vision of this insane world or something decent, I staggered from the rickety table with the flat wine to the trusting eyes of Luke the Barman. But he didn't look very trusting long. For a joke I lay on his bed one night, on the second floor—his bed was chained up. Luke came into the room and asked, 'What are you doing here?'

 'I needed a break from the Bar,' was all I could come up with. For some reason it seemed to work, as he refrained from bashing me. I walked downstairs and found $2 in the Gents. Spud was helping a dying guy wash up, as he had all his life savings of blood all down his front.

'I got stabbed by the cigarette machine,' said the scarlet man, washing blood off his tie with screwed-up dunny paper.

'There, there, old son,' said Spud.

But the man then fell down dead. 'I thought we'd have a drink,' said Spud. 'Too late now.'

The next thing there are two nervous rookie coppers click-clicking their biros and trying to hang onto their clipboards.

'How did this happen?' one of 'em kept on saying. I couldn't speak.

Sometimes it's important not to.

But Luke in the big bar just kept on serving alcohol. 'Last drinks,' he shouted, even when the cops escorted the corpse out through the side door to Lygon Street. Luke kept serving the beer up. And the wine. And cheerfully giving out change for the smokes. I started drinking with Charlie McGillicutty and Gail his girlfriend. Gail got hanged on Spud's motorbike the next day because she wore a great big woollen scarf and it got caught in the chain. This was right outside The Albion. Charlie got killed—hit and run outside Eltham by a guy in a white sedan a week later. They were all getting it.

'How you going, Charlie, mate,' I said.

'Look at all that dough in fuckin' Luke's bag,' he said.

To my surprise Charlie very neatly scrambled over the counter and put about $16,000 into his overnight bag—the one he kept the paper in and his bankbook and stuff.

'He doesn't need it like we do,' said Charlie.

We had to agree with him on that score.

Later on that night Spud and I walked to sober up to the ICI Building and he told me he intended to walk over it in these special suction-cup runners of his. Dunlop sandshoes with powerful black vinyl suction-things on. I watched him go up like a blowfly up ten floors and go to sleep up there— all that way up. He waved to me. Cheerfully.

'It's the air-conditioning fluid that I foolishly drank made me have a go at something like that,' smiled he. We lay prostrate in the Treasury Garden and drank a flagon of claret and spoke of God. I got so drunk I was stone cold sober. I told him I'd never work in an office. He gave me all his love and Winfield Red. He died a day later of heroin overdose. With a whole lot of bikies in the bush. About eight or nine of 'em. What an incredible loss. I still went there next day. To The Albion. I drank to overcome hangovers. I drank a pot of port mixed with brandy to overcome the shakes.

I was twenty. Over half my life ago.

This morning I lifted my ten-and-a-half-month-old baby boy out of his cot and he laughed his head off. So did my elegant wife.

I work full-time in an office now.

I have no high cholesterol or friends.

Well, yes I do, lots.

But none like Charlie or Spud.

Christ could they put it away.

R D Lappan

BRANDIED NANNY

Sure this job paid the rent, but it meant I had to put up with their children, Rupert ('Roopsie'), Cordelia and Clementine, whose names were indications of their characters. In the main I was required to drive these children to and from school and assorted extra lessons such as French or flute, and to do the grocery shopping, which I quite liked. I had to learn to cook Vichyssoise, which they ate twice a week, and I enjoyed the fact that you could buy ten different types of potatoes here, which may reveal that I'm fairly easily amused.

Concita, the charming Spanish housekeeper, took care of the rest of the housework. Sort of. To her increasing disgrace, and despite her charm, she frequently had accidents with ugly china ornaments around the house, and was working on borrowed time. The children called her a 'fat spic' (everyone was a 'fat' something), while the parents referred to her as a 'foreigner'.

My job was pretty cushy. I started early and finished late and scored several hours off during the day, when I swam in their heated indoor pool (sometimes nude, depending on how bored I was), and went home to my flat nearby in Highgate for lunch. Afternoons I spent driving through the streets and laneways that twisted from their house in Hampstead through to Golders Green, where I collected Roopsie, then to Swiss Cottage for Cordelia and back to Highgate High Street (so narrow in parts that you had to breathe in) to collect Clementine. On being introduced to me, the girls' first question was: did I know Jason Donovan? They didn't take much notice of me after they found out I didn't.

As soon as the girls got together in the car they started to argue, stopping only to badger me for money or cigarettes, whispering 'fat slut' under their breath when I ignored their requests. 'What did you say?' I'd turn around and yell at them. 'Cats' guts,' they'd say, and snigger. 'She said cats' guts.' Occasionally Rupert, who rarely spoke and when he did never said a nice word, would lean over and give one or the other of them a big whack. Lucky Rupert.

On a Wednesday in early winter I arrived home for lunch to find a telegram waiting for me under the door. I swiped it off the floor, turning it over and looking closely at the envelope. I raced to the phone and rang Tomas, then working in Edinburgh, a cold six hundred kilometres north. He made twelve hundred pounds a week writing some computer program for a bank up there.

His phenomenal earning capacity was a pleasant surprise to me, and I had early on resolved to enjoy it. We'd taken up together soon after I arrived in London, his ability to secure steady, highly-paid employment matched only by my inability to hold down a job for more than a month. We met in a bar playing pool; a friend of mine pointed him out to me ('check out the blond guy with the eyes') but I was too busy winning to pay much attention. After I'd beaten four guys in a row he challenged me. Then I beat him. He couldn't get over that so now we were having this affair to see who'd win. He'd just trekked across Asia and wandered through the Himalayas and, he declared, was here to make stacks of money. Unfortunately, soon after we'd begun exploring the most fabulously expensive shops and dining nightly in the best restaurants on his credit cards, he'd scored one of these high-paying jobs in Scotland. No doubt about it, though, he was spellbound by my charm and beauty still, ringing me at least twice a day.

My plan was to join him as soon as I could safely ditch this daggy nanny job.

I related my circumstances to him now: home for lunch, alone and scared with an unopened telegram. 'My poor darling,' he said. 'I wish I was there with you.' I loved the way he said that: *darling*.

He said: 'I wish I was there with you. Do they still have telegrams?'

'Apparently.'

'Well, open it now and read it to me.'

'I can't. I'm scared.'

'What of?'

'What do you think? Someone's . . . died or something.'

'Well, you're gonna have to open it sooner or later.'

'You reckon?'

'Yeah, I do. Just do it *now*.' He wasn't very original, but he was authoritative.

'No, I can't do it.'

'Just *do* it!'

'OK, maybe. Look, what if something's happened and . . . and . . . I have to fly home alone on a plane?'

'C'mon, you wouldn't be alone. Just open the telegram.' He knew how I felt about flying, but he didn't understand it.

'Yeah, maybe.' What if I had to fly home alone on a plane and then go to a funeral? What would I do on the plane? Would I cry and be scared all the way home? Maybe I would just cry. Would that cancel out my fear of flying, I wondered? Who would I be sitting next to and how would they react if I cried all the way home? Would the attendants be nicer to me or more intolerant? What if I couldn't get a seat on a Qantas plane and had to fly with some airline with statistics . . . ?

'I have to go . . . ' he said.

'Me too. I'll ring you later.'

'Look ... '

'Bye,' I said and hung up. I liked to be the one to hang up.

I looked at the unopened telegram again, then grabbed my coat and drove the BMW to the discount liquor shop down at Archway. To my continuing surprise, my employers entrusted me with the care of this brand-new, diamond-white sports car worth thirty thousand pounds. It belonged to the mother of the children with the names, who was laid up after a hysterectomy—a good thing, I thought. So the BMW came to me.

At the liquor shop I chose a large, cheap bottle of brandy, which I'd never liked, but nevertheless knew to be the spirit that comforted the shocked. At the counter I said to the cashier: 'I don't usually do this in the middle of the day, let alone with brandy.' He looked at me blankly, not understanding my accent perhaps, and slammed the change down on the counter.

Back at my flat, I stood drinking brandy, looking out the windows at the rain and the leafless trees, turning the glass in my hand, the images in my mind. I did this until half the bottle was gone. I still felt sober, only the leafless trees were a little blurred. Mist, maybe. I thought about the telegram again and looked at it lying on the table beside the fireplace. I took another couple of swigs of brandy, straight from the bottle. My head felt tight all over and I realised I hadn't eaten since breakfast. I composed myself, and strode over to the telegram and opened it.

RING YOUR BROTHER URGENTLY. That's all it said. Jesus, I thought. What did that mean, Ring Your Brother Urgently? Why hadn't *he* called me? Who was dead or dying? And why hadn't my mother rung me? How could I fly alone? How could they possibly *expect* me to? Would the dead one *want* me to, even? Would I have time to go to the hypnotist before the flight? Would I be able to get drugs, like before?

Again I rang Tomas in Edinburgh. I related the message of the telegram. 'Everyone here in the office is wishing you the best. We're all thinking of you.'

'Oh. I wish you hadn't told anyone.'

'Do you want me to ring your brother for you?'

'No ... no. Why did you tell everyone?'

'A burden shared ... you know.' He was good at these banalities.

Born to them, in fact.

'Oh, and my mother rang.'

'You told her too? Tomas, if she rings me I'm going to hang up.'

'Don't, please. She really likes you.'

'She doesn't like me at all.'

'Well just be nice to her, OK?'

'Tell *her* that.'

We argued on a bit until we were both bored with it. 'I'll call you later,' I said and hung up.

Then I dialled the long number home.

'Mick, it's me. I got the telegram.'

'Thank God you've rung,' he said, sounding excited.

'I've been trying to ring you all week and you're *never* home.' I held my breath.

'What is it then? Is it Mum?' I asked in a small voice.

'Is what Mum? Oh, the telegram. No, no, no. What's wrong with your voice? Picked up an accent?'

I was slurring a little. 'Yeah, sure, an accent. Tell me about the bloody telegram!'

'The thing is this: I want you to place some bets for me, they're really important ... ' he paused, and then spoke slowly and seriously as though imparting some marvellous piece of information: 'I want you to put some money on the British Open for me. But you've *got* to do it before Friday or the odds will be too low.'

'What?' I managed to get out.

'Now,' he was saying a businesslike tone, 'I've got quite a few combinations here—got a pen handy?'

'*What*? But why can't you do it there?'

'Oh everyone's bet on Greg Norman here, the odds are far too low. It wouldn't even be worth it,' he said disgustedly.

I should have known. I should have known that Mick would pull a stunt like this.

'OK,' I said tightly. 'But did you *really* have to send me a telegram about this?'

'Yeah. It's really important,' he repeated. Then, 'You're pissed!' he said with pleased surprise.

Mick had all the interesting news for me: our younger brother, Horse, had fallen up the stairs drunk carrying a carton of beer. Six stitches in his knee, saved four of the bottles. My friend Tania, after becoming pregnant and having an abortion (she liked to broadcast these details of her life), had become a born-again New Age person. Given up drinking, smoking dope, and shopping. Her parents, who'd supported her through the abortion trauma and regular other crises, had now disowned her. She herself wouldn't give you the time of day unless you'd read all of Deepak Chopra, did Hatha yoga, and believed cats were the true spiritual masters.

'Once a hippie ... ' I said.

'Yeah, typical,' said Mick. These banalities were catching.

And Mick was in love again, or something similar. She was a freelance financial consultant who apparently specialised in writing computerised betting systems. She actually owned a part share in Redhead ('Whaddaya think about that? A part share in *Redhead*!'), an up-and-coming two-year-old filly who had famous horse parents ('Someone out of someone' and 'Someone out of a mare that could stay,' he said, or something like that), and who'd had three wins, all on wet tracks. I was suitably impressed.

It could be serious with her, he wasn't sure. How would he know? I asked. He wasn't sure about that either. It was good to talk to him. I wouldn't have to fly home alone after all.

Tomas never could see the funny side. He would demand at fortnightly intervals when we saw each other: 'But why was it so important for your brother to have this bet that he would send a telegram?' Then I would explain again to him how you could never have got good enough odds at home because naturally *everyone* would be betting on Greg Norman. 'Good enough odds for what?' he would ask me meaningfully, shaking his head, and I would shrug my shoulders and smile, unsure what he wanted to hear.

Tomas actually wished that someone had died, I think, and this caused some tension in the relationship. I debated with myself whether his wish was an actual character flaw or merely an essential ego-boosting mechanism.

'I can't see how you can laugh about it,' he would say. 'And your brother must be extremely, *extremely* irresponsible.' Or else he would ask spontaneously as we walked to the Tube or shopped for pretentious food items, 'Tell me— your brother spent all that money on a telegram for a *bet*?' like he still didn't believe it, and he wanted me to explain it to him again. 'Well, actually, telegrams aren't that expensive,' I told him. 'They're cheaper than faxes ... ' But he wasn't listening.

And, he would go on to remind me, it was not only him who found the whole episode frankly shocking, but an office full of Scots people. 'I mean, they were *really* shocked,' he'd remind me further. 'A telegram ... for a *bet* ... ' He'd been unimpressed too, by my achievement after the phone call.

After I'd said goodbye to Mick that day and rung Tomas to tell them all up there that everyone had survived, I hung up the phone to find myself pretty drunk. Very drunk. Would it be best, I wondered, to ring my employer and explain my circumstances honestly? But probably she would be as disapproving as Tomas or a Scot. Maybe she'd even get in a sacking mood, seeing as how Concita had given her ideas already.

The problem was that it might have been time to leave to pick the children up from school. I couldn't quite make out my watch face but it seemed that it might be about that time. What would happen if I didn't go? The mother couldn't do it. The father worked out of town, in Surrey. Why didn't I just ring a taxi? Yeah, a big, black old-fashioned taxi where I could go for a ride in the back seat, and maybe even sit facing backwards, which you can do. Pretend I was somebody else. Preferably someone rich. You could do that in those taxis. You could also turn the heating on and off, and no-one would say anything if you didn't wear a seatbelt. I liked that. All over Britain you could see kids riding in the family car on that bit up the back, waiting to be thrown through the windscreen at the first heavy braking, and nobody noticed or cared that they weren't wearing child-restraining devices.

But you couldn't ring taxis in London, I remembered. There's some secret number, it's not in the book. Only the Queen has it. You could only ring mini-cabs, which aren't half as much fun. You had to go out on the street and actually hail a taxi. You said 'Taxi!' in an authoritative way, perhaps raising your arm and a finger or two as if about to begin a little dance, and then one just stopped in front of you. But sometimes there are none; and sometimes there are lots and they're all changing shift and won't stop, even if you are somebody and can dance well.

No, the children would simply be stranded, left waiting forlornly on footpaths. Appealing as this thought was, I had the vague idea I was due to be paid tomorrow. If only *yesterday* had been payday—I could have used that money. Now what was it I was supposed to be doing today again? I tried to gather my thoughts, and came to a decision: I would simply *carry on as usual* in the English tradition. I hoped that *was* the English tradition and not some other thing I'd mixed it up with, like the Protestant work ethic.

So I wandered out to that big ol' diamond-white BMW and propped myself behind the leather-covered steering wheel. The hardest part of the whole exercise was getting the key into the ignition: getting that small silver key into that other small silver thing. It must have taken longer than usual because Freddie from the flat next door to mine yelled down to ask if I needed a hand. This made me fall about laughing, I couldn't answer, and I lay down across the passenger seat for a while. I may have slept, I don't remember. Then I recalled that when I got really drunk this was precisely what I did: I laughed my head off and lay down and went to sleep, wherever I happened to be. When I remembered this, I had another laughing fit. I opened one of my eyes and saw Freddie leaning out of his window watching me. He always wore three-piece suits with one of those chain things on the button-hole. Was it some kind of secret signal for bondage fans, I wondered lazily? 'You can't drive like that, you know,' he said in a superior fashion. I sat up and tried to look sober. 'Wanna bet?' I said, raising an eyebrow and laughing softly. I turned the key, slammed the gearstick into D, and did a 360 in the gravel driveway.

Out on the roadway, however, I drove sedately. I slapped my face a few times and spoke sternly to myself. I was now at that particular stage of drunkenness when you're not unconscious but you'd quite like to be; that stage when your vision is blurred and you feel you may want to throw up sometime soon.

The streets in London are quite narrow, the traffic heavy and fast, or heavy and slow, the drivers surprisingly polite: traffic on a busy road might stop to let you out of a side street. My concentration was focused on the study of blurring, moving images. So far, I'd managed to steer around them. I was so busy concentrating on avoiding hitting moving images that I didn't notice the traffic lights. And now I'd stopped at one inappropriately, I think, and I heard the sound of horns, gently, timidly beeping. So polite. I moved forward at a slow rate and found myself on the winding road to Golders Green and then outside Rupert's school. The Something School, it was called, I couldn't quite remember what. Rupert strode up to the car angrily. 'Where have you been?' he demanded. 'I've been waiting,' he said angrily, as a ten-year-old can.

'Get in and shut your faith.' I'd meant to say 'face', and I almost started giggling again. He looked suitably shocked at my less than caring demeanour. 'And don't say one word to me,' I managed. I felt sick.

'I always told Mummy not to hire you,' he sniped. 'I told her you were totally unsuitable.'

'Don't say *another* word to me,' I said more stridently. We were stopped at another light, red or green I wasn't entirely sure, but better to stop at them all, I thought.

'Mummy said she only hired you because you were ugly and she felt sorry for you,' he said.

I turned to him and said: 'Roopsie . . . ' and then I leant over the dark and soft velour upholstery and threw up everywhere. The light had changed colour and we took off again.

The drive to Swiss Cottage was uneventful, apart from Rupert's gagging noises. 'Not one more word now,' I was saying jauntily, feeling on the up and up. Cordelia stalked up to the car.

'You're late!' she said.

'Get in,' I said.

'Quickly. Do as she says,' hissed Roopsie. By the time I got to Highgate, they were both sobbing and gagging. 'Aren't these BMWs marvellous with their centrally-controlled windows and their child-proof locks?' I asked, but they stayed quiet for once. I felt a bit sorry for Clementine when she got in, as she'd never been as nasty as the other two.

I drove very slowly through the streets and noticed occasionally the flashing lights and terrifying sirens of police cars as they came up behind me to race between the traffic and up over the footpaths where practicable. They were not after me, luckily, but I wondered would I just be thrown straight into jail for this or did I get a trial, if captured? The local lockup or Holloway? And what would my defence be—fear of flying or telegrams?

When I finally rolled the BMW into the redbrick drive I was so relieved I almost cried. I'd made it. Gotten away with it. No scratches, no bumps or dents, no dead children, no police. I rested my head on the steering wheel for a moment and then realised I hadn't really thought about the mother and the consequences until we entered the hall and I saw her standing on the staircase in her dressing gown and leaning on the bannister for support. I was perhaps a little unsteady on my feet and looked around for a bannister of my own. Her black curly hair was in a mess and she looked angry. I made a sudden decision.

'Well, that's it. I've had it,' I announced. 'I'm afraid I can no longer perform under these intolerable conditions.' The children stood behind me, excitedly expectant. The mother looked a bit stunned.

'What's that smell?' she asked. 'Smells like . . . '

'I can't be expected to drive around like this,' I went on. 'In *this* weather. In *that* car. Worried about every little scratch, every little raindrop on the duco. In those traffic conditions. Day in, day out. With twelve million other people all doing the same thing.'

'What?' said the mother.

'And further,' I said, picking up my politics as I went along, 'if you want to poison yourselves eating Vichyssoise twice a week made from the radioactive produce of Northern Europe then that's up to you, but,' I paused briefly, 'I can no longer partake in such a sick exercise.'

'What?' said the mother.

'I quit.'

When Concita arrived at my flat later on that evening I naturally thought she'd come to commiserate, to bitch about our employers, perhaps to get a dose of my courage. Instead she propped her feet up on the couch and said: 'Guess what I did tonight?'

'What?' I asked cautiously.

'I quit!'

'What?' I said.

'It has really been some day. First, the washing machine broke. The knob thing just came right off in my hand when I pulled it. Then the Senora decides she wants all of the shoes cleaned. Hers, his, the kids'—I've spent the *whole* day in the laundry cleaning the ... the,' she searched unsuccessfully for the right swear-word, ' ...shoes. And then—I broke something else.'

'What?' I asked, intrigued now.

'The car.'

'The car?'

'The BMW. Just as I was leaving I reversed into the driveway to turn my car around and for some reason you had parked the BMW in a different place in the driveway, and then it had ... body contact with my car, and then I went inside and had myself sacked.'

Tomas, when he arrived that weekend and found out about the driving episode, shook his handsome blond head, wagged his finger and said, 'You foolish, foolish girl,' in his deepest, sternest voice. 'Drink-driving is nothing to be proud of. It's unbe*liev*able. And in *that* car. Your brother gambles and then you drink and drive,' he said, his jaw set like stone and his finger poised, pointing at me. 'Well, don't expect me to come to the rescue when you lose your job,' he was saying now. I hadn't actually told him the *whole* story yet, or much of my employment history (how could it be of interest to him? I'd thought). I'd just maintained that I preferred casual work. Never having been subject to such a patrician manner, I giggled nervously now, unsure whether to take him seriously. His face became sterner, if that was possible, and I had to leave the room.

From the lounge room, I could hear the soccer on TV, and Tomas talking and laughing with someone on the phone. He was drinking Heineken and hadn't offered me any. In the kitchen I wiped the benches and stacked the dishes. As I filled up the sink, the gas boiler mounted on the wall made the same stupid thumping noise it always did. While I did the washing up, I stared out of the window with glazed eyes and could just see something over next door's rooftop which might have been the sun, only watered down. There was no one on the street.

As I put away the dishes, I found half a bottle of brandy at the back of the cupboard. I reached up for it, unscrewed the lid and sniffed it. I raised the bottle in salute to Tomas in the next room. 'Cin Cin!' I said quietly as I took a long swig. I was pretty thirsty as it turned out. Then I went to my room and started to pack. I was out of there.

Leonie Stevens

UNidEntifiED FLyiNG ConcRete

The chemical smell met us at the door.

'Oh, God,' I said.

'Phew!'

'What's that?'

For a second I couldn't tell—one too many dubious wines at Danny's opening—but I heard a familiar cough and I knew. China hadn't swallowed him whole.

'It's Harry.'

Chris sniffed the air. 'That's not a human smell.' Danny chewed on his disintegrating yeeros. With a wave of warning, I led them down the long narrow hall to the kitchen, where Harry presided over the table like the wiseguy who just beat a rap.

'Harry!' I said.

'Maaaaate!' he croaked, and three things were obvious. One, his head was bare. He'd bragged that he was going to get it shaven in a Shaolin temple, but I thought it was just one of his stories. I mean, what self-respecting monk's gonna shave some white-boy tourist in *his* holy place? Probably did it in his hotel room.

The second thing I noticed was that he was already well off his face. The whites of his eyes were fluoro pink, and his sharp crafty face was covered with a film of sweat and aeroplane grime, like he hadn't had a bath in the ten days he'd been away.

The third thing that struck me—probably the cause of the second—was the foul chemical smell emanating from the bottle on the table. It was small and the liquid was clear, but definitely not benign.

'You old bastard,' I said, and when I bent close to skirt my lips on his cheek I noticed he stank of the stuff. 'This is Chris—' I gestured to him, and noticed Danny coming up the rear. '—and Danny.'

They gave each other blokey nods, Chris genuinely friendly and Danny like a robot. The opening had taken its toll on him. Despite Chris's repeated assertions that it was a great success, Danny was an emotional wreck. He was shaking, sweating from the top of his bald head down to his beard. I sat him down in a chair and wound around to Harry.

'So tell me—how was it?'

'China?'

'No, Cabramatta.'

'No bullshit, it was fantastic.'

'Any trouble with Customs?'

'Mate, you wouldn't believe it They impounded my sword!'

'What sword?'

'Oh, fuck, it's a beauty. They thought it was a weapon!'

'Ignorant bastards.'

'I gotta pick it up at the cop shop next week.'

'What a hassle.'

'But I got this through all right.' He held up a golfball-sized lump of what looked like tan playdough. I looked closely and smelt it, but couldn't detect anything over the chemical smell of whatever was in the bottle.

'What is it?'

'Hash, mate.'

'No way.'

'Spotted some myself.'

'Well, make yourself at home.'

'You'll get yours.'

'How'd you get it through Customs?'

He patted his shirt pocket. 'In me cigarette pack.'

'Bullshit!'

'It's true. They were so freaked out about the sword they didn't check. Here, try this stuff.' He made a show of the little bottle on the table. 'Chris! Danny!'

He lined up some shot glasses and poured the stuff. Chris scooped his up without hesitation. I was a little shocked, considering he'd been holding his nose just seconds ago, but I guess he liked diving into the unknown. He came home with me, after all.

'Go on, mate,' Harry said, 'Go for it.' He pushed one onto Danny. 'C'arn, Danny, give it a go.'

They looked at each other and downed them in unison, and I was glad I held off, because judging by their faces the stuff was toxic. Chris pulled a terrible face and gave a jerky shudder.

'Phwoar!'

Danny's reaction was more delayed: he downed it and looked at the glass, a vision of complete calm until a horrified expression swept his face, as if he'd been poisoned.

'Good, mate?' Harry asked. There was nothing he loved more than getting other people shit-faced. If he could guide someone else to a state of collapse, he was a happy man.

'Ugh,' Danny said, 'Ugh—ah—Jesus—what IS this?'

'I dunno, mate, some kinda firewater. I bought back three bottles. It's insane stuff.'

'I reckon!' Danny looked at his glass again, then swayed towards the table. Harry could read the signs.

'The second's always better, mate.'

I smelt mine. No way I was drinking that. Danny downed another shot, and Harry turned to me. I knew he'd talk me into sampling it, because I'm the weakest sucker in the world, but I got a reprieve when he noticed the stove.

'The knives!' he said. I turned and saw they were red-hot. He'd already cut the bottom off a cordial bottle, and lined up some mouseshit-sized droplets of hash.

'Hey, Chris,' I said, 'Come on.'

He took two steps across the tiny kitchen and said, 'Look, I'm not really sure about this—'

'Who was the guy who said he wanted to get—what was that word again?'

'Apoplectic.'

'Apoplectic.' A linguist through and through. 'Here, grab these.'

Chris held the knives. I dropped a mouseshit-blob of hash and drew the smoke through the cordial bottle, pure, intense, and I was stoned before I'd exhaled. The lines of the cupboards were different and the floor was softer. Harry didn't look quite so grimy.

'My paintings,' Danny was telling him, 'are about the "thingness" of the chair. The aesthetic paradigm—hic—'

'Chairs?' Harry said. Danny nodded dreamily. Harry waited as long as was polite, then turned to me. 'What do you reckon?'

'It's hash all right.'

'What did you think it was? Asbestos?'

'I just can't believe you walked it through Customs.'

'It's all in the attitude.' He raised his shot-glass of fire-water. 'You ought to try this.'

'No way, it smells awful.'

'When's that ever stopped you?'

He was right, I suppose. I said, 'Hooley Dooley, here's to Customs!' and skulled the chemical drink. It went to my stomach, then straight to my head. Domestos must taste like this. It started eating away immediately, burning, toxifying.

I said, 'Oh, my God!' and ran straight to the bathroom, because I was sure I was going to be sick. And it would have been better if I had, but the stuff was like superglue, burning my mouth and throat and stomach with the worst taste I'd ever known.

'Are you okay?' Chris said, swaying in the doorway as I dry-retched at the basin. The flaps of his flying cap were down over his ears, and he looked incredibly whacky. 'It's not so bad, once you get used to it. It kills your tastebuds so you can't—'

I dry-retched again and said, 'No way, I'm not having no more ... I retched '... poison from the streets of Beijing.'

Of course, with one thing and another, the four of us polished off two bottles. Harry was generous with the blond hash, and after a few slugs and spots we moved out into the back yard, because that seemed safer. Harry told an amazing story about scoring it from some heavy guys out the back of a spooky little cafe. He elaborated to make it more enter-taining, if not believable, and the whole while Danny kept staring at him, getting closer and closer till he was just inches away.

'I know you from somewhere,' he slurred, 'don't I?'

'I dunno, mate,' Harry said, grinning and in control even when he was too drunk to walk. 'Maybe from the shop.'

'What shop?'

'My shop. Well, it's not my shop, but I kind of—well—'
'Work there?' I suggested. Harry shrugged.

'I guess you could say that. I did for the first week, anyway.'

'He works at a sex shop,' I explained to Danny, 'in the city.'

'Yeah, maybe you know me from there?'

Danny stammered, 'Er, no, I don't think so.'

'Nothing to be ashamed of, mate,' Harry told him.

'Yeah,' I added, 'Harry can get you a discount.'

'No,' Danny said, 'I've never been into that kind of stuff. Not that I'd be afraid to, mind. It's just—well, never occurred to me. In my day—'

'Danny,' Chris said, 'this IS your day.'

'Yeah!' I echoed.

'Does everyone know that my friend here just had two years' work culminate in a very successful exhibition?'

Everyone already knew, but we gave Danny a cheer anyway. He smiled proudly, and I tried to crawl over to him to slap his back, but found I couldn't kneel and speak at the same time. My head was full of sludge. I felt like Stimpy, brains leaking out of my ear.

'Hey,' Harry called to me, 'You right, mate?'

The concrete rose up to meet me, but luckily one of us was padded. I bounced. I heard manic laughter—probably my own—then rolled on my back to watch the clouds.

'Harry,' I said, 'You're an evil swine.'

'Oh, shit,' he said, 'That's nice. That's very nice.'

'You tampered with this—' I picked up a bottle. 'Stuff.'

'I didn't.'

'You put trips in it.'

'I didn't, I swear.'

'That's where I know you from,' Danny said, 'Last year Julie bought some—'

'The art crowd!' Harry roared. 'At the Uni! I remember!'

Chris looked slighted. 'No-one told me about it.'

'Well, it was staff only. And besides, you were a student. If I gave you LSD—how would it look?'

'It wasn't LSD mate,' Harry said, 'STP.'

Danny folded his arms. 'Should I be annoyed?'

The clouds above swirled and took on shapes of Greek gods. Big bearded heavy-looking dudes with solemn faces and no chest hair. One of them had a bow and arrow ... nah, it was a cricket bat. I was sure they were Greek gods, and they were extremely significant, but I was too far gone to do anything but think stupid things, like whoops, there goes Zorba.

'This firewater,' Harry was saying, 'It's crazy stuff. No wonder they're all so fucken mad over there.'

'Where?' I said, 'Greece?'

'Greece? Where the fuck you get Greece from? I mean China. They're fucken nuts. The way they talk—'

'It's called language.'

'Aaaah!' Chris wailed, 'Semiotics!' And he crossed his fingers at us like we were vampires. Harry pretended not to notice.

'The Chinese language—you ever really listened to it? I have, believe me. It's so fucken manic, up down up down, so fucken fast ... now, you take a nice ordered language like English—'

'Hey,' Danny said, interrupting with such clarity that I was sure he was going to say something important, like Check out the Greek Dudes. He leant close to me and whispered, 'I love my beard.'

100

I nodded and said, 'Yes.'

'I won't get rid of it.'

I shook my head and said, 'No.'

'English is slow,' Harry continued, 'Refined—'

'Rubbish,' Chris said, playing with the flaps over his ears. 'English is a disgusting language. It's got no style.'

'What? How can you say that?'

'Easy. Would you like it in Spanish, Russian, Swahili or German with a goosestep?'

Meanwhile, Danny was sidling up to me, staring up into the air. 'Don't look now,' he said slowly. 'It's a flying saucer.'

I looked up immediately, but I didn't see any aliens. Shit, even the big Greeks were gone. I turned back to Harry, because if Danny was seeing UFOs, then I wasn't the only one.

'Harry, you're a bastard!'

'I promise,' he said, 'I didn't slip you trips. I didn't. I wouldn't.'

'Yes, you would.'

'No way.'

'To see us squirm, just for a laugh.'

'At today's prices? No way!'

He was probably right. I turned to Danny, who was staring intently at the Hills Hoist.

'He'll be all right,' Chris assured me, 'But it might be an idea to ... '

He drifted away. I waited for a good two minutes, then tugged on his flaps. He came back with a blink.

'Yeah, find a nice comfy corner for him. Otherwise he'll

lock himself in the toilet and crash and you know what a disaster that can be.'

I snorted and jabbed Harry in the ribs, because he did it all the time. Collapsed on the floor so you couldn't even get the door open to drag him out. Compound this with a small back yard, no garden space, and you've got a very ugly end to a night's social drinking.

'Okay,' I told Chris, 'Wait here.' I went to the laundry and got a sheet from the Dirties basket, and we made Danny a bed of vine leaves. He curled up in the corner of the garden like a gnome, beard tucked down to his chest, still gurgling about the aliens.

'Too much *X-Files*,' I suggested.

'No,' Chris said, 'He hasn't watched TV in two years.'

Harry and I gasped 'Wow!' and fell into a general stupor, amazed that *anyone* could not watch TV for two years. God, Danny was *really* into this chair thing. I looked up to the sky and the Greek dudes were back, along with an amazing light show that made the new year's fireworks on the harbour look like sparks from a nylon vest. Planets, asteroids, moons, whole fucking galaxies flew by. And I knew I was seeing what Danny had seen, a hexagonal base to all of it, and I knew Harry hadn't tampered with the drink, it was just this weird Chinese firewater, and I knew this Chris guy was going to be a good thing, even though I only met him two hours ago. Even the Chicken People were okay, deep down. Agro floated in the stars, a giant muddy bathmat in space. There would never be another moment. I ran my hands over the warm concrete, cement breath, feeling the thingness of the ground, brutal grey. Suddenly I *knew* why they built those buildings out of concrete and left it exposed. It was reality, the bottom line. Why hide it?

'Guys,' Harry said, 'I've got something to tell you.'

Tim Baker

L'Absinthe

Dalí stood, his white prophet's robes vibrant amongst the green of his garden, waving. Frieda took the yellow scarf he had given her at lunch and held it aloft trophy-like, letting it ripple in the seabreeze. Delighted, Dalí pulled off his shirt and twirled it with all the fervour of a football fan whose team has just won the Cup Final. 'Now look what you've done,' Ellis said.

'What ...?' She turned back to Ellis, who held his

Panama hat sandwiched between head and hand, as though trying to keep it warm.

'Stop waving that thing, will you. It's like you're putting up a quarantine flag or something.'

Frieda laughed. 'More like a red flag with a bull. Look ... ' She flicked her scarf and Dalí's rhythm increased. 'See? It excites him.'

'Nothing excites him. He's just being Dalí.' He turned without waiting for her, taking the path that led through the rocks, sea spray infusing the air with a rich salt vapour. Frieda followed, holding her sunglasses against a brief gust that amplified the gulls hovering about her, distorting their cruel cries into a plaintive appeal for understanding. She turned and Dalí was spinning his shirt around his head like a lasso. The backhand flutter of her Italian farewell seemed modest in comparison and she broadened it into large, graceful sweeps of her arm that sent gold bracelets shimmering in the sunlight. Behind her Ellis said, 'What are you doing?' His voice was distended by the wind. She turned and ran towards him, laughing. 'It's beautiful here,' she said, feeling the breeze seize her words and carry them off the cliff.

'It's just beginning ... '

She could taste the salt on his lips. 'We have the whole of summer ahead of us ... !'

'We have as long as you want ahead of us ... '

In the fragile shelter of a lone umbrella pine, Frieda swept her hair back and captured it inside her scarf. From where she stood Dalí's villa occupied the whole of the bay, his diminished figure standing in the centre of the estate. 'God, he's still waving.'

'Of course the bastard's still waving. We could stand here like idiots for hours and he'd wave at us all the time, not once missing a beat. It's what he has instead of talent: tenacity ... Grim, bloody obsession.'

'I think it's admirable ... almost.' Despite the distance it was still unmistakably him: the white trousers hoisted high around the broad waist, the wispy black hair streaming away from the flat face, the self-startled eyes. She could almost make out the moustache. He was holding his shirt by the cuffs, flapping it like a tablecloth out a window when they reached the head of the peninsula and the real wind struck them, drowning out the ocean, the gulls, their own voices. Ellis pulled her towards the shelter of the cliff-face, his words warm in the seasalt air. 'Okay, we wait here a moment then sneak back. I swear he'll still be standing there, waving.'

Frieda looked past Ellis to the village of Cadaqués, white and patient in the sun, framed by treeless green hills and the astonishing and remembered blue of the Mediter-ranean. 'All right ... '

'Now!' They charged back around the point, the wind dying like a dream startled by morning sunshine and Dalí was there, triumphant and certain, whirling his shirt.

'Like a goddamn Spanish windmill ... !' Even Ellis waved back this time, then they rounded the peninsula, entering fully into the ancient, once-worshipped element, their clothes snapping in the crystallised white air. They hurried on in enforced silence till they reached the charmed shelter of a beach where they made afternoon love upon the placid sand, dozens of gulls wheeling high above them, their wings casting shadows and unveiling flashes of light; holding hands afterwards as they searched for the track leading from the beach and they were back in the village, Cadaqués alive with motion, wood-slate blinds rustling against balconies, blue-hulled fishing boats rocking inside what passed for sheltered mooring.

Ellis and Frieda took a table at the café on the beach and immediately a Guardia Civil came up and demanded their papers, leafing backwards through their passports like a diner lost in an over-detailed menu. He handed them back with an indifferent salute and left.

'Do you suppose someone saw us on the beach and reported it?'

'No, it's just . . . ' Ellis waited till the Guardia Civil was out of earshot before saying the word. ' . . .Franco's Spain. More than twenty years after the end of the war and things are still the same!'

'Almost the same. We're here, after all.'

'But that's not really the point. The point is that he won and he can't stop reminding every one. The only thing worse than a poor loser is a poor winner.'

'So I've noticed . . . '

'What . . . ? Oh, you're talking about Moore.'

'You didn't have to rub his nose in it!' Frieda shouted above the rustle of fiesta flags.

'Henry will get over it. That's why he puts in all those holes, so he's got somewhere to crawl out if he nee . . . ' Frieda was shaking her head. 'Come on, it's too windy to talk, let's find somewhere indoors.'

They walked through seaspray thrown up by rocks that

gathered like an insurrection at the centre of the harbour, the dazzling white of the town calming in the late afternoon to a more sustainable intensity. At the back of a little plaza with a wind-frantic fountain was a bodega, its green door-blind slapping rhythmically. 'A quiet refuge for lost souls,' Ellis said, holding the blind back and opening the door.

In the immediate black of the bar they could sense the hush created by their entrance, Ellis feeling the peculiar power of a man entering a room with a beautiful woman. They stood by the door, their eyes straining for vision, a zinc bar rising luminous and damp, the wall behind it loaded with mirrors and an unreasonable number of bottles. Beyond was a large, dark cavern, inhabited by men sitting at tables with cards and dominoes strewn in meaningful geo-metric patterns. —Buenos días ... Ellis said into a gloom livid with the sting of black tobacco. There was a long silence and then someone slapped a domino hard on a table. Ellis turned to a man sitting on a stool by the bar. —Hola, buenos días.

—Buenas tardes, the man corrected him. The barman came up to them, a towel over one hand, as though con-cealing a weapon.

—Señor, señora ... ¿Qué quieren ustedes?

—No sé ... Ellis looked up at the shelves above the bar. He'd need ten minutes just to read the labels. —Un momento, por favor...

The barman left them and Ellis turned to Frieda. 'What would you like?'

'What do they have?'

'From the looks of it, everything.'

'I'd like something to settle me down after that wind . . . '

'Cognac?'

'Something you can't get in Paris.'

'I see. Local colour . . . '

'But nothing too obvious.'

'Frieda, when have you ever known me to be obvious?' Her laugh was as unexpected and caressing as May snow. 'Thanks for the vote of confidence.'

The barman returned and placed a large tray before them. On it were diced pieces of grilled octopus sprinkled with paprika, a tiny dish of anchovies white and plump in vinegar, olives dark as a farmer's hands, and cubes of tortilla speared by toothpicks. The man on the stool examined it and then them with the intense, open scrutiny only ever found in children and small villages. Ellis glanced at the man's glass. 'What do you think of that?'

'Looks revolting. What is it?'

'I'll ask.' Ellis pushed the tray towards the man and gestured with his hand. The man shook his head and thanked him. —¿Qué es eso? Ellis asked.

—Absenta.

—¿Qué?

—¡Absenta!

Ellis looked at Frieda. 'I didn't understand.'

'I think he said it was absinthe, but that'd be impossible. It's banned.'

'Maybe not in Spain.'

'Everywhere. It's lethal.'

'I'll ask the barman.' Ellis gestured and the barman came, his towel still concealing his hand.

—Sí señor . . . ?

—Do you have absenta?

There was a pause. —Sí señor, but . . .

—Yes . . . ?

—It's bad.

—¿Malo?

—Sí señor. For your stomach. Ask Manolo.

The man at the bar nodded. —Muy malo.

Frieda spoke directly to the man at the bar for the first time. —But . . . if it's very bad for your stomach, why do you drink it?

The man shrugged. —It's my drink. Everyone has their drink. Juan Pablo here drinks tinto. I drink absenta. I have my cigarettes too . . . He held up a packet of Celtas.

—They are bad for you also, Juan Pablo said, —muy malo.

—Yes, said Manolo, —but they are *my* cigarettes . . .

—Exactly, said Juan Pablo. —They are yours and no one can say otherwise.

—Clearly. That which you have spoken is the truth, Manolo said.

Ellis turned to Frieda. 'Sounds to me as though they've been reading too much Sartre . . . '

'Cynic! So what are *we* going to order?'

Ellis held thumb and forefinger towards the bar. —Dos absentas, por favor.

—Very well, señor.

Ellis and Frieda sat down at a table in the corner. Through a lead-glass window they watched the fountain scattering water towards them. 'This wind, what's it called, the Tramontana? ... it's incredible! I've never seen such a windy place.'

'It happens on the Mediterranean. All the legendary winds—the Sirocco, the Mistral, the Lebeche—end up in its waters. They blow themselves out after a few days.'

'It gives everything such a strange, almost haunted atmosphere.'

'It's somehow appropriate, isn't it? This was the birthplace of Spanish surrealism. Buñuel and Dalí used to spend their summer holidays here back when they were friends, before success forced them to hire accountants. Gaudí stayed on long after building our hotel. Is it getting to you?'

'I love it! But it is tiring. Everything seems like such an effort, even just walking across the seafront.'

'It can get to you. Cadaqués is famous for suicides and locos ... like you know who, for example ... '

'As loco as a monkey ... '

Juan Pablo appeared carrying a tray charged with two opaque-glass goblets, a pitcher of water, their plate of tapas, a bowl of sugar cubes, a pair of perforated spoons and a quarter-full green bottle. As he set the things down, Frieda glimpsed the hand concealed under the towel, and looked away towards the bar, where she caught the eyes of Manolo through the smoke. She thought he nodded at her and she turned quickly back to the activity at the table, Juan Pablo half-filling their glasses with a flat green liquid, then leaving them.

'Did you notice his hand?'

'No, why?'

'He's missing the ends of his fingers.'

'Probably lost them when he was a fisherman.'

'I remember something about the Fascists cutting off the fingers of people caught writing in forbidden languages, like Catalan.'

'They did that with the Basques, not the Catalans. He probably lost them winching in the nets. Happens all the time.'

'That's what I read ... ' Frieda stared down at the two glasses sitting upon the newly crowded table. 'Now what?' she asked.

'Something about the sugar ... '

'I know!' Frieda said, taking a spoon and placing it over the glass. 'You put a cube of sugar here, and then pour water onto it, and the sugar dissolves through the holes in the spoon and drips into the drink.'

'That's exactly it! I remember now.' Ellis was already preparing the glasses. 'So how did a nice girl like you learn about a drink like this?'

'I saw glasses and spoons like these at a brocante once and asked about them. Only those spoons were flat and triangular and made out of silver.'

'So are these,' Ellis said, taking Frieda's spoon and holding it up to his eyes. 'There's something unique about silver spoons. If you put a silver spoon in an opened bottle of champagne it will keep its bubbles.'

'Any spoon will do.'

'It has to be silver ... just like the one you were born with.'

'Never miss an opportunity, do you?'

'Not if I can help it.'

'You're jealous. There's no-one I know who would have loved to have been born into privilege more than you.' Frieda raised her glass to her nose and sniffed, pulling away quickly.

'Dalí for one ... What's the matter?'

'It smells like paint thinner!'

Ellis swirled his glass under his nose. 'I get mainly anís but there *is* a resin smell there, hints of turpentine, and something almost like unripe mango!'

'Green fruit, that's bad for your stomach too! We're not really going to drink this, are we?'

'This is the muse of the poets—*la fée verte*—we can't stop. Now when we slowly add the water it'll cloud like pastis.'

'I don't like pastis.'

'Too late darling, we're in over our heads.' Ellis placed the spoons back on the glasses, balanced sugar cubes on them then gently poured the water from the pitcher, the sugar bleeding into the absinthe which stirred like oil receiving water. He increased the flow and the water began to penetrate the drink, forcing a concaved separate domain within the alcohol, sending a puff of whitish cloud expanding outwards. 'Look, it's changing now.' A few more drops and the spreading cloud was tentatively touching the borders of the glass, consuming the absinthe. Then everything settled, the liquid rendered a flat, murky white, like the flesh of an oyster.

'Magic! It looks much safer now. Cheers.'

The power of the drink took Ellis by surprise, an intense, deadly burning lingering in his oesophagus long after he'd swallowed, making him gasp as much in astonishment as in breathlessness. He felt the liquid's journey, the indencently heavy arrival, and then a second burning, melting into a rising heat that embraced his stomach, his lungs, his throat; his nasal passages preternaturally clear, as though cauterised. The thing that bothered him the most was that he enjoyed the cumulative experience. He looked at Frieda, who was holding a hand delicately but emphatically to her throat, as though she were an elderly matron receiving bad news about the imperial army. Her eyes were wide when she smiled. 'Some drink.'

Ellis looked at her glass. Frieda had drunk it all in one gulp. He drained his, receiving a similar yet diminished rush, then refilled their glasses. 'Take it easy,' he said, 'you should sip it slowly, the way you do pastis.'

'I didn't mean to gulp, it just happened.' She impaled a piece of octopus on a toothpick and offered it to Ellis. He shook his head. 'Not hungry?'

'After that lunch?'

'You have to eat. That's what the barman said.'

'I've never known a woman to eat like you.'

'I have a normal appetite.'

'*I* have a normal appetite. You have an immense appetite. Where does it all go?'

'I burn it off. It's normal. You must have been like that when you were young.'

Ellis smiled, tasting the absinthe without water or sugar. He felt the gravity of the drink on his lips. 'My God this is strong! Give me your glass.' He set up the spoons and sugar and began to pour the water in. 'The thing about absinthe is that it's not really an alcoholic drink, it's a drug. It even has the paraphernalia of a drug, like the pipe with opium, or the tourniquet, needle and flame with heroin. There's no other drink that has that.'

'Tequila,' Frieda said. 'It has the salt and the lemon, and the knife to cut it with. And the worm . . . '

'Jesus, sounds more like some 17th century *Vanité* canvas than a drink. All you need is the skull. Look, I don't know about tequila, Mexico is your territory. But this drink is in my domain. I understand it. It's Degas' painting, Lautrec's *oeuvre*; Van Gogh's life. It's art history. That's why your loco monkey, Dalí, would never drink absinthe.'

'He doesn't need it.'

'Now more than ever. You saw the stuff he's doing. The man's caught in a time trap, like the whole goddamn country. He hasn't taken one artistic risk since the war.'

'That's not exactly true, Ellis. You're always too hard on others, too competitive. They give *you* credit for what you're doing.'

'They give me credit because they're afraid of me, they're afraid of what I'm doing and even more importantly, they're afraid of who's taking notice. Talk to Lipchitz and Zadkine, talk to Braque—even Giacometti and Picasso. They all know who's doing what, who's selling, and why. Even Dalí knows and he's stuck down here south of the border. The pressure's on, forces are shifting. New York grows more powerful every day. I know what they're all thinking, I'm asking myself the same question: what happens to innovators and modernists when they begin to be left behind by the very forces they helped create?'

'Honestly, Ellis, these people are still at the height of their powers.'

'The art market doesn't think so.'

'The art market doesn't know what it thinks.'

'That's precisely why it's so important. It's an empty vessel. It doesn't know, so it has to be told what to buy. You find the right voice and the market will follow, no questions asked. I'm not saying it's right, I'm simply saying that's the way it is . . . We finished that bottle already?' He turned towards the bar. —Señor? Dos más, por favor.

Juan Pablo came to their table, solicitous yet anxious. —Perhaps you would like to try some tinto? We have excellent tinto, from Tarragona Province. Better than Rioja really. . .

—Thank you. More absenta and more sugar.

Juan Pablo brought a new bottle to the table, holding it under his bad arm as he broke the seal with a knife. He poured generous Spanish measures, the absinthe like a green snake coiled in the bottom of their glasses. Juan Pablo took the bottle away, then returned with first a bowl of sugar cubes, and then a large platter of Serrano ham and slices of bread smeared with olive oil and fresh tomato. —You must eat as you drink, he said. —Otherwise your stomachs will be bad, very bad.

Frieda felt a rush of affection for the barman, the bodega, for the whole village; a door was opening before her, about to reveal experiences she had always guessed were out there but would somehow never befall her. 'Let me do the honours this time,' she said, placing the sugar on the spoons. She poured the water onto the cubes one drop at a time, far more slowly than Ellis had done. 'See? You weren't doing it right.'

'You're the expert now, are you?'

'It has to be slow, *really* slow.'

'I did do it slow, slower than you.'

'No you didn't. You always rush things that need to be slow.'

'What does that mean, I always rush things?'

'You have to be careful not to bruise the absinthe.'

'What exactly do I rush?'

Frieda's eyes were level with the glasses, watching a bead of water swell at the bottom of the sugar cube and hover, crystal-enriched, for a long moment before plunging into the absinthe, sending shivers through the alcohol, its oily consistency quivering then reforming, absorbing the invader. 'What ... ?'

'I said what are you talking about?'

'The idea that you can tell what's happening just by knowing the end result is wrong. You have to watch the transformation take place. You have to be patient.' Each drop of water was enriched and transformed by the sugar and each took its toll on the absinthe until the evolution began, the alcohol slowly ceding its colour and consistency, roiling towards an opaque cloud of white with currents of dense, swollen green swimming through it.

'It needs more water.'

'It's perfect.' Frieda sipped it and her lungs ached, as though she were inhaling the inflamed air around a bonfire, and then there was a rush of warmth deep inside her, the kind of lulling profoundness she imagined must overwhelm mothers at the very moment of conception. 'Perfect . . . ' Her lips and mouth were drying.

Ellis took a long sip and received the turbid glow, an elevated astringency cutting through his breath, clearing his throat and nostrils, making his eyes water. And then there was the charmed settling, like stepping off a rocking boat onto the certainty of land. 'What were you saying about me? You were trying to make a point about me.' His tongue was heavy and he could feel the sharpness of his teeth around it. 'I have to be careful,' he said.

'About being too fast?'

'What?'

'You said you had to be careful.' Frieda was patient, savouring the irresistible allure of logic. 'Careful about what?'

Ellis was eating a piece of bread with the deliberate attention of a convalescent patient.

'Careful about what?'

'Careful I don't bite my tongue off . . . All right, you can laugh, but it has happened. I have heard of it happening. Do I sound strange to you?'

'Usually.'

'I mean now.'

'You're lisping.'

'So are you. See? We could bite out tongues off. Easily. We'd choke on them of course.'

'It's a metaphor for life . . . '

'What, biting off your tongue?'

'No, this drink. It's so hard at first; that first swallow. Then it's easy. Just like life, right?'

'That's not a metaphor for life, that's a metaphor for learning to ride a bicycle ... ' He pushed the plate towards her. 'Eat, eat, you have to eat. Otherwise you'll be sick.'

'My glass is empty.'

'Now that's a metaphor for life.' He turned towards the bar. —Señor? Dos más, por favor.

'I think we should go.'

'Where?'

'Home.'

'To Paris?'

'To the hotel. Gaudí designed it.'

'I know, I told you that.'

'I could tell without you telling me. That's the difference, you see.'

'Difference between what?'

'Braque, Giacometti, Picasso, even Dalí. All the people you were slandering.'

'They're artists, not people. And I wasn't slandering them.'

'Yes you were. They can tell without being told. That's what makes them artists. They don't need the art market. For them it's the equivalent of gossip, that's all. It's *Variety*!'

'It's Hedda fucking Hopper ... '

'I can't sit here arguing with you, Ellis, I have to go home. I need to lie down.'

'Are you all right, darling?'

'If I get home, I will be. My hands are going numb.'

Ellis stood, for the first time noticing the Serrano hams that swung like hanged bandits from the rafters. He used them to navigate a way to the bar.

—Sí, señor . . . ?

—The bill, please.

—Sí señor . . . Twelve pesetas.

Ellis handed him two ten-peseta notes, and waved the change away.

—Gracias . . . Are you all right, señor?

'Never better.'

—Perdón . . .?

—Sí, I'm fine, gracias. Ellis went over to the door and held it open, the evening wind coming in, full of contradictions: warm with the contained heat of the day, fresh from the sea. He waited there for some time, then closed the door and went back to the table. 'Are you all right?'

'I'll never be all right again . . .'

'Can you stand?'

'I think I'm going to die.'

'No, no you're not. Just here, give me your hand, that's right, now put your arm around me . . . that's right. Just a few more steps . . . ' Juan Pablo had the door open for them.

—Gracias. Buenas tardes.

—Buenas noches señor, señora. . .

They crossed through the fountain's spray, the moon lancing towards them from the sea, unexpected and strangely satisfying, like the face of a friend suddenly seen on the métro. The wind revived Frieda enough to make her insist she could walk on her own, leading them up through an archway, gusts pursuing them like porters at a train station, then turning down a steeply descending alley into an extraordinary, contained stillness, the high facades protecting them from the Tramontana. They followed the

narrow lane, their feet slipping on flint cobblestones sleek
with time, the alley deserted except for the mirrored glint of
cats' eyes and distant intimations of domestic life; the stutter
of kitchen dishes, football cried through a radio, the gentle
intrusion of a guitar and the sobs of a young woman. The
lane emptied onto a plaza, streetlights swinging in the
breeze, their hotel suddenly standing there, expectant and
satisfied at their cries of amazement. 'Thank God,' Frieda
said, already heading for the reception desk. Ellis took
charge of squeezing them past the astonished gaze of the
elevator boy and into the lift, their wrought-iron cabin rising
past ceilings that swirled like the sea, angles bending the
wrong way, misdirecting lines of vision. Just like the end of
a play, the key fitted perfectly and Frieda threw herself onto
the bed, the pillows refuge and salvation.

'Aren't you going to get undressed?'

'I want to stay dressed in case you call the doctor.'

'But why would I call the doctor?'

'Please turn off the light ... *please!*'

Ellis switched off the light. Outside their window the
square was still rocking. 'Why would I call a
doctor? ... Darling?' He leant over Frieda, her breath only
slightly laboured. 'Darling ... ?' The bed swayed under his
weight when he lay down, as though it were an air mattress
on a swimming pool. He waited for the water to settle,
Gaudí's ceiling flowing across his eyes like a river that never
ends. He closed his eyes to make it end and it went away,
taking him along with it.

Frieda had no idea what time it was when she woke,
nor what hotel she was in. She only knew that she was

dying. She stood up, unhooked her dress and let it fall, then stepped out of it towards the bathroom, the tiles freezing through her stockings. She peeled them off as she sat on the toilet, her life slowly passing out from her, clutching her ankles with her hands and moaning as it got worse, her perspiration-matted hair forlorn about her calves. She had never realised before how thin her legs felt, as if she were still just a little girl and she started to cry for her own fragility and for the childhood she had lost and for her parents who had left her an orphan, and she cried until her chest ached and she had to lean over into the basin, still sitting on the toilet, and retch into the cold embrace of porcelain.

Afterwards she felt completely enervated yet oddly determined. She was able to clean herself up and make a glass of water with three soluble aspirin tablets and to drink it, and even to clean her teeth afterwards. Naked, she went back to the bed, the coolness of the tiles giving way to the caress of carpet. Ellis was sleeping on top of the covers, half his body hanging off the edge. Through the window she saw the square was flooding. She watched water rising above doorsteps and shop fronts and she estimated how long it would take before the floodwaters reached their floor. She still had time to go back to bed. The sheets were cool and blurred and pulled her towards the white infinity of sleep.

Frieda felt remarkably alert and rested in the morning, using the powerful hot jets of water in the shower to test out any signs of weakness in her head or body. There were none. She had rid herself of the poison the night before and now she was stronger than ever, as if her body had been immunised. She admired her long, graceful legs in the mirror as she shaved them, legs which had felt so thin and childlike only hours before restored once more to those of a natural athlete. She combed her newly-washed hair, lustrous under the brush, and she was nearly dressed when Ellis awoke, a stunned look of dried surprise on his face.

'Good morning. How do you feel?'

'I'll let you know when I understand.' Ellis retreated to the bathroom, transforming himself in only thirty minutes into a passable representation of himself. Together they went downstairs and had breakfast in the dining room overlooking the still-drying square.

'You don't want those?'

'Take them. My God, it must have poured last night. Look at the puddles out there.' His eyes wandered inside, widening in amazement. 'Look at these carpets! They're drenched.'

'The whole square flooded. I saw it. Water was going in under all the doors.'

'The rain woke you up?'

'I ... I had a dry throat.'

'*Had* ... Mine's still as dry as a salt plain. How can you eat after last night?'

'You know what Juan Pablo said. "Eat! You must eat!"'

'Muy malo for your goddamn stomach all right! Listen, I was thinking, I'm not feeling that great today. Why don't we just drive as far as Collioure and spend the rest of the day there. That'll get us past the border at least. That's the main thing. We can take a wander around, look at the places Derain and Matisse painted, go swimming if we're up to it, all right?'

'They have a beach there?'

'Two, right on the port.'

'Sounds wonderful. When shall we go?'

'How about now? I just need to pick up a few supplies before we leave.'

'Can you get me some saffron while you're there?'

'Of course. Anything else?'

'You could order some more coffee and croissants on your way out.'

His lips were dry against hers. 'There's no stopping you, is there? *A tout à l'heure.*'

Even with the top down, the drive was something of an ordeal at first, going up the steeply winding hills of the cape, then descending the switchbacks towards El Port de la Selva, the sky wind-polished and optimistic with early summer. After la Selva the road became much easier, obediently following the coast north for the last ten miles, the border crossing at Portbou taken up with exchange receipts and the laborious counting of pesetas and francs; the officials abrupt and sullen, as though under instructions to leave as unpleasant a parting memory as possible so that only those who really loved the country would return to face the red tape and black patent leather of Franco's Spain. After more than an hour they were released into the welcoming embrace of France, a jovial-looking gendarme flagging them down at the Cerbère customs post. —Monsieur, madame, your passports please ... Ellis handed them over and the gendarme returned them without even opening them. —Do you have anything to declare?

—Nothing.

—Very good ... May I look inside those bags in the back?

—Of course.

—Merci ... Ah monsieur, you told me you had nothing to declare!

—But I don't.

—Mais monsieur, surely you are mistaken. What is this ...?

The gendarme was holding a large green bottle with *la vraie absinthe* written on its label in prominent blue and white scrollwork.

'Ellis! How could you?'

'Frieda, please ... '

—Et voilà, monsieur, même la dame est choquée!

—But ... but we are allowed one bottle of spirits, are we not?

—Of course monsieur, one bottle, we are civilised in France, but absinthe ... ? Non, monsieur, we are not *that* civilised. Elle est interdite.

—Really ... ? I had no idea it was forbidden.

—Mais oui, since many years. Monsieur, I am afraid that I will have to confiscate this bottle.

—Oh but ...

—*Monsieur*, please. I could fine you heavily for attempting to smuggle contraband into France, but I understand that you did not know this was the case.

—I had no idea. In Spain it is sold everywhere.

—They are like that in Spain, uncivilised ... Alors, monsieur, madame, bonne route!

—Merci ... They drove on in silence till they were well

out of Cerbère. 'Damn,' he finally said, 'I was hoping to take some back to Paris.'

'But Ellis, why on earth would you want to? Wasn't last night enough?'

'Curiosity value, I suppose. Besides, last night wasn't so bad ... No it wasn't! Look at you, I've never seen you as bright as this in the morning.'

'I'm bright because I remember how I felt last night and I know I'll never ever feel like that again.'

'Never say never.'

'I'll never let that happen to me again. Not with absinthe or anything.'

'We're certainly certain this morning. There's nothing like being certain in the morning.'

'How about you? I can't believe you wanted to take that poison back with you. And don't tell me last night wasn't too bad, I saw you. I know what you were like.'

'Listen, Frieda, I've had worse than last night and I suppose there'll be worse to come.'

'Doesn't that make you sad, to think that?'

'Why should it make me feel sad?'

'It's just that sometimes you go out of your way to have nights like last night. You're, I don't know, attracted to it ... to the romance of it.'

'I'm attracted to experience, to taking risks, that's all. And in a strange sort of way it helps my work.'

'It helps your work to feel as sick as a dog?'

'Darling, let's not go into this right now. Frankly, I'm not up to it.'

'My point exactly.'

'Darling, please ... '

'All right, no more arguments for today,' she said, gathering her legs up under her, the sea coming back into view. 'So tell me about Collioure. There are two beaches, you say?'

'One for the morning and one for the afternoon.'

Frieda looked at her watch. 'Good, we'll have time for both.'

In front of them the coast road began to drop towards the red cliffs of Collioure, the sea beyond dazzling in the intensity of its blue, the wind sculpting white cuffs of motion across its travelling surface. Frieda began to laugh.

'What's up?'

She shook her head.

'Come on tell me, what's so funny?'

'He's probably still standing there, still waving ... '

Ellis' laugh rose above the motor, even sustaining itself briefly against the blunt, heavy pistons working inside his head. When Frieda leant over to kiss him she noticed the sweat at his temples and how terribly pale and drawn he looked. 'Everything will be all right,' she said, caressing his brow, 'as long as we have one beach for the morning and one for the afternoon.'

Christos Tsiolkas

M argaret Kildare had just made the coffee and was involved in a polite argument with Denise, the Jehovah's Witness from across the road, when she heard a knock on the front door, answered it, and was breathlessly told by the awaiting police officer, a young woman in a neatly pressed uniform who was squeezing tight on her cap, that after shooting seven people in the National Unity Bank building, Margaret's son Patrick had turned the rifle on himself and had blown his brains out.

Margaret had no moment of disbelief. The impact of the police officer's brutal recitation was immediate. It marked the clear and sudden break of her life into distinct parts. Afterwards, everything was to divide into the before and after of that moment.

The police officer tried to put her arm around her, but Margaret shook it off. An apology flitted across her mind, but it easily vanished. She did not want to be touched, hugged or comforted. Her mind went immediately to order. Denise can make the tea and coffee. I've got to ring John.

Denise's reaction was pure bewilderment and she was praying softly to herself as she spooned out the coffee, arranged the cups. Margaret could see her lips quietly forming mantras. The policewoman stayed with her while two detectives came into the house to check out Patrick's room.

Conversation was, of course, impossible and Margaret excused herself to phone her husband.

'It may be better to wait and tell him when he gets home,' the police officer said. 'We can go and collect him from work.'

'No,' said Margaret immediately, 'you can't arrive at his work in a police car. People will talk.'

The young woman looked embarrassed, Denise choked back a cry, and Margaret bit down hard on her lip. It hit her, a freezing panic. This was something the whole world was going to know about. Stripped of the formidable reserve which was one of her defining traits, she collapsed with her face in her hands, knocked over a coffee mug and started to wail.

Anna Tagatti was on the phone when she noticed the strange man approaching the counter. She was talking softly to her boyfriend Steve. One moment, she mouthed to the stranger.

'Steve, honey, I've got to go.' This time she mouthed the words, I'm sorry. Steve kept on talking.

The man had a blue bag hanging over his shoulder. It reminded Anna of the bag she had at school, only bigger, and with an airline logo on the side instead of the school crest. The man was sweating, his neck and forehead glistened. She was saying goodbye to Steve when she noticed that the stranger had unzipped his bag and taken out the rifle. She stopped talking and dropped the phone. The rifle was astonishingly beautiful, a sharp ebony. That thought flashed by. Then he pointed the gun in her face and she started to scream.

She stepped back, slow, and he fired two quick shots into her temple, a bullseye, and she jerked back against the wall. There was a loud crack.

It was only the calm wave of the narcotic that brought Margaret back to sanity. The doctor was cool and professional, did not say much. John sat beside her on the bed, crying continuously, and holding her hand. She marvelled at the amount of tears; he wasn't howling, but his pain was open and neverending. His grief was surprisingly comfortable. He was only interested in the suicide of his son, he was hurting with the loss. She looked up at him. The thoughts of the murders slipped away. She kept coming in and out of sleep. He did not let go of her hand.

In Patrick Kildare's room the investigating officers found a half-completed essay on rules of evidence, a copy of the video *Falling Down*, copies of *American Shooter* going back two years, a pack of pornographic playing cards from Wrest Point Casino, seven pornographic magazines, a heavily notated copy of Barry Hines' *Kes*, a slashed Visa card, promotional material from Australians Against Further Immigration, from National Action and from the Macquarie University Anarchist Collective, a ticket to a Red Hot Chili Peppers concert, a bong and a quarter ounce of marijuana, two suicide letters dated five months apart, a copy of the Bible, the skeleton of a blue tongue lizard, a biography of Charles Manson, the autobiography of Malcolm X, a biography of General Powell and two other books about the Gulf War, a Monkey Punch cartoon novel from Japan, a card advertising a brothel in Altona, an outstanding invoice for mechanical repairs to Patrick's car, two empty Jim Beam bottles, a semen stained T-shirt under the bed with ants crawling all over it, a job file containing twelve job rejection letters, a collection of newspaper articles about the Vietnamese control of the heroin trade in the city's inner-west, a signed photograph of Geelong footballer Gary Ablett, unopened mail from the University, including a notice from the Head of the Law informing Patrick of an interview before an assessment panel, a photograph of his ex-girlfriend Victoria, and a three-hour video containing various segments of the *World at War* documentary series. There were two

posters on the walls: a theatre bill for *Platoon*, and an A4
photocopy of a quote from Revelations:

And in those days shall men seek death
and shall not find it; and shall desire to die, and death shall
flee from them

Directly beneath where the photocopy was Blu-tacked
on the wall, there was a savage indent in the plaster. A
murky smudge surrounded the indentation, which tests
revealed to be samples of Patrick Kildare's blood. The drip
marks trickled all the way down to the skirting rail; there
were dried stains on the carpet.

Margaret liked to drink. The day of the funeral she was
drunk by mid-morning. Her sister was running around,
taking charge and Margaret just sat floating at the kitchen
table, downing whiskey and smoking cigarettes. She was
being prescribed a strong dose of Valium that relaxed her
straining neck muscles. The whiskey, dark and lush, Irish
and smooth, was soothing. She slipped her tongue around
its velvet texture, felt it ignite her throat.

'Another one, Anne,' she ordered, and her sister reluctantly poured her another. She was swimming in the
whiskey, diving into the glass, shutting out the room. There
was her sister, a neighbour, and John. Didn't he keep
coming in and out? All the others, the neighbours, the relatives, they were just blurs. There was to be nothing of that
day that she would remember. Just how good the whiskey
was.

After he shot Anna Taggati, Patrick turned around and

pointed the rifle into the panicking crowd. The offices of
the Trentham and Delaney insurance company were cluttered with desks but it was open plan and Patrick had a
clear view of most of the people in the office. He walked
towards a blonde young woman, a girl really, no more
than seventeen, who had fallen to the floor, her hands
around her ears, rocking on her knees. She looked up as
Patrick approached, all tears and moaning. He pointed the
rifle at her, paused, and then kept walking. He fired on
Alistair Lee, big and burly, shot him twice through the
stomach, and then shot Bettina Kowper through the head.
He murdered Russell Dixon and fired twice on Alex Gian-
nopoulis. Gerald Geeson, forty-five and a supervisor, had
tried to hide under his desk. For some reason this outraged
Patrick who belted Geeson with the butt of the rifle, then
started kicking into him. He played with him, shooting
him through the foot, and leaving him screaming while he
shot Valerie Hodgkinson and Dagmar Vatsko. He then
returned to Geeson and shot him through the neck. Blood
had drenched the white bare walls, had soaked the carpet.
People were screaming, moaning, dying. Then there was a
sound of a war on the fire escape stairs, and a squad of
men, decked out in military fatigues smashed through into
the office. But they were too late. In front of young Jimmy
Brown, the work experience kid, Patrick shot himself.
Jimmy was not to forget the smell of Patrick's burning
skin, the spray of blood and brain. His sleep was to be
haunted by Patrick's flimsy body ricocheting from the
assault of the gunfire. A spastic dance of death.

The young woman who had been spared Patrick's

outrage was offered $20,000 by *Woman's Day* to tell her story. Alex Giannopoulis, who survived the shooting, was not so lucky. High on pethidine, he told his story, for free, to a pretty young journalist from the *Herald-Sun*.

John decided to tell few people about the funeral. Only the closest relatives, the most loyal friends. There was no announcement in the newspapers. People avoided mentioning Patrick's name. John's gut spun in lethal anger at this silence. The Priest mumbled through the service, confounded by the enormity of Patrick's sin. Everyone avoided John's eye. He realised Margaret had been right to get pissed. She moved about in her trance, ignoring everyone. He wanted to scream out that he loved his son, missed his son, cherished the memory of his son. A deep ugly hatred was forming in his belly, he could sense the fire. He had seen the faces of the people his son had shot on the front page of a morning paper. Seven newsprint portraits stared out at him. He loathed them. He couldn't bear his mother's compassionate sorrow.

'We must write to their families,' she implored him in her thick brogue. 'Not now, not now, it's far too soon, but we must acknowledge our shame. God help us.'

He had listened to her, had watched her grey clenched and frail body sob. Fuck you, mother. That's what he thought.

The day before the funeral they had received the first crank call. The media had been flooding the lines. After the first day, John had taken the phone off the hook. But after calling his brother to organise the cars for the funeral, he absent-mindedly put the receiver back in its place. Almost immediately the phone rang.

—Who is it?

Silence on the other end.

—Can I help you?

—I blame you.

—What? John did not understand.

—You and your cunt of a wife, you're equally to blame. You're murderers. The voice sounded middle-aged, small town and bitter.

John slammed down the receiver and screamed out gulps of pain. Margaret was sitting by the heater, a white robe wrapped around her body. She was holding tight on the bottle.

—John, who was that?

—Wrong number.

Margaret did not believe him.

Over the next two weeks, as the murders were to dominate headlines across Australia, Margaret and John were to receive fifty-seven letters of vile abuse. Most letters treated Patrick as Satan, an evil force that must have been created by the combined sins of the parents. The letters hinted at abuse, perverse incestuous humiliation, obscure cultic torture. On the television a psychologist argued that Patrick must have been, could only have been, abused as a child to go on and commit the murders. Bizarre stories, intricate and fantastic, were heard. First the street, then the neighbour-hood, and then it seemed the whole city, had turned against

John and Margaret. They moved into her sister's place but the callers managed to find them there. Margaret often recognised a tone or an accent but the whiskey mixed with the pills had dulled her memory and she could never place a face or a name to the sound. She didn't really care. No one could be trusted.

One of the letters was slipped under Anne's front door. It was addressed to Margaret. She began to tear it open and noticed the blood. Her fingers were sliced by the sharp edge of razor blades glued under the envelope's fold.

Margaret stared at her bleeding fingers. Her face collapsed and she turned old. John put out a hand to steady her. He bandaged her hand, stroked her hair, and he noticed that her lips were cracked and black from nicotine. He poured her a drink. She gulped at it gratefully.

After Anne's place, they moved to Cairns. But the local television station discovered them and they had to move again. They settled somewhere in Western Australia. And changed their names.

When Patrick was fourteen he got into a savage fight over a football game and had started kicking in the head of an opponent. Five boys had to pull him off and Patrick started belting into them. His outrage was ferocious.

'We could have won, we could have won, if that fuckwit Terry hadn't fudged that mark.'

Mr Lageti marched Patrick into the changerooms and threw him under the shower. The water was freezing, the drops stabbed into Patrick's skin. His anger kept him warm. The thick, sharp jet of ice water continued to bruise his body but Patrick refused to apologise. His electric dark eyes stared out at Lageti and it was the teacher who was the first to look away.

The offices of Trentham and Delaney were shut for three days. Cleaners were hired to transform the offices over the weekend. When the staff came back to work on the Monday following the massacre, there was no sign of damage, no specks of blood anywhere to be seen. A round of prayers were held and then everyone resumed their work.

Staff were discouraged from talking to the media. This was a memo straight from the top, from Mr Delaney himself, the great grandson of the architect of the business.

A representative of Trentham and Delaney attended all seven funerals.

Margaret listened to her husband deliver a eulogy to Patrick and she felt sick. Nausea. He looked thin and very unattractive up there. His suit was too big for him. The alcohol saved her from screaming, kept her mouth shut. She couldn't feel any love for her son—was there ever any love there? She couldn't recall his face. Margaret choked out a whimper and the small congregation all arched their necks to look at her. John smiled down at her. She returned him a valium-tinged grimace. She couldn't recall Patrick's eyes. She knew their colour, their shape, but she couldn't ever remember looking into them. He always turned away from her.

John finished the eulogy by affirming his love for Patrick. The guests shuffled their feet. Margaret was all spite.

I wish the little bastard had never been born. She remembered having that thought and then she quickly nodded back into her drunken trance, shutting out the church, the world, her husband and her friends. She daydreamed numbness.

After the funeral, she drank more, quick shots of liquid down her throat and she made her excuses and fell into bed. The bed was soft and she swam in it, rolled in it, letting the alcohol and the drugs send her into sleep. John came in to look in on her, and she clenched her eyes tight, pretending to be asleep.

One month before the murders Patrick Kildare visited a brothel in Spotswood called Shivers. He asked for an Asian girl. Emily remembered him because he refused to talk to her, he just handed her sixty dollars and lay back on the massage table. He unzipped his fly and tried to force her mouth down on his cock.

'No,' said Emily. 'Not without a condom.'

Patrick took out an extra twenty-dollar bill.

'The answer is still no.'

He took out another twenty.

She shook her head.

He pulled up his trousers and got up to leave, snatching the money. She gently sat him down on the table and pocketed the forty dollars. His crotch smelled foul. Bitter sweat caked his thighs and dry flecks of come coated the head of his penis. He forced her head hard on to his cock, pushing through into her throat, and as he came he tugged hard on her hair, wrapped it firm around his fist, and he would not let her wrench her mouth away from him. She was crying when he finally let go. She spat all over him.

Patrick had not washed for a week when he attended the brothel. For at least two months he had not washed his penis, had allowed a moist sheaf of semen to form under his foreskin. His diary plotted the methodical buildup to Emily's humiliation. On the night he returned from the brothel he had written just one line in the diary.

I want to kill.

Margaret had stopped watching the news. The first day she was sedated, the second day she did not get out of bed and on the third day John threw an ashtray through the television screen. It was in Cairns that she first saw footage of the massacre. Police vans and ambulances were lining up on Bourke Street, and there were bodies being carried out in stretchers. She saw a photo of Patrick flash on the screen. Eighteen, crewcut, eyes lowered. He looked like a thug.

The man from the television who found them in Cairns offered a couple of thousand dollars to interview them. When John refused the man started to swear and to threaten them. Margaret thought him vile and fascinating. His hair did not seem real—not a wig, but not natural either.

'Excuse me,' she interrupted, 'have you had a hair transplant?'

The next day there was a picture of Patrick in the paper. And a photo of their house in Cairns. SHAMED PARENTS FLEE PSYCHO'S MASSACRE was the headline. Their house was on the six o'clock news and again on television at seven the next morning.

Three years after the violence, for that is how she referred to it, Margaret woke up from a terrible nightmare in which a young Patrick, still a boy, was tearing apart the anguished body of a cat. In her sleep, Margaret recognised the cat. It belonged to the Donaldsons, the nice South African couple just down the road. She woke up with the cat's terror puncturing her into consciousness. She was wide awake.

She got up, left John snoring, and moved into the kitchen. She poured out a large glass of whiskey, lit a cigarette, and started drinking. Outside the world was still black. She drank a second, a third. She lit another cigarette and went out into the backyard, taking the drink with her. A mist had settled over the town, a gossamer halo encircled the moon. She sniffed the night air. When Patrick was five he had discovered an injured dove at the back of the garden. It's not going to live, John told him, it's dying. Patrick had taken the bird and cuddled it in his palms. Give it to me, John ordered, I'll take it away, put it out of its misery. Patrick screamed as his father took the bird out of the young boy's hands. Patrick ran to a corner of the garden, and under the canopy of giant ferns, he covered his ears and shut his eyes. John cupped the bird in his hands, and squeezed.

'Do you want to bury it?'

Patrick rushed up to his father, grabbed the carcass and dived back under the ferns.

Margaret had tried to hug the boy but he refused her sympathy. He remained in hiding, digging into the dirt, burying the bird. When he finally came into the house, it was dusk. She ordered him to wash his hands. He refused.

That night he ate his dinner slowly. His hands smelt of soil and feathers.

Margaret drank her whiskey and the comforting balm of the alcohol slowly relieved her of agitation. She gazed into the dark golden liquid and breathed in the fumes. The fog was moving around her, soaking into her, and she was drifting towards sleep. She looked up at the sky, at the stars obscured by the mist, and she was warm. She couldn't tell where the fog began and where it ended. The sky was in the whiskey and the whiskey had drenched the whole world.

Margaret wrapped the fog around her, drank from it, breathed it, and moved sluggishly back to bed. She descended into the mattress, plunged deep inside it, and when sleep came, it tasted dry; it tasted bitter and smooth.

Susan Errington

Tasting Prospera

So bright. So clear. It is morning in the house. As they fade away, the smells of the dead evening's entertainment seem caught for a moment by the patterns of sunlight falling on the floor. The smells linger like ghosts, fleetingly, and then they are gone. Out of the window. The stinking incense of the cigars and cigarettes. The whiffs of cooked meat, the pungency of dried sauces. Even the flowers in the vases and bowls exhale their tired perfumes and their water is already darkening to putrid.

It is morning in this room. It's quiet. There's a hushed air of expectation here as if somewhere someone is waiting for a curtain to go up. Look into the room. In this scene there is a bedroom and a bed and a girl, who is not quite asleep, almost awake. Her name is Prospera. She is eleven.

Waking, Prospera cannot remember what it was that broke her sleep. If she had dreamed, her dreams are forgotten. She thinks that perhaps it was a dream. The dream about trains. Of endlessly waiting on platforms or of getting lost or losing things and other people. Prospera saying goodbye. Feeling afraid, perhaps. The house is very still. Prospera lies on her side, with her knees tucked up under her chin. It's too early to get up but she can't seem to go back to sleep. Prospera has closed her eyes tightly but the sunlight is always getting in.

At last, she rolls herself out of bed. Her bare toes curl as they touch the floor boards. Instinctively, she feels cold. Feels as if she should feel cold on such a blue and cloudless morning in summer. Soon the temperature will rise rapidly, so everything is relative, and by reference, it is cool now compared to later on. Getting out of bed, Prospera cannot escape seeing her reflection in the mirror. She would rather not, if she could help it. Fat Prospera, they say so bluntly, so profanely, at school. This morning Prospera mostly sees the tangled mane of hair she is growing in the hope of concealing her entire body. Her sister has threatened to cut it all off while Prospera is asleep. Occasionally, Prospera drapes her bedroom mirror with an old scarf or jumper or some piece of underwear. The mirror will remain veiled for a few days, until she can no longer bear the suspense and absolutely must uncover it. Just to see if there is a new Prospera underneath. Disappointment cannot be avoided but she wants to look anyway, out of resentment, out of fascination with her own apparent ugliness.

Prospera is restless and she wanders around the house. It seems so deserted that Prospera imagines that it is empty and abandoned. That the house is not in the middle of some suburban street but in the middle of the desert, or on an island, standing alone like a lighthouse. A decaying building, on the point of breaking up, of falling into the sea. Even the gulls shun it. And everyone else has gone away, leaving Prospera alone. She wouldn't be afraid on her island, in her lighthouse. Not like at the train station. It would be her place.

A chair is lying on its back at the dining room door. It's half in and half out of the doorway. It looks like a watch dog that has fallen asleep on duty, its legs up in the air, head down, snoozing in the shade. A tatty, old dog. Prospera sees that it is not a chair which actually belongs in the dining room; it's a chair she can't ever recall seeing in the house before, of bent wood with a rounded back and plaited wicker seat. Absurdly Prospera is angry that some guest at last night's party has brought this invader and left it for her to pick up and care for. She carries the chair and stands it behind the door where it can no longer be seen and give offence.

Even the dining room looks different this morning. The furniture has been moved about. It's pressed up against the walls, creating a large square in the middle. Prospera spins in a circle in the empty centre of that room. It's a long, large room and the ceiling is decorated with plaster mouldings of vines and grapes, stylised as though part of a coat of arms. Her spinning startles a bird in the pine tree outside the French doors that look onto the garden. The flapping and flustering of the wings sound for a minute like a cough or a laugh. A hidden intruder. As if Prospera were not alone in the room after all. She stops spinning and when the room stops spinning too, Prospera is staring at the dining room table, which has been pushed back to the wall by the fireplace. A white tablecloth still covers it. An Irish quilt of embroidered linen bequeathed by a great grandmother. The table faces the French doors. It is what is on the table that surprises Prospera. On top of the clean cloth, someone has neatly lined up row after row of glasses. There are many of them, Prospera thinks, maybe there's fifty, maybe there's one hundred glasses on the table. Left over from the night before, they are the final flavours of the party. Most of the glasses are still half-full, not empty and washed as they should have been on the beautiful quilt. Someone could not bear to pour away the wine, to watch it swirl and gurgle down the domestic drain. This wine is left behind with great order and ceremony despite the knowledge of ultimate destruction. Prospera remembers how she once left a sand castle behind on the shore, knowing that the sea would take it in the end. The glasses sparkle on the white tablecloth. Prospera cannot resist them. You should see how the sunlight runs through the liquid. Yes, these glasses seem to Prospera to be filled with coloured sunlight. Prospera puts her finger into one of the glasses, watching it stain a deep red. She sucks the juice off cautiously, careful not to mark the quilt. Her pink tongue, also stained, relishes the last few drops. And there's more. Drink me, says the wine, as surely as if those words were written on the glasses themselves.

Prospera begins with champagne. Some of the flutes are almost full, others have only dregs. But Prospera doesn't pour all the alcohol into one glass, she tastes each one separately, treats each offering, each discovery, uniquely. Her hands travel over the collection on the table, her eyes searching. Eagerly, Prospera consumes the last of the champagne. She can distinguish this drink from the others because of the tall, graceful flutes, otherwise it would be harder to recognise the champagne. Shapely flute, like a woman in a smooth dress. Prospera holds the cool glass in her hands. She likes the shape. Why are they called flutes? Flutes are long and straight. At school, Prospera's friend has a silver flute. When you put your lips to that instrument it was hard to make any sound. Harder than you ever expected. Lip to lip, the champagne flute seems much easier to play. And the champagne, it's dry to the tongue, this liquid, not sickly sweet and frothy as she was expecting, Prospera licks her mouth. Her head feels light. It's a pleasant sensation after a while. When the juice has had a chance to go down.

A funny feeling. Floating. Her head in the clouds, her feet far below. The room seems far away, blurred somehow. It's suddenly so funny. Prospera laughs to herself. Laughs and laughs. To have your head floating. Your head is a balloon tied to your body by the pink string of your neck. Yes, laughs Prospera to herself. Very funny.

Prospera is thirsty. After all she has drunk, her thirst surprises her, but she knows that her mouth is dry; and her throat. The flutes are empty. Instead Prospera now has the colours to guide her. White. You should start with that colour, she thinks to herself, although she does not remember why. Has she heard her father say that? Nor can Prospera distinguish the different types of white wine. She only vaguely knows some of their names. As she makes her next selection, Prospera gives herself a little test on the names of white wines. A times table of wines. She imagines that she's at school standing in front of the whole class. Something she hates doing, when the knot in your stomach twists so tight you can hardly breathe. She hates the idea that from the safety of their desks, the other girls can look at her as if she's an exhibit in a zoo. But it's all right today. Everyone will be so impressed by her knowledge. How clever you are, Prospera! She lines up some of the glasses in front of her. Pay attention class. Prospera thinks hard to remember the names of the wines. It's difficult this morning, with her head floating around the dining room, but yes, she must pass her wine examination. Well—there are sharperays. Are they like stingrays? Prospera wonders. Her mother told her that if you step on a stingray, it's tail will cut your foot and the wound will never ever heal. It will always be bleeding and weeping. Prospera is angry with her mother for telling her about the stingrays because she loves to go to the beach. Now she is always watching for shapes under the wet sand. Prospera feels the hot swell of her anger rush up from her chest to her face as if her mother were there in the room warning her about stingrays. Her mother never listened; she only talked and talked. But yes, the wine test, she must go on. Prospera, the class is waiting. Speak up, girl. Prospera considers: there are also white wines called readaling, and mouse cell and sendamillion and . . .

Prospera is sitting on the floor. The empty glasses lie around her. Some of them have lipstick stains. Prospera wonders whose lips they are, whose drink she is sharing. Pink lips and apricot, orange and dark red. White wine. But this wine isn't really white, is it. Not white at all but the colour of pale straw. It's the colour of Prospera's hair. Her hated hair. Her too much hair. Prospera pulls all her hair forward until her face is completely covered. There's only a space for her mouth. She's just a mouth, ready to receive, to taste, to swallow. A sticky mouth. Some of the wine has run down her chin. Prospera's hands are less steady now and she's forgotten to be careful about spilling things. The hem of her night dress is splattered with the wine. She can smell the scent of wine on her skin like traces of soap. She'd like to bathe in this drink; so silly. Prospera giggles. She smiles and hums a few tuneless notes. What waste. What wickedness. Suddenly, Prospera up-ends the last glass of white wine. She tips it down the neck of her night dress. The liquid runs between her flesh and the cotton. She holds her hands against her ribs so that hardly any runs on the ground. She rubs the wine in her skin in slow, gentle circles. She loves the smell. Droplets of wine drip down on to her thighs. Prospera closes her eyes and thinks that she might go back to sleep after all. It's peaceful in the dining room. She puts her head down on the scratchy carpet. Prospera feels like she's in a boat floating on a lake. Not a boat, a leaf. The room is melting, is becoming a reflection of a room in the surface of the lake. Ah, the golden sunlight on the water. She can hear a voice calling her through the doors into the garden. It's very faint. Prospera, Prospera. She's not going to answer because she doesn't want to be disturbed although she likes the sound. The voice caresses her, as if someone were gently brushing her hair.

But the red wine is still on the table. Prospera knows that it's there. It's colours are the best of all. She wants to sample those colours. Prospera stands up and sits down again. Stands up and rests on her elbows on the table. The table is holding her up while she traces the detailed pattern of the quilt with one finger. Prospera rocks back and forward for a moment. Her eyes focus on the red wine. The last glasses.

Red wines have names too but today, girls, there will be no oral examination on their nomenclature. You only need to know what your tongue will tell you. And your nose. Red wines are like red roses, full of a solid perfume that makes your head swim and ache a little too, but you keep on inhaling.

Prospera takes the red wine and makes a circle. The glasses of red wine remind Prospera of the glass beads in a necklace which belongs to her, which she keeps wrapped in tissue paper in a drawer in her room. Prospera has always had his necklace. She has a vague memory of receiving it a long time ago, when she was small. At that time she thinks it might have been in a box, but now the tissue paper is all that's left. She likes to imagine that it belongs to a very beautiful woman. Someone who will return some day, not for the necklace but for Prospera and who will make everything right and fair. Sometimes, this woman is Prospera herself.

Prospera never wears the necklace. Only, some days or, more often, nights she carefully unwraps it and holds the smooth, coloured baubles between her fingers' tips. The beads are not all the same shape. They are quite irregular and Prospera likes to close her eyes as her fingers trace each one, studying, memorising their individual contours until their shapes are to her hands like familiar faces to her eyes. The beads are not all the same red but some are pale, just above pink, others gradually deeper in colour. If you stare intensely into the beads, you can be mesmerised by their depth, by your own tiny vermilion image at the centre. Prospera remembers that red colours, as do red wines, have their own unique names.

Prospera drinks the red wine just as quickly as she drank the champagne and the white. She drinks more carelessly, more clumsily. This is the wine that leaves its mark, the juices of the grape printing a strange pattern on her nightdress. Prospera is splashed with red droplets as if by paint or the petals of flowers. Or else she's adorned with jewels, with rubies. Yes, thinks Prospera, she's been wearing her necklace, the first time ever, and the string has broken. But the beads haven't fallen to the floor and rolled away, under the piano or the table or sideboard where she would never reach them. Magically they have stuck to her clothes and become part of her body. She's transformed and is rich and luminous like the beads. Prospera, how beautiful you are!

The last of this colour of wine is darkly red, thicker

than others, a little sweeter, fuller. It's from a glass that was standing away from the others, back in the shadows, almost completely full. It must originally have been chilled because it still retains a little of the feeling of extreme coldness. You could sink into this sticky drink, be held fast in its deep redness. Prospera has put this glass at the top of her red circle and now it is the only one that is left. It waits for Prospera's hand. Drink me.

How suddenly small the dining room seems; darker too. The sunlight has turned to shafts of dust coming in through the window and the doors. Dust that gets into your throat and eyes. The furniture is darker too and the curtains look so heavy, it hurts your arms to think of even touching them. Prospera sits on the ground, or perhaps, she lies down. Back to that peaceful boat on the lake, that's what she wants. The room begins to move around her in a slow circle. All the furniture joining in with the patterns on the ceiling. And the turn quickens, spinning around Prospera who lies very still. Even when you close your eyes, it makes no difference, or makes it worse, the room runs in faster and faster loops like a strange, frightening ride.

Prospera opens her eyes wide. The spinning has stopped for a moment, although the room still trembles with its exertion. What can she see? There it is, in the middle of the floor, the alien, bent wood chair, the intruder that she had placed behind the door, casting a hard and perfect shadow in the centre. As she watches, it seems to Prospera that the chair is tiptoeing forward, little by little. She thinks that if she shuts her eyes again, the chair will rush towards her and attack.

Prospera waits. But there is no attack. No nasty end.

The chair flexes its hooped back; it is bowing to Prospera. It is waiting for Prospera to acknowledge its invitation. Prospera and the chair circle one another in soft, rhythmic steps. Her body seems light, pleasant. Prospera is happy. She feels a sense of release as if a heavy coat has fallen from her shoulders but she does not know from what she is released. She could be naked for all she knows at that moment; that endless moment. How strange that the girl and the chair are dancing. They dance with such unexpected grace; such freedom. Just for them, there might be music too, as the room picks them up and carries them in its whirling embrace. Sweet music.

Until there is a breaking sound. A slapping, a crashing as if the chair has lost its footing and fallen over backwards. There are lights, too harsh. God, they hurt her eyes. There are laughing, scolding voices. And her head, her head is broken with pain by those voices like Humpty's shell. The dance is over. The room is full of people. And the bent wood chair is back behind the door. Dazed, Prospera wonders if that's where it always was. She is gathered up; she is questioned; the doctor is called; she is prodded and pumped but Prospera talks very little. Why should she? They all say, oh she can't remember a thing and they snigger again. Too drunk.

Prospera sits in the shade under a tree. Its branches spread out over her, casting a lime green light. It is afternoon in the garden. The shadows are long; it's cooler. Prospera is pale and has a headache. She reclines on a garden seat and old pillows from the cupboard which are vaguely scented with mothballs and coffee stains. She is gradually succumbing to the feeling of heavy, languid exhaustion that is creeping up through her limbs. As she drifts towards sleep, Prospera thinks that they are quite, quite wrong about her. About forgetting. She can remember. The flavours of the wine are still there in her mouth. What a dream. Prospera, the lotus eater, will never forget.

John Birmingham

The Tasmanian Babes Fiasco

The most fucked-up night of my life ended like this. I spilled through the girls' front door, pants around my knees, howling like a loon at the Gates of Hell. I caught my foot on something and went down. But it didn't matter because I felt no pain. I was so far gone by then I couldn't tell up from down. The world seemed to swim up to me through a watery red mist and all I could make out through this mist were a lot of very serious looking people.

Then the milk van exploded out on their front lawn. This was a piss poor turn of events, which I feel compelled to set down here, in the hope that others might avoid the same ruinous folly.

I'm not sure which domino fell first. The Babes? The Thunderbird? The mountain of drugs and tequila? I just don't know. I have trouble sorting it out. Perhaps I was too wasted or perhaps I just do not want to remember. Whatever. Trying to get this straight is a bit like pushing blocks of coloured smoke around my mind so you'll have to bear with me.

We might as well start with the Babes.

There were three of them. Three Tasmanian Babes. A tall one with big brown hair and cowboy boots; a short, cute one with a spray of freckles on her nose; and the other one, a blonde who liked to get around in bare feet and chew gum a lot. I forget their names. They moved into a house just up the street from my place. They were new to Brisbane, didn't know too many people and they were all a little bit dim. I think you'll have to agree, it doesn't get any better than that.

My house was a nice enough dump, one of those run-down old Queenslanders which are disappearing from inner-city Brisbane. In fact, the place I'm talking about is gone now too, replaced by the fifth or sixth in a line of shit-ugly apartment blocks. There is no sitting on the verandah in those sorts of places, no sipping hot sweet tea, eating chocolate biscuits, smoking joints and drinking beer. There is no stepping carefully in your bare feet on the weathered boards, vaguely aware of threatened splinters and old nails. There's no dozing in hammocks, no corridor cricket, no banana trees or magic mushrooms in the yard. There's no floating population of itinerant housemates, no half-dozen students avoiding late assignments, no communal trips to the DSS or cheap Chinese take-away. There *are* aluminium window frames, Scotch-guarded nylon carpet and, sometimes, an *en suite* in the 'master' bedroom. But no Thunderbirds, no mountains of dope nor lakes of tequila.

This Thunderbird I mention, his name was Ron. Thunderbird Ron. We called him that because he'd gotten into body building, and I mean *really* gotten into it. He'd grown so huge and monstrous that he moved around like a badly strung puppet, the way those guys do, like they've got so much muscle and bulk on them that their arms stick out from their sides and they don't seem able to bend their knees when they walk. His personality was sort of stiff and wooden too and he had a stilted way of talking, as though he had to bench press his own weight to squeeze out the words. He was a bit of a fuck-up and I took a real shine to him. He was studying sports science when he moved into a sleepout round the back of this big house. He knocked back about ten litres of this really foul wheatgerm and egg-based yoghurt drink every day and watched an unhealthy number of early Schwarzenegger vids but he was all right. He could pick up a lounge chair with his teeth, which was useful sometimes. He also had a problem with women. They terrified him. This came home one day—literally—when I was sitting in the lounge room playing some prehistoric video game, the last remnant of another long-departed flatmate.

The Thunderbird waddled in, really agitated. I think I

was the only one home at that stage. There were maybe six or seven of us living there but, for a change, the whole house had managed to work up some enthusiasm for whatever lectures or part time jobs or welfare scams were on the agenda for that day. I glanced up and noticed right off that Ron had this big white bandage wrapped around his hand but I didn't pay it much heed. Figured he must have crushed it between some dumbbells down the gym or something. I said howdy and turned back to the game. Thing was though, I just couldn't concentrate because Ron was looming over me putting out these psychic waves of borderline panic. I blew off the game, leaned back from the console and asked what the trouble was. He wanted to know if I could give him some advice on nightclubbing clothes, which is a laugh if you know me. I've got like one pair of jeans, another pair of King Gees and a couple of rotting tee shirts with advertising slogans on them. But the Thunderbird ploughed on regardless, explained in this tortured passage of dialogue that he wanted to go to a nightclub, 'to ... meet ... some ... women ... who ... he ... might ... be ... able ... to ... *havesomesexwith*'. He ran that last bit together really quickly.

I thought, No way, man! Never happen. I explained that those sorts of places, they weren't for him. They were terrible places, a bit like black holes, except they'd collapsed in on themselves under the weight of their own bad vibes. They were full of guys with attitude problems and chicks like Glenn Close in *Fatal Attraction*, or Sigourney Weaver in *Aliens*—the last one, that is, the one where she shaves her head and dresses in a grey sack. The idea of Ron in one of those places, it just didn't sit right. I tried to talk him out of the idea but it was a thousand miles of hard road. He was locked in and tracking. He was hot guns on the whole thing. He'd gone and got this Mr Universe physique, worked hard for it, suffered for it and now it was time to go out and get some sex because women, 'they ... wouldn't ... *have had* ... a ... chance ... to ... *have sex* ... with ... a ... man ... like ... me ... before'.

I thought, Thunderbird, you speak the truth.

I was getting a little keen to change the topic so I said he didn't look like he was up to much at the moment on account of the bandage he was sporting. Asked whether he'd broken his wrist at the gym, knowing that if I could get him onto the gym he'd talk for hours about carbo loading and steroid abuse and reps and sets and all that shit, perhaps even forgetting about sex altogether. At least that's what I thought. But when I mentioned the bandage he became even more cramped and down shifted than before. Explained that he'd broken all these bones in his hand the other day when the blonde girl across the road, the barefoot gum-chewing space-alien beauty queen had smiled at him in the street. He'd wanted to talk to her. He'd been burning to talk to her, in fact he wanted to ask her out to a nightclub, but he couldn't, he just couldn't, she'd smiled at him, and said hello, and he'd ... and she'd ... and ... and ... and ... So he'd scuttled inside, made a fist and punched out the wall in the hallway.

Okay. That was cool. There had been some talk about that mysterious giant cavity.

And also, I figured, who was I to criticise? I mean, I'm

the guy who was swept away by a bout of homicidal malice
for Glynn Nicholas, the comedian, because once, after some
show he did on campus, he spoke to Joanne, this girl I was
keen on. Sadly, while I might have been keen on her, it was
a one-way street and there was nothing coming back my
way. I had a method for dealing with it, though. I'd drink
a carton of beer and smoke some shit and drink some more
beer, or maybe some cheap whiskey and then I'd roll around
in the mud screeching like a madman and trying to rip my
heart out through my rib cage till I felt a little better about
the situation.

On this particular night, I'd tagged along to Nicholas'
show with Joanne and her friends just in case she came to
her senses. She didn't and I guess I was about eighteen,
maybe nineteen beers into the cure when I saw Nicholas and
her chatting away. I'm older and wiser now, or maybe just
tired, and I know they were just bullshitting. The way you
do.* But back then, unmanned by rejection, spastic with
alcohol and hash and unrequited lust I twisted and wrenched
these few meaningless seconds of polite schmooze around to
the point where I lay awake at four in the morning imag-
ining them in the throes of wild cheap motel room sex. I lay
there, spinning out, grinding my teeth and clenching my fists
until I'd cut bloody half moons into my palms like some
deranged character from a Stephen King novel. So I had
some sympathy with this poor bastard standing in front of
me, sweating and squirming and generally looking like all

---

* Not that you're off the hook, Nicholas. If I ever see you, pal, you're
a dead man.

of his vital bodily fluids had backed up and he was maybe three seconds away from rolling his eyes, sprouting thick, matted clumps of fur on his palms and punching into the nearest warm hole he could find. But better than sympathy. I had information.

You see I knew all about the barefoot one. I myself had been smiled at on the street, just one day previous. But unlike the T-Bird I had bounded over like a horny little pup and made ready to do the naughty right then and there, in broad daylight, in the middle of the street. She *had* smiled at me after all. But when I got there, after the usual hellos and so on, she'd said with the smirk of an arch conspirator, 'Your friend, the gym guy, he's a big boy, isn't he?'

'Oh yeah,' I smiled, slightly deflated, but not wanting to show it. 'All natural too, won't have a bar of them roids.'

'You know, you guys should come over,' she said. 'We're having a house-warming on Saturday.'

'You sure? All of us?' I asked.

'Whatever,' she said. 'Just be sure and bring He-man with you.'

You betcha, I'd said, and wandered off, mental cogs spinning and whirring at full speed. The thing was, when word got out that the Tasmanians were throwing a party, there would be no question of non-attendance. The house would in fact go ballistic. Come the first rustle of a chip packet or the pop of a Spumante bottle there'd be a stampede, a thunderous phalanx of lusty, beer-crazed youths spilling down the front steps of our house and charging up the road like one of those angry cartoon clouds with a riot of arms and legs and bolts of lightning exploding from it.

But, it seemed, we were dependent on the T-Bird's doubtful charisma for our *entrée*. There was only one thing for it. House meeting.

'Excellent!'

'Fabbo!'

'Outstanding!' they went, just like a Pepsi ad.

'I dunno,' muttered Thunderbird, deep in the grip of a Maximum Fear.

'Just wear your posing pouch and a pair of sandals,' somebody suggested.

The house was gathered around an ugly looking pile of glistening, grey bones and soiled refresher towels. It had been a bucket of the Colonel's finest, but that was a long time ago in a galaxy far, far away. I licked the rich greasy scum of secret herbs and additives from my fingers, already regretting my third Kentucky Fried Mistake that month. I'd told the guys about the party and about the T-Bird's extraordinary luck, although to look at the thin rictus of terror which had stolen over his features you'd think I'd told him he was facing a blindfold and cigarette at dawn.

They were a mixed bunch, this house. There was myself, not doing much of anything at that point. The T-Bird, of course. Brainthrust Leonard, a gawky, third year engineering student with an unrivalled back catalogue of *Star Trek* fanzines and Australian *Playboys*. There was Jabba the Hutt, who watched so much television his butthair had fused with the mouldering fabric of the brown couch, forcing him to live via the remote control because if he'd ever actually got up off that couch he'd have had to walk around with a couple of filthy, rotting cushions stuck to his arse like the post-it notes of a lesser God. There was Mick, the pommy yob, who liked to headbutt things. And then there was Elroy, who styled himself as the Milko from Acapulco, which was half right. He was a milko, with a van and a milk run, but he actually came from Gladstone which wasn't nearly as interesting.

We had only recently become an all-male house, and hadn't yet settled into the inevitable rut, but we were well on the way. For instance, Brainthrust Leonard had already announced that he liked to sit on his hands before a session with his bunny mags, because his fingers went numb and 'then it felt like somebody else'. That brought forth a chorus of salty yarns and masturbatory one-upmanship. It started with Elroy's confession that he liked nothing more than to park his milkvan on a high hill in the morning, drink a carton of chocolate milk and whack himself off as the sun came up. It reached a nadir with Mick's demonstration of penile 'push-ups'; a ludicrous exercise which involved draping a wet bath towel over his erect member and repeatedly raising it like a boom gate.

I'll think you'll agree, the omens were ungood.

You can just imagine how these barbarians reacted to the invite from the Tasmanian babes. Jabba wasn't much interested because it'd mean missing whatever dreadful off-ratings bilge the networks were planning to pump out that weekend. But everyone else felt certain that they'd been chosen by fate or karma or the Great Pumpkin or whatever to play their part in the binge of the decade. There wasn't a man amongst us who didn't think himself the object of those women's lustful intentions, 'cept for the T-Bird of course, that huge tongue-tied baboon with a pudding bowl haircut and the only one of us who was actually in with a chance.

The party didn't kick off until seven or eight, and we planned to hit the ground running. At three in the afternoon on the day of the gig, we gathered around the kitchen table to worship before a massive drug cache spread over the faded green formica. We'd agreed that those who intended to go to the party had a responsibility to ensure that it really was the ugliest, most debauched and bestial orgy these Tasmanians would ever encounter. (It never occurred to us that they might think differently.) To that end we had fanned out through Brisbane each of us shaking the trees of our various underworld contacts, dislodging a pharmacological cornucopia and, judging by the number of people crammed into our kitchen, picking up a fair swag of camp followers along the way.

I'd say there were an extra two dozen punters there over the normal house population, and all had arrived bearing bags of smoke. Some generous souls had also tossed in a few sheets of acid, some eccys and, I'm sorry to add, a whole case of really cheap, vile, generic brand tequila. Old El Gringo or something like that. The sort with a dead plastic scorpion bumping around down the bottom of the bottle. It was an impressive haul which held the room in a quiet, almost reverent sort of thrall for a while. Most impressive of all however was the dope mountain. You really had to be there and lay eyes on this sucker to believe that such a marvel could have ever existed. Everyone contributed, but it really took off when Elroy and one of his milko mates lobbed a football sized clump of hooch onto the pile. They knew of a small plantation behind a state school which they had ripped off early one morning a while ago. They donated half their score to the communal stash, believing the investment would pay off handsomely in gross carnality by night's end. As it grew and grew it reduced everyone to excited giggles, then to whispers and finally to awed and simple silence. It was maybe two feet across at the base, a rough circle climbing to chest height from the table top, a rich green tangle, a mound of green wound through with long, tightly compressed sticky buds and knots of purple heads.

But this was Queensland, of course. And wherever three or four were gathered together in one spot, it was probably against the law. Had we been caught gathered around this little lot it would have been so against the law that we would have all gone to jail for a million years. It was maybe three-thirty in the afternoon by then. Hours to go before the party. Hours to sit there, staring at the dope mountain, waiting for the Tactical Response Group to crash in through the windows and cut us down with tear gas and karate chops and a few bursts of sub-machine gun fire.

'*Less just smoke tha fookin' thing,*' said Mick.

And we fell on it.

I awoke hours later, on the brown couch boxed in by hundreds of people. The house was roaring. My chest shook and pounded to a 15 000 watt blast of *God save the Queen and her fascist regime.* I was still stoned, but it wasn't the trippy, free-falling pleasant sort of stone which had rushed on after my third cone in the kitchen that afternoon. It was a heavy, sludgy, turn-your-brain-to-treacle sort of stone. I pushed through the crowd, making my way to the kitchen, hoping to toke up and take off again. But when I got there the table was bare. I shook my head. I remembered there'd been so much shit to get through that we had stopped bothering to mull it up. People were just ripping handfuls of ganga out of the pile and stuffing them into improvised cones and joints and corn cob pipes. I remembered being so wasted that my vision had started to come apart, the colours and lines melting into each other. I remembered some friendly gay boy called Tarquin trying to tempt a skeptical T-Bird into a little snifter of amyl under the house. And then I woke up on the couch. There was still a pile of beer chilling in the kitchen sink so I took one and wandered around to try and find out what had happened.

People were hanging out of the windows and partying in the mango trees out the front. There were cars all over the lawn. Punters kept rolling in, and I was swept along by this roiling, thunderous, clamouring mob, this sweating seething tide of unwashed dreads and shiny domes, of torn jeans, yellow teeth, Apache girls with zulu spears, biro tatts and celtic runes, of bare feet and bovver boots, this savage caterwauling crush of human flux and flow which pressed in hard upon the mind until the vision blurred and time itself broke up and swirled around in little lost jigsaw moments of disintegrated continuity. I saw the T-Bird pressed up against a wall outside the bathroom but had trouble getting to him as I was pushed and dragged off balance, buffeted by the confluence of riptides and sucking currents which coursed through the dark press of the party. I saw him squeezed from his minor vantage point, rudely hustled past the throng who were also waiting at the bathroom, ('*Take it on the road, Arnold*'), emerging at last from the hot fug and crashing din to stand, briefly, atop the back steps. Someone elbowed him in the spleen and he stumbled down the stairs. I did not see him for three days after that.

A voice screamed in my ear, 'Get on the end of this one!'

It was Mick, with a spliff the size of a Cuban cigar, wrapped in bright pink paper. I shouted thanks and toked up, drawing the rich acrid smoke down deep, letting it smooth my jagged edges and take me deep. It occurred to me that I knew then why people called it being 'ripped'. I felt like I was being borne away from a shoreline at night, the lights of real things receding into the dark as warm water carried me off to negation.

I asked Mick what had happened. He misunderstood, I think, and told me some story about feeding some All Hallows girl a trip. He'd found her swaying at the terminal point of completely self-indulgent nihilistic drunkenness, swaying and drinking and talking to herself about how nasty the world was. Mick thought a tab might make her a little more receptive to his dubious charms, but she'd just greedily gobbled it down and disappeared. Hours later Brainthrust Leonard and some other guys had found her standing in front of a full-length window on a patio, holding the hem of her skirt out and twirling from side to side like a little girl. As they were watching, her face turned feral and she punched the window, left a big spider web of lattice work cracks in it, then turned around, saw them and freaked. They tried putting the soothers on her but she escaped by grabbing onto a small piece of rubber tubing sticking down from the gutter and trying to swing away like Cat Woman. It broke and she fell to the driveway with a big sick thud, but jumped right up and ran away. Damnedest thing ever, said Leonard. Must have been a good three-metre drop. Nobody saw her again but the phone kept ringing all night. It was her, but all she ever said was, 'No way out no way out no way out.' Then she'd hang up.

'*C-o-o-l*,' I drawled.

By the time Mick had finished his story I was starting to fly again. Elroy appeared beside us with half a bottle of over-proof rum and Coke and stupid satisfaction smeared all over his face. We bellowed like Vikings and passed the bottle and drank each other's backwash till it was gone. The angels were really singing for me by then, a high, sweet, loony tune that jammed out anything even approaching rational thought. We pushed our shiny, sweating faces close together, screaming at each other that it was just a damn shame about the destruction of the dope mountain until Mick let go a strangled little shriek and launched himself unsteadily off towards the kitchen. Elroy and I and lurched through the heaving crowd, coming upon the shaven headed loon a few seconds later waving quickly gathered fistfulls of Old El Gringo and cackling like a fiend bent on certain self-destruction.

But even in my advanced stage of moral decay I shuddered inwardly at the prospect of hopping into this evil looking toxic waste. It had a greasy, pissy colour, vaguely reminiscent of the ancient dusty jars lining the cabinets of my old high school science lab, jars of dark yellow saline in which floated the flaky, slightly rotten bodies of long dead tiger snakes and miscarried kitten foetuses. My stomach rolled over slowly at the thought. Tequila and I did not have a good history. The last time our paths had crossed—an ugly, senseless binge to celebrate Mexico's national day— I'd been forced to spend thirty-three hours spreadeagled on a polished wooden floor, convinced that I'd been nailed there, so great was the pain which spiked through all my joints and organs. The host of that party, now the curator of a major regional art gallery, had kneeled by me a number of times the next day to press a wet cloth against my cracked and ruined lips. He ignored my croaks and groans of 'Oh you filthy bastard', putting them down to the horrors of delirium tremens.

Still and all, a drink's a drink, so we fetched some Lucozade from the fridge and three plastic Ronald Mc-Donald glasses from the dish rack and set about lining up and kocking down a full set of Old El Gringo slammers. And an awful, terrible business it was too. Apart from Mekong Delta whiskey and some obscure brands of Ukrainian cabbage vodka, tequila is the only drink I know of which acts as a genuine stimulant. Bang bang bang went the slammers, sending frothy eruptions of alcoholic Lucozade over the rim of our glasses before exploding like sickly sweet tangerine hand grenades behind the thin dome of bone holding our sorry, fucked-up brains in place.

Then Elroy remembered that we had another party to go to.

The Babes!

I roared so loud at the memory that I hurt my lungs and had to lean against a wall for a little while. Then I was off, fucked, hysterical, crashing up the hallway towards my room with my jeans down around my ankles, intent on changing for their party. The tequila, the smoke and the lust all combined and sparked in a high octane, dangerously unstable mix which licked like fire at the base of my brain stem and seemed to cause a distant, fearful roar. I fell through the door, hitting the wall and leaving a huge dent in the fibre board. A couple of dykes were thrashing around in my bed but I ignored them and they me. I was so completely unco I couldn't get my jeans on or off. I simply rolled around on the floor, hysterical and spinning out.

Mick and Elroy stuck their heads in to yell that they were taking the van and going as 'the fuckin peppers'. I had no idea what they were talking about but I didn't want them getting there first so I shucked my pants up as best I could and staggered out after them, barrelling through half a dozen strangers sitting on our front steps. I caught a flash of a naked buttock climbing into Elroy's milk van, before the headlights blinded me. I ran. They drove.

The Babes' place was only two or three doors up but I beat them because they crashed into our mail box on the way. I hit the Babes' door at full tilt and, like I said, crashed to the floor with my pants around my ankles. The horrified party-goers—there were a few dozen of them, very intense looking folk, looked like opera buffs with martini glasses and little nibbly things held between their pinkies and thumbs—well, they had no time to react to my grand entrance, because my flatmates were bringing up the rear.

Mick and Elroy careened across the lawn like suicide bombers with the milk van's headlights on high beam and the Red Hot Chili Peppers cranked up to the max on Elroy's boombox. The Peppers had been in town just the week before and Mick had seen them do their socks on cocks routine. They had also worn space helmets with flames coming out. Mick and Elroy, morons that they were, had been laying plans to emulate them ever since. That afternoon they had pinched a couple of plastic witch's hats from some nearby roadworks. They'd soaked rolled-up newspapers in petrol, jammed them into the hole at the top and left the whole lot sitting in Elroy's van for a few hours. Then, as I was rolling around on the floor in my room, they'd both grabbed a sock, stripped naked, and attached them to their willies with rubber bands before charging out to the van.

They mounted the gutter, kicking the spotties to full beam and smashed through a picket fence. They jumped out and lit up their hats, forgetting that the milk van was full of petrol fumes. There was a massive flash explosion—WHOOF!—and then Mick and Elroy weren't the arse-kicking Chili Peppers no more. They were just a couple of fools running around with socks on their cocks and their heads on fire. I was trampled as the guests ran to put them out.

They weren't allowed to stay at the housewarming and neither was I so we all went home. The party kicked on until four or five. I had a few more spliffs and Lucozade and tequila surprises and remember becoming convinced that I could diffuse my atoms through the structure of the house by sheer willpower. I don't remember spending the better part of the night on my hands and knees butting my head against the lounge room wall until I passed out. But people tell me I did.

Christopher Cyrill

WHat WiTHeRS and WHat RemAinS

M y uncle had wanted to be a policeman. He is a tall man and when he was in his teens he made himself a set of weights by filling old ghee tins with concrete and setting iron poles between the tins. He trained day and night, drank buttermilk and ate at least two eggs with every meal, hoping to impress his examiners with his physique, preparing for the tests of strength the job would require of him. At dinner this evening, as his breath quickened and he reached for his pillbox, I could see along his arms, see where the muscle had withered and the flesh hung from the bone like wineskins and also the muscle that remained. He applied to the Lucknow Police Corps and sat and passed the exam but on the eve of his induction his mother had persuaded him to become a teacher.

My uncle lives on the grounds of the small Catholic school he founded and I have lived with him and his twin daughters for four months. We live near the Amhinabad Markets, close enough to see the Lucknow Square clock-tower, a brick spire with a broken face where hawkers sit in the surrounding weeds and roast corn. I sleep in a hammock in the room where my aunt's body was placed for the viewing. On each wall hangs a framed picture of her and in the corner of the room stands a statue of Mary garlanded with lotus flowers.

I rarely sleep more than five or six hours a night. I find it easy to fall asleep but often I'm woken by nightmares and when I wake I stay awake. I lie wide-eyed and afraid. I've had a recurring dream since I was a child of being pursued through a street of complete darkness. I never know what pursues me until the end of the dream when I realise that I am fleeing the dark, the dark which seems physical, as if it has hands and torso and feet, the dark I am within until I wake.

One night last week my uncle and I hailed a rickshaw to Arjuna's, a restaurant near Lucknow station where my uncle pays half-price. My uncle was carrying a small hessian bag with him and he smelt of tiger balm and brylcream.

We rode through the narrow dirt streets between roped cows and thin brown dogs scavenging in rubbish heaps laced with dung. My uncle held a handkerchief scented with rose-water over his mouth and nose. As the rickshaw driver passed through crossroads my uncle pointed out a grey building with smoke coming through a broken window, which he said was where my father had won his first boxing bout. I told my uncle that Lucknow looked like a city that had come through a civil war and he said that he would have left the city years ago if it wasn't for his school. Then he added that the previous autumn there had been a Holy War. Hindus and Moslems had rioted and fought with knives and sticks and stones over the desecration of a mosque and in the riots a friend of his had been trampled to death and my uncle talked of his friend's death in a way that made me regret having spoken at all.

We arrived at Arjuna's and my uncle paid the driver and told him to return in three hours. The driver looked away as he was paid. We walked into the restaurant, which was decorated with large fern trees and fraying tapestries, and the waiter called my uncle 'Mr Tallow' and called me 'Sir' and offered us the middle table. We sat down and my uncle waved away the menus and ordered in Hindi. He tapped his watch and said something else in Hindi after he ordered. He then took a bottle in a brown paper bag out of the hessian bag. The waiter returned with two shot glasses and two long glasses and a jug of water. My uncle unwrapped the bottle.

'This bourbon I kept saying was for a special occasion, you know, but no special occasion has come. Well, they've come and gone for the last twelve years. More than twelve years old, this bottle.'

My uncle poured two shot glasses and I said thank you and we drank. The drink left a sandy taste in the back of my throat and made my eyes blur and it had neither the sweet aftertaste nor the dark mahogany colour of bourbon. I wondered if the liquor was safe but kept drinking, not wanting to offend my uncle and hoping at least the alcohol would help me to sleep.

My uncle drank a few shots and sipped water. He said that he had taught the waiter when he taught at St Francis' College.

'Very smart boy, except in Latin. We thought he'd be an engineer,' my uncle said, as the waiter laid plates of mutton curry and potato chops before us.

My uncle pointed to two other men, who were sitting in one corner of the restaurant, their faces partly hidden by the leaves of a fern tree, and he said that he had taught them and their children.

I looked around at the tapestries hanging from the walls, tapestries depicting scenes from the *Mahabharata*, the headgear of kings and the chariots of gods strung with gold beads, the red, white and black thread of Kali's gown unravelling, a wheel of fire laced with yellow ribbon.

My uncle drank and nibbled at his food and then he smiled and began to speak of my father. He told me about the time they had raced on second-hand bicycles up and down the Hazratgunj, the main street of Lucknow, hoping to impress the woman who was to become my mother. My father had told me the story and in my mind I spoke the punch line along with my uncle, ' . . . and she was walking down the street with someone else.' As he said this he raised his hand in the air and waved goodbye to an imaginary woman and I heard the pills in his top pocket rattle in their box. He told me then of his wish to be a policeman, and how my father's only ambition before he took his law degree was to play hockey for India.

My father died close to a year ago, never having seen the school his brother had founded. The school is built within the same rectangle of flats where the brothers were raised, my uncle acquiring the bottom floors in the years after my father's migration, breaking down walls, hiring a guard and dogs to protect the desks and chalkboards and cement bags that he had trucked in from Delhi. In the years that I was attending primary school, my uncle was building his school, for Catholic girls between the ages of five and twelve, with the help of my father's cheques.

My father sent a cheque once a month along with short letters about our Vancouver winters, the starfish snow and the pink dawns above the Cascade ranges, the shop on Kramer St that made the best halva, the photographs: *Michael the day of his birth, Michael and me at the Cape Chidley lighthouse, Michael at the National Hockey trials.* My father never once mentioned himself in his letters to my uncle. I wrote short notes to the man I was named after, retelling what my father had told him, and I paid for the stamps. My uncle had framed the photograph of my father and me embracing the night of my twenty-first birthday, the night my father recited Tennyson's 'Ulysses' from memory to a crowd of dinner guests either stunned or bored, and I wondered if people were preserved by the things that they preserved.

As I sat with my uncle that evening, as he drank more and talked less and the plates of food cooled before us and were taken and reheated and set before us again, I thought my uncle had missed his brother for all the years of my life in a way I could never imagine.

I was too drunk to eat by the time the bottle was empty. My uncle ate only the small bunch of grapes that came with dessert, leaving the tender green stalk in a bowl beside the bottle. The stalk looked like a bonsai tree. The waiter packed the food into plastic containers.

Outside the rickshaw driver was waiting. He said a storm was coming and helped my uncle into the rickshaw. He then put his hand on my shoulder and helped me in. The wind pushed the canvas top of the rickshaw up like a sail. My uncle leaned back and fell asleep. I asked the driver if he knew the way home and he smiled and nodded. He started pedalling as the rain began to fall. I sat back and watched him. He was pedalling fast and cars stopped for him as we passed the clocktower and turned left into the main thoroughfare of the markets, where the streetlights hung on loose wires and swung in slack arcs on the wind. It began to hail. The driver covered his head with his hands and the rickshaw rolled to a stop.

In the swinging light I saw pedestrians run under the awnings of stalls, tucking their groceries and packages under their arms. Rickshaw drivers leaned in under the canvas hoods with their passengers. A woman tapped her children on their backs to hurry them up. A man tapped the hindlegs of his herd of cattle with a stick. Then the lights went out.

I sat in the dark and felt the movement of people around me, heard the grunts of a bull and the shouting of drivers. Water dripped into my hair. The hail glistened. The lights came back on. My uncle sat up, his eyes blinking, his arm reaching for mine.

When we arrived home my cousins looked as if they had been crying. They dried our heads with towels and scolded my uncle for being out so late. They did not talk to me. I offered my towel to the driver and thanked him and one of my cousins paid him. Again, he turned away as he was paid.

That night I lay in the hammock and tried to stay awake. I wondered how, after a lifetime of nights and mornings when I awoke trembling from the darkness I could not outrun in my dreams, I had found myself drunk in a storm in the dark of a street I could not name and I had not been afraid. I felt as if I had been there too many times before to be afraid, as if my nightmares had prepared me for the moment.

The next morning my uncle could remember nothing. He sat and looked at the egg paratha on his plate and asked me if he had paid the bill and the driver. He then asked me what we had talked about and I said he had told me that he had wanted to be a policeman. My twin cousins looked at him strangely, as if he had told a lie.

Rosie Scott

RAGing with RaLpH

A whole day to get through once I'd packed. In the end I turned on a midday soap and brought out Tyler's gin, a fresh pack of cigarettes, just to retain some equilibrium.

'My darling, I can't live without you. You must know that by now.'

'Brad. I'm a happily married woman. You can't just walk in here and talk to me like that.'

Well-nourished, vapidly beautiful, utterly self-absorbed, the actors walked about the coldly luxurious sets as if they were automatons. I watched in fascination as they mouthed the lifeless words in frame after frame. It was really like some kind of special American hell, a ring of fire, the terror of the undead reflected in their blank perfect eyes, their sur-roundings, where even the flowers in bowls were as flawless as plastic, the weather-beaten old world outside choked off forever. I had never watched the show before and now I wanted to watch them talking forever, especially after my third gin. My fascination with the pull of the flickering screen, their smiling smooth terrifying faces held me, cocooning me, shielding me from my thoughts.

'At least kiss me before I go. You can't deny me that. I've thought of no one else but you for months.'

'Brad. Oh Brad. Please don't tempt me.'

I had been half-expecting him, but when the shadow fell across the screen and I looked up, he still gave me a fright.

'Sorry to trouble you again,' Ralph said. I stood up and switched off the TV, motioned to him to sit down. Luckily, gin and despair had softened all my edges so I wasn't nearly as disturbed by him this time. We were equals, partners in humiliation.

'You've heard all about them,' he said. 'Your husband and my wife.'

'You're married?'

'In a manner of speaking,' he said smoothly. He sat down

on the sofa. He looked the same, as if he had been unto-
uched by the news.

'Well, you are or you aren't,' I said, argumentative.

'Not legally, but close enough. Does your husband know
what he's letting himself in for? Apart from dealing with
me?'

'Listen, Ralph. Don't come here with your threatening
talk. Talk to him. He's not here. Tyler's always been able
to look after himself.'

'Has he?'

Looking closer I could see that first impressions were
deceptive. Ralph was disturbed, but in a kind of deep glacial
way that was very hard to pick up at first contact.

I realised that it wasn't just his pride, his love, it was also
his source of income, his stock in trade as the unvanquished
macho man that was at stake.

'I don't let people cross me like that as a rule,' he said.

Out of the blue I felt a hysterical laugh start up inside me.
It sounded like he had come straight out of the show I'd
been watching, the guest gangster.

'Well, you're going to have to this time,' I said recklessly.
I realised blurrily that I was quite drunk. 'Anyway, I'm not
the one you should be talking to, I've got my own problems.'

He looked at me and, amazingly, said 'I know. It's hard
on you. I hear you've been married a long time.'

'Yes,' I said with distaste.

'Sky'll run through him in weeks, and then you can have
him back. She'll clean him out. I've never known her to fuck
anyone as poor as him. She usually goes for the old rich
suckers. I'm her rough trade.'

'Rough trade? You don't look it,' I said. 'Here, have a drink.' I kept trying to control the insane drunken laughter bubbling in my stomach. 'Tyler's good as rough trade. The best.'

'What are you going to do about this, Belle? If you don't mind a personal question.'

'I'm not going to hang around here and beg, that's for sure. You should go back to Sydney as well. You don't want any more crimes on your conscience.'

'I might just do that,' he said, his eyes as mean as flint, with a flicker to show he'd heard the word *crimes*.

'Tyler's got a lot of weird underworld friends. They're very devoted. You won't get away with much with Tyler. He always covers his tracks like that.'

'You're a tough little lady yourself, aren't you? Anyone would think he hadn't done you a bad turn.'

'I don't see it like that. This isn't the TV. He's still my friend even though I hate his guts.'

He laughed suddenly and his face looked younger and even soft, for a minute anyway.

'That's what it is. You've gone and put yourself under the weather. Why don't you come and have some lunch with me? Line your stomach. Have you got any decent dresses though? You'd look all right if you did more with yourself.'

'Honestly,' I said. 'This is like a time warp. Have you heard that women have recently become human beings? I'll spell it. H-u-m-a-n b-... '

'Yes,' he said, impatient. 'You'd be entitled to say the same thing if I came in here looking shitty. Wouldn't you?'

I felt helpless, out of my depth, almost reckless about the

bizarre turns my life was taking. Here was this gangster, this pimp, straight out of a Hollywood movie, that I suddenly, inexplicably, had a sick, intimate bond with. It was all so unreal I felt a kind of brainstorm descending.

'Okay, okay, I'm coming.' I got up and stumbled slightly with the rush of air to my head, lurched off into the bedroom trying to keep my dignity intact. I didn't even bother to change in the end.

When I came out he was standing looking out the window. He looked so concentrated in his reverie, so mean, so murderous, it gave me a shiver.

In the car, his body very tense beside me, he said, 'We've known each other for a while, Sky and I. We met professionally if you know what I mean. I was working for a company, interviewing potential girls for an establishment. Very high-class. They wanted only the best. When it was her turn, that was it.' He looked sideways at me. 'Once she gets under your skin, she's it.'

'What's the big attraction?' I asked, feeling sick. 'Besides her good looks?'

He gazed off into the distance, and I saw with a jolt that he really loved her.

'You can't really put a finger on it. Sometimes she's like a little girl, other times she's like a queen, but you always know when she comes into the room.'

It occurred to me that he'd invited me to lunch out of an urgent need to talk about her. There was probably no one else he could be that vulnerable with in his world, and here was I, tailor-made, my credentials of shame and dishonour as impeccable as his own. He could indulge in the obsessional, grieving, circular conversation of the wronged lover as long as he liked with someone like me because I could never pull rank. I tried to imagine what his kind of businessmen/criminals/friends talked to each other about besides money and deals. Sex maybe, but certainly not love, certainly not admitting to being dumped. I had an image of all these big dark-suited dead-eyed men earnestly confiding in each other about marital problems, saying things like 'Maybe we weren't spending enough quality time together', and smiled in spite of myself at the thought. He obviously needed the comfort of my presence so badly he was prepared to overlook my insolent manner and the fact that I didn't have the class to wear shimmering mini-skirts.

'She's completely out for herself, and in the end you come to really admire her for it. There's a certainty there if you know what I mean. She's run off with men before, but there's always a reason. Money usually. But she can be so go-go, that girl. She can make you feel like a million dollars. She can rage all night, and start again next morning. A barrel of laughs.'

I tried to think of Tyler having a barrel of laughs with someone who made him feel like a million dollars. It was inconceivable that he had shut himself in a cage like this, amongst people with minds so bleak and banal, a TV quiz show world where money was the ultimate truth, the fulcrum on which everything else rose and fell. Tyler, the ultimate sixties man whose life had been a testament to earthly immediates, my Tyler spinning in the fronds of plastic web which would eventually choke him.

I thought of Kate and Patrick, as if the booze had released

images too painful to look at in the sober light of day. Driving through the Brisbane streets with Tyler's new girl-friend's ex, I painfully catalogued their bewilderment, their disillusionment, their rejection, the shock that mirrored my own. For all the bloodbath of our relationships, we had a shared language, a common view of the world which did not include Tyler falling in love with someone else, let alone a woman like Sky. We were used to the deviant, the surprising, the off-line in our family life, but this, this was the real thing. In my drunken reverie I found myself resorting to an old habit of mine, of supporting Tyler in the face of the children's injustices. 'She's very beautiful and unusual. He's finding his lost youth,' I heard myself telling them. Even I couldn't believe it. I settled back in the car determined not to allow my mind to wander any more. Sometimes I couldn't believe myself.

'There's just something about her,' Ralph said, almost to himself, turning the car smoothly into a private carpark below a palmy hotel. It was as if I wasn't in the car.

The restaurant was filled with discreet business people in suits, a lovely luxuriant light-filled room gleaming with elegant glass tables and chairs, leafy trees in silver pots, a view of the river from floor to ceiling windows. Everything reflected light and glitter, it was such a delicate, luxurious edifice perched like a fairy castle above the city. The impassive waiters, all much more handsome than their fat customers, the expensive fragrance, the sheer *discretion* of everything, all spelled out a truly manic exclusiveness. Sitting down at a window table, the city humming below, deciding on lobster for entree, I realised I was both hungry and recklessly, drunkenly at ease. Ralph ordered wine and I started drinking again with a vague desire to stay drunk until I got on the plane.

'Nice place.'

'Not bad.' He was so at home, with his perfect restaurant suit and dark good looks, just the right amount of friendliness and contempt for the waiter, the way he placed his large white hands on the table as if he owned it.

'So,' he said, looking across at me without a smile as if he found my presence suddenly incongruous too. 'What does she see in your husband?'

'What does she see in my husband?' I echoed, insulting. 'Well, he's a kind man, he's funny and he's sexy. Very wise. Most women find him attractive. Usually very wise,' I corrected myself. 'Usually. Not recently.'

'Bit of a catch, is he?' he sneered, openly hostile.

'He sure is.'

'What does he do? Labouring work?'

'Sometimes.' I said. I thought of him, barechested, working in the sun, looking up to see me with his smile of complicity, sweaty curls clinging to the back of his neck. His work smell always devastated me, a kind of earthy, dusty, faintly acrid smell to do with hard physical work in the sun, a big peaceful male body, fresh sweat. The sort of professional men I worked with never smelt like that, their aftershave, deodorant, clean-clothes smell was not nearly so exciting. I suddenly noticed by the bruised, shamefaced look on Ralph's face that he was about to ask questions about sex.

'I don't want to talk about Tyler,' I said quickly. 'Can we drop this?'

'She told me he's great in bed,' he said, with great difficulty as if he was tipping a huge stone on the table that he'd been carrying around for days.

I said, 'I don't want to talk about him. I'll just get up and leave,' trying to swallow down a sudden flare of pain. The jealousy that was always lurking in my heart was very unpredictable. I never knew when it was going to hit next; just then it really felt like a soft explosion right in my innards as he spoke.

'I don't like talking about it either,' he said. 'She's never said it before about other men.' He was drinking heavily as well and his eyes were bloodshot. We must have looked a weird pair.

'I should have married the bitch. She wanted to, you know.'

'Why didn't you?'

'And you know something else?' he said. 'She *was* busking. It wasn't bullshit. I saw her myself. Standing on the fucking street. She was wearing those tight little shorts with everything bulging out and she was doing magic tricks and fire-eating for any old passerby. Now what kind of woman is that? I said to her. "All right. Forget the game. If you're sick of being a callgirl that's okay. Why don't you go on stage? The movies? You've got talent. I'll pay your way. Not on the fucking street, for Christ's sake." She just looked at me as if she was going to smile but hadn't quite got round to it. She was already in love with your hubby. That was the problem, only I didn't know it at the time.'

'Well, now you do,' I said, suddenly exhausted. I excused myself to go to the toilet, a hushed, pink, silvery affair with ferns in the corner and shining taps. Looking at my drunken despairing face in the mirror I was surprised to see how remote I looked, how bizarrely attractive, almost a stranger. My skin was deathly pale with booze, and with the violet under my eyes and bruised mouth I looked as if I hadn't slept for weeks. I was lost in some interior world, but glowing as if the pain had irradiated me. I put on some more make-up, fluffed up my hair in a mane and sprayed on some old sample perfume I had in my bag. 'Great in bed,' I said to test the sourness in my mouth. Already I felt desperately, if I could only keep confronting the pain it would lose its bite, but that seemed a forlorn possibility. Standing in the toilet I thought of the first conversation I had with Sky in Sydney about the director she intended to fuck. I remembered, with a tug of acute embarrassment, my patronising, older woman advice, and her enigmatic smile to herself into the mirror. How was I to know that I was dealing with the black widow herself, I thought to myself for comfort, but it was no help at all.

When I came out onto the soft carpet I found that I had great difficulty in making my way towards the table. It seemed miles away over acres of shimmering greenery, glittering glass. The floor swayed up and down to meet me and I wondered vaguely if I would ever get there. I saw Ralph like a sombre shadow, staring moodily out of the window and I set my sights on him grimly, determined not to let the side down. Even then I lurched gently into a waiter, and then hit my hip against a table. Everyone seemed to be smiling at me. He barely noticed my return, he was so preoccupied.

'I can't believe she's really left me,' he said, as if he was talking to himself. He had got through a bottle of wine just while I'd been in the toilet, although for all I knew I'd been in there for hours.

'She sure has, honey,' I told him seriously and cracked open a lobster leg so sharply it pierced my hand. 'Ow,' I said childishly and sucked my skin.

'Was it you who told me? That he said it was serious?'

'I can't remember. Of course it's serious. It's the first time he's ever done this.'

'The first time?' he looked at me with his expressionless handsome eyes. 'The first time you knew, honey.'

'The first time,' I said firmly.

I was suddenly bored with his flat ugly mind, the predatory way he looked at the world. The exoticness of it had faded on acquaintance, under all his beauty and neurotic glitter he was just a human adding machine. Even his pain over Sky had a metallic ring to it.

'Well, that's a first.' For some reason this seemed to cheer him slightly. 'Never had a one night stand, eh? Come on, Belle, I don't believe you're such a bunny as that.'

'Nah,' I said, noticing that I was reverting to my deep Southern accent, a sure sign of hostility. 'I was only kidding. That man was rooting like a darn rattlesnake the whole time I knew him, and there wasn't a thang I could do.'

For some reason it gave me great pleasure to launch into the extravagance of another accent, swim about in those honey vowels. It was like a release, my one true expression to lose myself in other lives. Ralph didn't even seem to notice it or if he did he gave no sign.

'I know a song about being abandoned,' I said. 'But it's about a mother. *She's gone, she's gone, she's gone, she's gone and no crying will bring her back. She's the only mother I ever did have, going down that railroad track.'*

'Keep it down, will you?' he said, annoyed. He was drunk as well, but there was no loosening in him.

'That wasn't loud,' I said. 'It was under my fucking breath. I was only trying to cheer you up.'

'That song wouldn't cheer anyone up,' he said argumentatively. 'It's degenerate.'

'It takes one to know one,' I said cracking another leg.

'What was that?'

'I said, it takes one to know one,' I said loudly, pausing in my work.

'That's where it was,' he said suddenly. 'I saw you on TV. That Oz show about the family. Out in the bush.'

'You sure did, honey. Ah been on quite a few of them damn Ozzie shows now. You can just take your pick. Families is my particular specialty. Out there in the desert, killing them snakes to save my kids as if there was no tomorrow.'

'You think that's funny, don't you?' he said furiously. 'No wonder your dumbshit husband left you.' He looked haggard, with his bloodshot eyes, sallow skin.

'Probably for the same reason your dumb girlfriend left you,' I said as quickly as was humanly possible.

We looked at each other, almost sardonic about the balance of terror between us.

'Settle down, will you. I take you out to an expensive restaurant—look at the way you're behaving, for Chrissake.'

'You talk to me as if you were my pimp,' I said. 'And you keep insulting mah husband. He may have left me, he may be fucking your girlfriend, but he's mah husband.'

'Can you stop that fucking voice?'

The plates of chicken arrived looking like works of art. I vaguely remembered reading somewhere that being truly wealthy meant that you ate perfect little baby vegetables—and there they were, white button mushrooms, like dots of butter, tiny glowing carrots the size of a baby's finger, miniature corn, pale with tenderness. We sat there looking at the food without making a move.

'Ah thought ah was hungry, but now I find I just ain't,' I said. 'Oops. Ah'm so sorry.'

'I can't eat either,' he said disgustedly. 'That's a hundred bucks down the drain.'

I picked up the fork and ate a mushroom, so soft it melted in my mouth like snow.

'I'll try and get rid of ten bucks at least,' I said, provocative, and speared some chicken. I felt such a hideous wave of nausea I had to stop eating.

'You don't act like a famous actress,' he said in his cold way. 'Where's your manners?'

I stared at him trying to fight down the nausea.

'Don't speak for a minute,' I said tightly. 'Or I'll spew.' I felt the sweat on my cold forehead, that sick wave going over me. After a minute though, my stomach settled slightly and I tried to relax.

'Now what were you saying?'

'Nothing.'

'Perhaps we ought to go. I'm not feeling too good. I can't eat any more. Thank you anyway. The lobster was great.' I even patted his hand. It felt as cold as bones. 'You know something, Ralph? She'll come back. Now that I know who

you are, I know it. It won't last between the two of them.
But you just gotta leave them to it.'

'You really think so?' he said. 'You don't know what she's
like.'

I felt sorry for him all of a sudden.

'How long was I in the toilet? Did you notice?'

He said, 'What makes you so sure?'

'So sure about what?'

'Them not lasting.'

'They're not compatible.' I was, for that moment, insanely
sure, even flippant. 'You can't keep screwing forever.'

'Sky can,' he said.

I felt the nausea rising again.

'I swear I have to go.' The restaurant, his face was suddenly a sinister swim of shapes and voices, blooming and
dreadful forms like an aquarium full of killer creatures
moving languidly but inexorably towards me.

'You go on to the toilet,' he said looking at my anguished
face, horrified. 'Quick. I'll pay the bill.'

I stood up obediently, my head spinning and started the
long terrible journey back to the haven of the toilet. I felt
the first retch about halfway there, and put my hand up to
my mouth to hold it in if need be, trying to smile nonchalantly as I passed table after table of hushed diners. Another
retch and I felt the awful flood rising up in my throat, the
vomit filling my mouth. I broke into a sort of shambling
run, all discretion gone and by the next eruption I was at
the toilet door, both hands cupped to my heaving mouth.
The last thing I remember for a while was half-kneeling,
half-lying in the cubicle, my poor face against the cold

loveliness of the toilet bowl, drained, purged, exhausted, almost happy.

Much later I opened the door and a whole blur of interested faces bloomed towards me, a pale mass of polite but obscenely concentrated interest. I stood at the doorway, taking it all in for a minute, keeping reasonably steady on my feet. Finally I bowed gracefully, a cheap trick, but all I could think of in the circumstances. There was even a scattering of applause as I made my way with what I hoped was great dignity to the lobby where Ralph, my friend, was waiting.

Driving home we hardly said a word to each other. I had the feeling that there would never be anything more we could say to each other ever again. There was no doubt he could see nothing funny in our lunch, and in my drunken haze I didn't know whether to laugh or cry myself.

Peta Spear

The Getting of Pleasure

She met him in the usual way. She was half-hidden, floating languorous in a cup of shadow. He was suspended in a beam of light, bumping arhythmically against the side of the bar. When she first saw him it looked like he was burning up in the light, his blondness was so extreme. She had the initial advantage—she'd been watching him in his halo of fire from her corner of the room without him realising it. What attracted her attention was the way he kept stroking the lovely green bottle, very gently, probably without any awareness of the delicacy of his touch. By then, it was getting late, the night was splitting into morning and the drink had done a nice job and relaxed her. Having a number of drinks in a place she felt comfortable in relaxed her more than just about anything else she could think of. Although it was sometimes possible for the drink to trick her into crying and she'd end up in the ladies' washing her face in cold water. And after that, catching her reflection in the sad mirror and feeling like a fool.

No foolishness tonight. Not tonight. A relaxed, almost happy night. She had gotten to the stage of feeling warm, runny, a little blurred. Soft. So far, it'd been one of those nights of tucking herself into the corner and being left alone. She liked the ability she could sometimes demonstrate of being invisible. It amused her to practise her invisibility so that it wasn't too awkward for her to be a woman drinking alone. On this night she stayed invisible until she saw him look over at her from his position of light, screwing up his eyes as if she was a ball of glare burning his skin. The way he contorted his face like a clown made her laugh out loud and he took that as an invitation, and it was, because she all of a sudden wanted to remember herself as someone who could effortlessly laugh and they went from there.

It was a fast courtship and an easy one. Her name was Maya. His name was Nick. When the barman called final drinks they hooked each other by the arm and went out into the spinning air. By then the night had cracked. When they went to bed it was with a bottle of white wine. When they kissed, Nick pressed the bottle hard against her and his tongue was a spatula inside Maya's mouth, folding the sweet acid grape into her. Maya shuddered as she caught the ferment of his tongue. Then he ran the wild circles of Bacchus over her ribs and around her hard nipples and syphoned more wine into her mouth. She poured a libation into the natural basin of his belly and lapped at the tributaries that trickled over the plains of his skin. The thought that she was drinking just like an animal made her start laughing again and because her laughing seemed to have a bad effect on his desire, she kissed his ear and whispered that, tonight, she was simply feeling very happy. That was the first time Maya had said those words in a while and she realised they were true.

'Give me the bottle,' she whispered. Nick took a long gurgling swig and handed it over. Maya proceeded to douse her belly with the warm colourless wine. It cascaded over her mount of Venus, pooling in her inner thighs, clasped tight together. 'Now drink,' she giggled. But it was only when she sluiced Nick's penis with the wine too, that he finally became erect.

'Quickly,' he said, taking the bottle from Maya, 'Get on top of me.' And she did and he told her that coming wasn't an issue for him, the main thing was, that she should take her pleasure and come. So he took another drink to keep it up but Maya was getting tired by then and almost straightaway, she came.

'You want to come now?' she asked.

'No,' he murmured, 'I don't need to.' By then the bottle of wine was finished. They both fell sound asleep immediately, clinging to each other despite the stickiness of Maya's fluids comingling with the coating of wine on their bodies.

The deep dreamless sleep that drink gives Maya is her best, most profound sleep. The sleep of drink is her favourite type of little death. In that sleep she is more abandoned than during her climax and she's more abandoned for longer. She even likes the moment of waking from this type of sleep, for if it's been as deep as she likes it to be, she wakes not knowing where she is, who she's with, why she is there. Drink has ushered her into some memorable places and the first thing she does when she wakes is think not: where am I? Or: how did I get here? But: what part of this is now part of me? It is the same with the people she wakes to. Which part of them will become a part of her?

Maya scrutinised the comatose Nick when she woke. It was the moment of realisation that drink has transformed a perfect stranger into an intimate. She counted the freckles on his browned, sunburned shoulders, noted how his almost white hair grew low down the nape of his neck onto his back, saw he had a nasty smallpox vaccination scar and that his legs trembled in irregular intervals as he slept. She touched his sacrum and felt the heat of his body travel into the palm of her hand. She wanted to make love again. It was a sudden and violent spurt in her, this urge, but his penis stayed nestled into his groin, placid inside the wrinkled gossamer condom, empty of semen but evidence of the sexual moment.

Maya had been kicking in the wide dragging river when she'd seen Nick. He had appeared like the flash of a life buoy, blur of light jetting in the dark, spinning salvation out to her. When she lifted a sodden arm to grasp him he had been solid and reassuring and she'd had second thoughts about any comfort that the pull of the current might bring. At least, that's what Maya told Nick about the way they'd begun. The metaphor of the river was one of her favourites. Men in bars often understood that sort of language. Especially the men she found clinging to the precarious and shifting edges of bars late at night.

Nick grasped Maya's forearm in one hand when she said this to him and brought the bottle of beer up to his lips with his other hand. Maya licked a fleck of foam from his mouth and took the bottle from him. 'Listen,' she said, 'this is not about literality. There's nothing we need be afraid of in each other.'

'Agreed,' replied Nick, slipping his hand off Maya and taking back his bottle of beer, fingering it in a way that was a lover's caress.

'For example,' Maya continued, 'Are you stiff right now? Are you stiff for me?' Nick finished his beer and motioned for another round. His eyes were fixed on the horizon of the bar. Maya put her hand on the lump that signified his sex.

'No,' Nick said. 'I guess I'm not. But don't take it too literally. It doesn't mean, for instance, that I don't want you.'

'What does it mean?'

He grinned at her. 'All it means is that I need another drink.' Maya drained her glass and watched how Nick seemed to like holding even an empty bottle. As she waited for the next round a wonderful feeling of softness began to fill her. She wondered if it was the feeling of happiness. She leant against Nick's arm and closed her eyes against every-thing she didn't need to know about and felt the solidity of Nick's muscles shifting then tensing around her. It was a shock when she felt his fingers against her cheeks blotting tears because she'd had no idea that she was crying.

Nick sensed a growing, formless, invisible turbulence in Maya. He could feel it building despite the ease of their togetherness, their intimate surveying of bars, their carnal passage from one watering hole to the next, their blind amorous fall onto the floor, against the wall, in the alley, between parked cars, behind the bus shelter, into the bed—places where the turbulence might at any moment erupt. Places where the sex flowered when the drink met the air and they grabbed at one another, keeping each other afloat. Times when he felt her reach into his soft centre and squeeze, trying to wring the softness out of him with her fisted hand, and it taking greater and greater force for her to summon an answering hardness in him.

That first raucous dawn when they had tumbled together into bed and Nick had kissed the wine into her, he'd said, 'Drink keeps me focused, I won't come if I have a drink.' But after a while of him not coming Maya said to him, 'I want you to come. I want to feel the heat of your ejaculation on me. In me. I want the smell of you.' And he tried but he couldn't. She said nothing more about it then, simply handed him another drink when he asked for one and she took one too because it made no difference to her. She wasn't the one who had the problem of getting hard. No, not true, the way she could get hard was a problem too. But it wasn't a hardness of the body. Something else. Connected with the sex, with his lack of hardness despite her softness. She had thought hardness and softness went together, an equation of togetherness. What she hadn't considered was that he would be soft and she would be hard. Nick was so often soft that after a while, Maya could feel herself growing spontaneously hard whenever they were together.

How—the transition from softness to hardness—how it happened, Maya did not know. Perhaps it was something spontaneous, something deeply secret that occurred within, and then floated, *fait accompli*, to the surface, offering itself as indication of a whole lot of other things that too, happened below the surface. When she made love with Nick she felt first, the hardness of his belt buckle, then the hardness of the metal zip in his jeans, then the hardness of his calloused hand, then the hard probe of his finger, then the malleable organ of his sex. 'Don't touch me there,' Nick would say to her. 'Let me touch you instead. Let me go down on you.' And instead of his hardness she would feel his soft breath, his soft lips, his soft tongue, his soft sighing against her soft flesh. And then Maya would fling out her hand and encounter his hand and they would lift the bottle, one after the other, to their mouths and the drink would further confuse the hard softness, the soft hardness, the switch of one for the other, the other for the one and they would spurt the drink down each other's throats until she would yell, 'Now! Put it in me. Now!' And each time, Nick would tell Maya that for him coming didn't matter. That he knew other ways for her to have her pleasure.

Maya's pleasure. Maya's pleasure is the pleasure of the floating raft. A tough hard body to carry her is Maya's pleasure. Sodden, but still sailing, that's Maya's pleasure. Riding her over the deep water, carrying her away, somewhere she hasn't been before, somewhere she wants to go, somewhere she should be going. That would be her pleasure. Maya goes alone into a bar and picks the drink in which she sinks. And after a number of drinks Maya can't recall what it is exactly that is her pleasure. She feels only a familiar turbulence and the feeling that she better watch herself or she'll end up crying, an outburst that for a woman sitting on her own is a sure sign that the woman is in a bad state. Out of control. Unhappy. Maya quickly gulps down her drink but the very thought of control brings tears to her eyes at the precise moment a schmalzy love song starts playing on the jukebox and it's as if she's one of those sentimental fools weeping over a failed love affair. Because all of a sudden she's weeping despite not meaning to. And she sternly tells herself to stop it, because the one thing that might make everything right is in her hand. The bottle blends beautifully into her hand.

That night when they fell into the bed Maya said, 'I want you to do it to me.'

'Do what?' Nick asked, even though he knew she meant—I want you to put your hard dick in me. Instead of answering, Maya went limp and soft in his arms. 'You want me to fuck you?' he prompted. 'You want me to give it to you?' Then Maya pushed her hand down between his legs but Nick's penis wasn't erect.

'I want you to have your pleasure too. But you're not hard,' she breathed, sliding on top of him.

'No,' he replied.

'But this is,' she told him. Nick felt the curve of a small, slender beer bottle roll over his chest. Heard the swell in the bottle, felt it spill over him and run across his belly. Maya hauled herself up and rubbed her crotch along the path of foam the drink had made between them. 'And it's so wet,' she added.

'Do you mean,' asked Nick, putting his hand over her hand on the neck of the bottle. 'That you want me to make love to you with this?'

'Yes,' replied Maya.

'Uh huh,' said Nick.

He rolled her over and crouched above the blur of her body in the indeterminate terrain of the bed and took a long pull from the bottle then leant over Maya's mouth. When the neck of the bottle entered her he cried, 'I'm going to give you my fuck!' and began to gently make love to her with the bottle. It was the sort of long sustained indolent fuck that Nick had never before been able to give Maya. His whole being now concentrated for the first time in such a way that he at last, through the bottle, was giving her the hard rhythmic fuck pleasure. And it was not only Maya's pleasure. The aphrodisiac of the bottle affected him, with it in his hand, it in Maya, it was as if Nick felt an overwhelming erotic connection between himself and Maya and for the first time, when Maya moaned and bit his shoulder he too, had his pleasure. He came, with a great shout and at the same time, Maya threw back her head and bucked her hips but it was a pretence, and she could not come.

Afterwards Maya lay awake beside the sleeping Nick. She looked at the familiar walls, the familiar ceiling, his familiar form. A part of him is now a part of me, she thought. She sighed and picked up the green bottle cradled close to him and sniffed it. Despite the sex, it smelt of nothing but beer. She got out of the bed and dropped the bottle in her handbag. In the bathroom she rinsed Nick's cum from her leg and splashed herself with cold water. The mirror seemed friendly enough. She told herself she didn't feel in the least like crying, not at all, she simply wanted a nice quiet drink somewhere, in a place she hadn't been before. Somewhere new. Where she and Nick had never been. When Maya got out into the street, there was a band of pale pink lighting up the sky, the night had been broken. As she walked down the street she took the green bottle out of her bag and flung it into the air. The action made her feel girlish and carefree. Almost happy. Then the bottle burst against the gutter and shattered into sharp little pieces and the feeling was gone.

Richard Lawson

On Jungle Juice

It was overcast that Friday morning when Skinny Pete arrived on deck acting chirpier than usual and spruiking that he was in preparation for a big 'un. Being an off-pay week, I asked whether he'd had a windfall at the races or whatnot, seeing as how the money was usually drying up for most of us diggers by that time in the normal run of things. The reply he gave Sean O'Riordan and me sounded guarded, if not a bit sly.

'Nah, nah, nothin' like that, let's just say that something has fallen off the back of a ship, which needs lookin' after. Me mate Dougie's found a walker on an African tug, and she looks like a little ball-tearer. All I can say is that they're gonna be legless in Matto come midnight. Who knows? She might even turn out to be a weekender.'

The most we could wheedle out of him was that his mate Doug Blake, who rigged for a quid on the Port Botany night shift, happened across this 'walker' on a freighter just in from Africa. I spoke enough Wharfian to know that a 'walker' meant any item in a shipment which arrives without much in the paperwork department; hence no-one knows where the walker walks from or where it walks to when the walker walks as walkers do. More's the point, nobody bats an eyelid when the item or items get reported as 'missing on the high seas'. That Pete was talking wharfies and weekenders only meant the booty was booze and knowing that mob's thirst, then a power of it. So the day was spent digging and filling and cheerfully chipping away at Pete, certain he'd eventually drop us a clue or two about the secret gathering. But it was soon very clear that protecting the venue's location, rather than improving Sean's or my meagre social life, was the main concern.

'Nah, nah, sorry fellas, I'd love to 'elp yers but I can't. This one's stayin' classified, top secret, 007.'

When he refused to give us the oil by lunchtime it was clear, at least to me if not to Sean, that he was under some oath to keep his trap shut or else. So, lunching as usual beside the floral clock on the crematorium's lawn, we threw proceedings into reverse and gave him the cruellest cold shoulder I'd seen dished out to anyone on the job since the last time he'd come the tight lip with us (which I vaguely recall had something to do with a mystery party also).

In the washrooms after work Sean continued to bombard him with references to traitors and liars while I soaped my hands into a lather fit to please Pontius Pilate. Eventually Skinny Pete obliged us by caving in, as only a grave-digger can.

'OK, OK, you two, O-friggin'-K!' he cried. 'For Christsakes I give in! But please, please, please: no more fuckin' quiet! Let me find ya a piece of paper and I'll give ya the friggin' address!'

'Ah I jes knew ye'd come through for me, Petey!' said Sean as I caked the back of Pete's shirt in suds, 'I knew ye were jes bein' a bit of a stubborn ol' mule!'

'Whatever you do,' said Pete, 'don't for Christsakes turn up before me. I'll 'ave to smooth it over with Dougie first, all right?'

I assured Skinny Pete we'd arrive at the festivities fashionably late. Now, thanks to our general spite and meanness, we all had something to do that weekend, even if it did mean hanging out with wharfies for a spell. Tyranny had again triumphed in the workplace and all in the world was well.

By my timing it was eight-thirty sharp when we knocked on the frosted glass of 59 Iroquois Crescent, Matraville, and got a reception cooler than even I had expected. We might well have been a pair of Jehovah's Witnesses turning up to god-bother on Grand Final day.

'Yep?'

The tip of a rum-pocked nose poked through a narrow slit in the door. Sean shoved me ahead of him and we hovered under the pale porch light like a pair of clumsy moths drunk on the rays. I said that we were friends of Pete Brophy Esquire and that we sought kind admittance.

'Who?'

I repeated the spiel.

'Don't know 'im,' said the nose, and shut the door in our faces. I turned and asked Sean if he'd had as good a time as me.

'He probably don't know Pete's real name,' he moaned. 'Give 'er another go, Dix, go on!'

I sucked a deep breath and tapped again.

'What is it?'

'We's mates of Skinny Pete,' said O'Riordan over the top of my head. 'He told us to meet 'im here.'

'Wait 'ere,' snuffled the nose, and again withdrew.

Behind the glass a shadow approached and opened the door. Stepping onto the patio came a gaunt and slightly potted Elvis impersonator; tall with slicked back hair, in a denim jacket and jeans which hugged the bony hips. I adjusted my night sights and did a double-take, realising that before us stood none other than Skinny Pete. He wrapped us both in his wiry arms, casting a furtive glance to either end of Iroquois Crescent.

'Yers like vodka, guys, doncha?' he said as if counting words. ''Cos there's a swag of special black stuff in here! Come on, let's go get rotten!'

We padded over the shagpile of Doug's suburban

bungalow through several rooms lined with laminated feature walls and lit by the blue light of an unwatched giant TV. In the kitchen out the back an awkward looking blonde, mascara-lined and wearing tight purple stretch-ons and hula skirt, stood po-faced over the stove. In the hubble-bubble dozens of cocktail franks bobbed away like devil's dicks in a cauldron.

'Out there, loves,' she said, pointing to a sprung back door, 'it's all out there.'

Outside we could've been forgiven for thinking we'd stumbled into a jungle clearing, for there we found some local wildlife blinking on at us suspiciously. Hovering beneath a string of party lights were Doug Blake, his nose, three mates and a couple of their wives, all swigging from little shot glasses filled with a jet black brew. Maybe it was the pith helmets and loud, fruity shirts that made me mutter, 'Doctor Liverspot, I presume?' Skinny Pete heard and elbowed me in the ribs.

Off to one side two tables crammed with crystal snifters sparkled with bright reds and blues and greens, a long banner with 'Happy 45th Dougie' flapping gently above on the evening breeze. But the happy gleam of glass was overshadowed by a grim-looking object sitting on its pat out in the backyard. Perched on a wooden table above the lawn sat the mother lode that Pete had so dismally failed to conceal from us, a pair of bamboo flares burning at either side. The party's core was a huge blackwood keg, about twice the size of a forty-four gallon drum and looking for all the world like a pot-bellied idol amongst the voodoo light and kero smoke. Pete breezed over and proudly slapped a bony hand against its dark side.

'Well, 'ere she be, boys. Whaddaya make o' er?'

A string of foreign words in white paint offered some finer details of the contents. I confess the sight of all that mumbo-jumbo had the hairs standing up on the back of my neck.

'Probably says, "swallow at own risk",' hooted Pete, seeing me pawing over the hieroglyphics.

Across the way big game hunter Dougie, roused by the sight of unfamiliars ogling his pressie, excused himself and sauntered over. It was hard to decide at that point which got my vote for the most bulbous object on site: the barrel or the beak. I reserved judgement as Chief Doug extended us the stevedorian hand of friendship.

'So these must be our trendy waiters, eh Skinny? Sorry 'bout the mix-up there before, fellas, but ya can't be too careful you know, least not tonight, eh, know what I'm sayin'? Why doncha 'ave some of the good gear yourself and then bring the boys and me a fresh round. Don't go gettin' pissed on me though; some poor bastard's gonna 'ave to be still standing to pour breakfast!'

Doug Blake winked and let his hull slide away like a cargo carrier slipping its moorings and heading for sea. Once he was out of earshot Sean hauled Pete in by the jacket collar. The host's passing reference to waiters hadn't been lost on my date.

'Waiters, Petey? Did I 'ear 'im right? You got us in by sayin' we'd be frickin' servants for him and 'is bunch, didn't ye, Pete, yer sneaky li'l bastard?'

'Look mate,' flubbed Pete, 'I 'ad no fuckin' choice. You

would've stood a snowball's chance of gettin' in if I hadn't come up with sumthin'. Why doncha just try bein' grateful for a friggin' change?'

'Oh me lordship!' snapped Sean. 'Beg pardon I do. Could I get ye another, an' maybe giv yer old fella a tweak while I'm at it?'

I butted in saying that it might be overdoing things. We were in mixed company, or least that's the way it seemed.

'You'll keep, mister,' said Sean, letting Pete go again.

Skinny Pete smoothed out the crushed collar of his jacket and staggered off looking most peeved at Sean's ingratitude. Rather than stew over the matter with Sean I grabbed a tray of empties and crossed the lawn to pay homage at the black idol. A rickety tap stuck out from the base, leaking its payload onto the ground below. I stuck a finger under and trapped enough for a sample. All things considered it wasn't a bad drop, smooth and very drinkable for all its blackness, but with an aftertaste I put down to the wood of the barrel itself. But it was the quantity alone which declared the theft something of a coup. I sank a couple of nips listening to Dougie giving his guests a brief history of the heist.

'So it's knock-off and I grab some casuals, slave labour, all right? I say to Jeff, the overseer, that I'll need a hand with this one, that there's a prob with the freight sheets and I don't know where the fuck it's s'posed to go. Annoyin' thing what with it being so late and all. He says that customs will 'ave to come on down and have a look-see and I say, "Now whaddya wanna go and do somethin' stupid like that for, Jeffy?" Right? See I've already sussed 'er out days before and know the bloody thing's loaded with the ol' Bongo-Congo, right? So I says to 'im, real quiet like, "You know, Jeff ol' mate, it's me birthday, didya know?" "No," he says. I says, "I never saw the thing come ashore, did you?" So I cut the bullshit an' spot 'im fifty right there and then and 'e walks off feelin' like fuckin' Santa's lobbed early. Straight-forward she was, boys, I tell yers. Clean as a friggin' whistle.'

Clean indeed. Doug's fellow explorers tumbled about yelping with laughter, back-slapping the big pirate and con-gratulating him on chalking up another for waterfront reform. I strolled over with a fresh round as a new tide of weather-beaten faces entered the gathering. All carried slabs or gift-wrapped boxes of the same size, which were just more slabs dressed up. A mad galoot out in front was hol-lering for the birthday boy.

'Beak, yer mad bastard! Happy bloody burfdee yer lazy big keg-swipin' animal!'

The bald six-foot bruiser in tank top and ball-hugging jeans shot out a calloused hand which looked as if it had come straight off a pub meat tray. Dougie grabbed the giant claw and bear-hugged its owner.

'Reggie, Reggie! You bloody great big hunka vegie!'

The incoming guests milled about in the amber glow muttering awkward 'howsitgoin's' to me and casting wary eyes at the sulky Sean, who swanned past divvying out black manna from his tray. The wharfies were all regular-looking blokes in the main, in straight shirts and plain trousers. But their women were quite a menagerie, mostly over-tanned, over-tizzed or over-tinted, and covered in everything from cave-woman frocks to frilly cowgirl jackets. Skinny Pete slotted in just fine, moving around hugging and kissing and carousing with the wharfies and their women and generally just being one of the boys. I listened as nicknames and greetings rang out in the night and each guest stepped up in turn to be introduced to the great barrel. As the yard began to fill and I cast a quick waiterly glance at my watch. Quarter past nine. From there on in, time would never be the same again.

'Cripes, Dougie! She'll 'ave a friggin' kick and a 'alf to 'er,' said the Meat Tray, wrapping his arms around the dark idol. 'But I'm keen, son! Keen as friggin' mustard!'

'Thought yer might be, Reg, so I got in the economy size,' roared Doug.

'No good bein' caught short, eh ol' mate?'

'We're talkin' gallons of high-octane el primo, ol' son,' chortled the host, rubbing his hands in glee. 'Black an' beautiful and free! Go on, folks. Get amongst it!'

'Too right!'

'You betcha!'

'You're a bloody bottler, Dougie!'

Yowls of approval continued from the faithful as I charged around on the backwash, plying the happy revellers with nips. Meanwhile my fellow servant was over by the fence plying a couple of slender ladies with a few evergreen gags. I was pleased to see his demeanour on the mend.

'So anyhow the Irishman turns up at the stadium with 'is barbed wire and says, "I'm 'ere for the fencing. Which way?" '

O'Riordan's captives smirked and raised their glasses for refills.

'Ah, yer darlin' girlies, you is,' said Sean, his face aglow, 'darlin' li'l girls.'

Without warning Dougie's bride flung open the kitchen door and ambled past, toppling several of my best pours. She seemed an unlikely match for Dougie. Tall and ungainly, I wondered how long had passed since Sir Douglas rode into her life sprouting the promise of thirty-two perches in a shining suit of brick veneer. I watched her blonde bouffant sashay through the throng and whisper something in hubbie's ear. She adjusted a colossal cheese 'n' jatz platter then returned to the misty confines of her kitchen. Doug took his bride's communique, whatever it was, and vanished into the laundry.

'Righto, righto, righto! Servant make way! Servant make way! Here comes the guest of honour!'

A fanfare of horns blared from the rafters. A handful of guests jumped in fright while others rose to their feet in anticipation. Sean, telltale slosh stripes on his blue polo-shirt, wandered about topping glasses, his own in particular. For a reluctant conscript, he seemed to be laying on the codswallop pretty thick.

'And more f'you, sir, and f'you . . . n'er mind I'll get ye another quick as a wink, marm!'

Sir Doug and his fellow missionaries fell in next to the kitchen's fly-screen door, doffing pith helmets and coming to attention in a guard of honour. Out rolled the special guest, a plump grannie on a fluoro-striped oldie's scooter. A round of cheeky gags and general hoopla passed around as she brought her ride in for a perfect three point landing on a patch of concrete painted with the single word 'Mum'. Once she was safely docked, a tottering Doug stepped up onto a bench seat and proposed a toast above the sea of bobbing faces.

'Darlin' Mumsie! Friends, Mormons and country bread,' he slurred, 'bend, I meant lend me ... ah stuff it! Hope yers get stew'd, 'ave a fat time.'

With those lofty thoughts the girth of Sir Douglas Legless was laid out to recuperate on a nearby banana lounge. His Mum gazed about through eyes of glowing green, a layer of pancake plastered over the family conk which stood out like a piece of space shuttle. I surprised her by swooping in with a couple of heart-starters and could tell right off that she was eyeing me with something more than casual interest.

'And who might you be, lovie, 'aven't seen you 'round this neck of the woods before.'

I replied I was the help and that she shouldn't hesitate to beckon should she need anything.

'Anything, eh? Ooh, I like a slave boy who'll turn it on for an old duck.'

With that she gave me a very toey pat on the backside. After that it seemed likely that I'd been singled out as a mark and that to escape this harasser wouldn't be easy, considering she was motorised. I made a note to put Sean on her table from there on, knowing a septuagenarian on a trike probably wasn't that far out of his league. I excused myself but not before she'd got in a second well-aimed grope at the front of my crotch.

'Hmmm, Samson,' she cooed, 'plenty to go round there, I bet, eh?'

I gasped and broke free, lurching across the yard to narrowly miss Sean, who was veering in the opposite direction.

'Better be watchin' dis stuff, Dreggsie,' he mumbled. ''Tis a filthy li'l sting it's got to 'er I can tell yer. Four down and already I'm sailin'!'

O'Riordan tottered before me, his tray tilting to bow then stern, looking like a crowded ferry ready to keel over. I helped him right himself, and reissued the host's warning about slaves getting pissed. At the same time I realised I'd managed to stumble backwards a pace or two myself. I put my tray down on a pile of house-bricks and checked my watch once more. Quarter to ten. What was happening here? Either my watch was out or the minutes were expanding. Nor had many yet realised that those in the advance party hadn't handled the pace at all well. The host was down, so too his three fellow trail-blazers who were snoring away loudly in deckchairs. So much for the drinking dynamos of the docks, I thought. These louts were just a bunch of big pansies.

I tripped over a chair leg and felt the night air swirl past my ears as I tried to regather my poise without anyone seeing. I saw that most, after just a few rounds, were already well gone and beyond casting judgements. Behind us, on its backyard altar, the idol cast a curved and ominous shadow across the flickering grass. The yard was crammed with docklanders knocking back the black stuff like there was no tomorrow. The way time was crawling, I wasn't sure there would be.

'How's about a li'l musak?' yelled somebody from the house.

'Yeah, givusa tune! Somethin' for the worker, eh?'

'Or the buccaneer!' bellowed the Meat Tray.

'I'll handle this,' yelled Skinny Pete. 'Got jes the tickit!'

The king of self-appointments stumbled over to the laundry where the stereo was stationed. I put him a drinking hour ahead of me at least. That gives me some leeway, I remember thinking, maybe just a couple more and I'll finish up. Twenty past ten? My watch must've been broken because it felt as if we'd been there for years. I went to say something about this to Sean, but forgot the point. He meanwhile was back at the idol, raising an accusing finger and belting another one down.

'Who are ye,' asked O' Riordan of the keg, 'an' whence do ye come?'

I toasted the question with a nip of my own. Down it went, the warm buzz of fluid creeping across the walls of my gut like a vine. But it was the clamour of Pete's voice rising from the laundry which rang the first alarm bells of the night for me. The doctor of spin obviously had a problem on his hands.

'C'mon now, yer bloody li'l smartarse! You aint gunna make a goose outa me, you're not. Now friggin' play sumfing 'fore I letya bludy 'ave it.'

I raced over to the laundry and stuck my nose around the corner. Inside Pete was manhandling the three-in-one and trying to ram a CD into its half-open mouth. This was causing the unit some distress for the hole in question normally took cassettes. The meters along its front panel flashed silent screams of red and green as Pete regressed steadily backwards through human evolution. When he reached Australopithecus I swung to the three-in-one's rescue. There were one too many pithecuses in the yard as it was.

'Garn git in there,' he shouted, 'before I make a bludy mess o' ya! Garn! Jessee if I don't!'

Skinny Pete finally tried folding the CD in half and jamming it in, a last ditch attempt to get some merry melody into the proceedings. No machine, I thought, not even an el cheapo, should have to die like that. I wrenched him away saying I'd handle things from here on in. What remained of *Al Martino's Songs of Love* I stashed under a wash basket where it would do no further harm. This was as much a relief to me as it was to the cassette player. It gave an appreciative blink and shut down of its own accord.

'Ta, Dreggsie, ol' mate,' Pete moaned. 'Nothin' works, eh? Nothin' works the way they tell yer it does ...'

The keg's fifth victim slid down the front of the household's washing machine and passed out. I stuck a couple of dirty towels under Pete's head and left him with the rest of the white goods. His bondage session with the hi-fi had come as a timely warning. From there on in, I thought, it was customer service only.

'Where's-a-Dougie? A-where's-a-Doug? A Dougie-wuggie-wuggie ... A Dougie-wuggie-wug! Ah wohhhh! Ah wooohh!'

Being otherwise occupied I hadn't seen the gorilla arrive. All I did see was the top of something very hairy watoosiing through the throng and blurting into a tiny party trumpet. Some of the ecstatic closed in around the poor beast, patting its head, while others, Meat Tray and his ilk, were busy pinching it hard on the backside. Jesus, I thought, what a way to earn a bloody quid.

'Who's a pretty monkey,' grunted the Meat Tray, 'who's a pretty boy then?'

The beast spun around tooting each time its behind was stung and growling for a little decorum from the wharfies. Sean was of no use here seeing as how, in my absence, he'd already sacrificed himself to the volcano god. He lay in a purple carpet next to the keg, gently melting down the trunk of a jacaranda. You bloody useless louse, I thought, if anyone's going to keep for this, it's going to be you. I grabbed him by the heels and, discreet as one can be dragging a body across a lawn, laid him out on a garden bed up back. At least I knew the clump of wisteria I left him under would stop him getting on the nose. I turned to find I wasn't alone.

Doug's mum had tracked me up the back and judging by the look on her face, she was there for a little private service of her own, but not of the liquid kind. She held a half-nip in one veined claw, a full one in the other, and God knows how many under her belt.

I asked if she was OK to drive.

'I's missed ya, kiddo,' she slavered. 'Where yer bin? Come 'ere an' sit on ol' Rae's lap for a bit, eh?'

This, by a street length, was the evening's new low. Here I was doing the right thing, laying out the fallen, when I'm suddenly cornered by Hell on wheels. I didn't feel like being chatty, and wasn't about to cop any more touchy-

touchy, so I strung her along a bit suggesting she try and crack onto the one called Reggie. Failing that I suggested she call road service and get someone qualified to have a poke around under her boiling old bonnet. Neither option appealed. She just kept up the 'me Jane' look, sipping away at the dark venom and fixing me with a boa constrictor stare.

'Bit o' slap 'n' tickle never 'urt a big grown-up bloke like you, did it, darl? Cum an' sit on me lap and let me 'ave a good look at ya.'

Grim thoughts of geriatric scooter sex gripped my brain.

To my horror I realised that this old boiler meant to jump me even if it meant running me down to do it. Why couldn't it be O'Riordan or Pete copping this? I thought in despair. No, they were off in vegetable land, leaving me to fend off the mobile mauler. Ma Blake instigated foreplay by chugging towards me a pace or two, then tried to steer me into the nearest dark corner. In desperation I looked around for something to shove in her spokes but, finding nothing handy, changed tack and resorted to begging.

''Ere now, lovie, don't get shy on me ... promise I'll be gentle wif yer, darls. Swift an' gentle.'

It was then that the terrified gorilla broke free of his tormentors and charged into the shadows looking for a tree of his own to climb. He came on, waving his little silver trumpet like a sword, hotly pursued by the Meat Tray and two mates who looked set on groping some more monkey. Finding me and Ma Blake lurking there, the hapless beast appealed for help. I said I'd love to but was about to be raped myself.

'That's right,' drooled Ma, 'if ya likes it rough, I gives it rough.'

'Shit a brick!' cried the gorilla. 'What are these arse-holes on?'

Life, my friend, I remember saying, they're high on life. Ma turned her attention momentarily to the gorilla and was clearly sizing him up for conquest after she was done with me. I found myself bewildered to realise she was not only insatiable but a species-jumper to boot.

'Well, they're not gettin' me!' growled the gorilla. 'Here, lady. Come here a minute!'

With that the ape took a hostage. In a flash it stepped around the back of Ma's trike and boarded it as pillion. He then ordered her around to face his pursuers. Seeing the threat to Mumsie's person, the Meat Tray and Co. stopped dead in their tracks. Seizing my chance I wished the gorilla well and slipped out of the way.

'Hold it right there, dickheads!' it yelled. 'Or the old girl's gonna have a nasty prang.'

Ma twisted about on her scooter seat, trying to inch away from her captor and let out a scream to wake the dead.

'DOUUUUUUGIEEEEEEEEEE, HELLLLLLLLPPPPP MEEEEEEE!'

From the depths of his coma Doug Blake wafted back to life and rose zombie-style from the comfy recliner, his face stained a hideous green by the party lights. Squinting about, he zoomed in on the source of the anguished cry. Dougie wasn't a man to be monkeyed with, which was a pity really.

'Ma? What the fuckin' hell's goin' on?' roared Ma's offspring, knocking pissed guests out of his way. 'What the ...? Why you dirty ...!'

'No, Doug, no!' cried his missus, stepping to the ape's defence. 'It's a Gorillagram I booked for your party! Reggie and his crew were pinchin' his arse and now he's scared to come out. He's not up to anything with yer Mum, Dougie, honest he's not!'

The good wife's assurances only served to further raise Dougie's ire.

'He'll be fuckin' scared when I've finished with 'im. Hold on, Mumsie, I'm comin'!'

It was uncharitable of Dougie, I thought, to ignore his wife's gesture and the extenuating circumstances which led to the gorilla's desperate act. Those watching drew a single breath as Dougie advanced towards the spot where the gorilla was hunkered down behind Ma's chair. This is going to be ugly, I thought. It was, but more than anyone could ever have guessed. The crowd hushed and somewhere a clock chimed. I counted a paltry eleven beats as Doug and his posse closed on their quarry.

'I'd stay away if I were you, pal!' the Gorillagram Man cried. 'We don't want 'er gettin' hurt, now do we?'

The beast's bravado wasn't fooling anyone, least of all sonny boy. Out the corner of my eye I glimpsed the skulking Meat Tray silently closing from the left flank, the Gorillagram Man looking all but done for. None of us, however, had counted on cunning old Ma becoming her own saviour.

'WATCH OUT, YOU MOB! GET OUTA ME FRIGGIN' WAY!'

Ma Blake threw the scooter into first and planted it, sending the gorilla rocketing off the back into the open. In disbelief I watched him spring to his feet and in a single bound leap the neighbouring fence—a good six to seven feet—in sheer, sightless terror. Ma shot forward with a fearful spin, barrelling a couple of floral floozies too pissed to get out of the way, she and scooter on a direct collision course with ... well, I guess I don't need to say what. The look that dawned on Dougie's face at finding himself too big, slow, pissed and late was priceless. I stifled a guffaw as the rest of the crowd braced for impact.

'MUMSIE! NOOOOO!'

It was a nice piece of forethought on Ma's part which saved her neck. With a gut-wrenching crunch she slammed into the table, stockinged legs stuck straight out in front, the snap of bone and wood heard in one sickening crack. The keg thudded onto its side on the grass and, with gathering speed, cannoned towards the rear of the house.

'JESUS WEPT!' screamed Dougie. 'NOT THE BOOZE! NOT ME GORGEOUS BLOODY KEG!'

Doug's ill-gotten trophy slammed into the wall, rupturing on impact, its blood and that of the party spewing out over the concrete in a molasses-dark tide. Tiny waves fanned out under the laundry door, where they would soon wash against the shores of Skinny Pete. Deservedly so, I thought. Hope it seeps through his duds and burns that miserable excuse for a backside. Next time he felt like being narky with me, I'd let him.

A first-aid brigade bearing Ma Blake swept past and

though I tried to ignore it, believe I saw her wink at me as they hustled her inside the house.

'It's OK, Rae darlin',' soothed Dougie's wife, bumping me out of the way. 'You're gonna be fine, just fine. Just hunky bloody dory.'

That I doubted. While an ambulance was rung and Ma's hide was heard gibbering within the inner sanctums of Blake Manor, I, like any good waiter, grabbed a straw broom and began to sweep the pond off onto the lawn. It was my horrified screech at seeing the limp, hairy arm dangling from the splintered side of the keg that brought across a dozen or so curious onlookers, the Meat Tray among them. As a group we stood in silence trying to comprehend the thick, sausage-sized fingers of a huge primate drifting on a pool of embalming fluid.

'Root me ragged, Dougie! What's this yer dishin' up to us, ya bloody big burk?'

But Dougie was with the wounded. I could tell that Meat Tray's biggest problem was working out how his Gorilla-gram quarry had managed to wind up inside the keg. I began to explain that all was not what it appeared but gave up, seeing it as a lost cause at that point of the festivities. Instead I moved that we quickly dispose of any evidence, but naturally enough, the Meat Tray overruled me.

'Nah, no way. Leave it to the big dickhead to clean up. C'mon, boys, let's go 'ave an ale.'

The Meat Tray, Indian-giver he was, hoisted a carton of gift-wrapped cans onto his shoulder and left with a few wharfie mates in tow. Again I was very glad to be sober, for once the revelation began to dawn on those who remained, the sound of emptying stomachs filled the Matravillian night. Some stunned-looking blokes stepped up and stared agog at the mysterious limbs of whatever it was that had once occupied the keg. Two drunken dulcies fainted in a clash of heads on the lawn. Other types, sensing police involvement, quietly left the scene. It still hadn't gone midnight when I yelled for last drinks.*

* There is no truth to the rumour that the Australian Ambassador to the West African republic of Burkina Fasa has, on behalf of our government, convened a maritime inquiry into the matter. Nor is it true that the Curator of the Australian Institute for Anthropological Studies was in attendance incognito at Iroquois Crescent on the night in question. Finally, the decomposed remains of a large primate of unknown origin were never discovered, nor reported in a local news article entitled, 'The Link in La Perouse?'.

Tim Moltmann

Fibonacci Sequence

There's a time in the temperate zones when winter ends. It's not so much the start of spring, a capricious season not to be relied upon. No, it's much more accurate to say that winter is over. The cold stops short of the bones. The sun, when it shines, has vigour.

I was contemplating the change of weather as I walked away from my office building and headed uptown in search of food. I crossed a one-way street and walked diagonally through the park. Gardeners were mowing lawns and the cut grass gave off a fecund smell, as if anticipating more warmth and light. I crossed another one-way street and turned a corner into the central business district. What I called the CB Deebies.

I glanced across the road and saw a pub I usually avoided. The doorway was filled with a man whose body appeared to be in spasm. He lurched across the footpath and out into the traffic. Cars braked and horns blew. The spasms continued to drive the man's body across the road towards me. Bile flew from his mouth and streams of shitty piss left a trail of his zigzag route. He fell at my feet and with one last spasm, sucked in a bale of air. I swear my trouser cuffs stretched towards him. He was motionless then, but continued to ooze. A snail crawling across the footpath was surrounded by the man's liquid and I stared at its shell, so perfectly proportioned. I closed my eyes and saw a spiral where the snail shell had been, turning, turning. I opened my eyes again but the man was still there. I had to resist a strong urge to prod him with my shoe, to see if I could get one last reaction. But I knew it would be futile. The body reeked of death. Hey barman, I'll have one of those.

I'd yet to become particularly infatuated by death before that day. Being on the scene of a car accident had not excited me in any way. Media accounts of natural disasters and wars had rarely held my attention to the end of the column space. Perhaps I'd just never been close enough. Whatever the reason for my past indifference, this was clearly something to embrace. It's not every day that you get to watch someone reduce themselves to a pile of fabric and skin, oozing at your feet as you walk down a city street. I grabbed a sandwich (and a strong coffee) and headed back to the office to share the details of my brush with death. Selwyn occupied the work station next to mine. He was playing a golf game on his computer.

'You won't believe what happened to me in the street just now.'

'Try me.'

'Some guy up and died at my feet.'

'Did he have a heart attack or something?'

'Or something. It looked to me like he had a super-tanker of booze inside him and he just ... erupted.'

'What do you mean "erupted"?'

'I saw him stumble out of the Vic and onto the road. He was out of control. Somehow all of the cars approaching the lights managed to miss him. He kept coming towards me, like I was a magnet. I just stopped and stared, glued to the spot. His movements looked pretty funny, but there was stuff coming out of his mouth and his pants were stained. I could see he was in big trouble. Both ends burning. Then he collapsed on the footpath in front of me, took one last gasp and died.'

'How do you know he was dead. Did you check for a pulse or a heartbeat?'

'No way. It was the smell. He smelt of death.'

'Maybe he just smelt like drunks usually do.'

'No, it was something else. Anyway, he didn't look like a drunk. He looked like your average conservative. Like dozens of others you see out there every day.'

'Did the cops and the ambulance turn up?'

'I didn't wait. I'd seen enough, and uniforms make me nervous. Besides, people were gathering like crows on a road kill. I can't stand that sort of voyeurism.'

'You can talk! It sounds like you had a pretty good look at the spectacle.'

'Honestly, I didn't have any choice. I was just . . . there.'

It wasn't until I'd recounted the experience a few times to other people that I became aware of how ridiculous it sounded. I didn't feel the need to embellish as a bland, faithful rendering should have been trenchant enough. But as I spoke I also stood apart, watching and listening to myself speak. I felt this second self roll its eyes and glance sideways to confirm its scepticism. I began wondering whether or not I'd actually seen the things I was describing. My physical eyes, the ones in sockets in my skull, scanned the faces of my listeners for traces of this imagined betrayal. I saw none and as the afternoon wore on and further intelligence entered the building from other people who'd been in the city at lunch time, I felt more confident in my telling and retelling. The paranoia didn't completely evaporate though, and I was left feeling a little tarnished by the end of the day. Having experienced such an amazing thing first hand, I'd expected minor celebrity status. Brief, vicarious, but certainly a feeling of enhanced importance. Instead I felt insecure and uncomfortable.

The TV news ran a brief item on a man who'd collapsed and died in a city street earlier that day. It said the man had died of heart failure and didn't mention booze in the equation. Not enough detail for my liking, though I reasoned that the authorities (whoever they were) had not had long enough to investigate all the aspects of this intriguing event.

Next morning's newspaper was scarcely any better. Man. Dead. City street. Heart failure. Only his name, age, suburb and occupation were included by way of further information. The lack of curiosity outraged me. This guy obviously had a huge amount of booze in him and for some reason he erupted so violently that it killed him. Heart failure my arse. This man drank himself to death. How did he manage to do it around noon on a Tuesday? It may sound strange to say that a newly dead body, clothes soaked in the secretions of its final rebellion, could look ... respectable. But I knew this man was no drunken vagrant. The first time I saw him framed in the pub doorway, his body slack then stretched by spasm, he registered as absolutely normal. Black shoes, grey pants, white shirt, red tie, blue coat, balding, bespectacled. Normal. OK, his pose may have evoked a club dance floor rather than a city street. But it was clearly an ordinary body doing an extraordinary thing. It certainly didn't evoke empty flagons and a cardboard box under a bridge. How had this man got into this state? Why had it happened?

I started to think that some kind of cover-up was taking place. I thought about ringing the hospital, the police, the press. Maybe my eye-witness account would be valuable to the investigations which must surely be continuing. Something so fantastic, something I'd seen with my own eyes, had to be attracting attention. I picked up the phone book and thumbed the pages, then put it back down. That second self was there, rolling its eyes again. I went back to the paper. The rest of it was filled with crap. Local politics, small issues blown out of all proportion to create an aura of significance, to try to give us some sense of a place in the world. And here was a real-life mystery played out in our streets, reduced to the size of a small advertisement. Wanted, absolute indifference to the spectacular demise of someone like you and me, right on our front doorstep.

Selwyn didn't so much sit at his work station as tolerate its presence in his personal space. I walked over and leaned on one of the partitions.

'I've been thinking about that guy I saw the other day.'

'I'll bet.'

'I can't believe there hasn't been info about him in the paper or on the news.'

'People die every day. Just because you saw the corpse doesn't make it special.'

'But it was special. There was definitely something weird about it. How could he drink enough booze to kill himself without having any adverse reaction beforehand?'

'You don't know that for sure. You're making it up. Anyway, the paper said he died of a heart attack.'

'Fuckin' bullshit. I saw what I saw.'

'Settle down, Dave. You're getting yourself all worked up over nothing.'

'Sorry. It's just that the image of him stumbling towards me keeps running through my mind. I can't forget it.'

'Try thinking about something else for a while. Why not something really radical? Like, work.'

'Piss off.'

'Good idea. I'm going out for a gasper. Cover for me will you.'

I couldn't think about anything else. I continued taking every opportunity to discuss it with others in the office, trying to get some insight into what had happened by talking it through, exploring the possibilities. But interest was waning and the more I tried to sustain it the faster it slipped away. People were becoming reluctant to engage me in casual conversation.

The phone rang. I knew it was an internal call. I picked it up.

'Dave Johnston speaking.'

'Hi Dave, it's Mandy from Human Resources.'

'Right. How can I help you?'

'Dave, I understand that you had an unfortunate experience at lunch time the other day.'

'If you call seeing someone die at your feet "unfortunate", then yes.'

'Well, as you're aware, the Department has an Employee Assistance Program and trauma counselling is available. The service is free to all employees and their families and is absolutely confidential. I thought I'd give you a ring to encourage you to use it if you're having any difficulties.'

'Thanks.'

'The number is listed under "E" in the telephone directory.'

'OK. Bye.' I hung up.

I didn't feel traumatised. I felt angry. Frustrated by the apathy of others. Their inability to acknowledge something exceptional in their midst.

Saturday morning was damp and chilly. Spring. I took my hangover down to the shops, bought a weekend newspaper and crawled back into bed with a pot of tea. Two pages into a national broadsheet and I'd officially awoken.

CONCERN OVER ALCOHOL DEATHS

Authorities in several states are coordinating investigations into a series of deaths from alcoholic poisoning. Seven people have died in seemingly unrelated incidents over the last four days. All have displayed the symptoms of massive alcohol abuse, yet none was found to have been drinking heavily at the time of death. Police investigators and public health officials are working with manufacturers and distributors to determine whether a common cause can be found.

The story went on to provide details of the seven deaths, starting with my man. Bingo. Vindication.

The shit really hit the fan in the papers on the following Tuesday morning. Thirteen more deaths occurred over the weekend. Certainly cause for concern, but at least relative to the amount of booze drunk on those days. Then another thirteen died on the Monday, a quiet drinking day for most of us. This took the cumulative death toll to thirty-three and mass (media) hysteria kicked in.

The share market was the first thing to give. Whilst there was nothing to suggest that all of this was enough to completely dry up demand (not in my circles anyway), it was clear that a lot of people were going to think twice before having a tipple. The brewers, distillers and wine makers took an absolute hammering. A flow-on effect hit a number of primary producers and manufacturers of glass and packaging. The entertainment sector also took a beating, media companies dived and a few advertising outfits with large brewing accounts looked like disappearing completely. Interestingly, some importers actually surged as theories sprang up about the source of the problem being localised. This was seen by most analysts as an aberration. We'd never import more booze than we'd produce locally.

There were calls for calm, assurances that everything possible was being done, recall of batches of product associated with the deaths and in some cases total product recall. I followed all of the media coverage as if it were about my own group of family companies. I started a journal and hoarded newspapers and magazines normally discarded. I thought about clipping the relevant articles but there were so many I decided to keep all of the publications intact.

I'd been on nodding terms with the newsagent for a while, but my sudden fascination with every utterance of the media took our relationship up a notch or two. He was in his mid to late forties, wiry, fit and tanned. Serpent tattoo on his right forearm. He'd always struck me as an interesting

sort of bloke, but I'd never managed to get beyond the pleas-
antries before.

'I hope you don't have too many shares in the
breweries.'

'The sum total of my personal wealth is invested in
what you see around you.'

'What do you make of all of this?'

'Newsagents with their own opinions are headed for the
loony bin. I'm here to peddle other people's opinion, not
donate my own.'

'But people all over the country have been dying for no
apparent reason.'

'People have died for no apparent reason throughout
the history of mankind. The only thing that's amazing about
it is that we continue to find it amazing.'

'Aren't you even slightly curious as to why?'

'I know why. People die because their lives are finite.'

I'd been told by someone else that he was a Vietnam
vet. Perhaps he'd had a bit more time to think about this
stuff than I had.

What I found incredible about the economic impact of
these events was that they demonstrated the fragility of the
system so beautifully. A man died at my feet from a cause not
yet properly determined and in little more than a week the
future of several large companies with international affilia-
tions was in question. What kind of ruse had been going on
here? Why all the talk about structure, value, wealth, strategy,
when the whole thing could be dispersed by the loss of a body
or two? Like breath on a dandelion wish.

I began drinking regularly in the pub the man had lurched from. Gradually I encountered a number of people who'd been there on the day. A merchant seaman called Jacko was the most responsive to my questions.

'Did you see that guy in here who died in the street on Tuesday?'

'Saw more of him than I'd have liked, mate. Breakfast and lunch all over the bar.'

'He'd only had a couple of beers, hadn't he?'

'Only saw him have a couple. But then he wouldn't be the first two-pot screamer in this place. Parking a tiger they call it in South Africa.'

'What?'

'Throwing up. Parking a tiger. Can you believe that?'

'It all sounds pretty weird to me. People don't just die from a couple of beers at lunch time.'

'All I know is he parked a tiger on the bar then took off out the door with the wobbly boots on. Maybe the tiger came back and bit him.'

Others told a similar story. Ordinary-looking guy walks in, drinks one beer while reading the newspaper. Part of the way through his second beer he vomits across the bar, reels and staggers into the street. I knew more about what happened next than any of them. I continued asking questions but as happened in the office, people began to withdraw. The bar staff became quite hostile towards me whenever I mentioned it. Obviously management didn't see this sort of thing as being good for business.

I'd decided to take some time off work so that I could devote myself to an investigation of what was going on. My daily pattern involved taming a hangover, checking the media at the newsagency, going to the library to do some research and drinking in the Vic. I'd unplugged the TV. Its treatment of the events was far too superficial. At the library I read about brewing, distilling and wine making to see if I could find a common thread that might link all of this together. Water? Sugar? I read about the effects of alcohol on the body. I read about economics and the workings of the share market. I followed each lead methodically, in search of a logical solution. The library assistant seemed bemused by the range of my requests.

'Where would I find information on unexplained disease outbreaks?'

'What happened to home brewing and the All Ordinaries index?'

'It's all related.'

'I'd love to know what you're studying.'

'Death.'

'Well, I suppose it does tend to level things out.'

The more I concentrated on this one event, the more I came to understand a wide range of things, to see their connectedness. I spoke to fewer people but our conversations seemed to be of greater significance. My life was gaining potency. By embracing an unknown I was losing my fear of uncertainty.

'How's the peddler of other people's opinions this morning?'

'Better than you I'd say. You look like shit.'

'My personal appearance is of no importance to me. Successful research requires total dedication.'

'Research into what?'

'Death.'

'You know nothing about death.'

'Precisely. That's why I'm having to work so hard. So, what happened yesterday?'

'More of the same. And now we've got the bleeding politicians involved.'

'That should make all the difference.'

It being only a matter of months before election time, the politicians weighed in big time. The conservative opposition reached up and grabbed family values off the shelf, gave them a quick dust and held them aloft without fear or favour. The policies of the government had so estranged the average person in the street that they were turning to the bottle and drinking themselves to death in alarming numbers. A conservative government would look at subsidies for low alcohol beverages, review licensing hours and consider ways of legislating maximum daily limits for the purchase of alcohol.

The Left took a far less emotive approach, being in power at the time and having an interest in hosing the whole thing down. Additional funds were pledged to help with the investigations. A national hotline was established, support provided for the families of victims and a major new initiative in drug and alcohol education announced. The minor parties walked a line between the two majors and a few independents provided their personal views.

The words of the politicians failed to touch me. I'd encountered this 'epidemic' first hand. I knew something about it. It was not a political issue and the whole machinery revealed itself to be impotent in the face of an unexplained reality. I felt that somehow it all had to come crashing down. To be replaced by what I didn't know.

I stopped going to the library as the people contact had become too distracting. I stopped drinking in the pub. I had nothing more to learn from them. My range was shrinking, from home, to the newsagency, to the bottle shop and home again. I walked this route several times a day, like a pilgrim circling the Kaaba. The days rolled by, the bodies piled up and as the media cast its net wider in an effort to maintain fever pitch, the religious leaders were the obvious next choice. Beneath a veneer of understanding and support, a solid plank of divine retribution was pushed into the arena. The plank was wedge-shaped, thin at the liberal end, thick at the fundamental. But it was sawn from the one log. The traditionally hard-drinking Catholics were the most conspicuous. Come with us, they said. Let us replace your fear and uncertainty with an absolute. Faith. Unbeatable. Also unprovable. I wasn't buying at any rate. The man who died at my feet was not fingered by a deity for being a naughty boy. He'd somehow managed to get so much booze into his system that it just shut down. I still didn't know how or why, but God and the devil were not on my list of suspects. Neither was my newsagent.

'Do you believe in God?'

'I believe that people will believe anything. I couldn't stand in here all day surrounded by this crap and think anything else.'

'So what determines what people believe?'

'Their fears.'

'And what determines what they fear?'

'Their beliefs.'

I grabbed a cold stubby from the fridge and walked back out into the garden, twisting off the top as I went. A horde of newspapers and magazines had been spread out on the table. My notebook lay on top. I turned to a clean page and began to summarise the events of the last couple of weeks.

Day One: A man lurches out of a pub at lunch time and dies on the footpath (at my feet). Found to have massive amounts of alcohol in his system, though the evidence suggests that he'd only had two beers all day.

Day Two: A woman dies in similar circumstances in another part of the country.

Day Three: Two people die (in separate parts of the country). Found to have massive amounts of alcohol in their systems despite moderate intake.

Day Four: Three people die. Blah, blah, blah.

Yesterday, one hundred and forty four people died in the same way in various parts of the country. All had swallowed one or two alcoholic drinks before turning into incontinent rag dolls. None had drunk heavily in recent times. None had a history of alcoholism. No amount of testing, analysis, withdrawing of product or scaremongering seemed able to stop the sequence of events.

I wrote the daily death tolls on a single line.

1, 1, 2, 3, 5, 8, 13, 21, 34, 55, 89, 144 . . .

Strangely, each number was the sum of the two which preceded it. Somewhere in the back of my mind I knew there was a name for this sort of sequence. A friend had told me about it years ago. It was a word from another language, though the way my friend had mangled French I wasn't sure I'd ever be able to recall it. All I could come up with was Phoebe and Archie.

Nothing in the dictionary under Ph. F. Fi. Fib. Fibonacci sequence or series. The infinite sequence of numbers in which each member is the sum of the previous two. Infinite. Holy shit. I ran inside and located a couple of old maths textbooks. I read that Fibonacci sequences abounded in nature. They were named after a thirteenth-century Italian mathematician who developed the sequence while studying the breeding of rabbits. Leaves grew around plant stems in these sequences. The spirals on the surfaces of pinecones and pineapples followed them. Sunflowers. Snail shells.

I lay on the lawn and took a swig from my stubby. It had rained earlier in the week and the sunshine over the last few days had given the grass a head of steam. I thought I could feel it pushing up from beneath my body, stretching towards the firmament, oblivious to a fate of mower blades and compost. The grass felt omnipotent. The grass felt . . . infinite.

This was my third beer of the day, though I'd knocked the previous stubby on to the lawn with a few sips left in the bottom. Good for the grass, I supposed. I was calmer with some booze in my system, looking forward to leaving the danger zone of one or two drinks per day. It occurred to me that what had been killing people was moderation. I theorised that all of the small amounts of alcohol they'd imbibed during their careful, measured lives had somehow managed to accumulate in their bodies and hit them at once with a knockout punch. Give me excess, give me abstinence, but rack my body in the throes of death if I succumb to the evils of moderation.

The next number in the Fibonacci sequence was two hundred and thirty-three. If the pattern continued to hold, this plague was going to keep slicing the top off the bell shaped curve of our drinking population with ever-increasing ferocity. Only those at the margins would be safe, the middle ground no longer a haven from choice. What's it to be, careful or careless? What might our world be like when dominated by teetotallers and drunks? Would the righteous have their day and rule in smarmy indignation? Or would we lurch into bacchanalia, run on some kind of pickled intuition? A bit of both perhaps. Two poles, apart, to keep the whole thing spinning.

I turned over and bathed my back in the warm grass. Rather than being soothed by the beer as was usually the case on the morning after, my guts were feeling queasier by the minute. I stood up again, thinking that if my stomach didn't settle down soon, I'd have to park a tiger on the lawn. And as the horror of that thought took hold, my body bent double in spasm and my mind's eye looked on, removed, detached, as if watching from across a busy street.

Max Cullen

BoTTLED Up

When it came to partaking of vast amounts of
alcohol, Marc Thyme was fully cognisant of the
pitfalls—he had fallen into several pits that very
evening. Christmas was coming up and the obligatory round
of parties had filled his cup of life to the brim of deliverance.

Overflowing with pique, Marc was delivered to the
desk sergeant by two bemused young constables—

'Here's a Lulu for you, Sarge. Found this one in a

vacant lot—reckons someone knocked off his house.'

'The shing was devvinately there ten years hago, Shher-geant—can I help it she moved house?' Marc became swamped with self-pity. 'Took the lot she did: kids, the car, the housh an' all me sheventy eights: King Oliver, The Rhythm Kings, Johnny Dodds, Tiger Rag with Jelly Roll Morton, the original 1923 recordings of The Wolverine Orchestra with ... '

'Name?' barked the sergeant, a red-faced giant, a lot more gruff than *buff*.

'... Bix Beiderbecke ...'

'Empty your pockets, Bix,' the big man snarled. And then said to the young coppers: 'Did 'e give yez any trouble?'

'Nah,' said one. The other shook his head.

'Pity,' the sergeant muttered as he watched Marc's fumblings. For the sergeant too was a victim—the son of a violent drunk—and as he observed Marc's pitiful possessions appearing he felt an instinctive disgust.

PRISONER'S PERSONAL EFFECTS
One only handkerchief—filthy
$4.63 cash
Receipt: Bathurst Street Loan Office
Nine TAB tickets
Journalists' Club membership badge
Keys—2
2 raffle tickets/Christmas hamper
Passport/EXPIRED
Address book—tattered
Comb—DISGUSTING

Watch with broken strap—not going
Paperclip
Box of matches—3 left
Ballpoint pen—leaking
1 mouthpiece for bugle/trumpet/cornet.

'Stand over there,' the sergeant said, directing Marc to a quaint enclosure, adding with emphasis, '*BIX*.' And snarling, 'Now, *BIX*, tell me your full name.'

'Leon Bismarck Beiderbecke, I play trumpet, I was just resting between gigs when your men found me ... ' Marc was *nearly* going too far. 'I'm not drunk,' he said, going too far.

'YOU'RE SUNK, BISMARCK!' roared the giant, and ho-ho-hoed at his merry joke.

The two young constables joined in the laugh, but soon stopped when they detected the senior man's animosity towards Marc.

'I don't like being taken the mickey out of, son. Your passport here tells me your name is Marcus Xaviour Thyme. I just hope for your sake this stuff we got from your pockets is stolen property, 'cause if it's not that means you *LIED* to me about your name, and I really HATE thieves, but *LIARS*, well ... tell 'im boys.'

'You'd better tell the truth, Box o' Wheat Bix or whatever-y'name-is,' one constable said earnestly. 'The last prick who was in here and lied to the sergeant about his name had to be buried in an unmarked grave—because no sod knew who 'e was!'

'Unrecognisable,' added the other.

By this time Marc was deadly sober. 'Bix is what most

people call me, and that's the truth,' he said, lying. 'If I say my name is Marc Thyme, most people who don't know me think I'm being a smart Alec. So I usually say it's Bix, Leon Bismark Beiderbecke. It's the name I use when I'm not using my name.'

The sergeant examined a small, very tarnished metal shield and addressed Marc with a new contempt. 'The Journalists' Club. Well, well. You're a journalist, are you, Marcus?'

'No, *I'm* not,' he said with true conviction, 'my father was.'

'Your father was a *journalist* was he, Marcus?'

'He was the BEST.'

'There's no such thing as a good journalist, is there, men?' he said depositing Marc's belongings into a large envelope.

The less vocal of the two constables answered, 'All journalists are scum.'

'They're nearly all alcoholics, aren't they, Sarge?' prompted the other.

'That's right,' said the sergeant. 'Most of them are alcoholics, all of them are liars.'

'I'll bet your ol' man was a cop,' Marc said, putting his foot carefully into it.

'Did *it* speak?' rumbled the Terrible Hulk.

'I hope not,' gasped Starchy.

'What did you say?' demanded Hutch.

'My old man used to say,' said Marc, in full flight, 'Scratch a policeman and you'll find a human being.'

'We say something else in here, Bix,' said Hutch,

'Scratch a cop and you'll get yer fuckin' head bashed in . . . '

'Is this *your* trumpet mouthpiece?' interrupted the big man.

'Yeh.'

'Are you any good?'

'I get paid for it . . . sometimes. I had to hock the horn today to buy Christmas presents,' Marc confessed coyly.

'Looks to me like you bought TAB tickets and a skin full of grog.'

'Yeah. Well that too—and don't lose those betting slips, will you? I haven't checked them out yet.'

Then, hit with a sudden sense of loss, Marc asked. 'Where are my parcels?'

'Take him away,' ordered the sergeant.

Marc was herded away bleating, 'I had a plastic bag full of stuff! Little toys for my children . . . thieving mongrels!'

The Drunk Tank was not yet crowded, the long night still a pup, but Marc was cast in with several hardened drinkers. The heavy door clanged shut.

'I want to make a phone call. I'm entitled to one phone call—it's the law!'

'You're not entitled to anything, Box,' said the departing constable. 'You're drunk.'

Marc appealed for help from his distinguished cell mates: 'That's the law, isn't it, you're allowed to ring your solicitor?'

A heavy, monolithic bearded person wearing a purple velvet evening suit, black bow tie and shirt with frilly lace cuffs answered in a mumbling Neanderthalic accent, '. . . Iron a baddister annay wooden net meek all a slithertor. . . '

Marc caught the gist. 'You're a BARRISTER and they wouldn't let you make the ONE phone call to which you are LEGALLY entitled? That is CRIMINAL! Did you tell them who you are?'

'Sapiently ... ' slurred the suit. 'Told them I was [hic!] Perry [hic!] Mason: made no difference at all.' And in brief he rested his case.

'I'm going to write to the *Herald* about this,' said Marc.

Then from a pee-stained corner adjacent to the exposed Brasco there uncoiled something foul. A vile thing of breath the rank quality of bile and stale Guinness. 'YOOOO-UUUUU LIIIIITLE MAAAAANNNNN!' The creature spoke in an amateur stage Gaelic roar, giving each word more volume than value and projecting its spite with all its might at Marc, who now stood rooted to the spot and 5'10" in his pre-Christmas stockinged feet—a good foot shorter but not as dense.

Marc's father, who had been an amateur boxer and could have been a contender and maybe even world champ if he hadn't been KO'd by booze at an early age, once advised him that inside every bully there lurked a frightened little runt of a man trying to get out. And so it was that Marc considered sagely appealing to this oncoming bully's inner man. He could see at a glance how his use of bygone pugilistic training might prove ineffective. This person was thick. He had thick orange hair and thick eyebrows draped like awnings over blood-encircled eyes which stared blankly like stagnant, stinking, lifeless pools where a twinkle long ago had drowned, sunk in a thick, purple face which was emitting thick unintelligible sounds. Marc thought quickly and asked evenly, 'Are you talking to me, runt?'

The creature pulled up short. *Slowly he turned, step by step...*

'What's your name, champ?' Marc added, with true Costello pluck.

'BRENDAN EFFIN' BEHAN!' it roared, raising beefy paws.

As the refugee from Paisleyland descended and severe censure seemed certain for Marc, from beneath a grey, threadbare prison blanket there squinted the professionally pummelled visage of a true Australian son. He spoke low and darkly, saying 'I'm Muhammad Ali, if yuz don't shuddup I'll punch yer plurry lights out.'

'Plurry?' thought Marc. 'Not a locution one encounters every day.'

A deadly hush had descended, followed by an awesome silence, then a heavy calm.

Next to Marc there sat a young man wearing T-shirt, jeans and tattoos. He emerged as a closet intellectual, very hip, as he said quietly to Marc, 'I told the dude with the stripes I was Jack Kerouac, you know, the "beat" writer.'

'On The Road,' murmured Marc, all-knowing.

'No,' said the tats, 'out at the desk. What did you say your name was?'

'Bix Beiderbecke.'

'Craaazy,' said Jack with a fast fading smile. 'Christ, I could use a smoke.'

A commotion outside was duly followed by the introduction of yet another miscreant.

'Get in there, you dog!' said one constable throwing the dusty man heavily to the concrete floor.

'Get on your feet when you're being spoke to!' said another and kicked the wretched soul in the guts.

'I want to make a phone call,' he gasped, spitting blood from his lacerated lips. 'I'm entitled ... '

'You ain't titled to nuffink, DOG!' said the cop and reefed a size twelve into Dog's groin.

CLANG! went the cell door.

'Whimper ... ' went Dog.

'Jim?' said Marc, beginning to recognise under the blood and dirt the face of a fellow traveller. 'Aren't you Jim McNeil, the famous prison playwright? What are you doing here, Jim?'

'Research.'

Jim had honed his way with words doing fourteen years languaging behind bars, and was a big fan of the twelve-bar blues. He recognised Marc the trumpet man from quite a number of bars.

'How are you, Marc?'

'Shhh!' shhhd Marc, 'you don't give your right name here.'

'Now you tell me! I told them my name and they called me a liar.'

'Is that why they bashed you up?'

'Christ no! Usually after they knock off my pension cheque they just let me off with a warning. But I haven't had a cheque since the Social Security mob went on strike, so ... '

Jack Kerouac then squatted near them. 'Got a smoke for a bloke, Jim?'

'Sure,' he said. And handed him the pack.

'I saw what happened, comrade,' said Perry Mason. 'I'll take your case.'

'I'll take a smoke,' said Muhammad Ali.

'When we get out of here,' announced Brendan Behan, 'I am going to buy each of you a jar of Irish Whiskey. I love you ALL.'

Marc signed for his belongings at the desk. The young constables had returned to the scene of his arrest and retrieved a plastic bag full of Christmas presents. There seemed to be nothing stolen. Seven TAB tickets were missing, the remaining two were attached to a neatly folded form guide by a paper clip, and the winners were marked in red.

There was enough from the win for Marc to get his trumpet out of hock and buy himself a long cool beer. He drank to Bix, and Jim and all alcoholics anonymous.

Jean Bedford

The Night they Planned Iris's Wedding

S al was in a foul mood. Robert had been back in
town for two days and already, she said to Iris, she
was having deep anxiety symptoms. After seeing
him two days in a row she was falling, she said, into the
black hole. She lay on her bed all through the second
afternoon, after Robert had gone, telling herself she would
not fall into the black hole. Fuck it, she thought, my life's
nothing but a series of having to be *friends* with people,

whether I love them, or hate them, or both or neither.

Her mood was not helped by Tony ringing to make dinner arrangements. Things between them were already going wrong—there had been the night Otto arrived at midnight and Sal had had to get out of bed to talk to him and had ended up drinking all the champagne Tony had brought, for a start, and Tony had already said once or twice in this previous week that he thought they were seeing too much of each other, that perhaps they should cool it a little. So when he rang she was flustered. She'd meant to convey something with this phone call, but, still thinking about Robert, she didn't remember what she'd meant to convey.

'At least,' she said to Iris later, 'I hung up first.' But she'd also crawled back into bed with her Arthurian romance, thinking—it's all fucked. She'd been obsessed with this statement lately, it was coming to seem a most elegant summation. This time last week, she thought, Tony was ringing to say he was knocking off early and he'd come round for a drink before his official dinner. This time last week ... Athena Starwoman in the *Mirror* had told her she'd be on cloud nine, and she was. She heaved herself off the bed and went to see if Spiro, her other house-mate, had bought the paper. Spiro was unable to get through the day without reading his stars, too. The paper was under the ginger cat on the kitchen bench, but her stars were boring: a partial eclipse of the sun and the new moon in Scorpio, a most unreliable sign. Athena said to put everything off. Tony's stars said that problems would be resolved after the weekend. Sal wished she hadn't agreed to dinner on Friday.

She went back to bed. Robert had the kids and she had

stacks of work she wasn't doing. She put her book down and tried to think, but thoughts wouldn't come. The phone rang.

'Hi. Sal?' It was Iris.

'How'd it go?' Sal asked. Iris had been to see Sal's (and Robert's) truly amazing accountant.

'Wonderful. Everything's OK. Come and have a drink.'

'Well, why not?'

She went to comb her hair and the phone rang again. Leo and Spiro were playing chess in the living-room so Sal answered it.

'It's me again,' said Iris.

'Yeah?'

'I forgot to tell you we're technically corporate conspirators. Ken said we've done what Harry M. got five years for.'

'Oh shit.'

'He says you'd better see him.'

They were both laughing so much Sal hardly heard her.

'OK, I will. I'll ring him tomorrow.'

Peg, who shared Iris's house, arrived at the wine bar after a while, and Sal had to bring her up to date on all the stuff Iris already knew. Peg was nearly as upset as she thought Sal had been. She'd kept saying how brave Sal was, even to think of falling in love. Sal was beginning to think it had been a recurrence of a chronic stupidity.

'And I suppose you and Phillip are still *happy*?' Sal said bitterly to Iris. She knew they'd been away during the week.

'Yes, very,' Iris said, but her voice was troubled. She

explained: 'I think he wants us to get married, and I won't do that.'

Sal looked at Peg.

'Yes!' they said together. 'Get married. What a wedding!'

Iris laughed.

'No, Iris,' Sal said. 'You don't have to live with him or change your name, people don't these days. But the wedding! Imagine it! No-one's been married for ages.'

They did begin to imagine it until they were all crying with laughter. Peg and Sal were to be matrons-of-honour in mauve guipure lace over white satin. Peg described the dresses—strapless, boned, a fish-tail pleat, chiffon shoulder slips. Old friends of Iris's, Jenny and Dianna, neither of whom had ever married, would be bridesmaids, in reverse colours. Sal's daughters and all their friends would be flower-girls and carry baskets of roses. The ceremony was to be in the derros' park outside Kinselas—they'd take over the restaurant for the reception. Harry would give Iris away, Phillip would have a famous and awful communist writer as best man. The colour scheme throughout would be mauve and yellow. Cabbage roses featured prominently. Leo and Ariel would write the Epithalamium, a four-hour epic in medieval Latin (Leo had done a classics degree) and Old Norse (Ariel, a thriller-writer and one of Sal's closest friends, had studied Icelandic languages once). There would be choruses which all the guests would be required to chant.

'I want to wear a yellow going-away suit,' Iris said. 'With a waist and a peplum and a pleat. And very high yellow shoes.'

'And a pill-box hat,' said Peg, her eyes very round.

'And Harry's suit has to be mauve,' said Sal.

'Absolutely,' Peg said, 'with a purple Liberty tie.'

'We'll all smoke all through the ceremony.' Iris was remembering Jenny graduating in Arts at the age of fifty-seven—the photos showed them all smiling, cigarettes dangling from every hand.

'Can we have picture hats?' Sal asked Peg.

'Absolutely. As long as they're covered in cabbage roses.'

'I want a dress like Lady Di's,' said Iris.

'Of course,' said Peg, like the Fairy Godmother. 'And Phillip should be all in white with mauve-tinted sunglasses.'

Sal looked worried. 'Do you think he'll come at it?'

'It doesn't matter,' Peg said. 'Anyone'll do at this stage.'

Louise at the wine bar said they'd turn on the shower tea and that the cigarette companies would probably sponsor the whole thing. That got Sal and Iris enthused about who should have the television rights.

'It could be a series,' Sal said.

Eventually they left, and Sal walked home thinking that women together, laughing, could apparently heal anything. She fell into bed with hardly a thought of the next night, Friday.

On Saturday morning Sal burst into Iris's kitchen. Phillip was there and he and Iris were having breakfast.

'How's it going?' Iris said. She knew that Sal had been anxious about the dinner date last night.

Phillip looked slightly annoyed—this was the second

Saturday in a row Sal had interrupted his papers and bacon and eggs with Iris. He was clearly wondering if it was going to become a habit.

'It's truly fucked now,' Sal said savagely. 'It's the *friends* routine again, only this time he means it. We're not even going to *see* each other for the rest of the time he's here because he can't trust himself to stick to it. I'm some sort of Delilah figure or Devil Woman or something . . .'

Phillip had a funny look on his face, almost as if that idea struck a chord somewhere. Iris glared at him and he turned sympathetically to Sal.

'Perhaps he's jealous,' he suggested, 'Otto turning up last week . . .'

'No,' Sal dismissed that with a grimace. 'It's all about *him*, what *he* can and can't cope with . . . *Bloody* men!'

She sat down and began to pick absently at Iris's bacon rind. Iris poured her a cup of tea and she drank it without appearing to notice. Iris sighed.

'Sal,' she said. 'We're thinking of going to Bondi for the day. Do you want to come?'

'Nah,' Sal said, then, 'sorry, thanks, but no I can't. The kids are coming back to my place for the weekend while Robert gets himself settled in again. But I'll drive you to the train if you like.'

On the way, Sal told Iris and Phillip that if they didn't stop holding hands over the back of the seat they could walk.

The election was the next weekend and Sal watched it on television at the coast house with Mary.

'What happened to Tony?' Mary asked. Mary was pissed off—she had had to vote for a local right wing independent in order to prevent an even worse Labor candidate getting in.

'He's back in Melbourne, probably,' Sal said. She half expected to see him on the screen when they showed the counting and the politicians crowding in the Party rooms.

Mary looked at her but said nothing. She understood, there was no call for her famous acerbic comments here. Sal was grateful—Mary's marriage had broken up at around the same time as hers, in fact Mary's husband Jack blamed Sal for it. It had provided a bad example, he said. She looked around the large room that she and Robert had designed from the derelict shell they had bought years ago and gave a shiver.

'What's the matter?'

'Nothing—just, lots of ghosts here.' She laughed. She had told Mary why Robert wouldn't use this house any more—'Too many ghosts and bad memories,' he had said and she had been deeply hurt, because some of the memories were good and there were benign ghosts, too, from the years they had lived here. It had been a hospitable house—always food in the fridge for Sydney friends en route to somewhere else or locals who dropped in; regular Sunday lunches with city people who enjoyed the charming train trip or the drive through the park. She had not wanted to move back to Sydney, nor had the children. She had a flash of resentment that she had given in for Robert's convenience. Then she thought, No, I would have gone mad here that first year, on my own.

Now, there were new ghosts—Tony, waking in the afternoon from the mattress in Maria's old room (because Leo wouldn't give up what he called the master bedroom), reaching for her, already dressed and distracted because she had to make the girls their dinner. Tony, at the beach, and their starfish competition. Tony, sitting in the chair Mary sat in now, telling her about his first marriage, about how he had come to work in party politics. Tony, tentatively teasing her daughters, winning their approval. She thought she could see what Robert had meant.

'Come on. Don't get maudlin on me,' Mary said. 'This shit,' she gestured at the television, 'this is enough to cause a deep depression. Who needs *lurv* when you can get angry about politics?'

Later, when Mary had gone, Sal moved around the large house turning off the lights. She had drunk a great deal of wine, and she sat on the bed in the spare room that Robert had sometimes used during their increasing periods of separate coldness. But sometimes, she thought, sometimes I crept down here and we were happy for the night. She wondered if she would ever work out what had been *her* mistakes, and what had been unavoidable.

264

Rosemary Creswell

Epithalamium

I t was after Sal and Peg planned Iris's wedding that things between Iris and Phillip really went wrong.

Iris and Sal and Peg were idling away a few hours at the wine bar one night. Iris and Sal had been idling away the afternoon at the wine bar since lunchtime and Peg had joined them on her way home from visiting a spiritualist. Peg was writing another book and they were discussing whether the narrative should be in the first or third person.

'The first, I reckon,' said Sal whose own books were a mixture of persons.

'The trouble with that,' said Peg, 'is that I always get it muddled up with myself.'

'Who *is* talking?' asked Iris.

'Well, I don't know. I'm writing this book backwards. I know what she does, but I don't know who she is because I'm not up to the first chapter, which is last, in my head.'

Iris talked about that not mattering and people being defined by their action and not having any central persona which she vaguely remembered from first year philosophy twenty-five years ago but she couldn't remember which philosopher.

None of them could remember anything much that week. They were having a lot of trouble with nouns, especially proper ones. Only that morning Iris had needed to look up something in the *Shorter O.E.D.* but couldn't find the dictionary. She had asked Peg, who lived with her, if she had been using it and Peg had said no. But later when Peg was making her bed she had found one of each volume under her pillows as though the words were going to seep into her head in the night.

They worried about this failure to remember substantives. Peg, who was a nursing sister, referred to the problem as dealing only in connective tissue not with muscle and bones. Sal said it was caused by drinking but as Iris pointed out only she and Sal drank a lot, not Peg, but Peg had just the same problem. Iris was annoyed that Sal said it was drinking.

Sal then thought it was the full moon.

'Well, even if I don't quite know who I'm writing about, she's got to have a certain age and appearance and so on, and a name I suppose.'

'That's immaterial,' said Sal.

'As a matter of fact it's very material,' Peg snapped. She was having trouble with this book.

Iris tried to explain the doctrine of Nominalism to them—she was in a philosophical frame of mind—but she couldn't remember much about that either.

They were silent for a while and Iris squeaked the wine glass by running her finger around the rim.

'Phillip asked me to marry him last night,' she said.

'What,' Sal screamed, animated, leaning forward. 'Why didn't you tell us before?'

'I forgot.'

'You forgot! You mean we've been here seven hours and you've only just remembered?'

'When is it?' asked Peg.

'Oh I'm not going to. It was just drunken talk at five a.m., but even if it was sober I'd have said no.'

'You will say yes,' said Sal. 'You are going to get married. It's your duty. We need an uplifting human emotional event for 1985 and your marriage will be it. All of Sydney needs an uplifting event for the rest of this century and your wedding is it.'

Peg agreed. 'Absolutely,' she said. 'All of Australia. Don't be selfish.'

'Harry will give you away,' said Sal. 'He likes ceremonies and Peg and I will be the bridesmaids, no I mean matrons-of-honour.'

'And Jenny and Dianna will be bridesmaids,' said Peg, 'because they are nearly sixty and will enjoy it.'

Sal said it should be colour co-ordinated and thought of red because Phillip was left wing.

Peg felt that was too garish for such a subtle event, and such a significant one. 'Harry should wear a mauve suit,' she said, 'and Phillip will wear a mauve shirt and tie with a white suit. White for peace.'

'And mauve lace over white satin for us,' said Sal. 'And bonnets, mauve bonnets.'

Peg thought matrons-of-honour shouldn't wear bonnets.

'Big crownless picture hats is what we'll have,' she said.

'With mauve cabbage roses on them,' said Sal.

'And sweetheart necklines,' said Peg.

'And white lace over mauve satin for the bridesmaids,' said Sal.

(Later, when they explained the colour scheme to Jenny, Jenny said she wanted pink. Sal got annoyed with her for wrecking the co-ordination but Peg said it was alright, Jenny and Ida could have pink tulle kick pleats in their mauve and white dresses.)

'And in the derros' park opposite Kinselas with the reception in Kinselas,' Sal went on.

'Absolutely,' said Peg. 'With the honeymoon at the Marxist Summer School.'

'Yellow for your going-away outfit,' said Sal. 'Mauve and yellow and white will be the colours, with a dash of pink for the bridesmaids.'

'A lemon linen suit with a pill box hat and a half veil,' said Peg.

'Mauve and yellow and white with a dash of pink will become the fashion colours of the decade,' said Sal. 'Jenny Kee jumpers, Maggie T. shirts, Prue Acton dresses, Stuart Membery jackets. We'll patent the colour combo.'

'And lemon patent-leather high-heel court shoes,' said Peg.

'And Leo and Ariel will write a long epithalamium,' said Sal, 'which will be read at the reception. With rhyming couplets in Old Norse at the end of each verse which will be recited by the guests.'

Peg felt this would take some of the spontaneity out of things, but Sal explained that great events have to be planned or they get out of hand, so Peg said, 'Absolutely.'

'Don't just sit there, Iris,' yelled Sal. 'Take notes or something. It's going to happen and these things have to be prepared and co-ordinated.'

Iris was embarrassed. It was getting out of hand. Even though Phillip had been drunk and it was a silly idea, it was a gesture of love. And she did love him. She explained this to them.

'We're not knocking it, Iris,' said Sal. 'We're celebrating love in the last fifth of the twentieth century. We are giving thanks to love in a loveless world.'

'I think Phillip's very brave saying that,' said Peg. 'I mean I don't mean brave because he said it to *you*, not brave because he wants to marry *you*, just brave for saying it. Like a knight in the middle ages or something.'

'Yes, courtly,' agreed Sal. 'He's courtly. *Fin amour.*'

And gradually Iris was drawn into it and they planned

it over four bottles of Dom Perignon which Sal couldn't afford but which she bought on her Bankcard because she said it was worth it. And they laughed a lot and in the end all the customers in the wine bar were drawn in and Louise the proprietor wanted exclusive rights on catering for the shower and kitchen teas, and the guitarist wanted to be a troubadour at the wedding reception and Peg said there should be ten, and Louise said Marlboro could sponsor it, and Peg wanted to organise the sale of the film rights and Sal said she would write the book of the film. It was a great night.

It had all seemed very funny at the time, but when Iris told Phillip he was not amused. He was much more than not amused. He was very angry.

It was the following night and they were at the movies, *The Big Chill*. Iris tried to explain that they had not been mocking his emotions, they had been celebrating them. It had been a eulogy to love between a man and woman. An epithalamium, a *chanson d'amour*. A testament to his honest courage. A paean to the institution of marriage in the twentieth century.

He was unconvinced and angry. He told Iris he would never ever reveal his emotions to her again. He said that she and her women friends were dedicated to trivialising all male feelings. That they were interested only in drinking and the emasculation of men. That they didn't deserve love. That it was no wonder Sal's and Peg's husbands had divorced them years ago. That it didn't surprise him that no-one had ever married her.

No matter how hard Iris tried to defend the planning of the wedding it just made things worse.

She felt wretched.

Alone in bed that night, she wondered if she shouldn't have said yes.

Venero Armanno

The WEREwolf Who fell from GRACe from the BathRoom WiNDow

A side effect of living in one of any country's fabulously entertaining urban sprawls is that most people, this writer included, sooner or later experience a time in their lives when their inner werewolf must break free of the chains society has taught us to restrain this fantastic and hungry creature with. When such an outbreak occurs most people experience a wonderful sort of exhilaration, and, conversely, an almost total and terminal inner derangement.

A freed werewolf, it must be understood, will rampage through a city without so much as a backward glance, or an attack of conscience, or any sort of desire to repay a debt; this werewolf, by its very nature (you might know such a randy, slobbering creature as the Id, or the lizard part of the brain, or by some other name), will have to get the better of its owner. What happens then is not too dissimilar to what F. Scott Fitzgerald wrote of Americans in the Jazz Age: werewolf and owner will engage in the greatest and gaudiest spree of their personal histories, and there will be plenty to tell about it.

It was in the mid-eighties that the werewolf's strange and beautiful hunger first came upon me. It was a moment of a kind of reawakening because sometime before then life had lost its lustre and I'd lost that spring and charge to my step I'd always felt so good about. The beginnings of this hunger, or this revitalisation, lay in the fact that I'd become single again—and completely traumatised by the event. As they say, when you go to the bottom of your personal pit you either stay down or you find a way to claw your way back out, tooth and nail. The funny thing is I thought I might as well stay right down there; I had no urge to come back into the light. As Paul Simon had written, darkness was my friend, and I was well pleased to settle in for a lengthy visit. Then, without really wanting it or caring about it, life somehow regained the glowing sort of allure I hadn't experienced since my adolescence.

This was a revelation. Each day was another type of revelation.

I remember the process happening; day by day the

world around me was morphing into something altogether beautiful, but still, frustratingly, altogether unattainable. Life was turning into a thing so attractive and so utterly delicious that I actually wanted it, and more, I had to *devour* it as if it were the most succulent deer gambolling in a glen. Yes, I wanted to devour life piece by bloody piece and swallow it all down into the chasm of my belly. Maybe this was a sort of survival instinct kicking in. Maybe I didn't want to allow myself to act like a dead man at all; that wild part of me that used to like a risk or a fight or a feed and that spat on authority had finally crept into the open again. Hunger and fear made it emerge from captivity: hunger for life, fear of death. So this werewolf sniffed at the air and cast its red-eyed glare around. For, in truth, all a werewolf will ever know is *need*—and there can never be any one thing quite so important in the werewolf brain, not in this world anyway, and so the time had come to tear the world to bits.

I tend to confuse hunger and thirst. At times they can be just the same, like this:

In the Underground Nightclub, one three o'clock in the morning, INXS and Spandau Ballet and Simple Minds playing rinky-dink dance tunes, I realised that despite drinking Heinekens one after the other for an amount of time roughly equivalent to a normal human being's working day, I really wanted to keep on drinking from those gorgeous little green bottles for plenty more hours to come. Overtime of the soul, I thought, with no grizzling and no questions asked. In the Underground that early morn, ten years ago, it seemed that what I had acquired was an insatiable and inexplicable thirst; the perpetual motion machine of the gullet. I didn't have a clue about this. What I did know was that when I looked around at the crowded, smoking, yelling, hollering, pouty, pudgy, pretty, aloof, available, androgynous, motionless or radiantly dancing young women in fake gold and silver sequin fit-outs, I wanted to go on drinking till the cows came home, that I needed to go on drinking till the cows came home, that I *had* to go on so—no choice about it.

As days and weeks passed it wasn't just this thirst that consumed me, it was appetite as well. I felt always at the point of being ravenous. Grasping at the straws of life, my metabolic rate had somehow soared so high that I could eat anything I wanted—pastas, curries, fish and chips, bean nachos, beef burritos, chicken and cheese enchiladas with buckets of sour cream and guacamole on top, and buckets of beer to chase them down with—and not put on a bit of weight. On the contrary, I was burning up—losing weight—from the crackle and sputter of angst and fury and need, all of it aimed at putting a pyre under the past and getting me a piece of the new, alluring world. Yet, I wonder now, was it really angst, fury, despair—or were those things just show? Maybe what was really firing me up was *overwhelming delight* at finally being free to play the wolf man of the urban jungle.

Back then, who could tell—and more to the point, who cared?

This was living.

So, the appalling heart of the matter was that I didn't

drink for forgetting, I drank for fire, to fire me up, to get me going, to make me attractive and to make me success-ful—and I actually believed this strategy worked in spades and aces and hearts. Heineken or Fourex or Crown Lager, Minchinbury or Asti Spumante or Carrington, Johnny Walker and Stolichnaya and Gilbeys Gin, they were high octane werewolf fuel that burned into pure motivation—and what motivation! A lean and efficient monster was what I became. Half-nuked, I could nightclub sweet-talk and schmooze and booze as if these things were the world's most noble callings; I could dance with rhythm and charm and never tire; I could tell a story that would make you laugh and cry. And in the midst of these nocturnal feats of magic there were daytime feats no less astonishing. My business career grew exponentially. When I spoke in meetings I made sense. When I wrote business proposals they were tight, lucid, and fully reasoned. *On the money.* Whenever I got around to asking some General Manager of this company or Managing Director of that company to put his name on the dotted line of a one or a three or a five million dollar contract, he eventually did, and then would call his secretary in to get us both a cuppa and a bikkie so we could have a good old chat. Not about cricket, not about politics, not about technology, just about things.

Life, maybe. Human need. Love.

You see, my werewolf was an affable sort of beast, the most canny sort of urban creature, and its hands didn't shake and its eyes didn't burn and its mouth was never dry. It understood human need because that's all it itself really was, a walking wound that made money and drew people in, that drank and feasted—but always with tears behind its wary eyes.

That's why werewolves, in my opinion, are the most attractive of night creatures. Beyond all spine-tingling postulations about hunger for food and thirst for drink and lust for life, there is one overriding need that we relate to on a soul-level: the need to be loved. At the three o'clock in the morning of a smoky nightclub that need is ever the strongest, and—to draw a little on F. Scott Fitzgerald again—in the dark night of a werewolf's soul it is always exactly three o'clock in the morning.

A werewolf, then, unlike a vampire, cannot be alone. A werewolf cannot choose solitude. For me, one of the strongest images in early cinema is of Lon Chaney Jr desperately fighting against the chains he himself has wrapped his body in so that he will not go out into the night while his werewolf side is free. In a way that's what happens when our true wolf is inspired. We'll find a way to fight off shyness, tiredness, fear of rejection, two left feet, insipient halitosis, anything, because the wolf can do just about anything on this earth—except be alone. No wonder a werewolf must howl at the moon; no wonder booze is the perfect werewolf fuel.

Somehow I can barely remember a hangover, not from the mid-eighties. Except of course for one, which I'm about to write of. Life in a silly sort of way was awful and beautiful all at the same time. It was life spent balancing on a precarious ledge—and a werewolf, really now, with all that wild hair and rage and limitless yearning, well, it must have just about the world's most appalling sense of balance.

So this is what happened.

Alienated from what used to be my home, I had to find a new home. 'Home' is of course one of the most loaded words in language, like 'mother', like 'country', like 'hope'. Try replacing any of those things in a hurry and watch how *anything* you come up with will seem a poor substitute. The best you can do is find a path of least resistance, an easy or at least easier option, and the path of least resistance I came across was the happy coincidence of a good friend just having made his first home purchase and needing a house-mate.

I packed up my belongings and loaded them into a hired van, and at the other end of my journey there was my friend Joe to take me in and care for me like the saint he was and still is. It took me a few weeks to fully comprehend that what I'd done was move from the leafy inner-city of Brisbane, from a cool and charming renovated old Queenslander with acres of sloping back yard and a high rear deck that was like peering over a mountain ledge down upon a green and lovely valley (this entire place was, in my mind, always 'Home'), into a hot and flat southern suburbs semi-rural seventies estate where all the square brick and plaster houses all looked like one another, where all the neighbours and their kids and their pets all looked like one another, and where there was not a nightclub or decent restaurant or cinema within cooee (forever now, 'Hell').

Where we lived, the rear of about four or five homogenous blocks all met in the back yard. Separating these lots were unattractive wire fences and gates. In our street people drove four-wheel-drives and paraded fishing rods like badges of honour, and wore stubbies and thongs to the supermarket, to the local KFC, to the school P&C meetings. All the kids seemed between three and six years of age. Any local teens were local toughs, and they hung out by their hotted-up push-bikes around the front door of the local video store and stopped you using the pinball machine inside. In my single bed, the last thing I would hear at night was the hoarse barking of our many neighbours' many pit bull terriers. Everyone in that neighbourhood, except for Joe and me, who could barely feed ourselves, much less pets, much less ravenous dogs, owned pit bull terriers. The first thing I would hear in the morning—dawn, of course—was that self-same hoarse barking, and some deep-throat growling, and some whimpering too. This was explained by another sound I came to know very well in the mornings and sometimes in the afternoons too, something quite different: the frantic rattling of the back-yard fences and gates as the various neighbours' squat dogs tried to have sex with one another through the wire.

I had a new goal in life, and it was to move, very quickly.

The partnership in that house lasted six months. At night I would head off into the city and its inner-city surrounds and drink myself stupid and dance myself blind and sweet-talk myself hoarse, and start some trouble. During the day I would engage in the commercial world with all the hasteful enthusiasm of Doctor John Faustus selling his soul to Lucifer. Weekdays and weeknights were a dizzy, happy blur. Saturday nights out were usually fine, but what I came to dread was the weekend itself, those dead Saturdays and

Sundays of the suburbs. I was neither sportsman nor sports fan, so there was nothing to thrill me during the dragging hours of closed shops, of hot and deserted streets, of afternoon cricket shows and nature documentaries, and of pit bull terriers growling with ecstasy or frustration through the wire fences.

Six months in Hell.

Then I found a house back in that green inner-city suburb. It was another renovated Queenslander, even more spacious than the last, big cool bedrooms, big kitchen, and it was surrounded by rose gardens and spreading camellia bushes, plenty of bougainvillea and many, many trees. The house was low at the front and high at the back, where a cherry blossom tree flowered, and where the largest jacaranda tree and the two tallest palm trees I've ever seen grew. There was all manner of wildlife to be found basking on the various terraces of the descending slopes; lizards craggy as progeny of the Jurassic era, scuttling scrub turkeys, butterflies, grasshoppers, bees, and no pit bull terriers. It was paradise, a cool paradise, and the city and the nightclubs were less than a twenty-minute stagger away.

Once again I'd found 'Home'.

I told Joe I'd be moving out from his place. He asked me where I was going. When I told him he considered things for all of a second. He said,

'Mate, can I come with you?'

So he came with me.

We threw a house-warming party. Everything should have been all right then, but it wasn't, because it was a day full of beer and an evening full of Minchinbury, but mostly,

I believe, because it was the clear night of a fat full moon.

By about ten in the evening only the stalwarts of the lengthy Saturday afternoon housewarming were left, and the alcohol was gone. There wasn't a drop to be had. Nowhere in my nice new home was there a spit of booze left, and no-one was in any kind of condition to drive to a bottle shop. But soon, as if by magic, a ute from the Toowong Royal Exchange pulled up outside and a hairy-headed gent with a black eye and a bad limp came singing to the top of the front steps, and he was carting a carton of Minchinbury sparkling plonk.

The person responsible for this was Jane, a nightclub pal, and despite being thoroughly plastered she hadn't lost the power of looking up a pub's home delivery service in the telephone book. So we popped bottle after bottle and drank to her ill-health—by then Jane was throwing up. The stereo played loudly and couples smooched in the corners of the big rooms, and by and by the neighbours came over to introduce themselves and politely complain, and the stereo played even more loudly after they left. Past midnight more people dropped out; a bottle would fall to the ground, empty, another dead soldier, a cab would arrive, the party would thin. When we couldn't stand on our feet any more we slumped around on the furniture. When we couldn't slump any more we lay on the carpet, bellies sloshing and distended, belt buckles loosened, skirt clasps unclasped, eyes bleary, feet in socks touching fluffy hair-dos, stockinged feet touching growing bald spots, padded shoulders touching chunky thighs. Hands still managed to grip Minchinbury bottles.

Someone with a higher threshold for boredom than most had the bright idea of digging out a Trivial Pursuit game that lay somewhere in the house. Some searched for that game with renewed vigour, on all fours, crawling on bellies, staggering around and connecting with walls or door jambs. When the Trivial Pursuit game was found we sat cross-legged or lay flat in a semblance of a circle. I can't remember who was winning or losing. I can't remember who was playing. I can't remember how much time passed into the wee hours, but then:

'Who played the Wolf Man in the 1941 movie of the same name?'

'Lon Chaney Jr.'

Someone growled deep in their throat. Me, Joe, someone else, I don't know. Jane, who had ordered all the new drink, and thrown up, and come good, screamed.

'Don't!'

'And it's a full moon,' I said, giving my growl a great deal of conviction. And then, just like that, Joe and I were chasing Jane all around the house, her screaming, the two of us grunting and barking like idiots, the others watching uninterestedly or maybe just having another drink and another hand of Trivial Pursuit.

Still, we chased Jane around every room of the house, and she screamed all the more, and when we herded her toward the bathroom she ran in and slammed the door, locked it, and Joe pretended to beat at it with his shoulder.

Joe said to me, 'You climb up the window from outside!' and I thought that was inspired.

I ran out into the night and it was warm and the air

was sweet and a great yellow moon hung low over the not-so-distant Brisbane city-scape. Fresh air hit me in the side of the head, a great friendly fist, and I stood still and took in the moment: ah! my friends inside drinking champagne, Joe, good old Joe, playing a good old game with his good old buddy, Jane scared half out of her wits and screaming in the bathroom. The neighbour's kids were hanging their heads out the windows, eyes wide with terror and delight. I thought of this day, of my freedom, of my wonderful home, of *my wonderful life*. Could it ever be any better than this?

And so I howled up at the moon, a nice roar that came from deep in my chest, deeper down in my belly, right from the soul. The neighbour's kids were dragged away from their windows. The shutters next door went bang! bang! bang! one after the other. I'd never known a happiness like this, such fulfilment. The moon hung over that city skyline, all fat and low, and it was my brother.

In the darkness—of what? three o'clock in the morning?—I went around to the side of the house. I could feel the way my legs were all rubbery. I could feel the way I wanted to fall right off my feet. My head was throbbing. The thorns of unseen rose bushes dragged at my clothes as I went past. But I could hear Joe banging with his shoulder against the bathroom door and I could hear Jane squealing, a sound that was like the mewling of a cornered deer to a werewolf. I felt my hunger swell and I started to climb up the side of the house in order to get to the bathroom window. I had no idea just how high that window really was. The bathroom windows were barred; I didn't know that either. There would be no way in and only one way down.

By then I was pure werewolf anyway. My fingers scraped at the crumbling timber of the window ledge and I pulled myself higher. I got a grip of the bars at the windows and hoisted my legs up. It was like being on a high mountain peak, and there was a valley below, far, far, below, and the world was spinning and careering. Bleary eyes looked from dark night into the crazy-bright of a renovated old Queenslander's renovated bathroom. Jane was behind the door, keeping Joe out, and she was managing to laugh and cry at the same time. Then she turned. She saw the shape spread-eagled at the window, behind the bars: an axe murderer come to get her, a spider man.

The wolf man.

Jane shrieked the way Fay Wray once shrieked at King Kong.

My fingers lost their grip on the bathroom window's bars. In mid-air, in space, I half-turned and started slowly, poetically, to fall from the ledge. The moon and the stars and the milky way flashed brightly in my eyes. A werewolf's howl started from my throat but I thudded to earth before it was out. My face was buried in the dirt until Joe came out of the house to find me. Some bushes and trees covered me.

Joe said, 'Mate, you did a little pruning on the way down,' and when he found I couldn't walk he put me over his shoulder and carried me inside, a dead, deflated, werewolf weight.

Laying me flat onto the carpet, he rejoined the Trivial Pursuit game and the Minchinbury. Jane came out of the bathroom and lay down, wiping her face with a handkerchief. I lay there and stared at the cracks in the ceiling until a friend named Margaret turned up a little later. She was a nurse's assistant at the Royal Brisbane Hospital and had just finished her late shift.

Margaret took one look at me and said, 'You'd better get to Casualty.'

I couldn't feel a thing.

'Look at your ankle,' she said. I tried to but couldn't, and the others gathered around. There was a suitable hush. 'Joe,' Margaret went on, 'I'll bring my car to the front, you and Jane'll have to carry him.'

Joe and Jane carried me into the waiting car. All the way to the hospital we joked and laughed, except of course for Margaret, who was dead sober. At Casualty, I hopped to the front counter with my arms around Jane's shoulders. It didn't look like a hospital, it looked like a hotel.

'Yes?'

'A room for me and my bride. Make sure it's got a view.'

They stuck me in an overnight observation room along with some poor old guy who'd come in with a gaping head wound: his son had gone nuts with an axe and had let him have it. Full-moon fever maybe. The old guy's skull should have been cleaved in two, but somehow it wasn't. He was as dopey as me. Sometime in the night, in a strange bed, in a strange room, smelling hospital smells, I woke up to dark-ness—and to the imposing silhouette of that old guy, his head wrapped like an Egyptian mummy's, as he leaned over me and stared at me with great empty eyes and said,

'Why did you do it, my son? I should kill you with these hands. Oh, why did you do it?'

I was sobering up and the pain in my leg was giving me a good old thrashing. I spoke in a voice as even and reasonable as I could: 'Why don't you climb back into bed now? You're tired and it's late. You're good and tired, aren't you? Doesn't that bed look good?'

And the poor old guy did climb back into bed, and I didn't really sleep again, and in the morning they came for me and through the red bloody haze of the hangover of the century I had to start explaining.

I got to spend weeks and weeks in my nice new house, in plaster. I wasn't allowed to drink. It was the best thing that could have happened. So was the crashing hangover that seemed to last as long as it took for my leg to get better.

These things were my salvation.

I'd come off—fallen off—a booze-induced high that had lasted months and months. It was a high that had turned me into a werewolf, and somehow I'd built up a life while at the same time tearing myself apart. I look at drunks now and I know I was and still can be the same dribbly, vomity, shouting piece of scunge as them. My old nightclub friends had been the same as me. We barely knew we were plastered. When I met Jane again in the cold light of day I barely knew her. Every time I'd met her in the past we'd been beyond rational conversation. She was a stranger, a complete and utter stranger, and she went away and so did most of the others, and I didn't miss one of them. I never knew them anyway, and they never knew me.

I sat in plaster for a long time, alone and broken up inside and out, but scared straight too. I came to understand that everything I'd done those past six months was just smoke and mirrors to hide me from heartache. Even corporate success—just a bit of mental trickery, but nice work if you can get it.

I've learned to balance the bottle, I think.

Yet the werewolf—that wolf man, whisky man, Heineken man and Minchinbury man, with his appetite and spine-tingling roar—some three o'clock in the mornings of course I know he's there, yearning a little, ready and waiting for me to fall.

Mandy Sayer

DreamTime Alice

I n the four months we knew each other, the only time Waldo and I left the New Orleans City Limits was on the occasion of my twenty-first birthday.

St Valentine's Day, 1984. It was a chilly, cloudy morning in the South's last month of winter. It was the day, with all its original and romantic associations, that I sensed our affair could not adapt to the open spaces of longevity. As the live oaks and magnolias grew thick above the road

Waldo's VW rumbled along, as the swamp mist deepened and a flock of blackbirds netted the sky, Darwin's ghost leaned against Eros and snickered into his ear.

We all know why the dinosaur died out for good—the earth suddenly changed and he couldn't shrink himself into a fish bone fast enough.

Lust, I was thinking on the day of my twenty-first, Lust is a big Brontosaurus, a bloody T-Rex.

I sat in silence beside Waldo as he drove and drove and allowed the scent of the swamp orchids to chide us on.

None of us had much money, so it was decided we should celebrate my induction into adulthood by packing the car with provisions and driving into the woods to have a picnic. My companions on this day, my benevolent role models, the tribal elders initiating me into this great ceremony of Mature Life, this sanctified state of grown-up-hood, were a five-foot-one frustrated Errol Flynn called Woodhead, a towering juggler who couldn't make love with the lights on, and my hung-over father in the pair of studded cowboy boots he'd found in the garbage outside the bondage shop on St Phillip Street.

The problem was that we had no destination. Gerry and I never ventured much beyond Canal Street's invisible border. Woodhead had never jogged further than the terminal where the streetcar tracks ran out on Carrollton. Waldo only traced the vertiginous but regular route between Uptown and the Quarter about eight or nine times a week.

He decided to drive east, toward the bayous and

canopies of Spanish moss, but at a vital intersection on Napolean Avenue we found the crossroads clotted with cars, trapped behind the debris of what looked like a head-on collision.

Waldo swung the car up over the median strip and headed back the other way. My father had already begun sipping from one of the flagons of red we'd just bought from the A&P. Woodhead sat in the back seat beside him, head tilted back, jaw extended, and gulping at the air like a starved guppy. It was all part of his chin-tightening regime, along with witch hazel toner and this weird thing he used to do with two elastic bands.

So Waldo nosed the car south and headed toward the river. We followed the curve of the levee for a while, in search of a pleasant spot. But when he finally pulled up and we clambered out not fifty metres from the Canal Street Ferry Terminal, we all gave each other slow and disappointed looks. The river was low and shit-coloured, and there was a man in a pair of brown house slippers asleep under the cabbage tree palms.

When we got back in the car, Waldo began gnawing at his bottom lip and absently steered the car toward Uptown, along his usual route. I was feeling stupid as I sat there beside him, sweating and braiding my fingers together in the silence. I was wearing an Edwardian silk blouse the colour of egg yolk, with layers of cream lace stitched around the neck and bodice. The skirt looked a little Spanish, I suppose. I'd made it from the leg of a wide pair of wide bell-bottoms. The pants, cast-offs from a former Sydney teen talent queen, had two ruffles of yellow satin stitched around the bottom.

Now they rested about three inches above my knee, and sat there, almost mocking.

'Where did you get that outfit?' Woodhead had asked when they'd pulled up outside the Witchcraft Shop earlier.

I remember looking at the ground and my skin rising into a quick, nervous dance. Woodhead's tone had been warm, almost friendly. Suddenly my fingers were running across the lace and I was telling him about my dubious inheritance from the former teen talent queen, how I got two skirts from one pair of pants. As we got in the car, I prattled on further about my tailoring expertise, the dress I'd converted from a Colombian coffee bean sack. The motley-coloured skirt which appeared after I'd snapped off the metal spokes of a golf umbrella. As I fastened my seatbelt, I detailed how I'd hemmed and threaded the waist with ribbon, assuming he found it all mildly amusing, until I glanced in the rearview mirror and saw the smirk on his face. Had his original enquiry been motivated by sarcasm, too? How long would he have let me rattle on about the fashion potential of discarded fishing nets and parachutes before he'd reveal his incredulity, his judgement of me as a mere dingbat?

I sat next to Waldo in the shuddering car and wished I'd worn something plainer. After all, it was only a picnic, and in the woods, at that.

Waldo hunched over the steering wheel and kept his eyes nailed to the road. The prodigious fumes from Gerry's furtive gulps from the flagon filled the car. Woodhead was busy doing eye exercises, glaring from left to right, up and down. For a while there, his eyes rolled along a diagonal

plane as we idled in front of a red light, as if he were checking to see if his right temple and left jaw were still intact.

In retrospect, it seems silly to have worried so much
over a facetious remark made by a stunted, unemployed
actor called Woodhead, a man who flossed his teeth three
times a day. But between his perpetual exercises and
Waldo's silence and my father's reclination into the posses-
sion of red plonk, a thread of inadequacy unravelled in my
groin and unfurled itself up my spine.

Waldo turned the radio on, and the billowing howls of
Ellington's 'Creole Love Call' filled the car. I closed my eyes
and breathed it in, suppressing the desire to unknot the bow
at my side and rip the troublesome skirt to shreds.

We hit a bump in the road and, when I opened my eyes,
I found Waldo steering us onto a long, concrete bridge. His
hands, the way he held the steering wheel, the way he slowly
changed gears, betrayed a sudden sense of purpose.

I straightened, clapped my hands together, and
declared, 'Oh, Master, where dost thou take me?' (It was a
mixed impersonation: something between Shakespeare's
Ophelia and Barbara Eden's Jeannie).

But Waldo just grinned and stared straight ahead. 'This
is the longest bridge in the world,' he said. 'Twenty-four miles.'

And then the green road sign rose up before us: Mande-
ville—24, and Woodhead asked if anyone had any nail
clippers.

The eggshell-coloured bridge over which Waldo's blue beetle
winged was called, aptly I thought, The Causeway. With
every mile we covered, Lake Pontchartrain's beguiling green

shimmered further into the car, deeper into my nervous hands still gripping the culpable buttons of my shirt. The light was implacable and serene, a watery silver aura humming toward the horizon. And there were small breaks in the cloud formations as narrow as my finger, where fine shafts of biblical light yawned down to the water like a seamless Jacob's ladder.

Woodhead stopped biting at the ravished stumps of his fingernails and Gerry finally burped and screwed the top back on the flagon. The azure capsule that was Waldo's VW propelled us on and on. The DJ on WWOZ, our only link with the land behind us, persisted in his duty to garner the New Orleans metropolitan area with copious amounts of musical romance on this day of the heart's most valued saint. Sandman from the Ninth Ward called in and requested 'Do It to Me One More Time' for Honeybucket Mama in Metairie. Antoinette from Tammany parish purred through the speakers, asking for 'Love Child', dedicated to her 'milkman on the other side of the river'. And then a request for Billie Holiday's 'The Man I Love' came bawling in after that, intoned by a suicidal drag queen called Surreal, who said she was calling from the public phone inside the Marriott Hotel's Women's Powder Room.

Was it an elaborate joke? I wondered. Conceived by some hapless homophobe living on the edge of the bayou? I shrugged to myself. The call might have been legitimate: everyone in New Orleans was so bloody literal and melodramatic.

Over the miles, The Causeway seemed to rise imperceptibly. Towards the middle of the bridge, I looked around and could barely see the shore we'd left behind. Just water, inexorable green water swelling against every horizon. Periodically, a sign would appear recording the distance covered or, rather, how far we still had to go.

The undying love songs pulsing through the speakers seemed to propel the beetle on, charged by the dulcet melodies of 'The Tender Trap' and 'Sweet Lorraine'. When Aretha Franklin howled out 'Muddy Water Blues', I rolled the window down all the way and allowed her voice to peal out over the liquid universe.

But when the first traces of civilisation appeared, when distant shapes began to form, a little knot of sadness loosened within me. It was my big day, and we had driven across the longest bridge in the world to celebrate it in a town whose name bespoke my own, at least phonetically.

A village began forming itself before us, a scintilla of cottages, shopfronts, and dust. Waldo swung the car off the bridge and turned right. Little black kids in shorts were crowded around a huge puddle in the earth, sailing what looked like hand-crafted boats, made out of paddle-pop sticks and paper. I remember wondering why they didn't walk down to the shore and sail them on the real lake, but perhaps so much water brought with it both fear and anonymity. How softly that green seduction beckoned, how easily it could pull one down.

Waldo was scouring the right side of the road, trying to find a clearing through the bare oaks and tall Judas trees. Calla lillies, having rioted through April and into the summer, were now beginning to brown and curl into themselves.

Our persistent need for water, whether it be bayou swamp, river, gulf beach, or lake, spurred us on. Waldo perhaps sensed intuitively my need to return to it, to that rapacious, cool substance from which all life springs.

Things were not looking good, however. Dead foliage and scrub clung to the earth between the road and the water, and the leaning magnolias looked haughty and judgemental as I gazed at them, as if offended by our presence.

Gerry sighed and started drinking again. Static began teasing the speakers and grew so imposing I finally leaned over and spun the tuning knob, but all I could cajole from the other points on the dial was a raspy monotone. I switched off the radio and allowed the creepy sounds of outer-Mandeville's bush to insinuate themselves into the car. I could almost hear the muted ruminations of dying poplars, the swamp orchids' tender gossip.

Red dust formed a fine veil across the bottom of the windscreen. Woodhead suggested in a deadpan voice that we all sing a song. ' "Ten Green Bottles",' he said, 'or "Do the Hokey-Pokey with Me".'

No one responded. Waldo just straightened and changed gears. Gerry, melancholy and half-pissed by now, made a vaguely-related comment to what appeared to be the back of Waldo's seat: 'I'm just a fucking jazz drummer, not a singer. Why do bands these days always advertise for drummers who can *sing*? I said to this one bloke, I said, Listen mate, I'm a drummer born with a hare lip, I'm flat-out *talking*.'

Waldo allowed a vague smile to surface on his lips, but his eyebrows were still knitted into his perplexed pursuit of a decent picnic spot. A chain-link fence, about twelve feet high, and choked at the top by coils of barbed wire, suddenly appeared on our left, divulging, perhaps, the promise of a clearing or grassy knoll. Waldo leaned on the accelerator and followed the long, impervious fence around the curves of the road.

I wondered what was behind such a barrier, and why it was so high. Through the fence's steel web, I saw nothing but the same wilting honeysuckle and ivy, the same recalcitrant oaks. Not even a child or solitary gardener. Not even a hint of a single fruit of domestic labour.

Soon a sign appeared on top of the wasteland of grey wire: *Trespassers will be Prosecuted* in bold, official red letters. The place was looking more and more intriguing and formidable. Waldo continued to trace its trajectory into the Gothic wilderness of Louisiana, where, I imagined, alligators languished in lush, deep mud, and water moccasins slithered through a swampy nirvana. I surrendered myself to the car's insistent rumble and Waldo's wide, purposeful gaze, which would surely get us somewhere, I decided, if I could just believe in it enough.

I folded my hands and made an effort to hope, to feel confident in God's great design: I was twenty-one: it was St Valentine's Day; and both the man who fathered me and the one with whom I thought I was in love were right here with me. But I couldn't stop thinking of my mother asleep in her double bed on the other side of the world, lost to a different season, dozing against the heat of the last month of Australia's summer, the humidity into which I was born.

I was drawn from my meditation by the sudden appearance of cut grass, of a manicured, tidy lawn rolling like a wide green carpet towards the edge of the lake, where two picnic benches and a solitary wire garbage can stood like a lost family of artefacts from another life, an obscure venue for ghosts.

Waldo swung a hard right and we followed the gravel path up to the lake, close to the concrete levee. We crawled from the beetle and stretched. Gerry staggered over to the nearest bench and crowned it with the now somewhat-diminished flagon of deep red plonk. Woodhead announced he was starving and whisked the picnic basket—a cardboard box stamped with Dixie—from the open boot of the car.

Waldo cubed cheese with his Swiss Army knife, and Woodhead was soon relishing in his appointed task: tearing up a breadstick almost half his size into manageable, bite-sized pieces.

It was only after I'd poured the wine and we'd all sat down together that I noticed a sign on the other side of the street, above a pair of heavy iron gates: Waldo had driven us to the family reserve in front of the Louisiana State Hospital for the Insane.

To make a relationship, you've both got to fit into each other's stories, further each other's plots. My story, I thought, demanded a serious love interest, something to scintillate my narrative and open me like fruit. Enough of the dubious sub-plots gleaned from one-night stands, enough of the solitary lingering on the edge of another life.

Enough exposition and raw dialogue. I wanted a real twist, a pulsing tendon in my song.

But what about Waldo? What was his story, and what kind of character was I playing in it? What lines did I utter, what moves did I make to ensure me a minor role in his motley theatre?

For every first date, I think, is an audition for a part in someone else's play. The problem is, that the work is perpetually writing and revising itself, and you often get called in to tighten up the sagging narrative of someone else's life. A plot whose lines and reversals you do not yet comprehend because you haven't known the guy long enough. But the casting director and writer—the man you've been seeing—he'll let you know how well you did. You might get a call-back in a day or two, which could lead to weekly rehearsals.

Sitting outside the Louisiana State Hospital for the Insane, with Waldo opposite me in his dark, 1950s sunglasses, after having known him for three weeks, I felt as if I were still in rehearsal for a play I didn't understand and that wouldn't be opening for a very long time.

Woodhead's story was simple, and went a long way toward explaining his sarcasm that day. He'd had to leave his girlfriend in Boston during his four-month foray down south, and was obviously missing her. I saw it in the way in which he allowed his shoulders to round in on themselves as he sat across from me, morosely munching olives. The way he'd lift a piece of cheese to his lips and pause, as if he were about to reveal something profound to the piece of gouda before bringing it to its ultimate end between his thrice-flossed molars.

What kind of leading lady was Woodhead in performance with? I sipped my wine and quietly wondered. She'd have to be short, I decided. No average-sized or tall woman in that story. And the costumes? She'd have to be fitted out, I mused, in a conservative yet fashionable line. She'd be the kind of diva who wore pantyhose underneath her jeans. And pastel blouses made out of a cotton/polyester blend. No little Spanish skirts constructed from the bell-bottomed leg of a pair of hand-me-down disco pants. No silk and Edwardian lace.

I was being disingenuous and I knew it. I munched on a hunk of bread and slowly brushed the crumbs from my lap. What did Waldo *want* from me? How was I supposed to be playing this scene? There was no direction in this story, no pattern or rising action. If only he would beckon me over to a quiet corner and whisper in my ear—*Do something with your hands ... Stop playing for laughs ...* Or, *Project your voice a little further during the longer love scenes ...* But Waldo just stared out over the water, absently shelling peanuts and popping them into his mouth.

My indomitable father was the only person in our silent quartet who felt duty-bound to clown about and make this miserable Act bristle with the conviviality for which it was intended. Gerry burped and farted and told the story about how he passed out on his father's boat after drinking two flagons of port and woke up two days later on a beach off Newcastle. And then the one about his teetotalling Irish Catholic mother, who reluctantly began to imbibe one glass of the same Ruby Red port, upon her doctor's instructions, before she retired at night. The prescription was to soothe her nerves and cure her chronic insomnia. Clara, the ginger brunette, who never missed a Sunday mass, ingested her medication each evening with a mouthful of guilt: drink was a dapper demon masquerading as a demi-god. Still, she swallowed her one snifter of Ruby Red before she crawled into bed at night, and soon the devil went to work inside her, drawing down her eyelids and inviting her into the sanctity of her own dreams. Over the weeks, if she were feeling particularly restless, she sometimes took two drinks instead of one. She kept the flagon in a cabinet beside the bed. And if she occasionally snuck a mouthful while she was baking bread or ironing, it was only because she had seven children practising either violin or piano throughout the day in the living room. And that little bugger Gerry banging on cake tins in the backyard.

But her husband, Aub, Sydney's Deluxe Hairdresser, with a chain of sophisticated salons throughout the city, he knew things were getting out of hand one day when he came home and found her swaying as she divided herself between the two tasks of chopping vegetables for soup and grating Sunlight soap for the boiler which was washing his uniforms. Not only did she sway, not only did she break out in a bawling rendition of 'Amazing Grace' when Aub returned to the kitchen after his evening bath, but he found handfuls of yellow shavings melting into the chicken broth and what must have been half the back yard's spinach and carrot crop floating about with his white coats and cotton underwear in ravaged, irregular pieces.

'And Aub went tearing down to the doctor's joint there and then and abused shit out of him,' said Gerry, smacking his lips and grinning. I wondered if it occurred to him that he was now cradling the neck of a flagon of red not too unlike the large bottle of Ruby Red which had caused his family so much consternation almost sixty years ago.

'Told the quack he'd reduced his God-fearing wife to a hopeless boozer who couldn't get through the Lord's prayer at night without hiccuping!'

Waldo smiled and Woodhead erupted with a chuckle. Sometime during the monologue, Gerry's plastic cup had blown off the table and was now skittering across the buffalo grass toward the solemn iron gates of the asylum.

Gerry took a swig from the flagon, wiped his mouth, and laughed. 'But Mr Sayer,' said the doctor, 'I told her to drink two *fingers* of port, not two *bottles*.'

It was at times like this that I loved my father, that I was conscious of the loving. How he was sticking to the edict of The Show Must Go On, in spite of the hollow theatre of that day, and the solemn house to which he was playing. His mother was one of the few female characters who was secure in his bawdy comedy, the rollicking, circu-itous story he was still plotting through his sixty-fourth year.

Soon he was off on a gambling tangent, how the pooled talents of his individual brothers conspired to produce a betting system so tight and impenetrable that one night his older sibling, Ernie, arrived home with three suitcases full of cash, and threw fifty quid at the teenage Gerry just to help him count it.

How did he make the transition from his mother hiccup-ing through her nightly prayers to a fountain of crumpled bills cascading onto the kitchen table in 1936? I tried to trace his soliloquy back through the labyrinthine logic of the fraternal betting system, but could not find the seam. I lifted my plastic cup and drained it. Sometimes, with Gerry, there was no connective tissue. Occasionally, when he was working a particularly hard crowd, one anecdote seemed to randomly follow another without joining or furthering that thing he was making, that long epic that was himself.

But that afternoon he was a man with a mission, ensuring the flagon continued to circle, and that we might all laugh, just a little, on this supposedly significant day.

I knew Woodhead was succumbing to Gerry's incantations when he stood up, tottered a few feet toward the lake, and collapsed onto the grass with a big, goofy grin on his face. Waldo, the man responsible for transporting us back to the world on the other side of the lake, sat across from me and swallowed mouthfuls of water for every sip of wine, unable to relinquish himself to my father's ribald magic.

I abandoned my cup and began, like Gerry, to swig from the flagon directly whenever it was passed to me. The more I drank, the more I wondered about Waldo's possible motivations and intentions. Had he driven me here deliberately? Was it some perverse joke, this picnicking outside the Insane Asylum? Did he know it was here all along?

In spite of being aware of the fact that he'd hoped for the bayous or a spot by the river first, I wrestled with the possible subtexts of the afternoon, and Waldo's disturbing gift for metaphor.

I uncapped the second flagon and wandered across to the levee. I kicked off my shoes, sat down, and dangled my

black-stockinged feet in the lake. The water was cool, and I
didn't let it lap up beyond my calves. I lifted the flagon and
swallowed a mouthful of wine: it wasn't Ruby Red Port, but
it was close enough.

From *Dreamtime Alice*, a forthcoming memoir.

Matthew Condon

The Abattoir Party

Edward Pinkerboo lifted the silver foil off the tray and
saw a blood spot in his egg.

He felt his stomach turn. He had not had a blood
spot in an egg since he was a child. He remembered that first
blood spot well because it was more than just a blood spot.
For there, in the yolk, was a milky, partly formed chick curled
in on itself, a hint of wing and beak through a film of jelly. He
had taken the day off school that time. Now, seeing the small

red dot of blood, he felt embarrassed to raise a finger to the air hostess, to have his breakfast replaced. He held his breath, swallowed with difficulty, and placed the silver foil back over the top of the tray. He opened the air vent above his seat and looked out the window.

It was a Saturday morning, and Edward Pinkerboo was seated in Row Five of the aircraft. It was his first trip Out West. He had bought a pair of Cuban-heeled, square-toed R.M. Williams boots, two Miller shirts with mother-of-pearl clip buttons, a black Akubra hat and a pair of moleskin trousers that, through a miracle of design, could be both shorts and slacks via the two zips that ringed his legs mid-thigh. He had a Swiss Army knife attached to his belt, a torch and a water bottle in his overnight bag, and a First Aid kit in his hand luggage. He felt slightly conspicuous in his new Western outfit. He imagined people were staring at him at Sydney Airport. He had tried to rough up his Akubra the night before, smearing it with soil from his potted plants at home in his flat in Elizabeth Bay. He sprinkled water over it and trod on its rim and threw it like a frisbee into his lounge room wall over and over. Now it just looked like a grubby and misshapen new hat.

Still, he reasoned that the further he travelled West, the less conspicuous he would seem. That it would happen in the air, in the aircraft, as it passed over the wooded mountains and then the green plains around Dubbo and finally the strange scorched earth towards Broken Hill. He had somehow missed the transition. Suddenly the ground was red and brown and covered in a lattice of veins the colour of the spot in his egg.

Edward Pinkerboo closed his eyes and thought of his mate, John. He had not seen John for seven and a half years, when they shared a flat together at Potts Point. They had gotten along well, considering. And they had always managed to keep in touch, considering. Even when John moved to The Bush to clear his head. The Bush had caught him, he wrote back. Had taken hold of him. And now he was getting married, to a girl from The Bush, and it would be John's pleasure if Edward Pinkerboo could come out for The Buck's Night, to recall old times, to catch up, to reacquaint over a few beers.

The plane lurched and Edward Pinkerboo opened his eyes. They had dropped several hundred metres and he felt hot. The blister on his heel had burst. You see? he said to himself. Lucky you have the First Aid kit. He didn't like to dwell on the fact that he was injured, already, having not even alighted from the aircraft. The low hills around Broken Hill were dark red and treeless. He saw rusted iron rigs rising from some of them. He saw giant holes in the earth and brick stacks. He saw the grid of the town as the plane banked. He produced a sachet of wet hand towels from his hand luggage and dabbed at his forehead and neck.

'Please secure your trays in front of you and make sure your seat is upright.'

The breakfast tray had, at some point, disappeared. Edward Pinkerboo held his hands together tightly, excited and a little afraid. Perhaps it was the scorched earth, the savage rips and tears in it, the rocks. Perhaps it was the town itself, hunkered down in the heat. He had been told it was 'rough and tough' Out West. The blister on his heel stung.

Edward Pinkerboo closed his eyes as they landed and saw two pinpoints of red behind his eyelids.

'You'll be driving alone, Edward?'

'Yes, Jean,' he said.

He was amazed at the friendliness of the lady at the hire car counter. How she instantly called him 'Edward'. No need for formalities here. He adjusted his hat. It didn't fit as well as it had at Sydney Airport. Either his head had expanded, marginally, during the flight, or the hat had shrunk in the cool of the overhead locker.

'Just overnight, Edward?'

'That's right, Jean.'

'So you'll have the car back tomorrow afternoon?'

'Yes, Jean, tomorrow afternoon.'

Edward Pinkerboo, despite Jean's comforting, motherly voice, felt uneasy, just as his hat felt uneasy on his head. It may have been the crazy Pro Hart ants painted on the walls inside the airport. The giant ants tangled together, at war, ripping and tearing at each other's big heads. He felt prickly all over.

'You have a lovely time, Edward,' she said, handing him the keys.

'See you tomorrow, Jean.'

He collected his luggage and found the car outside. The heat hit him like a wave. He threw his hat on the passenger's seat and revved the motor for a while to get the air-conditioning going. He took his Explore Australia book from his hand luggage and checked the map. He had already marked it elaborately in pencil, having traced the route to John's property as John gave him instructions over the telephone. He had sat in his Elizabeth Bay flat overlooking the bay and the yachts and John had taken him down the highway north of Broken Hill, off the bitumen at The Roadhouse, left at The White Letter Box, and on to The Property.

'You can't miss it,' John had said.

And it had been a breeze, by pencil. Now, as he sat in the hire car, it all seemed so confusing. John spoke about the drive from the airport as if it were a quick trip to the corner store. But it was hundreds of kilometres. He wondered, with the air-conditioning roaring, if he shouldn't have rented a four-wheel-drive. He had been too shy to enquire, what with the ants and his ill-fitting hat. He didn't know how to drive a manual, and thought it might have embarrassed him, not to have been able to operate a manual, Out West.

As he headed into town he started to shiver and it hurt to use his foot on the accelerator and the brake, on account of his blister. He thought of all the explorers that had perished in this part of the country, of their bones bleached against the red earth alongside the curled ribcages of their horses and mules. He swigged from his water bottle, misplaced the cap and spilled its contents onto the passenger's seat. The brim of his hat darkened.

'Shit,' he said. By the time he had righted the bottle and screwed the cap back on he was out of Broken Hill on the Barrier Highway and heading for Wilcannia. He questioned why he had come all the way Out West anyway, for a Buck's Night. He questioned his friendship with John. What had made him do it, he asked himself. What, in the end, was the point? He could have said no in an instant. For a start it would have saved him a lot of money—the hat, the boots, the shirts, the trousers, the Swiss Army knife holster, the flight ticket, Jean's hire car. And did it matter if he ever saw John again? He had been a lousy flatmate anyway. Never cleaned up after himself. Came home drunk at all hours. All the nude women skipping from his bedroom to the bathroom. John and Edward Pinkerboo were, in fact, like chalk and cheese. Something, though, had kept them together. A fine thread of something.

'On the road agaiiiiiiin,' sang Edward Pinkerboo. He was flying now—up to 120kph—and convinced himself to make the most of The Trip. He was like that. He sang himself out of depression, out of misgivings. They flew off him, like the bugs that were fired out of the jet stream of his hire car. 'Just can't wait to get on the road agaiiiiiiin. . . '

He did admire John, deep down. He really did. Because John, as he remembered, was a Real Man. That was the basis of their friendship. In John, Edward Pinkerboo saw the sort of man he would like to be. Edward Pinkerboo saw all the masculine attributes he lacked being lived out, in action, in three dimensions, with John. It was like that with most men. They never truly felt comfortable with their own manhood. It was only through a friendship, through an attachment with another male who filled in those missing blanks, those missing bits of manliness, that they could achieve a level of comfort with themselves. That's what John did for Edward Pinkerboo. And there were lots of men like

John, surrounded by males like Edward Pinkerboo, who knew the score, who knew what they gave in a process that galvanised their own worth. But would it be the same for the two of them—Edward Pinkerboo and John, John and Edward Pinkerboo—Out West?

'The life I love is makin' music with my friendsssssss ... ... sssshit!' Edward Pinkerboo reefed the steering wheel to the left. His left-hand tyres kicked up dirt and rock, the car slid a little, but he righted the wheel and got the car back on the highway. A hundred metres further on he stopped.

Edward Pinkerboo had hit something. His heart pounded. He slowly got out of the car and went round the back of it. He looked down the highway and saw nothing but a fading cloud of dust. He walked to the front of the car. There was no damage. Then he saw the fine spray of blood, like the tail of a comet, across the passenger's door.

A small feather was fixed to the front of the rear vision mirror by a globule of blood and yellowy grey matter.

He looked at the feather and the guts and the spray of blood and the egg came back to him and the unformed chick of his boyhood and all of a sudden he was seven-years-old, his heel stinging in his new cowboy boots, his mouth open in fear and wonder, alone in the middle of a red desert, in the heat, except for the body of a bird, somewhere in the pink dust that was slowly settling to earth.

Edward Pinkerboo stopped singing Country and Western songs in the hire car. Instead, he counted carcasses. By the time he reached the ghost town of Wilcannia, after two-and-a-half hours' driving, his tally had come to eleven kangaroos, four galahs, two wombats and a fox. He learned to spot a carcass hundreds of metres before he reached it. He could see, in the heat haze above the road, the movement of black birds then, closer, a silver and red and brown spot on the road or beside it. Then he would be on top of the carnage, the black birds skipping only a short distance from the animal's body as the car got closer, the litter of the impact—pieces of flesh and blood and fur and feather—covering the road or the dust and tiny shrubs at the roadside. It was unlike a dog or cat struck back in the City. They were comparatively gentle deaths for animals, in the City. A knock on the head. A crushed limb. A quiet extinguishing. But here, Out West, the deaths were spectacular, the splitting of the atom, metal striking body at a great speed and death an exploding star.

As he pulled into the service station in Wilcannia he saw two dogs tearing at the mudflap of a road train.

'How ya' goin',' said the attendant. 'Fill 'er up?'

He nodded and got out of the car. Edward Pinkerboo was not feeling well. He took in the town without really seeing it. The old Plaza cinema for sale, the two corner pubs, the grocery store, the Post Office and the bridge over the Darling River. He went into the small diner and tipped his hat at the three truck drivers waiting for hamburgers. They nodded to him and looked him up and down. The diner smelled of cooked meat and fried egg and blood. The warm air was filled with it. He ordered a coffee and left quickly. He could barely walk on his right foot and he hobbled back to the car. Edward Pinkerboo was not functioning right. He felt he was doing everything for the first time—handing over money for the coffee, paying the attendant, starting the car, sipping the hot coffee. He felt he had just been hatched into the world, still unused to the fit of his shirt and trousers and boots, still unused to communicating with other people. He felt—what?—a brittleness about himself. That a sudden noise could crack him.

'They're good people out here.' John had told him on the phone. 'Make you feel right at home.'

He parked the car down by the river so he could finish the coffee and he saw his hands shaking. Perhaps it was the carcasses of the animals. So much blood. He had never been good at the sight of blood. He had hardly seen a lot of it in his life. Finance managers don't come across a lot of blood in the course of their work. A paper cut, perhaps. The slip of a letter opener. He finished his coffee and checked the map again.

The Roadhouse was a further ninety-five kilometres, The White Letter Box another twenty, and The Property another thirty-seven. He rubbed his eyes and sat back and looked at the river for a while. He tried to imagine John's fiancée. He saw her, for some reason, on a horse, mustering cattle. He saw her in jeans and a checked shirt. He saw her brown hair in a ponytail, the ponytail poking out from under a weathered Akubra. He heard her whistling to her work dogs, rising slightly out of the saddle, the saddle oil and horse sweat rubbed into the inner-thighs of her jeans. He saw the cattle with wild, frightened eyes, kicking at the dogs, a frothy saliva at their mouths catching dust, and he heard their screaming as if they knew where the trucks in the distance were going to take them.

He dozed off. Only for a few minutes. He woke with a start, his head full of red dirt and hooks, and hoofs lined up like the keys of a piano.

Edward Pinkerboo crossed the river for The Roadhouse.

Concentrating on the bottle of bourbon in his luggage made Edward Pinkerboo feel more at ease. He had bought the bottle especially for John, remembering he had liked bourbon. It was not your ordinary bottle of Jim Beam or Jack Daniel's, either, but a special limited edition Jack Daniel's, over fifty per cent alcohol, with a special label and two complimentary shot glasses in a bed of straw in a wooden box. He had wrapped the wooden box in a towel then secured it in the middle of his bag. He felt warmed and safe just thinking of it—in the straw, in the towel, in the bag, in the boot of the hire car.

Flocks of galahs rose from the sides of the road as he drove on to The Roadhouse. Not a single car had passed him, nor had he passed anyone. The smell of the cooked meat in the diner had finally left his clothes in the cool cabin of the car. He thought of the bourbon and then wondered how The Buck's Night would unfold.

Edward Pinkerboo had been to only two Bucks' Nights and had had one himself, before he married Becky. His was a terrible Buck's Night. Edward Pinkerboo hadn't even been able to get his Buck's Night right, let alone his marriage. He had mishandled his Buck's Night. He had eaten with several of his friends, including John, in a restaurant, with the promise of strip clubs and all manner of misbehaviour to come. But he had never made it past the restaurant. He had drunk too quickly and the meal of raw fish and rice and tangy pickles hardly arrested the roar of alcohol in his slight frame. He had sung 'Rhinestone Cowboy' on the karaoke machine and lost his way, the subtitled words on the screen swimming into each other. He and his friends had sat at the sunken table in their socks and talked at length about what they planned to do when they left the restaurant, the bars they would drop in on, the nudie shows they would view. They talked it up so much they had almost lived it out. Edward Pinkerboo nearly fell into the urinal in the restaurant toilet. He had returned for one final skull of sake and it had turned the evening. The one thimble of warm wine. The bamboo shoots on the sides of the ceramic cup so deft, as fine as the wings of a hummingbird. But it had triggered a flywheel inside Edward Pinkerboo. One that began slowly then gathered speed, quick, quicker, quickly, more quickly than he had sense to realise, gathering momentum, and more momentum, until the Buck could not get out of it. He saw white horses and rhinestones and chopsticks and napkins and socks and then he was on the floor, at the foot of the stairs down into the restaurant, and he was climbing, climbing, up through a warm corridor of air thick with fish and lemon grass, and then he hit a wall of lights and legs and tooting horns and he was tipped into the back seat of a taxi and the neon throbbed like his head and he was waving to the creamy faces that stood outside the cab, wavering his fingers, then someone closed the door and his fingers didn't move anymore, his hand, stuck in the door, four fingers outside the cab, in the cool air, then it was released suddenly and he fell back into the seat and awoke the next day in the arms of a monstera deliciosa outside his flat.

The other two Bucks' Nights had been little better than his own, although he remembered flickerings of nudity—a thatch of pubic hair, a distended nipple pierced like the nose of a bull, and candle wax dripping onto a buttocks—and the hangovers.

As he came within ten kilometres of The Roadhouse he queried the whole concept of the Buck's Night. There was really very little that had differentiated other Big Nights of his youth, although there hadn't been too many. Why was there a need for men to 'farewell' the Buck from singlehood into marriage? Was it an attempt to compress everything— the boy, the youth, the man—into one evening? And why was the Buck's Night more a state of mourning than of celebration? Like waving off an ocean liner, the streamers tearing away from the dock. Another element of it that Edward Pinkerboo disliked was the competitiveness of the drinking. The Buck, and indeed all members of the party, were somehow forced into displays of drinking prowess as if this, in essence, was the barometer of the Buck's Night's success. There was something frightening about men getting together under these circumstances, Edward Pinkerboo thought. There were so many undercurrents. So many expectations. It was something that flowed through the lives of all men, not just exclusively on a Buck's Night. It never went away, like malaria. It sat in the blood stream. That's what terrified Edward Pinkerboo.

He passed The Roadhouse and checked his tachometer. Twenty kilometres to The White Letterbox. He found it easily enough, and turned off the highway. He opened the gate, drove through, closed the gate behind him, and got back in the car. It was pure bush in front of him. Gnarled, leafless trees. Clusters of boulder. Sheep droppings. A twin-rutted road. He drained his water bottle and drove on.

The car bumped and slithered and the undercarriage was troubled by tussocks and rocks. He began thinking about the men he was about to face. At John's Buck's Night. The ringers. The shearing contractors. The farmers. The Tough Men of the West. He always felt uncomfortable in large groups of men. He had always believed himself infe-rior. Less experienced. That he had somehow missed out on the World of Men, and that he was perpetually on the fringe of it, looking in, putting his toe in, pulling it out again. Perhaps it was why he had accepted John's invitation. Why he had come Out West in his cowboy outfit. To force his way into the circle once and for all, at thirty-two years of age. To face his fear.

He passed small cairns of skulls and bones as he drove down the rough road. The air conditioning blasted into his face. His hat had dried. He imagined the bottle of bourbon jiggling in its straw bed.

Perhaps it wouldn't be as wild as he imagined. Just a few cowpokes sitting on logs around a fire. There was nothing out here. No bars to terrorise. No strip joints to roll into. No women at all. A Buck's Night without women, he thought, was like a stick of dynamite without a fuse. That's what did it, every time. The women. They just had to be around. There just had to be a hint that they were in proximity to set off drunken packs of men. Just a whiff of female. It was how drunken packs of men related to each other— by bouncing their drunkenness off women, off the idea of women. Out here, thought Edward Pinkerboo, a little more relieved, a little more relaxed, there was nothing but the stars and the bones, the exploding sparks above the campfire and the exploded carcasses of animals. Beer and bourbon and dust. Edward Pinkerboo whistled a little bar of 'Rhinestone Cowboy'.

Shortly after the seventh gate he saw it. He stopped the car and a bole of dust rolled over the top of him. When it cleared he saw it again in the distance. A tent town, the shelters arranged in a loose circle in a paddock, the shelters themselves ringed by utes and motorbikes and the occasional horse tethered to a tree. A coil of smoke rose up into the sky from a central fire. There was a caravan with an annexe and a crudely painted sign—PUB. There was an open-sided marquee with another sign—TUCKER.

Edward Pinkerboo parked the car and gingerly emerged from the cabin. He was struck by flies, and an eeriness, a loneliness. It was lonelier with this empty ghost town than just the bush itself.

'Hello?' he said quietly. He walked into the centre of the tent town, his heel throbbing, his hat pinching his head. 'Hello?'

He walked up to the fire. The small flames embracing the red hot coals were the only things moving, apart from the flies. He sat tentatively on a log beside the fire. He looked around. He brushed the flies off, knocking his soiled new hat to the edge of the fire. He scrambled to retrieve it, but already the front fringe of the brim had seared.

Edward Pinkerboo held the hat in his hands, and almost gagged at the smell of the burnt felt.

'Eddy, you old bastard!'

Edward Pinkerboo finally found his former flatmate behind the homestead. He had approached the empty house and been attracted by the barking of dogs, the mewing of sheep, and a faint wash of dust. He walked with difficulty to the makeshift crutching shed and pens, where several men were working, all caked in dust, all khaki, except for the blood sprays up their wrists and across the fronts of their shirts. They had all looked up at him. 'Hello there,' he said, waving briefly, and they had gone back to their work. It was John, though, fixing the lambs for crutching, a pair of shears in his left hand, a container of antiseptic powder in his right, who had recognised his old friend Edward Pinkerboo.

John washed his hands in a bucket and vaulted the pen.

'You old bastard,' he repeated. 'Haven't changed a bit.'

They shook hands and John slapped him on the shoulder.

'Fucking great you could get out here, mate. Fucking brilliant. How ya been anyway? How's the city treatin' ya? Eddy, Eddy, come and meet the boys.'

They approached the pens and Edward Pinkerboo shook their hands, mishearing their names above the crying of the sheep and the barking of the dogs. By the time he had

319

done the rounds his hand was covered in blood.

'We got about an hour's work left, mate. Make yourself at home. Have a look around.'

They were the toughest men Edward Pinkerboo had ever seen. Not to mention John. He had a handlebar moustache Edward Pinkerboo had only seen in the movies. He had a Harley Davidson tattoo on his right shoulder. He was leathery and strong and a part of the pens, the skipping of sheep, the dogs that bit into the sheep's necks and skittered across their backs. He was a part of the earth. Edward Pinkerboo felt more ridiculous now than he had back at Sydney Airport.

The men were totally consumed in their work. They didn't even glance at Edward Pinkerboo. He leaned casually on a fence as if he had leaned on country fences his whole life. He tried to see himself leaning on the fence, how he appeared to them, how he crossed his legs nonchalantly at the ankle, how he occasionally touched the burnt brim of his hat, how he squinted his eyes, just a little, in recognition of their work. Not bad, boys, his eyes tried to say. Just give us a yell if you need a hand.

But the last place Edward Pinkerboo wanted to be was inside the pens. He watched as John fitted the lambs into a sort of rusted metal carousel, their legs secured beneath two hooks. Then he cut the raggedy tails clean off with his shears, and a small font of blood, as fine as ink squirted from a fountain pen, pumped into the air, over John's hands and arms and onto his already bloodied shirt. Edward Pinkerboo thought he was going to be sick.

He turned away from the pens and strolled up to a ute,

casual as you please. He rounded the ute, admiring the country, or appearing to admire it, seeing nothing before him, the wash of brilliant red blood in front of him, the expanse of red earth, and walked, without realising it, towards the carcass of a sheep hanging from a yardarm.

It was only the dogs, a few metres off, tearing at something on a fence, that brought him out of his blindness.

The sheep hung by its two hind legs before him, headless, gutted, skinned in this portable, outdoor abattoir. A small pad of concrete beneath the sheep was sticky with blood. Then he saw the sheep's skin on the fence, the dogs trying to rip it from the barbed wire. And then the head, a few metres away. And then the pile of entrails, attended by three more dogs.

Edward Pinkerboo stepped back, bumped into the ute, turned, put a hand on the bonnet, and vomited into the dust.

'You been drinking already, Eddy?' John yelled.

Edward Pinkerboo heard nothing, and the bile touched his throat like a branding iron.

'So how the fuck are you anyway?' said John.

The tent was filling up, and John and Edward Pinkerboo had taken a position together around the fire. It was still daylight, but only just, and the men were starting to pour in, from properties hundreds of kilometres away, from Wilcannia and Cobar, from the roadhouses and camps, from shearing quarters on other properties. There were shearers and roo shooters, truckies and farmers, butchers and horse breakers.

As they sat talking the tent town lit up, and Edward

Pinkerboo swore he could smell baby powder in the air, coming off the men who had all showered and changed and slipped into their identical best—the brown boots, the beige slacks, the pale blue shirts rolled up at the sleeves, and their hats. It was odd—the men all the same, and that sweet fragrance working its way through the makeshift settlement.

'And Jimbo?' John went on. 'Whatever happened to that sad and sorry bastard . . .'

Edward Pinkerboo felt better after his second beer. They had not commented on the vomiting episode, but sometimes he caught the eye of one of John's sheep men over in the beer annexe, or the food annexe, and blushed at their roars of laughter.

'Jane was a good sort, that's for sure,' said John. 'She was a bloody gorgeous looking thing . . .'

John looked into the flames of the fire as if his past life in Potts Point could be found there—the many faces of his time in the City, the old motorcycle he rode, the view from his bedroom. It was all there, in amongst the charred wood and the ashes and the coals.

'Claire? Let's see, I met her about four years ago now, yep, have to be about four. She come round with her old man, checking out a few of me sheep when times were tough, tougher anyway. Yep, had to have been about four years now . . .'

He spoke at length of his fiancée, Claire, and chuckled at the thought of her 'in town' as he spoke, on her Hen's Night in Broken Hill. 'She likes a gin and tonic or ten,' he said, smiling.

Edward Pinkerboo knew, even during their short

discussion by the fire, that the John of Potts Point was unrecognisable to the John of The Bush. He was much more at ease, almost philosophical. It seemed to be Edward Pinkerboo's experience of people from The Bush. Everything they said was so pared down, so earthed and simple, that it had a double meaning. They spoke in metaphors without realising it. It took Edward Pinkerboo a while to adjust to John's conversation.

'Glad you could make it, Eddy,' John said again, slapping him on the back.

Edward Pinkerboo wandered around the tent town trying to catch people's eyes, nodding, bleating a limp 'Gidday' here and there. It was, he slowly began to realise, a very real and concentrated microcosm of his fear about men. Of being a man. It was all here—the ring of simple, temporary structures, the men from The Bush, the fire at the heart of it all. It was that tiny spot in Edward Pinkerboo's brain being lived out in the middle of nowhere, twinkling with bare bulbs, dusted with fine red earth. He had never felt such an outsider, despite John's presence. For John had gone from him as well. That slender line between them had, somewhere down the track, snapped. He drank three cans of beer in thirty minutes to hose down his fear.

The trace of baby powder disappeared, pushed out by the sheep that turned on a spit over an auxiliary fire near the TUCKER tent. Edward Pinkerboo wandered over to it. He knew this sheep. He had seen it, bloody and raw and exposed to the world, crucified on its metal cross, just a few hours before. It turned gently. He took in the delicate aroma of its cooked flesh, watching it go round and round, and within the smell he felt more secure. It may have been his seventh beer. Or was it his eighth? He nodded to the sheep in respect. He watched it go round and round. Maybe it was his ninth. Go well, he said to the sheep. Go well.

Other men had joined him by the sheep. They held their cans of beer and stared at the carcass. It went round and round. Edward Pinkerboo brought the can to his mouth and, miraculously, found that it was chilled and full. How did it get there? In his hand? Was it ten? Who? What?

The men were speaking to him. He could see their mouths move. He smelled something strange. He knew that smell. He took off his hat and batted out a small fire at the rear of the brim. A practical joke. He saw open mouths and teeth, tears streaming from eyes and men doubled over on the ground around the roasting sheep. It went round and round. And Edward Pinkerboo simply put his hat back on, and they slapped his back, shook his hand, offered him another can, this time with its own foam cooler jacket. He bounced from one group to the other. He told them jokes that were nearly as funny as his smouldering hat. They said things and he howled with laughter.

They produced a yard glass and cheers went up. Edward Pinkerboo finished his can of beer. Was it eleven? Or twelve? He was pushed to a clearing in the group, the men lit by the raging bonfire.

'Eddyeddyeddyeddyeddyeddyeddy . . .' they clapped.

He took up the yard glass, staggered a little, spread his legs, and slowly brough the long glass flute to his lips. He opened his throat and drank, and drank, and drank, and as he neared the end, the screams deafening around him, he saw a hundred distorted demons, their faces fiery orange, twisted, evil, as the scud of beer lowered in the bulb of the yard glass.

Edward Pinkerboo lay on his side in the shadow of a log near the fire. He was happy to sleep there, in the shadow of the log. His hat lay under his head, scarred and pitted with cigar burns. He had been there for an hour and was happy to die there at first but then the world became soft around the edges and his option shifted from death to sleep. If it hadn't been for the helicopter he would have gently closed his eyes and perhaps woken at a reasonable hour and perhaps returned the hire car on time to Jean.

'Hello, Edward, did you enjoy your stay?' he heard Jean say to him.

But somewhere in the back of his head he heard a helicopter and then the tent town was shaken by a dust storm and men's hats flew high into the air and came down and it rained hats over Edward Pinkerboo and he was suddenly lifted up from the dust, his new Cuban-heeled, square-toed R.M. Williams boots dragging, his own hat shoved down onto his head which was lathered in sweat, and was dropped closer to the fire, propped up by the legs of men behind him. He wiped a small dribble of vomit from the left side of his mouth, opened his eyes, and through the fire he saw two women in silken pantaloons and glittering brassieres dancing around a naked man sitting in a chair.

He had no thoughts of John because he didn't know where he was. He saw the women remove their clothes and caught flashes of nipple and firelit buttocks and golden pubic hair. He saw long, exquisitely curved thighs, rounded hips, the perfection of a breast. He caught the odd phrase in the roar that surrounded him, saw beer spurt in long arcs from cans, saw the naked women sit on the naked man. Edward Pinkerboo breathed deeply and the roar faded away and his head was filled with the cries of cattle and sheep. Dry, throaty cries. And the flashes of naked women tumbled with the glint of knives and shears and the moist frightened eyes of animals.

'On ya John boy!' he heard. 'Bit 'o wood there, Johnny! Bit 'o wood!'

Edward Pinkerboo fell backwards and awoke again and saw the flames tearing wildly at the air and heard the helicopter fade away and was picked up again and then he was running, running in a pack, the vomit strong behind his nose. The men around him were grunting, almost growling. He had his feet now, Edward Pinkerboo, and ran with them, lurched, branches tearing at his face, stumbling, regaining his balance. He tasted blood, was lifted again, and was suddenly face down against the cold tray of a utility. Then they were flying through the scrub, bouncing across the black earth, the tussocks tearing at the undercarriage. Edward Pinkerboo heard the started trampling of hooves.

It was a short drive. The ride had somehow jolted Edward Pinkerboo into some measure of consciousness. He sat up in the tray, and followed the other men to a small shed.

'Bring her out, Red,' someone said.

'Bring that bitch out,' he heard.

A cow suddenly emerged from behind the shed, led by

a rope. It skittered and backed off at the sight of the other men.

'Easy, easy,' said the man with the rope, belching.

'Let's get it over with,' someone said.

'Give it to the bitch.'

'Give it to her.'

'Fuck! Come on!'

The cow was illuminated by the headlights of the ute. It tried to pull itself out of the light but by now three men had hold of the rope, and another took its tail.

The wrestled it over to the steel post and concrete pad and it stopped struggling then, its eyes wide and dewy in the headlights, looking directly into the light, hypnotised by it, as if it saw, in the twin circles of white, its own fate.

'Do her,' someone said.

'Fucking do her, man.'

And a man emerged from the shadows, pulled out a bolt gun, put it to the head of the cow, and fired.

The cow dropped down instantly. Its hooves made little clicking sounds on the concrete before, finally, the clicking stopped.

'Fuckin' yo!' said the bolt gun man.

Its eyes remained wide open, still looking into the head-lights. Then the men went to work. Edward Pinkerboo heard the sharpening of knives in the darkness beyond the light, belching, dogs growling. The men moved over the cow, hoisted it onto the cross, then hacked its head off.

Something had happened to Edward Pinkerboo. He didn't turn his eyes from the slaughter of the cow. He didn't move. He watched them cut off its head, slit it down the middle and empty its entrails. He saw the dark wet tubes slither onto the concrete pad. He saw the flashing of the knives and silver on the surface of the blood pool and blood all over the men, and the dogs darting into the light and snapping and a glinting as clear as the jewels on the women's brassieres back at the fire and the milky white tissuey sack as fine as their pantaloons and veils. He heard the men whooping and grunting as they worked, just as they had done during the striptease act.

Edward Pinkerboo was drunk and the stars were bright and another spot of vomit appeared on his lips, but he understood everything about his fear then, as the shadowy men worked over the dead cow, its entrails slipping from the concrete pad, or snatched by a dog. He swallowed and took another swig of beer and looked at the head of the cow. He looked into its eyes and the pinpoints of light in them, before it was dragged off into the darkness.

Edward Pinkerboo woke the next morning in the backseat of Jean's hire car. For a moment he didn't know where he was. Then he saw the smouldering fire and the tents and thought yes, John's Buck's Night. He then thought it was right and proper that he should have a hangover, but he didn't have one of those fuzzy, painful hangovers at all. It was one of those rare post-drink miracles—he was perfectly clear-headed, without a headache, and everything was sharp and so distinctive he felt he was looking into the cells of the leaves, the minerals in the dust. He felt fantastic. He had felt like this once or twice before after a Big Drink. It was a mystery of drinking. That sometimes the joy of still being alive, of having made it through the night, made life itself so much more precious. It was that force of life that triumphed over the evil of abuse. His body seemed to be rejoicing, holding a little celebration inside itself. He checked the clock on the dash. It was 6.27 a.m.

Edward Pinkerboo got into the front of the car and drove away. He stopped at The Roadhouse and had coffee, toast, steak, eggs, more coffee, more toast, and a litre of bottled spring water. They were the best eggs, sunnyside up, that he'd ever tasted.

The air was cool and he drove straight through to Wilcannia. Small clouds of black birds rose away from the road as he passed. He didn't look across or down. He kept his eyes fixed on the horizon.

He checked the clock again and knew he'd make his flight with plenty of time to spare. It was only then, a few kilometres out of Wilcannia, that he remembered the special bottle of bourbon in its little straw bed in the boot. He thought of the dark amber bourbon rocking and gurgling with the motion of the car. He could almost hear the crackling of the fine straw. The clinking of the two complimentary shot glasses. Edward Pinkerboo thought of sending it to John when he got back to Sydney. But he knew it would never make it, no matter how much straw. It would never survive the journey Out West.

He slowed as he approached the bridge into Wilcannia. He didn't plan to stop. He figured he had just enough fuel to make it to Broken Hill. He passed the grocery store, the Plaza, and, to his surprise, saw a crowd of people standing outside the Post Office. He glanced at them, drove on, and was heading out of town again when something made him turn back. He couldn't explain it. He pulled up outside the Plaza, locked the car out of habit, and walked over to the crowd in front of the old sandstone building.

The air was still fresh and Edward Pinkerboo felt it gratefully on his hot cheeks. He noticed, for the first time, a burn on his right hand, a cut on the heel of his left palm. There were splotches of dried blood on his trousers. He wasn't sure if it was his blood or not. There was too much of it, as if he had jumped into a puddle of it and it had splashed to his knees. His blistered heel was stinging, and he felt a twinge in his left knee. He joined the back of the crowd and tried to peer over. He saw, through heads and over shoulders, animal hide, a hoof, a tangled tuft of tail.

Edward Pinkerboo nudged his way through. Nobody spoke. They moved at the slightest push, as if they were asleep. He made it to the front, stopped, and pulled in a huge draft of that fresh, cool air, laced with the essence of eucalyptus, the mud of the river, diesel, the whole country.

The giant carcass of the cow rested on the three steps up to the old sandstone Post Office. The steps had caught the morning sun and the whole scene was shrouded in yellow light, reflected back at the crowd from the granules in the sandstone. The legs of the cow had been neatly straightened, the tail extended. It had crude stitchmarks along the base of its belly, and on its side someone had painted: To Claire Fitzgerald, Urgent Delivery. The cow had no head. In place of its head, though, poking out of the stitched-up carcass, his hair matted in blood, and snoring, was John.

Edward Pinkerboo was at the airport, sitting beneath the fighting Pro Hart ants in the tiny terminal, with two hours and fifteen minutes to spare. He sat quietly with his luggage at his feet and stared at the clock until the plane came. He watched the second hand glide around the clock, the minute hand click by, one by one, the hour hand creeping secretly.

He alighted the plane and sat in Row Seven. He buckled himself in and watched the propellers turn then blur then saw the ground outside the plane blur then saw the whole country below him with its blood red veins and blood red hills. He even saw the highway he had taken to John's. He closed his eyes and remembered the bottle of bourbon disappear out the driver's window as he gunned Jean's hire car at over 160 kph, saw it explode in a million shards and droplets on the bitumen in the rear vision mirror, and the black crows skipping towards it, towards the site of the explosion, before it all disappeared behind him in a silver haze of heat.

Ben Widdicombe

One Floor Down from The Top of The World

G ina couldn't park because the space was covered in glass. She stopped her Fiat and peered back through the underground gloom, trying to catch the attention of the attendant.

Through the copse of concrete pillars she thought she could make out the light from his booth, though her eyes were still stunned from the bright day outside. She stripped the gears trying to put the car in reverse and swore.

'Excuse me?' she called. Nothing.

'HELLO?'

A shadow shifted in the background, and the silhouette of a baseball cap began to shamble slowly towards her. When he was up close the attendant leant his shoulder on the pillar nearest her car and she told him: 'Bit of a mess in the space.'

He looked at her blankly, as if he were translating the message into, or out of, English. Gina nodded towards the patch of bottle-green shards.

'In the parking space. I can't park there.'

She saw now that his jaw was slowly moving, like he was chewing on a stick of gum or tobacco or some deep, deep thought. The name on his shirt said *Leon*.

'Mr Lewis don't use his space much,' he said, at length. 'Hasn't had a car for almost a year.'

'Oh. Well, can I park somewhere else, then?'

He looked at the glass and then at some rust on the bonnet of her car and finally, back at her. 'Nup,' he said. 'All the other spaces're spoken for.'

Gina sat there for another moment, motor idling. She twisted her grip slowly over the ridge of the steering-wheel, and back again.

'Leon ... ' she said, hoping to disarm him with his name.

'*Name's Donald*,' he said, perking up suddenly. Gina started and he peeled his lips back to reveal a vast, gap-toothed grin. 'Old shirt,' he said, and then: 'I'll get a broom.'

Gina blinked. 'Thank you,' she said.

'No worries.' Donald turned and shambled off.

When he had gone, she ran through her mind the things she needed to take with her from the car.

Samples of rock, six kinds. Diagrams. Photographs of sculptures already completed. A reference from her sculpting tutor. Her black folder, containing notes from her telephone conversation with Paul Lewis and directions to his apartment building. Fifteen instant-print business cards.

When he rang he said he'd seen her sculptures in a student show, and traced her through the gallery. She'd never met him but he sounded interesting and didn't flinch when she gave him an estimate for the commission he described. She wondered whether this was the person who'd bought her most expensive sculpture from the show, Sad Madonna, optimistically priced at $1,000.

Donald returned and moved the glass to one, badly-behaved line at the side of the parking space. She eased the Fiat into the bay and collected her papers beneath Donald's lop-sided stare.

'Mgh,' he said, and smiled.

'Huh,' she replied, and bolted for the lift.

Safely inside its air-conditioned arms, Gina examined herself in the mirror. She was wearing a short green skirt with a double-breasted blouse to match. Tan-coloured shoes, no stockings, and tousled brown hair that would need more help than nature if it was going to go blonde like she wanted it.

DK, she thought of her look. *DK with creativity round the edges.*

The lift was well-appointed and when Gina pressed the button the ride was so smooth, it was as if the seventeenth floor had knelt down to meet her. She was a little disappointed her pigeon lived one below the penthouse level, *but*, she thought, *mustn't be greedy.*

When she stepped out she realised his apartment covered one half of the entire floor. An ugly brass knocker hung out of a lion's mouth on his door, and she banged it.

'Come in,' came a faint voice from within the apartment. Gina hesitated; although she thought she'd heard correctly, she was not the kind of woman to let herself into someone else's flat just because she was asked to. She banged again.

'Come in,' said the voice again, a little more clearly and a lot more tersely.

Shit, she thought. *I've done the wrong thing. I've messed everything up already. He'll think I'm stupid and nervous and deaf.*

Then she thought: *joviality. Let yourself in and be bright and artistic, like an artist should be. Like this isn't the first time anyone's suggested they might actually pay you to do a piece of work. Like . . .*

The door opened in front of her. The flat was dark, in contrast to the hall, and her patron was looking distinctly hung over.

'Come *in*,' he said, and turned away immediately. She swallowed and followed him in.

The flat smelled distinctly of bachelors, and not just the one. Although she knew he lived alone the odours seemed to infinitely reproduce themselves, like her own reflection in the double mirrors of the entry hall.

She followed Paul's shape into the darkness and once

again was temporarily blind. A large frame of light suggested where the afternoon might be, if it hadn't been gagged by an industrial-sized black-out curtain.

There was a flopping sound and she surmised the Paul-shape must have disappeared into the couch-shape by the wall. Two bits of marble dropped out of her folder and rolled towards freedom.

'I'm over here,' he said.

She bent to look for the marble and a triangle of basalt fell out the other end. Her fingers found popcorn, paper-clips, sweat socks.

'*Ugh.*'

'Are you all right?' he asked.

'I've dropped some things.'

'What things?'

'Samples. . . '

'*What?*'

'I've dropped some samples.' Her hand found something which could have been a large walnut, if it hadn't been furry and wet.

'Yeuch,' she said.

'You want some light over there?'

Gina thought she might like to leave the mystery of the walnut unsolved, but she needed to find her samples if she was going to sell her pigeon a sculpture.

'It'd help,' she said.

There was a long rustling sound, followed by a thump, and then the kitchen light. Gina saw she was kneeling by a peach pit, the contents of an upturned popcorn bowl and an empty bottle of lambrusco.

Paul leaned across the counter-top. 'Find 'em?' he said.

She looked up and saw he had shaggy, licorice hair just beginning to grey. His skin was slightly sallow and clung indifferently from his cheek-bones, as if waiting for a better offer.

Yet for all that he was handsome, with dark eyes that glistened like the moon on Loch Ness. He leant heavily on his elbows, and Gina reckoned he was supporting most of the contents of that lambrusco bottle and a lot else, besides.

'Do you mind if I turn the lights back off?' he said. 'I've got something of a headache.'

Her hands recovered one lump of pinkish marble and one of veiny-black. She straightened, forgetting the basalt, and said: 'But I've got things to show you. Drawings, and diagrams . . .' She held the folder out, as if for proof.

Paul looked at her for a moment, squinting. 'Oh, all right,' he said, wearily. 'If we have to.'

Then the top half of his face frowned at the same time as the bottom half flashed a dimply grin, a more boyish expression than Gina would have thought his drink-softened face could possibly have managed.

'But you'll have to come and sit by me,' he continued, 'I'm *terribly* short-sighted.'

He turned to go back to the couch and Gina was about to say something when he paused, as if he'd just had a very good idea.

'Drink?' he said. The prospect seemed to cheer him up.

It was at that moment Gina saw her Sad Madonna, head bowed, in the middle of a table in the corner of the room. She looked at Paul and beamed.

'Good,' he said. 'Pour one for me, too.'

It took her a moment to connect his message with her expression, but when she did, she composed herself and said: 'Oh, I couldn't. Well, I mean, not for me. It's too early.'

He looked at her as if she'd told him she was born with gills, and shrugged. 'Suit yourself,' he said, settling back on the couch. 'But mine's a very large Scotch. With ice.'

'Um, right,' she said. She stole another proud look at the Sad Madonna and went behind the counter, into the open kitchen.

Gina found a glass and a Scotch bottle readily to hand, but when she opened a door she thought might be a freezer, she found a fridge instead. It contained a bowl of yellow jelly, an uncharismatic looking pizza box and about half a dozen bottles of beer and wine. A gold-coloured cap which would have looked at home on a Stolichniya bottle hung suspended in the jelly.

Opening the door below, she found the ice. A wall of it. Although motionless, its rounded edges seemed to ooze ominously toward her, like a suitcase full of liposuction.

'*Um?*' she said, 'About the *ice* ... ?'

Paul was lying on the couch with the crook of one elbow draped listlessly over his eyes. 'Mmm?'

Gina looked more closely at the freezer and could see a hole cut in the centre of the block, just big enough for the handle of a knife. The hole was scored with scrape-marks.

She looked at the knife and then back at her sculptor's hands which, apart from waitressing, were her only livelihood. 'You've run out,' she said, and closed the door.

'No worries,' mumbled Paul, 'I'll take it straight.'

Gina picked up his drink and carried the folder over in her free hand. He lifted his legs to let her sit down, but she drew a straight-backed chair and sat to one side of the small coffee table. Paul downed half the Scotch in one swig, and it seemed to revive him.

Gina opened her folder and laid out the papers one at a time. As she was sorting Paul smiled at her. It made her pause for an instant and cock a questioning eyebrow, but he just kept smiling.

'Nothing,' he said.

Gina cleared her throat and teased one page out of the pile. 'Now,' she said, 'this new project. This sculpture.'

He nodded.

'You said you'd tell me what you wanted it for. I did some preliminary designs but it's a bit difficult to work on a commission, you know, when you don't know where it's going to end up.'

'I'll tell you, I'll tell you,' he said, 'but show me your ideas first.'

She lifted up the page. 'This is what I was thinking, after our conversation on the phone.'

Her first sketch suggested a woman's figure in pink marble, with a black stone shroud. The shroud could be made from one of a number of different kinds of stone, depending on how much he wanted to spend. The options were listed in a column at the side of the page, next to prices.

'I like it,' he said. 'It reminds me of your other piece.'

Gina blushed. 'I thought it might have been you. Who bought it. The Madonna.'

'I liked it the moment I saw it,' he said. Gina raised her

eyes and expected to see him looking at the statue, but instead he was looking at her. She squirmed a little under his gaze.

'Alternatively,' she said, peeling out a second piece of paper, 'you could have something like this . . .'

Paul touched her hand. 'Look,' he said. 'I'm sure this is all very nice and well thought-through. I've seen your work and I like it. Why don't you write down on a piece of paper how much you think you need to do this project properly and I'll write down on a piece of paper how much I'm willing to pay you.'

Gina batted her eyelids, surprised. She'd met sleepy drunks and boring drunks and even the occasional musical drunk, but never a business-like drunk before. Paul reached over, picked up a loose pencil from her things and looked at her, expectantly.

She tore off a generous corner of unused drawing paper and divided it in two, handing one piece to Paul. He started writing.

Gina tried to think of everything she'd been taught about negotiating skills in three years of art school, but all she could remember was her father telling her to cross her ankles whenever she sat down. She found her own pencil and wrote a figure on the paper.

Eight thousand dollars. She stole a glance at Paul and he was still writing, left hand shielding his script like a student. Panic struck her and she thought—there's no way he'll pay $8,000 for an unknown artist. I'll jeopardise everything.

She turned her pencil over and erased the eight,

replacing it with a six. She tried to make it look like it had been a six all along, but rubbing harder she just smeared the lead and ripped away a fine layer of papery fibre.

Gina looked back at Paul, but he was still writing. Intently.

Finally a blush hit her face which she supposed passed for daring, and she tore her paper in half once more and wrote $8,000 on the unspoiled portion in large, confident figures. *If it were done when 'tis done, then 'twere well it were done quickly.*

She looked up at Paul and when he noticed her looking, he stopped writing. She folded her scrap and handed it to him. He smiled sweetly, and slid his casually across the table.

She swallowed once, discreetly, and lowered her eyes. On the paper was written: 'Anything you want', and the rest was a collection of little flowers, drawn in to fill the time.

Her heart bounced and she looked quickly up, her cheeks hot and cold with excitement. Paul smiled, like a cat with a single yellow feather in its teeth. But she didn't quite see it.

'I can't believe it,' she said.

'Believe it,' he replied.

'It's ... *amazing!*' She beamed, and he beamed back at her.

'Now,' he said, 'how about that drink? I think this calls for champagne.'

Gina sat in her straight-backed chair, her mind swimming between the figures on the paper in front of her. More money than she had expected to make from her sculpture in a year. Or two years. And the *credibility* it would bring ...

Paul collapsed delicately back into the couch and plonked a champagne flute in front of her. The contents were a deep sunset-colour and there was a sugar cube disintegrating gaily in the bottom of the glass. She looked at it, quizzically.

'Champagne cocktail,' he said, and smiled.

'Champagne cocktail,' she repeated. That was one of those things she was never quite sure of on the menu, like 'capers' or 'bok choy', but now she was twenty-three she felt too old to ask without being embarrassed.

So she pressed the glass to her lips and found the liquid heavy and sweet, which she put down to the presence of the sugar cube. But it wasn't just that the champagne felt heavier, or thicker, but it tasted ... deeper, somehow.

She enjoyed it. When she took the glass away from her mouth, she even giggled. Paul took a generous sip, and then leant forward awkwardly to chime their glasses in a toast.

'Congratulations,' he said.

She grinned. 'We've got so much still to talk about. I've got questions ...'

'After the drink,' he interrupted. 'Everything, everything after the drink.' He began to smile and then he winced, leaning slightly again back into the couch.

'What's wrong?' she said.

'Oh, it's nothing. Just my head, my head. I suffer a bit from those, those what do you call them? Migraines.'

'I think I've got some aspirin in my bag.'

'Never touch the stuff. No, no, the only thing that helps

is—do you mind? If you'd put two fingers just there … '
He leant forward and indicated a spot on his temples.
'That's great, ahh, that's great. And just, if you wouldn't
mind, the same on the other side … ooh, yeah. And rub,
that's it, just rub gently … *wonderful.*'

His skin was slightly oily and she looked at him, eyes
closed, as she circled her fingers on his brow. She wondered
how handsome he would be if he hadn't soaked his body in
so much alcohol. *Impossibly so*, she thought. He was still
pretty stunning. As she was thinking all this and looking into
his eyelids, he opened his eyes.

'Oh,' she said.

He leaned forward, out of her grip, and kissed her
lightly on the nose. She pulled back.

'*Oh*,' she said again. He grinned.

'I hope you don't mind,' he said, picking up his drink.
'Your nose was just there, and it's such an adorable nose.'

Gina sat back in her chair, nonplussed. Paul took
another long gulp from his glass, and just when she was
going to speak he stood up. 'I'll get the bottle,' he said.

She opened her mouth to protest, but somehow the
words didn't quite come.

When she drank again and fancied she could feel her
head slowly filling up, like one of those fundraising ther-
mometers they put outside churches and paint red every time
someone donates another thousand dollars.

Well, she thought. *Today I can afford eight notches.*

Paul came back with a bottle in each hand. She was
surprised to see him add a generous slug of brandy when he
topped up her glass, and was momentarily suspicious as to

whether that was *really* what is in a champagne cocktail. But then, it *did* taste rather good.

They talked and she drank, and let him fill her glass up just once more. He apologised they'd used the last of the cubes, and she agreed stirring sugar in with a spoon wouldn't have the same effect. He said he'd tried it once and cracked a glass.

Slowly, Gina began to feel uncomfortable on the straight-backed chair. She slid the flats of her hands underneath her haunches and rocked slowly from side to side.

Paul reclined on the couch and they talked easily . . . He said he did something that seemed to be a combination of working in a bank and doing things with computers, but she didn't quite understand what. Moving money places. He was dismissive about it and she just smiled, unfussed about not comprehending.

'It's so dark in here,' she said.

'I like to keep the light out.'

'But it's such a lovely apartment. I'd like to see it.' He looked dubious.

She lifted herself up and went towards the window; he protested, but she folded back the curtain and admitted a single triangle of light.

The furniture was expensive but without personality: black lacquer surfaces and harsh, geometric lines. Her mind flickered with pleasure as she regarded the bleakness of the room.

He needs a woman to cheer the place up, she thought.

And then: amid the compact discs and charmless nicknacks which cluttered the standing bookcase, a photo-frame.

A photo-frame with a picture of a girl with beautiful, beautiful, curly blonde hair.

'Who's that?' she said, and hated herself instantly for asking. She let go of the curtain and the corner of light blinked shut.

There was silence for a moment and he said: 'An ex-girlfriend.' Then he added: 'The last one.'

Gina stood by the window and rolled that over in her drink-slowed mind. She was tempted to believe that was a pretty good answer—it showed he was single, yet sentimental enough to keep the ex-girlfriend's photo around, as if he didn't just use women and throw them on the dungheap when he was finished.

Yet she wondered whether she could *trust* him.

'Come back over here,' he said, swinging his legs off the couch once more. Gina returned to the straight-backed chair, picked up her drink and they regarded each other carefully.

'You're very cautious,' he said, at length. She nodded. 'I like that.'

In spite of herself, she smirked. 'What was her name?' she said. 'Your ex.'

Paul frowned. 'Why do you ask?'

'I just wondered.'

'Well, you would have found out sooner or later anyway,' he said. Gina's heart skipped—she thought that was a *very* encouraging thing to say.

'Rebecca.'

Rebecca, she thought. Even that cheered her up. She was terrified the girl was going to have been called Bambi or Sunshine or something else completely unsuitable to follow on from.

''Nother drink?' he said.

'Sure,' she said, and shrugged. 'Thanks.'

Paul heaved to his feet and went to fetch a fresh bottle. Gina found herself wishing there was enough light to check her make-up in a mirror, but when she sensed him returning she held up her glass.

But then. But then instead of filling up her glass he loomed above her for a moment and planted a warm, whisky-tasting kiss on her lips. His tongue darted over hers like a tequila worm on reconnaissance.

As quickly as it happened, it was over. Paul plonked himself back on the couch and assumed the expression of a choir-boy.

Had he kissed her for a moment longer she would have complained. Yet now he'd pulled away she wished she was there on the couch next to him.

He refilled her glass and smiled politely. Her mouth opened and closed like a goldfish, and she was sure her make-up must be ruined.

'You have beautiful hands,' he said.

'Um, thank-you ...'

'You want to get something to eat? We could order in.'

She was feeling hungry, and distinctly like she'd had too much to drink to go out in public. And besides, ordering in would keep her in his company for at least another hour or two.

'Sure,' she said, 'why not?'

'Great. I'll open a bottle of wine.'

Something in the business lobe of Gina's brain stirred, like an aged aunt buried just a little prematurely.

'Just before you do,' she said, 'I have to ask you a couple more things about the statue you want.' She was aware that she, too, was beginning to get a headache.

Paul looked at her as if he was indulging some ridiculous, girly whim. 'All right,' he said, 'if you want to.'

Gina struggled to remember what they'd sorted out so far and what they hadn't. As far as she could tell, they'd settled almost nothing except the fee. That was when the drinking started.

'This piece. I assume it's for outdoors?'

'Uh-huh.'

'What kind of, um, what sort of setting do you envisage? Is it a gift or is it for you?'

'Sort of for both,' he said.

'Hmm?'

'It's, well, it's for a grave.'

'Oh,' she said, and stopped short. She cleared her throat. 'Do you want the person's name included on the statue?' she asked.

'Sure. On the base.'

She had the dim feeling that she should start writing down details at this point, but she was too drunk. She thought she could always ask again if she forgot anything and besides, with any luck she'd still be there in the morning when they'd both sobered up.

'Is it for a family member?' she asked.

'No,' he said matter-of-factly.

'Oh. Well, what's the full name of the person it's for?

I need to know how big the base has to be.'

'Rebecca Bull,' he said. 'I'll have to check if there's a middle name or not.'

A dim, dim alarm went off in the back of her head. Like a bell with it's clapper wrapped in cotton-wool.

'Rebecca . . .' she repeated. He nodded. 'Oh, my gosh.'

She looked up through the gloom to where the picture stood on the bookcase and Paul kept slowly nodding.

'Paul, I'm so sorry. How did it happen?' She could have kicked herself when she said it, but she was too drunk for discretion. 'Wait, you don't have to . . .' she added quickly.

'No, s'alright,' he said. 'It was drunk driving.'

She flinched involuntarily and he said, 'I didn't have anything to do with it.'

She was guilty, now, trapped with her suspicion written all across her face. 'Did they get the guy who did it?' she said, trying to make amends.

'Nah,' he said, stretching out his legs. 'It was her who was driving drunk.'

Gina stopped short. She thought—*but, that's so unfeminine*, then wiped it from her mind, embarrassed.

He went on: 'We hadn't been going out that long. I barely even considered us *together* . . . but then the accident happened, you know, and her parents have like *no* money,' he indicated the apartment with a short jab of his hand, 'and they figured like I could *afford* it . . .' He took another swig at his drink, draining it. 'And I'd seen your work. Admired it . . .'

He was back to being charming now, and Gina felt her mouth begin to tug at a smile, despite herself.

'. . . and seen *you*, at your show, and admired *you* . . .' he continued.

She was aware that Paul's hand had moved towards her, that it was resting on her knee. But the alcohol had left her uncomfortable and confused, uncertain what to think about Rebecca. She wanted space to think.

'I have to go,' she said, getting up awkwardly. Her shin bumped the coffee table and her drink wobbled in its glass. Paul stood up quickly after her.

'You can't go. Not like *this*. You're *drunk*.' He took her elbows in his hands and looked at her, wide-eyed and puppy-dog sincere.

She looked back and then dropped her eyes to the table, clumsily evaluating how long it would take her to pack up her papers, get the rocks together and make it back down to the car. But the frame of light behind the curtain had begun to fade and she realised she was, objectively, drunk.

She had a dim recollection of ordering food, but she couldn't remember whether they'd actually done it and were waiting for it to arrive or if they'd just *talked* about doing it.

Paul was very close to her, now, smelling of whisky and deodorant and eighteen hours without shaving. She swore she could smell the length of his whiskers.

He let go of one of her elbows and closed her hand around the stem of a champagne glass. 'I *can't* let you go.'

She frowned, but before she could speak he said: 'Do you know what I think you should do? I think you should drink this, and then I think you should kiss me.'

He let go of her second elbow and she tottered back

slightly, almost as if she was going to fall. But she kept her balance and looked at him through narrowed eyes.

'You've filled it with, you've put brandy in it ...' She looked at the bottle in his hand and then down at her glass, as if they were two broken halves of the same picture. He shrugged.

'We've run out of champagne,' he said, matter-of-factly. 'Drink it. Drink it and we'll get comfortable.'

Gina looked at him, beautiful and drunk and helpless in his filthy apartment, one floor down from the top of the world. She thought: *the right woman could save this man.*

Then his hand was resting gently on the bottom of her glass, tipping it towards her lips. He made a funny face and she drank, the brandy sliding warmly around the back of her mouth, spilling a little at the corners of her mouth where she was beginning to smile.

Nick Earls

Green

In our year at uni Frank Green is it. The style council, the big man on campus, the born leader. From day one Frank G has been the definition of cool. Frank Green, frank in all colours, shameless and sure as a peacock. Peach jeans, pink jeans, Frank Green.

Queensland Uni, Medicine, 1981. Nothing counts here if Frank's not part of it.

Frank Green juggles so many girls he's nearly juggling

all of them. He juggles so many girls they all know. They all know and don't care. It's the price to pay, if it's a price at all. Frank Green has magic in his hands, the poise of a matador, the patter of a witless irresistible charm.

I juggle girls the same way possums juggle Ford Cortinas. I'm road kill out there, bitumen paté, seriously unsought-after. Quiet, dull-dressed, lurking without impact on the faculty peripheries. Lurking like some lame trap, like a trap baited with turd and I'm not catching much.

I have, my mother says I have, a confidence problem.

Frank Green has bad bum-parted hair, mild facial asymmetry and teeth like two rows of dazzling white runes, but he ducked the confidence problem like a limbo dancer.

Frank Green makes entrances, I turn up. When Frank Green is the last to leave, I'm still there but no-one's noticed. Frank Green dances like a thick liquid being poured out of something. I dance like I'm made of Lego, like I'm a glued-up Airfix model of something that dances. Better still, I don't dance. I retreat quite imperceptibly like a shadow in bad clothes.

My mother says I have lovely eyes, and just wait, they'll all get sick of Frank Green. My mother thinks he has no staying power, but I beg to differ. Frank, those pants and Countdown, I've told her, three things that are here to stay. And she says, If you say so Philby, if you say so.

And I've told her there's no more Philby now, but does she listen? I've told her I'm Phil, this is uni, I'm Phil. And I'm sure I was only even Phillip for above five minutes before Philby surfaced in Moscow loaded up with Orders of Lenin. Philby the Russian spy. Philby the Third Man. Philby the bug-eyed black-haired baby just born in London. Me. Seventeen years of Philby now. And what chance does a philby have? Philbies sound so pathetic you shouldn't let them out. Philby: a soft hopeless marsupial that without a great deal of mollycoddling will drift into irrelevant extinction. A philby. A long-nosed droop-eared wimp of a marsupial with lovely eyes, destined to die. Inevitably nocturnal, and very afraid.

Outside the house you don't call me that, I tell her. Okay? Outside the house, no Philby.

On weekends I lie on my back with my physics book open over my head and I dream of girls. Girls who come up and talk to me at faculty functions. Who approach quite deliberately and talk to me with a calculating seductiveness. Glamorous desirable girls who tell me quite openly that they crave me with a painful urgency, that Frank is all style and no substance, they they hope they're not making fools of themselves, but they know what they want. And in the dream under the physics book I don't shake with fear and lose the grip on my burger, I maintain calm, I sip at my plastic cup of Coke, I let them have their say and I acquiesce to their outrageous desires. In my dreams, I am a peach-jeaned man of cool. I am lithe and quite elegant. I am all they could want, I am highly supportive of their expectation of orgasm and I treat them kindly.

And unlike Frank, I'd be happy with one, though admittedly any one of several. I have a list, a list of four girls I would be quite unlikely to turn down, should I figure in their desires. I have spoken to one on three occasions and another once. Other than this, nothing happens.

But that's okay, I've got six years in this degree.

Chemistry pracs begin on Fridays, and this is where things get weird. I'm in Frank's group (alphabetically) and his friends aren't. Week Two and the group divides to do titrations and I'm standing next to Frank and a little behind him when the division occurs so I'm his partner.

I learn things about Frank. Close-up things. Unglamorous things, but quite okay things just the same. Frank twiddles his pencil when he doesn't know much. Frank says Hey several times whenever he has an idea, or has something he thinks is an idea. Frank is very distractable and has no great interest in organic chemistry. In the first prac we talk a lot about bands we like. Frank sings like someone with terrible sinuses and fills beakers up with varying amounts of water and plays them with his pencil with no concession to the dual concepts of rhythm and melody. Our titration goes very poorly. Our tutor takes us aside and says, Listen guys I'm worried about your attitude, that prac was piss easy. Frank sings several lines of 'The Long and Winding Road', but all on one note, and the tutor doesn't know what to do.

Frank says Hi to me three times over the next four uni days. Frank actually says Hi to me, and people notice every time. People look at me and I can see them going Hey, he's Frank's friend.

Friday in the chem lab Frank says, I think I can get it right this time, and he sings 'The Long and Winding Road' again, but still all on one note. We spend the first forty minutes of the prac (Caffeine Extraction from a Measured Sample of Instant Coffee) discussing how profoundly the death of John Lennon has affected both us as individuals and society as a whole. The tutor asks if we could please do the chem prac and I tell him he should treat Frank's deeply held feelings about the death of John Lennon with respect. The tutor says he feels really bad about the death of John Lennon too, and agrees that the implications are undeniably global, but could we please do the chem prac. And he says 'The Long and Winding Road' is actually one of his favourite songs and could Frank please possibly never, ever sing it again, because Frank's version of if makes him very angry. Frank starts to sing 'Hey Jude', all on one note (the same note as that used for 'The Long and Winding Road'), and then thinks better of it.

We take a look at the chem prac. Frank admits he's done none of the prep we're supposed to and apologises to me, saying he's not really doing his bit for the partnership. I tell him I spent a few minutes on it last night, and as I see it we have two options. The first is to do the prac the way the book says, bearing in mind that this involves several titrations and the result will be very bad. The second option has two parts, which I explain to Frank quite quietly. The first part is the maths. I have done the maths, and I know exactly what our yield should be. The second part is the extra instant coffee in my pocket.

Frank chooses option two. We end up with a hundred and twenty per cent of the caffeine we are supposed to, and we tip just enough down the sink to give us an impressive but subtle ninety-six per cent yield.

After the prac Frank asks me if I'm doing anything tonight, not realising how unnecessary the question is. He says We're going down the pub if you want to join us. I say

Sure, but I try so hard to be cool when I say it that I gag slightly. I try to disguise it as a cough, but that only makes things worse. Frank looks at me. It seems I have to say something so I say Mucus and he says Sure, I've got these sinuses, you know? So I get away with it. When Frank's not looking I take my pulse. It's one fifty-four. I hate the confidence problem.

So I go home after the chem prac. I have to think about this and I can't do that in lectures. This is it. This is a big moment. This is tribal. This is right out of our anthropology subject not out of my life. This is the bit where the anthropology lecturer said All tribes have rituals and if you don't know them you're not in the tribe.

There are problems with this. It took me seconds to realise I'd never had a drink in a pub before (and this is where the gritty issues of ritual will come into play), but it wasn't till I was in the back yard thrashing the guts out of the Totem Tennis ball at 4.20 that I realised I didn't know which pub to go to. With the Yellow Pages and a map I work out the half-dozen pubs nearest uni. At some point this evening I will enter one nonchalantly and probably fashionably late (if late's still fashionable) and say Hi to Frank and whoever he drinks with and I won't say a word about the other pubs I've been to first. I understand ritual. Step one—appear to know which pub.

I shower and put on a lime green shirt with a yachting motif and regular jeans. Will there be girls? I wish my teeth were straighter, my lips more full. I lace up my white canvas shoes and my mother stands me in front of the body-length mirror and I just can't believe this is as good as it gets. I don't know what she expected, standing me here. I don't know if she thought I could still go out after seeing this.

I think I'll tell Frank I came down with something, some bug. If I was a real contender I could tell him I got a better offer. Sorry I didn't make it Friday Frank: girl trouble, you know? I'll go with the bug. I'll see him Monday morning and affect some queasy face that suggests a whole weekend of gastric discontent, and this'll all be fine. And no prep for chem pracs in future, that's where this trouble started.

My mother will have none of this. She's seen the map and tells me I'll need a driver. I'll drive you round till we find the right place, and I'll give you the money for a cab home, she says. And even though I'm protesting and telling her I'm really not feeling well, we seem to be having this conversation in her car and I seem to be taking ten bucks from her when we're stopped at a traffic light.

This is really bad, this whole thing. I'm aware of that. Imagine if Frank sees me, being dropped off by my mother, my mother fussing over me before I'm allowed out of the car. I say none of this, but she knows it anyway. This is the plan she says, slipping on sunglasses even though it's early evening, driving faster than she needs to, braking late, talking with maybe just a hint of an accent. And I think it's a hint of the accent she used sporadically but to good comic effect in a minor role in the Arts Theatre's recent production of *Uncle Vanya*.

I'm hating this.

At the Royal Exchange I'll park in the back car park, she says, going on in that damn accent. There appears to be a lane leading south-west from there, between two shops. You will walk down that lane. You will then turn right and walk along Toowong High Street until you arrive at the hotel, as though from the bus stop. I shall wait ten minutes, during which time I shall be reading this book. She holds up a Robert Ludlum novel she has borrowed from the library. If you are not back in ten minutes, I shall assume you have been successful. I shall drive down the lane, turn left and be gone.

My mother, when she takes the piss, really takes the piss, I am hating this evening even more. Hating this evening, hating Uncle Vanya and his whole family, hating Chekhov, hating my parents whose abiding strangeness means I don't have a chance out there. You've damaged me, I want to tell her. You've given me no idea of normal, damn you. If I die like a philby in there it's all because of you.

She parks in the most secluded spot in the car park. I do the lane thing as she has directed. The Royal Exchange, it seems, has several different parts to it. I hadn't expected that. (What had I expected? A barn? How could I not expect rooms?) It's amazing how relaxed the people are in here, all of them, how conversant with ritual in a way that seems innate. How none of them has white canvas shoes, but maybe Frank won't notice. I'm running round working up a sweat, running down my ten minutes, finding new bits of the Royal Exchange Hotel, not finding Frank Green.

I run back to the car park, to the secluded spot where my mother has opened her Robert Ludlum novel but is only pretending to read.

He's not there, he's not there, I tell her, and I don't like the slightly desperate tone I use.

Calm now Philby, she says. The mission has just begun. All will be well.

She guns the car out onto the High Street, loops back and parks in front of a panel beating shop round the corner from the Regatta.

Usual drill, she says, and reaches for Robert Ludlum.

I run to the Regatta, telling myself not to run. Telling myself Frank Green wouldn't run. I'm sweating quite a lot now. I'm smelling like a wet dog, I'm sure of it. And I don't see Frank Green, despite copious amounts of stupid looking. Everyone here is so relaxed. No-one's wearing a shirt like mine. No-one's wearing white canvas shoes. I feel sick, some bug maybe.

Hey Phil, Frank says from behind, tapping me on the shoulder and catching me quite unprepared. We're outside, on the verandah.

Pink Floyd Dark Side of the Moon T-shirt, peach jeans tonight. White canvas shoes. Frank Green is wearing white canvas shoes.

I just came in to buy a round, he says and we walk to the bar. So what do you want?

I'm not prepared for this moment. Damn it, I didn't think this through. I'm an anthropological idiot. What do I want? My palms sweat, my tongue rattles round in my mouth like a cricket bail. What do I want? I'm thinking all those beer words, but I have to pick the right one. I've never done this before. Do I want a pot? A schooner? A middy? Do I have to say which beer? What are the names of the beers? I'm dying here. How many Xs was it? Or something involving spirits, spirits mixed with something. Frank's waiting. Frank's becoming confused. But Frank isn't dizzy. Frank's heart rate is well short of two hundred. Frank isn't about to throw up and get frog-marched out of the tribe on his first day. I'm visualising my parents' drinks cabinet. Damn them. Damn them and their stupid English people's drinks cabinet. You amateur theatre loving bloody G and T drinking British colonial bloody bastards, I'm thinking when Frank says What do you want? again.

I tell him beer, Fourex, a pot. In my head this is what I tell him, but my mouthparts are against me and say Crème de Menthe.

Frank looks as though I've slapped him. Cream de Menth, he says. You want Cream de Menth?

Yeah. I say yeah, because what else can I say now?

Righto, he says and shrugs his shoulders. You want ice?

Yeah.

So he orders three pots and a Cream de Menth with ice.

He carries two pots out to the verandah. I carry one pot and the Crème de Menthe. And I visualise my parents' drinks cabinet and I curse the bright green bottle at the front. I see my father pouring it, offering me a glass with a con man's smile and a white linen napkin over his arm, saying And do we want it frappé, sir?

The others, Vince and Greg, friends of Frank's from our year, stare at my drink from some distance away. I am about to begin a long journey into the wilderness. The urge to apologise for my drink choice is almost irresistible. I want to go outside and pay a cabbie ten bucks to drive over my head. I want to start again. I want a pot.

What's that? Vince says, pointing to my drink (as if there's any need to point).

I tell him and he nods, nods like he knew but he hoped he'd been wrong. He wants to ask why. He wants to ask why, but he doesn't.

And I want to tell him. I want to say Look, it's not my fault. My parents are so nothern hemisphere, so insufferably strange. They drink this. They've made me drink it three times in company, but you shouldn't think I'm one of them. I meant to get a pot.

We drink quickly.

My shout. Greg says, and goes inside. He's back in a few minutes with three beers and a Crème de Menthe with ice.

And I can't change now. I know I can't change now. To say No, I'll have a pot would be to admit a gross error of judgement, so I sit in my lonely soft cloud of mint, sipping away. I take the next shout. Three beers and a Crème de Menthe with ice.

Frank is looking comfortable, leaning back in the white plastic seat and crapping on about uni, specifically about the chem prac and the coffee in my pocket, pinging a finger nail repeatedly against the rim of his beer glass and grinning at me while singing 'The Long and Winding Road' with the aid of no actual notes at all.

Shit, ninety-six per cent yield Vince says, shaking his head. We got eighty-eight and we thought that was okay.

I'm smiling, laughing with Frank about Vince who

doesn't quite get it and thinks we're champion titrators, laughing with him about the coffee in my pocket, about how we wouldn't have got fifty per cent without the coffee in my pocket. I'm sweating peppermint. I'm stinking of sweet mint and many parts of me are starting to relax, starting to become loose and less interested in direction. I'm laughing at almost anything now, just thinking about turning up at the chem prac with coffee in my pocket and laughing heaps.

This is very refreshing, I'm saying. Very refreshing with a little ice you know. But I think I'm only saying this in my head, doing a secret ad for Crème de Menthe, turning to camera with a James Bond smile and saying Damn refreshing, and giving a little tilt of the head.

Vince says Hey what's that like, that Cream de Menth? and he takes a sip from my glass. He scrunches up his eyes and thinks hard. He passes it to Greg and says What do you reckon?

It's not great with the beer, Greg says. It's not great after ten beers, but maybe it's not the best time, you know? Jeez it's strong though. I reckon if you wanted to get pissed, you'd get pissed pretty quick on this. What do you reckon, Phil? Get pissed pretty quick on this, do you?

I want to say Shit yeah. I really want to say Shit, yeah, but I can't work out with any confidence which order the words go in, and while I'm thinking about it, while I'm trying really had not to say Yeah, shit, he says I reckon Phil's pissed on this, you know?

Well he would be wouldn't he? Frank says.

I can't get up when it's my shout any more, so I just hand Vince the money and he automatically comes back with three beers and a Crème de Menthe with ice.

My sinuses feel very clear, I say to Frank. Very, very clear.

And Frank says Good on you.

I tell him it must be the mint. The mint clears the sinuses I say quite loudly. I can recommend it. And Frank thinks I am recommending it, in an immediate and personal way and, aware that he has a problem with his sinuses, orders himself two Cream de Menths with his next beer, taking them both quickly and earnestly, like medicine.

I am now feeling hot all over, and there is a ringing in my head coming from a long way off. I want to warn Frank about this, to say there might be side effects, but I can't possibly be heard over his singing, particularly while Vince is shouting Yeah I think they're a bit clearer, your sinuses. Yeah. That's sounding bloody good mate.

So he joins in.

Hey, how about some Five Hundred, Greg says, pulling a deck of cards from his pocket. Just for small stuff, for ones, twos and fives, hey?

First I think he means dollars and I wonder what I've let myself in for, and then he scoops a handful of small change onto the table and organises it into three wobbly piles. So I say Sure, and then realise I've never played Five Hundred before.

And just when I think I'm about to be thwarted by the tribal problem, I remember the Solo my father taught me to play. The Solo he had played when in the British Armed Forces in India. No-one in the Punjab could touch me, lad, when I had a bit of form going, he told me once. And he's always said that Five Hundred was an inferior version of the great game, and that anyone who mastered Solo could make the best Five Hundred player in the world look like a fool.

So, after a brief clarification of house rules, we play. We play, and I hear myself shouting, but, I hope, not ungenerously as I take hand after hand. Boldly, flamboyantly, elegantly, like a matador, like a hussar, feeling nothing below the waist, watching the table sway in front of me and rise on one occasion only to strike me softly in the face. And I feel nothing, nothing at all but mint and victory. And there are times when I'm sure my brain is resting and my arms play on without me, flourishing strategies that haven't been seen outside the British Armed Forces in India since the late nineteenth century, passing Crème de Menthe to my shouting mouth, raking money across the table.

From this point, my recollections are non-linear.

I lie on my bed with my room full of well-established daylight and stinking of old mint. Crusty green debris around my nostrils, hidden Crème de Menthe oozing from my sinuses whenever I roll over. There is a bucket on the floor near the bed. A blue bucket with a slick of bubbly green swill on the bottom.

We sang 'Across the Universe', I recall. Sang it, or at least shouted it at the cars on Coro Drive and they honked their horns, and I think I saluted. I recall myself shouting at all stages of the card game, loudly and in a ridiculous English accent, and saying very pukka things that today mean little. I remember giving the anthropology lecturer the bagging of a lifetime in his absence. At least I assume it was in his absence. I can see him rearing up through my rickety dreams saying You just got lucky kid, but I don't think he did.

And some of my large pile of small-change winnings went on a bottle of Crème de Menthe and we toasted many things, including the way the game is, or was, played in the Punjab, back when it was played by experts and the sun had yet to set on the long twilight of the Empire.

And I took the pack and started ripping out card tricks at high speed, just the way my father showed me, shouting at the others in a private parody of his voice Come on then Charlie, pick a card, any card. And I fooled them every time, baffled them and I can hear Vince's voice saying The man's a genius, a genius.

And I'm still in the middle of this slow green glorious death, heaving up some more unnecessary gastric juices into the blue bucket when my mother comes in.

Your friend Frank's called a couple of times, she says. He says to tell you that there's a barbecue at his place tonight, and that three of the four girls you mentioned last night will be turning up. He said to tell you that it's BYO, but don't worry, he'll have plenty of ice.

She watches me nod and lose a little more gastric juice.

You're doin' well, Philby, she says, perhaps in the accent she used to try out (unsuccessfully) for the part of Blanche in *A Streetcar Named Desire*. Doin' fine.

RumBle in The JuNgle

'How do you say "I need to go the the bathroom"?' the Reverend Raymond Stiller asked a little anxiously as the minibus rounded a corner and dipped down onto the flat stretch of road.

'*Chauffeur*,' I said to the driver, a Zairean called Gerard, '*Il faut faire pi pi!*' The battered van screeched to a halt at a clearing and the Reverend alighted first, unzipping the fly on his desert storm fatigues as he strode towards a cluster of recently-hewn tree stumps.

His hennaed hair glinted rosily in the afternoon sunshine; overhead a few puffs of cloud hung high in the African sky.

Desiré, our Tutsi chaperone, averted his eyes as the four-man entourage followed the Reverend across the roadside and onto the grass.

Gerard slipped a silver flask from his pocket. Furtively he gulped down a draught. 'Mademoiselle?' he proffered and I held up a hand in protest at my aching head.

He insisted, grinning. 'Yes, yes,' he said in French, 'it's better.'

So with my heart beating hangover fast and from the knowledge that seven innoculations and two courses of tablets need not protect me from the million exotic organisms which possibly flourished behind Gerard's brown teeth, I sipped. The straw-coloured liquid coiled down into the queasy pit of my stomach and burned all the way back up. I was feeling cheery when the Reverend and his cohorts climbed into the van.

'I just contributed more to this country,' said the Reverend, timing his words as carefully as an aspiring New York politician might, 'than the average US senator.'

Elwin Reuber, the former rearside guard for the New York Giants football team who formed Stiller's jumbo security wing, let out a huge guffaw and thumped a meaty black fist on the thigh of his capacious camouflage pants.

The publicity man, Theo Timms III, smiled generously and the five Americans slapped each other's palms. Elwin exclaimed to Desiré, 'Praise the Lord, brother!'

Gerard was trying to slide shut the door of the minibus, but it had run off its tracks and was jammed open. Shrugging, he eased back into the driver's seat and the vehicle took off with its new-found air-conditioning.

'How do you tell him to hurry up?' the Reverend Ray asked.

From the mid-western sky the sun poured through the van's back window, although it was only pleasantly warm. Rising ahead of us were lush slopes scored with terraces of coffee, tea, the ripe red plumes of sorghum and endless banana groves heavily laden with the September harvest. They were devoid of any humans.

'*Allez, allez vite!*' I called to Gerard, who leered at me in the rear-vision mirror. The van lurched into a higher gear as we made our ascent through the rolling hills of the verdant Rwandan countryside.

'Hey man!' said Winston Deans, a minister from the New York Baptist Church, 'this is too beautiful to be a war zone!'

I watched Desiré, his hand casually resting on his AK47, as his eyes rolled lazily sideways to fix on the Reverend Deans for a second and then back to Gerard at the wheel.

A few hundred metres along the road at the top of a hill, four soldiers stood between a corrugated iron shelter and two milk crates strung with a red cloth across our path. We had already passed through a dozen of these checkpoints. Gerard drew the van to a stop.

Desiré spoke with two boys in a language full of booming sounds and short *oogoos*. The boys carried assault rifles and wore new white running shoes with an assortment of army greens and the black berets of the Rwandan Patriotic Front. Neither of them looked yet fifteen.

Desiré turned to Ray Stiller with a raised eyebrow. 'They go to Kigali?'

Theo Timms opened his mouth and the Reverend Ray stopped him. 'That's okay. They're brothers, aren't they?'

His team mumbled in agreement, except Theo who whispered about vehicle speeds, crowd counts and how long it would take to get to the Rwandan capital.

'Hey man,' Stiller shushed him good-naturedly, 'you got as much chance here of hitching a ride as in Brooklyn.'

Elwin Reuber shuddered again like an enormous jelly. If he counted for two, my wet brain told me, there were eleven bodies on this tiny bus en route through the 'land of a thousand hills'.

Gerard had taken another sly gulp at the checkpoint and was chuckling as we sped down a gully. He had two hundred greenbacks in his pocket and, if he safely returned the five Americans, another two hundred due—the equivalent of one-and-a-half times the per capita gross national product of the country we were passing through.

I fingered the wad of Zairean dollars in my bag. Gerard was in for a big tip, a golden stack of notes each stamped with a lunging leopard and the face of Zaire's President Mobutu, even if its value was plummeting back in town as Gerard drove east. It was now about the width of *Dr Zhivago*, the remnant of a pile stuffed into a large manila envelope after I foolishly stumbled into the town bank waving a hundred dollar note.

It had been around four encyclopaedias thick. But that

was at dusk the evening before, in the terrace bar of the Karibu hotel when the bongo drums were going tim-tum and the sound of the band swaying to an African pop song was drifting down to the shores of Lake Kivu: When I was lightly acquainted with Primus, 'the queen of beers' and with the Reverend's plan to save his black brothers and sisters.

On the north-eastern edge of Lake Kivu on the border of Rwanda and Zaire lies the town of Goma, a picturesque cocktail stop for tourists journeying north to see the mountain gorillas. One morning halfway through the long dry season of 1994, several hundred thousand people with no prior booking surged into Goma, and from the *Office Des Douanes et Accises* down the Avenue Des Volcans to the lake's edge, they set up camp, past every hotel, by the concrete shops marked Las Vegas Fashion and Boutique du Goya and all the way to the airport.

The refugees ripped out the civic gardens by its roots and every other tree and shred of greenery to make thousands of tiny fires in the street each night. They started getting cholera and washing up dead on the lake shore.

The mayor of Goma went beserk. His friend President Mobutu, who liked to holiday in Goma, sympathised. The refugees were herded off—soldiers and perpetrators of the Rwandan massacres to camps close to town and those less well connected up a scoured track to the north.

Goma suddenly found itself busier than in the post-box-office rush after *Gorillas in the Mist*. Twice a day a Hercules would dip down between the low hills clustered with smoking humpies onto the lumpy tarmac. The giant jaw at the plane's rear yawned open and emptied out UN officials, nurses, doctors, aid workers, journalists, administrators, statisticians, blankets, vaccines, logisticians and thousands of bags of rice.

And Christians. When God screwed up in a watching-over-mankind scheme of things, the God botherers bothered. Big time.

Some were seasoned visitors to trouble spots: Lutheran World Relief, the Mennonite Central Committee, Norwegian People's Aid, the tea-towel nuns. Self-appointed bearers of the word. A Houston housewife with photocopied leaflets 'A child of God. PEACE BE WITH YOU' wandered the camps spreading Truth Justice & Peace In The World (Inc) to the illiterate.

They flew in from the four corners of the earth. It was a time for mercy. It was *biblical*.

The scene at the big camp north of Goma stunned them all. Including the Reverend Ray.

Kibumba was strewn across a vast African valley, between the smoking mouth of Nyiragongo, *the great one*, and two bluish peaks which descended into hills scattered with cypresses and eucalypts. As far as the eye could see, lean-tos fashioned from UN-issue green plastic stretched over lava-hard ground littered with football-sized lumps of volcanic rock. A sort of giant car park under garbage bags.

In a culvert by the roadside rows of bodies wrapped in woven canoes of papyrus lay heating in the sun. Across the sprawling filth of the camp which was shrouded in a haze of smoke, Mary, a Quaker with whom I shared a rice bag seat on the plane, was treading gingerly in thonged sandals among the refugees who were prostrate on the cholera-infected dirt.

At that moment, two large trucks pulled in from the road and began slowly ploughing a path through the refugees until they could go no further. Suddenly a multitude of those who could walk took up from their shelters and began thronging around the truck, beckoning and shouting as they fought over the boxes being tossed from the truck.

The scene looked familiar. Was it *The Ten Commandments*? Where was Charlton Heston? Where was Cecil B De Mille? In the wake of the exodus stood a group of men dressed like great white hunters. They were black and well-fed and they were holding hands. Four of them stood in a circle, their heads bowed as a fifth rolled a camera on the scene.

'Excuse me,' I whispered, 'but who are these guys?'

The cameraman looked up from the viewfinder in surprise. 'You never heard of the Reverend Ray Stiller of New York? He's going to be a US Senator.'

'Um, no. Sorry.'

'His congregation raised fifty thousand dollars. Five-oh, so we could come here and see what was happening to our black brothers.'

The Reverend Ray's lightly oiled hair fell in soft waves to his shoulders, giving him a rather girlish look. His cherubic face was tucked back at the chin and his voice rose in a soothing plea: 'Bless this troubled land, oh Lord, and keep it from disease and bloodshed between its people ...'

A woman dawdled past. She was a thin woman and she carried a bale of twigs which she clutched possessively to her scrawny chest. She saw the Reverend and did a double take. She stared for a moment, then began to speak in an agitated manner to herself, her precious booty forgotten in her arms.

Another woman joined her. They spoke in the language of boom and oogoo, pointing vigorously at the Reverend Ray Stiller. He had finished his prayer and was staring nervously at the pair. They approached, hissing a name again and again.

The Reverend Ray gestured. 'Can we help the sisters here?'

'I don't know,' I said. 'They think you're Idi Amin.'

There was only one place to stay in Goma in the middle of 1994 because only one place had running water and that was the Karibu, away from the ravaged centre of town and back into picture-postcard Africa, with hibiscus trees and purple bougainvillea tumbling over white walls, red clay tennis courts and neat green lawns bordered with daffodils above the intense blueness of the lake.

At the Karibu, which meant 'welcome', it was possible to forget the black hole of the day's business and pretend, in the feverish downing of extraordinarily well-chilled booze, that you had been merely out spotting rhino.

Waiters in faded blue uniforms delivered tall, sweating bottles of the queenly Primus to rows of long tables in one room.

The Reverend sipped mineral water as he sat silhouetted against the gathering dusk like a mountain peak, surrounded by his aides.

'I never seen anything like that in all my days,' he said, shaking his head.

'Lordy Lordy,' Winston Deans followed suit.

'No, man,' Elwin Reuber's eyes were pale and troubled.

'Well, as I always said, sometimes you've got to holler like hell to get what you want and I'm going to holler like hell to tell people what I just saw,' the Reverend exclaimed. 'People will not believe, will not bee-leeve!'

A waiter approached the table with his pad. '*Oeufs a la russe* and lake fish, suh,' he said to the Reverend Ray.

Elwin repeated, 'erf ah la roose,' licked his lips and frowned. 'Hey, Ray, does this fish come from that lake?' he pointed out to where, far below us, the waves were lapping on the shore.

The waiter gave an impassive nod. 'Suh.'

'I've been eating it for weeks,' said Moncef Bouhafa, an old Africa hand on crisis detachment from Liberia. He patted his tummy. 'I haven't been sick yet.'

'It is found in long waters,' the waiter said helpfully.

'Okay,' the Reverend nodded, 'we'll take the fish.'

It was called *tilapa* and looked like a fossil on a lab tray when it arrived, whole, black and steaming from the kitchen. I bit through the crunchy coating and it was fresh and sweet and slid moistly from the spiny bones.

Elwin Reuber finished his fish and sat rock still for a long while, his head cocked above the hill face of his belly as he listened intently to the faint gurglings in his gut.

Meanwhile, the Reverend Ray was formulating his plan. 'We must go to Rwanda. See the US Ambassador. Talk to him. Ac-tee-vate! We will go tomorrow.' He turned to me, 'Would you like to come, sister?'

Across the room, the tables were forests of the empty long-necked Primus bottles. There were journalists, photographers, aid workers, tired and dirty and more than a little drunk.

One said, 'I'm not at all religious, but this is retribution.'

Another said, 'It was a great shot, in the morning light, just a skeleton in a habit!' One shouted, 'A hundred and fifty? A day? A hundred and fifty!'

One ventured, 'All this death always makes me think of sex. It's the instinct to repopulate the earth, you know.'

Another asked, 'Do you know who that guy over there is?'

I said, 'Yes. The Reverend Ray Stiller.'

She said, 'He is one wild and crazy preacher.'

I said, 'How crazy?'

A man with eyes glassy as the fish lined up five glasses of beer to different levels and was chiming out a tune with his fork.

The Primus was ice-cold and malty and the night rolled on. People boasted about their exploits in the crisis spots of Africa and Europe, in Chad and Somalia, Liberia, Ethiopia, Mozambique and Bosnia, then back to Rwanda. All the trouble in the world.

The bus was smaller than expected. The driver spoke no English. The hangover was very bad. It was twenty minutes to the border and when I opened my eyes, Gerard was at the door of the van.

'Passport, Mademoiselle,' he said softly and he seemed

to undulate where he was standing. 'You are sick?' he asked in French and smiled the smile of one who understood the sickness.

We were outside a squat yellow concrete building. Machetes, rifles and ammunition lay in piles where they had been stripped from the refugees as they arrived, as much as you could disarm five hundred people a minute. Two Browning machine guns on tripods were trained on the road.

Inside the building, Elwin Reuber was standing at a wooden counter, one foot pawing the ground unhappily. His eyes were like golf balls, round with indigination and perplexity. His lower lip jutted.

The officer of the Rwandan Patriotic Front would truck no opposition.

'You will take escort. The road is *dangereuse*,' he said and Desiré emerged in his neatly pressed khakis from the shadows, grinning shyly.

It was late afternoon and still we had not reached Kigali. We had passed through ghost towns and miles of beautiful empty country. Only twice had we seen people, heavy with luggage, trudging along on the eight-day trek to the capital.

The Reverend Ray was looking gloomy as we shuttled on and he ruminated on the scene in the Goma camps. 'It's like in the Bible. Pest-ee-lence and plague! How could this happen to our brothers? I'm going to tell the American people what's happening here. They're gonna know what's going down with our black people here. We're gonna stop this suffering. Man, we gotta fight!'

The brothers nodded, 'Yeah!' 'Alright!' 'Stand up for what is *right!*'

Desiré looked on with mild interest. The boy soldiers had turned around to watch, their eyes wide at the sound of the Reverend's voice. He did not require a translator. The Reverend had begun preaching at the age of four. The boys were enraptured with the sound of the language of hey lord and praise you.

'You know when I went to England they called me the Beast from the Bronx but I told them that the way they were treating black people was genocide. Gen-oh-cide! And they wouldn't get away with it forever. Black people would be free. But that's what we seen there in those camps. Gen-oh-cide!'

The brothers murmured in hymnal strains. To remind the Reverend now that the refugees had committed the genocide seemed churlish.

More people were appearing on the road now as the van's shadow stretched to limousine length and Theo Timm's hopes of arriving back in Goma before nightfall evaporated.

The Reverend was thinking. His face turned from morose to thoughtful. An idea brimmed on his lips. 'I learned something yesterday,' he said, turning to the brothers. 'You know what I learned? I learned that where we were with all those troubled people was almost in the exact same place where Cassius Clay beat George Foreman in the world heavyweight title. At the rumble in the jungle. The *Rum*-ble in the *Jun*-gle.'

'That was more than twenty years ago,' Winston Deans whistled.

'Man!' said Elwin.

'Yeah, twenty years ago,' nodded the Reverend. 'And this here, this has got to be the Rum-ble in the Jun-gle Part Two!'

The brothers high-fived all round and Gerard caught the mood in the front and let out a wild shout. He was quite drunk now and flying down the hills with abandon.

The Reverend Ray said to me, 'Do you know how to say where is the American embassy?' Gerard answered with a simultaneous nod and shrug. On several pitstops I had shared his flask and it was rattling emptily about the driver's seat floor.

We shared a snigger and the van plugged on, an afternoon wind whipping in the open doorway as we drove on past abandoned cars and people carrying mattresses and pots and bags and food through the terraced hillsides down into Kigali.

On the footpaths in the city centre, children played in cars but the streets themselves were bereft of traffic.

On the Avenue Paul VI the stars and stripes fluttered above a bunkered building. It seemed deserted but a harassed-looking man eventually answered the buzzer at the gate. He was unimpressed by the Reverend's demand to see the Ambassador and Ray Stiller seemed wounded at the response. The man wore a grimy shirt and he looked exhausted.

'The Assistant Secretary of State, Mr Shattuck, is flying in,' he said. 'There's a press conference.'

'Where's the airport?' the Reverend Ray asked, his mood brightening.

At the airport gate, Ray Stiller alighted from the bus and patted his hair. We strode past the security guards. He spoke in a low voice to Theo, Elwin Reuber struggling to keep abreast.

Up a short hill a soldier balanced a television camera on his shoulder, squinting through the lens at an enormous US Airforce Starlifter which was taxiing in on the apron.

Sharpton walked purposefully towards the posse of media which clustered at the wire fence. A GI with a furry phallic microphone on a stick swivelled round and did a double take at the Reverend.

'Aren't you—?' he asked, clutching his forehead.

Stiller extended his hand. 'The Reverend Raymond Stiller!' announced Theo. A group of soldiers began to buzz around him. 'You guys are doing a great job here,' the Reverend Ray said and the camera started rolling.

It was almost dark in the old blue Fairlane parked in the driveway of a deserted building. Alphonse was translating from a sheaf of papers, the cone of light from his torch bouncing over the text.

'Rwandis of the movement who are here I want to tell you some words. You will hear me. In the last days I told you that we don't want to be ignored. We don't want it. If the snake bites you and you leave it to stay with you it is very dangerous. You will be dead all of you . . . ' Alphonse paused. There were many documents to read. 'You want me to go on?'

In the front seat of the car, the wire service man nodded. In the back, the freelance man said, 'Yeah, for a bit.'

'Everyone is having money.' Alphonse continued. 'You must bring the money to the party so they can cut off the heads of the Tutsi.

'They are animals with tails and floppy ears. They are *inyenzi*. Cockroaches.'

I was feeling dizzy and my gums tingled painfully from Gerard's aperitifs.

Through the dirty windows of the car, I could see the blackness falling across the city of no lights and the distant hills where the Reverend Al and his boys were on the road back to Goma, the night air swirling in the door as Gerard free-fell down the gullies.

Alphonse's torch bobbed on the page. It was not his Fairlane but he was sharing the two hundred a day. When he could locate his fiancée he wanted to get married.

'People Who Masterminded Rwanda Genocide and Massacres,' Alphonse read. 'Casimir Bizimungu, Agatha Habyarimana, Faustin Munyazesa, Agnes Ntamabyariro, Pascal Simbikangwa, Paulina Nyiram-asuhuko ...' The cadence of the names flowed from him in a smooth and sinister rhythm into the night.

Several hours later, during yet another wrenching of 'Buffalo Soldier' from the ghetto blaster at the Come Back Bar, a soldier fainted. He crumpled to the dirt floor at a girl's feet and she yelped. They picked him up and carried him through the crowd.

Tutsi girls and men and journalists packed into the small room hung with flickering oil lamps where the air had metamorphosed into a gas of beer, dope, tobacco and sweat.

Outside in the cool, the Boulevard de la Revolution milled with people.

Below avocado trees black against the sky, men and boys swigged on warm, dusty bottles, chattering excitedly and sliding on the overripe fruit which was scattered around like little hand grenades.

Propped against the low concrete building, a familiar lanky figure opened his eyes and smiled groggily up at the sky. The soldier's uniform was streaked with red dirt and the girl was giggling as she dribbled water onto his face.

'Desiré, it's you!' I exclaimed. 'Are you all right?'

He looked up unblinking for a moment, then smiled.

'Desiré! You didn't go back to Goma.'

Desiré looked at me, his expression calm. 'They forgot me,' he said apologetically.

'How come? Where?'

But Desiré had closed his eyes and was succumbing to a mop of his brow with the dampened end of the girl's white skirt.

I backed away and watched his eyes squeeze tighter as he breathed in her scent, his teeth flashing white in the glow from the doorway.

David Ireland

Liz the Large

E lizabeth Large was her name, but so many people
called her Big Betty that when she moved up the hill
on the Mead, she told everyone her name was Liz.
Better she should have christened herself afresh, but she
stuck with her parents' choice.

They called her Liz the Large. She had a big mole,
brown as a scab, on her cheek, and one single hair poking
up out of it.

She wasn't always a big woman. Twenty-five years ago she had been fifteen and she and her girl friends had nothing better to do on weekends than follow the football round. When young girls follow football they get to have some liking for footballers.

Johnny Bickel—he later played second row in grade, but never made it to representative teams—thought she'd be an easy root and began to take notice of her, and she responded to what seemed to be the new world opening before her. The other girls had to watch from a distance and eye off other boys when Johnny let Liz go with him to the games and sit there waiting for him to shower and come to take her out after he'd had a few beers with the team.

Johnny was pleased at the prospect of a whole new girl opening before him, too. However, that's not the way it happened.

In later years, when she was drunk, which was five times a week, she'd come out with her story, and everyone would pretend it couldn't possibly be true. Just to keep her going.

'Don't come that sorta bullshit with me,' they'd say. 'There never was a time you were like that.'

Sometimes when she insisted and they kept on at her, she'd squeeze out a few tears. It wasn't easy. She was a big horse and hard as nails. Two years before, I hit her on the arse with an airgun slug and she didn't even twitch.

'You believe me, don't you?' she said to me.

'Course I do, Liz. Believe what?'

'You know, about me and Johnny.'

'Johnny who?'

'You don't really know?'

'Not yet.' I took a swallow, put the glass down and listened.

'I was only fifteen. Not fat like now. A skinny kid. Johnny was a footballer.'

'Johnny who?'

'Bickel,' and her voice had a shade of alcoholic reverence.

The name rang a bell. There was a real estate agent called Bickel, his name plastered all over the place, vacant blocks, houses. You know the thing: Sold By, etc.

'He wouldn't believe I was a virgin. But I was. He took me down by the river, you know where the bridge is in Parramatta Park, where the willow trees come down near the water. It wasn't a car park then, it was all grass down to the water. I wanted it to be nice for him, but he couldn't get it in.'

'Couldn't?'

'Couldn't. Something about the way I was made, or just being so young. He got the tip of it in, but for a long while he couldn't get the rest. He got it out and put spit on it and kept trying. At last he got me to put my legs up against two trees—I was hurting in the back from the ground and little stones, but he kept trying—and with the tip in he sort of drew back and set himself and dug his feet into the ground and drove. Later he said it was how he was supposed to push in the scrum, but he wasn't laughing then. He looked very grim. It was hurting him, too, poor Johnny. But he got it in. When it went in, it went so fast he knocked all the breath out of me. And kid I didn't need all the breath I had.

'But you should have heard him. He was quiet for a second, then this look came over his face and his hands dug into me and he started real low: Oooooooooorrrr, and he didn't stop till he was yelling.'

'Sort of a victory yell?' I suggested.

'Don't give us the shits, Meat. He pulled it out as slow as he could, it was hurting something dreadful, and when it was out I looked and the skin was peeled right back from the tip like a banana.'

'Tough,' I commented. 'What did you do?'

'Do?' she almost yelled. 'You shoulda seen me! When he pulled out, there was blood everywhere!'

'Poor Johnny.'

'Poor bloody me! I was all torn inside.'

I looked at her stupidly. It had always been part of our boys' culture that as soon as girls were big enough they were old enough and when they were old enough they were big enough. It had no place to accommodate this bit of body news. Big enough to drive a team of horses through, big as a horse's collar, yes, that was the extent of our caring. But torn?

Poor bitch.

She didn't want to say any more, maybe because then the bloke came in that she was living with. For years she was cocking it up for all and sundry, but now she lived with a bloke.

All the time she was cocking it up she was married, but that was different. He was only her old man. She lived with this new bloke in a station wagon parked near her husband's place. When they weren't there, they'd be at the Cross.

They'd been there so long, the milko delivered milk to the car.

As I said, she wasn't a skinny kid now, she was big and fat. And sometimes she liked to pretend she was being bullied.

I was going past the station wagon one night around tea-time, taking Danny up the hill to his place—his pains were bad, too bad to keep drinking—and I passed the car which was the home of Large Liz.

'If you wanta sleep with me tonight,' she shouted, with a laugh in her voice. 'You'll have to sleep in the bath.'

It was a hot night, there was no bath, and sleeping with her would be like sleeping in a bath anytime.

In the pub she had a habit of getting her drinks when it was her turn to shout, and backing away from the bar stern first. That was OK, but instead of sort of sliding sideways and back, she'd charge backwards out into the main stream and rarely did she miss backing into some poor bastard with a beer, or since it was near the taps, more likely three or four schooners in his hands.

'Hey!' the bloke would say, surveying the damage and looking at her.

'Sorry,' she'd say.

A man would have felt bound to replace the spilt beer, but that sort of equality hadn't reached Liz. The man would see it was a female, shake his head and say lamely, 'That's all right, love.'

Next time she got a beer she'd do it again. Never seemed to make the connection between this time and last.

Funny thing. About three weeks after she told me the story of Johnny's getting peeled, she was passing me to get a drink and said out of the blue, 'I had to go to a specialist with it. But they could never fix it up. Not the way it was before. Johnny opened it right up.'

The guy with me gaped, but when I didn't say anything he didn't ask.

Poor Liz. We heard only a while ago something was the matter with her. Her attendance at the pub had been a bit erratic; when she came in she didn't have the same old bounce, and she went down from schooners to middies.

One day, a bit curious—besides, she wasn't a bad poor bugger—I drove up to the station wagon and parked opposite, putting the bonnet up and fiddling with the hose clips. A doctor was with her. They'd called him from the glass-sided public phone up the street, and she lay in the back of the station wagon. The doctor opened the side curtains to get a good look at her, and he was hunched up on the floor of the wagon trying to examine her.

There were sounds of arguing.

'Look,' he was saying. 'I'll tell you when you're dead. I'm the doctor, not you. I'm an expert and the instruments say you're dead. You've got no pulse for a start.' She was so massive, her pulse was miles under the surface.

'But I'm here talking to you.'

'So there's life after death.' He was a young doctor.

'How could I talk if I was dead?'

'Any more lip out of you and I'll sign the death certificate now.'

390

He folded his arms, looking down on her from where he knelt on the wagon floor. There was very little room, but he managed to look imposing.

She began to yell a bit weakly, Help, Help, and the like.

I walked over, rubbing my fingers on a piece of scrap rag.

'I'll show you up! You'll never get the better of me!'

She saw my face round the end of the vehicle.

'You're my witness, Meat. He's making out I'm dead. You can see I'm not dead, can't you?'

She didn't sound too sure herself. But I can tell movement and the sounds of sensible speech.

'You'll never die, Liz,' I said. She cheered up.

'Yeah, wouldn't be dead for a million bucks,' she said defiantly.

The doctor was uneasy with a third person present, and I was about to chip him about the way he treated people. Then I remembered I might have an accident or something one day when I was full. He might come to my accident and treat me, as they say, conservatively. You know, just leave you. Do nothing. I decided not to offend him.

What? What was I thinking of? Bugger him. 'I heard what you said,' I told him. 'You do what you can for her.'

She sort of recovered for a while and went back to schooners but she always looked peculiar. Then she went down and down over the next two months, to middies, then to sevens, and finally got so low they moved her to hospital over her protests.

She didn't know and the doctor didn't know, but when

the ward sister saw her after they'd bathed her, she moved her to Maternity.

'What's all this?' Liz wanted to know. 'Come on, what's the strength of you mob? What am I doin' here?'

The other ladies with big bellies in the ward, and nice coloured tops over their nighties, sitting up in bed reading magazines and sniffing the big bunches of flowers that were all round the place, smiled at Liz the Large.

'Just rest, dear,' they said. 'Sit back and rest. There'll be a cup of tea along in a minute.'

'Rest be buggered,' says Liz, undaunted by the prevailing kindness. 'I'm crook and they go and stick me in here. It's unreal. Me, in the pudding club! They're bloody mad.'

'When is it due?' asked one young lady in a nice voice.

'Due?' she choked, although her voice sounded, they tell me, as if the volume had been turned down quite a bit. 'Due? I'm not due. Nothing's due. I'm not having any kid. Jesus Christ, this can't be happening to me!' And she turned her face away. In the other direction, actually, but there was another woman with a fat belly smiling at her. Liz groaned and looked away.

'Will you all stop grinning at me? You give me the pip.'

The day before she would have said shits. They were wearing her down already.

And she could feel it. When they brought her some pink nightwear—Liz didn't have any to bring to hospital, she always slept rough—she made a fuss, but in the end the young nurses got her into it and combed her hair and fluffed it up a bit around the sides—Liz always had it drawn back tight out of the way so it wouldn't get in her beer—she looked a lot less like the old Liz and a lot more like the rest of the ladies waiting for their babies.

At first she resented this. Why did they have to doll her up like the others? She didn't feel right. But by next morning, after the best sleep she'd had since she was a little girl in pigtails, it somehow didn't matter so much that she was different.

When the night nurse hovered near her, she woke instantly—she always slept light in the station wagon, all sorts of characters got up near the Lake—and was just about to tell her to get to buggery, when her eye caught sight of the other beds and several of the bellies that were facing up, what with their owners sleeping on their backs.

Instead, she said, 'You don't have to worry about me. I'm all right.'

The nurses told stories to each other when they had their tea break about difficult patients they'd had. It wouldn't have done Liz any good to know she didn't even get a mention.

The next two weeks were a new life, even though both kidneys were failing and they were trying to keep her alive till the baby came.

As she sank lower, she still didn't believe there was a baby. Not even when it was kicking. She'd always had a full belly, and the little thing inside her didn't take up enough room to swell her out any more than she already was.

Word got around and we made sure the boys gave her a visit. Sharon was always on duty in visiting hours, so we fixed it with the publican for her to take an hour off in a slack time. When he looked a bit doubtful, we pulled all the boys out of the pub and showed him how slack business could get and he agreed right away.

Most of them said later they never knew Liz the Large would come up so well with a bit of care and soap and looking after.

In a fortnight she sank as far as she was going to, then fell right through the world. As she seemed to go, one of the women noticed—it was ten in the morning, opening time at the Cross—and called the sister. They got screens round in a hurry, saw they couldn't do anything for Liz and then remembered the baby. They looked at each other. What now?

There was no doctor around, so they pulled the blanket down and Liz's nightie up, spread her legs wide, lifted her knees high and had a look.

The top of a little head—only a square inch of it—was on show. They smiled then, and spoke to Liz. Quietly, but close to her ear so she'd hear if she was still conscious.

'It's your baby, Liz. He's coming now. Just a little squeeze now. Bear down, love. Bear down. Can you hear, sweetheart? Just a bit of effort. Come on now, help us. You can do it. We'll see it gets looked after.'

She must have heard, because the muscles in the big thighs tensed and the huge stomach moved and the little head slid out. It was covered with short, but very dark hair. Liz had black hair.

'Bit more now, love,' they said. 'Better is *you* do it. Come on, don't go away. Liz! Another effort. Push now. Bear down. Come on, one more time.'

The stomach moved again, very slowly, but it was

enough. The baby slithered out into waiting hands. They upended him quick and got him to yell and clear his throat.

The sound made Liz open her eyes. They held him up on the cord so she could see.

Her lips moved. Very softly she said, 'Well, bugger me!' And rested. They waited, still holding him up.

'Is he all there?' she said.

They held him closer, turned him round, showed her the face and ears, the arms and legs—right number of fingers and toes—and his little prick and balls.

The slowest smile moved the corners of her mouth and the puffy skin under her eyes.

She said no more words, but the smile stayed until her bottom jaw dropped. By that time the cord was cut, the little fellow washed all over and wrapped up and put in one of those cots with the wheels on in a big room with about sixty other newcomers to the world.

They cremated her and gave the ashes to the bloke she lived with in the station wagon, but he thought they might get lost or something and gave them to her husband to put on the mantelpiece.

The husband took the boy and got his married daughter to live in and look after him along with her own three.

They had a big party up at the house to wet the baby's head and everyone went. So many went that the publican— who knew about it the required number of days in advance—told his casuals not to come in, and helped in the bar himself.

There were four fights and the police came around three

o'clock. One stranger wandered over towards the Lake and got himself drowned in one of the eighty-foot holes, but the party was for the baby and Liz the Large, and no one took much notice of this event.

Luke Davies

VENom

*I*n my dream I'm walking through the butterfly dome
and everything else is flying. It's warm and green and
wet in there, and the beams arch away to a central
point in the roof where through a small hole you can see
the real sky. Between the larger beams the plastic ceiling is
held in place by a series of interlocking triangles.

I'm walking through the rainforest at ground level. Way
up there the sprinkler system is working but the drops of

water seem weightless and never hit the ground. They fill the dome and move around in the same motion as the butterflies, hovering and flitting.

The butterflies are everywhere. Even in dreams, there is no insect more pleasant to bump into. They're every colour and every size and they're in my hair and in the air and the trees and ferns are filled with them. In real life the sun can't get through the plastic and the light in the dome is muted but it's a dream and the sunlight glints on the droplets of water until they look like thousands of tiny balls of silver jiggling and swirling without regard for gravity.

Then Roy appears, only younger and more handsome. His red hair is slicked back and his freckles are glowing and the blood vessels lining his face have disappeared. He's grinning at me and all his teeth are perfect. He's hovering above me, above the trees, and he's got the biggest butterfly wings of all. They start orange at the edges and they go through many colours and they're blue in the middle.

His wings are flapping slowly, but I can feel the slight breeze from them moving my hair. His hands are free to caress the snakes that are floating all around him and nuzzling him like puppies. He lets them slide through his hands and he's laughing as he names each one that passes. The beautiful names: bandy-bandy, ophidian, fer-de-lance, mallee snake, diamond python, copperhead, amethystine, night tiger.

Then slowly Roy is turning black, and all the snakes are becoming white, and the dream, like Roy, begins to fade.

Roy the snake man turned fifty and threw a big drunken

party the night before my class excursion. If it wasn't for the way these events linked up together, things might have turned out a little different. This is 1973 I'm talking about. For a year, whenever I wasn't at school, I'd trailed along behind Roy, scraping out the algae in the ponds in the domes, helping him get ready for the snake shows, feeding the spiders in the spider house.

In 1972 my dad had announced we were moving to the country. Dad was throwing in his white collar job to manage a tourist attraction which would be called—bravely, I see now—the Butterfly Farm.

Friends of Dad had picked up for a song a run-down caravan park on thirty six acres at Wilberforce on the Hawkesbury River. It was called the Wilberforce Caravan Park and they must have figured a name change and a face-lift would do it a world of good.

The Butterfly Farm was to have two functions. Firstly, the caravan park would continue to operate. It remains always in my mind as the no-man's land of these two years of my life. The park consisted of permanents and casuals. The permanents were down-and-outers, drifters and psychopaths. I don't remember seeing them much, or talking to them ever. The casuals came for the water skiing. Speedboats could be launched by tractor from a rough dirt boat ramp. It was a popular part of the river for skiing.

I suppose the newer part of the venture was the part that could be said to be vaguely related to butterflies. Away from the caravan park, the Butterfly Farm proper was to spread over twenty-five acres of rolling fields and willow trees and creeks. In keeping with the spirit of the times—the

Whole Earth Catalogue had recently arrived in Australia—three large geodesic domes were built. Small rainforests were established in them, humid ecosystems with walkways and waterfalls and burbling creeks, all maintained by an elaborate network of hidden sprinklers.

The idea was that the domes would be filled with tropical birds and butterflies of all varieties. In my eleven-year-old imagination I had seen myself walking through butterflies so thick that visibility was reduced to a few feet. A blizzard of butterflies. The reality was different. These things are hard to do, I guess, especially on a budget. I wanted Dad's venture to be a success, but I remember my disappointment at the stillness inside the hot, wet domes. My eyes searched the lush foliage, but all I ever spotted was the odd butterfly hanging upside down from a leaf.

Maybe the butterflies were having some kind of siesta. I admit I didn't spend much time in the domes, and, after all, the Butterfly Farm *did* last for a year or two. Then again, maybe everyone who walked through those domes was disappointed.

The Schroder Exhibit gave the place some added educational respectability. It was a beautiful collection of mounted butterflies and beetles, gathered from all over the world earlier in the century, housed in huge cedar cabinets.

We lived in an enormous house built from convict sandstone, on the highest point of the Butterfly Farm. What began as our lounge room became the Schroder Exhibit. It was roped off from the rest of the house and called 'Museum'.

A miniature train ride wound through the property. There were ponies and minibikes and camel rides. Barbecue pits and swings dotted the green fields. On Sundays the highlight was the Daredevil Waterski Show. A team of lunatics in colour-coordinated wetsuits would leap from floating ramps and ski barefoot and backwards through walls of flame.

Somehow Dad became the MC at these events. A tinny speaker system was strung up from trees. The picnickers reclined on the banks of the river, eating their lunch and watching the show. For a summer or two Dad's previously dormant thespian talents flourished as he sat at a desk on the riverbank and described over loudspeakers, in a language verging on histrionic, the precarious and potentially fatal nature of the next stunt.

The snake house, between our house and the butterfly domes, was a small two-roomed structure built from Besser bricks. It consisted only of the heat-controlled rooms, a short hallway, and a storage closet. The public could walk along the hallway and watch the reptiles through the glass interior walls.

One room contained the lizards and the other contained the snakes and pythons. The snake room was further divided by a knee-high wall, which separated the venomous from the non-venomous snakes. Slithering over the wall wouldn't have been a problem, but the snakes were too lazy and well fed to bother in that heat. There were a couple of tree branches in there, and some rocks, and a bit of hay scattered about.

I was allowed in the non-venomous section. Roy the

snake man put on the snake show on weekends. I'd help him place the snakes in their calico bags and we'd carry them down to the snake platform.

Roy was kind and gentle, and keen as mustard when it came to snakes and spiders. Over the years he'd been bitten many times, but like all snake catchers he'd developed quite an immunity.

His face was mottled in a weatherbeaten way. His nose was red and he always smelt of alcohol and aftershave. He wore a hat against the sun. In 1973 he was still tipping it to ladies.

He lived in one of the caravans, a deluxe model with extra canopy. Sometimes we'd see him, pottering about in the morning sun, cracking his first beer for the day. Beer was like soft drink for Roy.

For my brothers and me this was a world of sandshoes and mud, creeks and adventures. Sleep came early and deeply. We'd be going to bed, I suppose, just as Roy's evening of drinking was beginning. But in the morning he was always there, shaking and polite, always ready to tell a joke or take us on a tractor ride.

One day I overheard some of Dad's friends—the investors—talking about Roy. I was lying on the roof of the verandah, where I would climb sometimes and gaze out for hours over the farm. They stood beneath me drinking beer. Nobody ever looked up.

In the distance Roy emerged from the snake house. The conversation swung around to snakes in general and Roy in particular.

'He's been drunk since the forties, you know. More

whisky than blood in his veins. Snakes wouldn't stand a chance. Still, he knows his stuff.'

I looked at the tops of their heads and listened to this betrayal. The way adults talked.

Roy took his job seriously. On Saturdays and Sundays he gave his snake shows at eleven, one and three. I'd see him spruced up in his blue safari suit, his hair Brylcreemed back, as he made his way across to the snake house. On the days I helped him we'd stand together in the small entrance chamber, out of view of the public. Roy would pull from his coat pocket a silver hip flask and take a long swig.

'Clear those cobwebs out, eh?' he'd say.

Or: 'Luck of the Irish, old son.'

Or my favourite, the delightful and mysterious, 'Ahh— long filthy hair of the dirty dog that bit me. Nothing like it.'

And he'd look down at me with that big gap-toothed grin. Chuckle a little and wink. Sometimes pat me on the head. It was a ritual I loved. Then he'd fling the door open and together we'd walk into the bright heat of the snake rooms, with the tourists watching on the other side of the glass.

I was in sixth grade at St Dominic's College at Penrith, a fifty-minute bus ride from the Butterfly Farm. There were about seventy boys in the year, but it was a new school and I'd made few friends. So I was pretty chuffed when our teachers organised an excursion to my own place. I saw it as a chance to raise my stature in the pecking order.

Midweek not much ever really happened at the Butter-fly Farm. A school excursion would trundle through, look at the museum, the snake house, the domes, have lunch, play around, go home.

But for the St Dominic's sixth grade, Dad organised a treat. He rustled up the carnies who brought in the horses and minibikes on weekends. And he promised me he'd get Roy the snake man to put on a show.

The excursion was on a Wednesday and the Tuesday was Roy's fiftieth birthday. So on the Tuesday night the caravan park experienced what must have been the party of the year in tiny Wilberforce. The wild festivities spread over several caravans but the focus was Roy's place.

I was aware of the party, of course, only as a forbidden zone. I was part of Roy's birthday and the weird fun that adults had—my experience was it always went from good to nasty—only indirectly. My brothers and I went to bed at the usual time.

In the middle of the night I woke. I lay listening to the hooting and laughter and music that drifted from the party and past my window and across the fields down to the river. A woman's hysterical screaming stabbed the air. It might have been laughter. Then I fell back into sleep thinking about my classmates and my teachers.

The first thrill of Wednesday was waking up and not having to go to school. At breakfast I teased my brothers about being in school uniform and having to rush to catch the bus. Dad came into the kitchen and saw me in my jeans and T-shirt.

'What are you doing?'

'It's the excursion!' I reminded him.

He stared at me as if trying to work something out.

He'd been to Roy's party for a while and I think he was a
little fuzzy at this time of morning. He took in my information. Suddenly he winced.

'The snake show! I forgot to ask Roy about the snake
show.'

'Dad!'

I couldn't hide my disappointment.

'Not to mind. Not to mind,' he said. 'Listen. When does
your school arrive?'

'About ten.'

'Okay.' He was thinking on his feet. 'Okay. It's a bit
early now. But at nine o'clock I want you to go down and
knock on Roy's caravan. Be very polite. Tell him I said I'm
sorry, I meant to ask him earlier, but could he please do me
a big favour and put on a show for you kids at eleven. Tell
him we'll work out the money later.'

By nine the day was becoming hot. The bland shrill of
cicadas filled the air. I walked down to Roy's caravan and
picked my way through the debris of the party, the cans and
bottles and ashtrays.

A ripped record cover lying in the sun showed a fat
balding man in a green and white striped jersey lunging at
a surprised lady in a red-and-white striped jersey. Her face
was turned to the camera and one finger touched her lips in
a kind of 'oh dear!' expression. The bald man had half
pulled down her crisp white shorts, exposing her right
buttock. It was called *Sinful Rugby Songs*.

Roy's door hung open and he snored loudly in the stale
ticking silence of his caravan. I stood at the door and
knocked gently and whispered, 'Roy. Roy,' for five minutes.

Then I knocked loudly and said, 'Roy!' more urgently.

Finally I moved into the caravan. Roy's leg protruded from the sheet and hung over the edge of the bed. It was yellow and hot in there and I didn't want to be there. I took hold of his foot and started to shake it. He swung around with an almighty moan and turned towards the wall and began to snore even more deeply.

I stood still for a minute, looking at the sunlight fall on a cigarette butt floating in a glass of wine. The snake show was important to my day. I left the caravan and hurried back up to the house to find my father.

So Dad got the job of waking Roy and I went up to my bedroom to watch for the arrival of my classmates. When the buses pulled up I ran downstairs in a frenzy.

'Mum! They're here!'

Then I composed myself and sauntered from the house to greet my classmates and teachers spilling out.

We went through the butterfly domes and listlessly tried to fill out our geography worksheets. As usual the butterflies were a non-event. I was in a heightened state of awareness and self-consciousness, ready to punch any kid who made a negative comment.

At a quarter to eleven I went to the snake house to wait for Roy. I stood at the doorway nervously searching for a sign of him in the caravan park in the distance. Dad had assured me that Roy was awake and the snake show would go on. At five past eleven Roy's caravan door opened, and his tiny figure began to stagger across the field.

I knew something was wrong—or at least different— before he was halfway there. No safari suit. No Brylcreem.

He walked with a stoop, a timid, defeated man, and he kept coming towards the snake house in long erratic curves. Veering off and heading back. As he came closer I saw that his red hair was wild and matted. His skin seemed pink but his face was very pale. He wore blue slacks and a stained white shirt with the sleeves rolled up.

'Hi Roy!' I said as we walked together into the entrance chamber of the snake house.

'How are you, Sonny Jim?'

He smiled weakly.

We stood at the door to the snake rooms. This was normally the moment of the little ritual. But Roy merely patted his chest, where no pocket was, no hip flask, and licked his cracked lips. He looked down at me nervously. He didn't grin or wink.

He took a deep breath and opened the door. My classmates and teachers crowded around the viewing windows as Roy and I stepped into the snake room.

He pointed to the snakes he wanted and I started placing them in their bags and tying the tops as he'd taught me. I felt unsettled by Roy but at the same time I was enormously conscious of the beauty of this moment. I was sure the rest of the sixth grade were looking at me with awe.

I finished bagging the snakes and stood at the small dividing wall to watch Roy at work in the venomous section. He kneeled on the floor and flexed his fingers and he looked up at me with big sad eyes, as if he was saying sorry for something. I couldn't work it out.

Roy's hands trembled, almost imperceptibly, as he reached for the snakes and put them in their bags: taipan, death adder, red-bellied black, the beautiful blue-bellied black. He picked up a tiger snake—the second-deadliest in Australia—as he'd done hundreds of times before, gently and slowly. But things were not smooth. Roy's hands were not smooth. The snake jerked unsteadily in the air.

It reached around and bared its fangs and struck him three times—wham! wham! wham!—on the web of his right hand, between his thumb and forefinger. It was a sudden blur of movement in the dreamy lethargy of that overheated concrete room.

'Shit! Shit! Shit!'

Roy dropped the snake. It slithered away.

He brought his hand to his mouth and sucked on the tiny wound for about five seconds.

'Damn!' he said, as if he'd merely locked his keys in his car. He dropped his brow into his good hand, shaking his head slowly. He looked at the wound, then began sucking it again.

'Are you okay, Roy?'

'Yeah, yeah. It's all right, matey. Listen, just to be on the safe side, run down to the kiosk and get me a pint of milk, will you? There's a good lad.'

I burst through the squeaky screen door of the kiosk. Breathless with the urgency and responsibility of my task, I took a pint of milk from the fridge.

'This is for Roy!' I waved the bottle in the air. 'He's been bitten by a snake!'

I didn't have to pay, of course. My Dad was the boss.

I sprinted back up the hill to the snake house.

By now Roy had put the rest of the snakes into their bags, including the tiger snake that bit him.

'There you go, Roy.' I handed him his cold bush cure.

He popped the foil top, tipped the bottle to the ceiling, and drank it in a single long mouthful. I watched his Adam's apple move up and down.

'Ahh.' He wiped his mouth with the back of his bitten hand, looked down at me, grinned and winked. 'That should do the trick. Until I get a real drink after the show, eh?'

I was relieved to see his sense of humour coming back.

I picked up six of the blue calico bags and their writhing cargo. I followed Roy down the hill to the snake platform. The other boys and my teachers followed us.

The only other visitors to the Butterfly Farm that day were about twenty spastics and their minders. They'd come in a bus. They had sort of twisted bodies and it made me feel sad to look at them. The minders pushed them around in wheelchairs. Everyone spread out around the wooden platform, which was roughly the size of a boxing ring. I climbed the stairs and put down the snake bags in a pile. Brimming with pride, I went back down among my classmates.

Roy would open a bag and take out the snake and hold it aloft with both hands, like an Aztec priest. It never ceased to thrill me the way the crowd oohed and aahed. He would walk around the platform in circles as he carressed the snake and gave his spiel. This little fellow is the such and such. It's found in the north of Queensland. It can grow to eight feet. It eats blah blah blah. Its bite is generally deadly to humans.

They were beautiful, rambling stories of snakes, utterly hypnotic. I knew them by heart. On this day all my senses were attuned not to Roy's words but to the responses of my classmates and my teachers, to the way their eyes followed him around the platform.

He milked the death adder, bending down low in a wide circular sweep. Everybody strained forward to get a slimpse of its huge fangs piercing the rubber lid, and the venom rolling down the inside of the glass like teardrops. His hands trembled holding the snake and the jar.

I remember how pink he looked in the hot sun. He was sweating more than usual.

He put away the adder and tied the bag. He took out a small thin snake that stretched away from his hands and tried to swim the air like a seasnake. It was a vivid green against his white shirt.

'Well this is the green tree snake and as you can see he's a frisky little chappy today—'

Roy stopped, as if confused about something. All eyes were on the snake. It continued to writhe from his out-stretched hands.

That's right Roy, I thought. It's the green tree snake. You've got the right one. Don't be confused.

For two or three seconds he stood motionless.

'Well, ladies and gentlemen,' he said. 'I'm afraid we're going to have to stop the show there, because—'

He began to sway.

Then his hands went limp and his body relaxed.

The snake fell from his hands over the edge of the plat-form and landed neatly in a spastic's lap. At the same time Roy began to keel over backwards. His red hair traced a long slow arc like a brushstroke across the sky. He made no effort to break his fall. He sailed gracefully downwards and hit the wooden boards with a ferocious slap and clunk.

In my memory now, time becomes infinitely stretched at this moment. A stunned silence settled on the crowd and everybody's gaze seemed to turn towards me. As if somehow my connection to the place could serve as an explanation or a solution.

Brother O'Grady looked at Brother Connor and then looked at me and said, 'Oh dear. Oh deary me.' I was trying to take in the scene. I was eleven years old. The tree snake skewed back and forth across the spastic's frail thighs. I guess the snake was about as surprised as anyone there that day.

The first person to break the trance was the spastic's minder, a plump woman of about fifty. She held her hands to her face and screamed and stumbled away from the wheelchair, backwards and fast. All her friends took her cue and did the same. There were minor collisions and entanglements between wheelchairs as they pulled them away in the panic.

The spastic's eyes rolled in his head like the eyes of a frightened horse. He took in the sudden emptiness of the circle around him. He looked down to his immobile hands resting on his immobile legs. The snake slid across his wrists.

I looked up to the snake platform. Roy lay sprawled on the wooden planks, arms and legs spread in an almost perfect star. His blue slacks began to darken, first around his fly and then rapidly down his legs. In seconds his face turned blue, then a dark purple heading towards black.

The urine continued to flood out of him, on and on, foaming in the cracks of the wood and running in bright yellow rivulets down past his shoes. The sun beat hard on us all. The spastic opened his mouth wide but could only exhale three short puffs of breath. Then a high guttural growl emerged strangled and twisted from his throat.

I just kept staring with morbid curiosity at Roy's sunlit shame. The piss everywhere. But I had to do something about that damn snake. After all, I was second in command.

I rushed through the forbidden zone to the wheelchair. The spastic's eyes were locked on the snake in his lap. I touched his face and made him look at me. 'It's all right,' I said. 'It's all right now.'

I lowered my arm slowly, in front of the snake's line of vision. I placed my hand palm up on the spastic's left thigh. The snake flickered its tongue to smell my hand and slithered up along my palm. I let it move through and closed my hand softly behind its head.

I took it by the tail with my other hand and lifted it gently away from the spastic. I ran up the stairs to the platform, dropped the snake into its empty calico bag, and tied the knot.

I looked down at Roy, purple, lifeless, and soaked from the waist down. Two things were dawning on me. Firstly, this was a very serious situation. Which was bad. Secondly, I was looking like a hero. Which was good.

The green tree snake was poisonous but not deadly. A good bite would lay you up in bed for a few days. A bit of fever and vomiting. I figured there was no need for my classmates to know these kind of details. Roy certainly hadn't got around to them yet. A snake was a snake. Scary. A snake could kill.

I looked down at Brother O'Grady. He was about Roy's age. Even on excursion he wore all the Catholic biz, the full black robe get-up.

'I'll get my Dad!' I shouted. It seemed a good solution to our problem.

I ran up the hill to the house.

'Dad! Dad!'

He came running from the office.

'What is it?'

'Dad! Roy's been bitten by a tiger snake! He's collapsed! You better come quick.'

My father always got around in gumboots in those days. It must have been some psychological thing—some kind if symbolic relief from the pressures of the city. But it sure made for an awkward sprint down that hill to Roy hardening in the sun.

Halfway down the hill we could see that Brother Connor was now kneeling with Roy. Obviously Brother O'Grady had delegated this responsiblity to the younger Brother Connor, who only wore the black trousers and black shirt with the white dog collar. Nonetheless, even without the robes it looked from a distance as if the last rites were being performed. The sandy-haired Brother slapped Roy gently on the face. It might have been the sign of the cross.

Brother Connor was kneeling on one knee over Roy. He was looking towards Dad and me the way people standing around an accident victim look towards the arriving ambulance. He seemed tiny and frail beside the bloated mass of Roy. His cheeks were flushed and I realised then how young he must have been.

Dad took the stairs to the snake platform in a single leap and Brother Connor respectfully stood aside. Dad took one look at Roy. It wasn't hard to see there was a problem here and he didn't bother to inspect him closely. He turned to Brother Connor.

'I'll get the car.'

Now he had to run all the way back up the hill. In the hot sun. In gumboots. So off he went, and I must admit it was pretty fast. The downhill trip alone had made even Dad look a bit purple.

The wheelchair crowd were all pretty spooked. Not much noise coming from their side of the show. Brother Connor and I stood on the platform, the only vertical bodies up there in that loneliness. It felt a little awkward looking at Roy for too long, so our eyes met for a couple of moments. It was like getting to know each other, out of context. A kind of bonding experience. I always liked that guy.

When that, too, became awkward, we looked away from each other and up the hill to where Dad had disappeared. I saw the yearning in Brother Connor's eyes. We were caught in an awful trance which only Dad's return could break. Our ears strained for the sound of the Hillman Hunter starting.

In the meantime Brother O'Grady was trying to shoo seventy boys away from the most fascinating thing they'd seen all year. It was a little difficult to get them all moving. Their bodies moved in one direction at a microscopic rate, but their heads remained fixed as one on the lifeless wet purple mound that was Roy.

I was exempt from Brother O'Grady's commands. I was the Snake King, in charge of these deadly calico bags spread all over the platform. And I was the Keeper of the Dead, proxy for Dad while he prepared the chariot for the sacrificial run to the Windsor District Hospital. Sun Gods all of us.

Time was no longer fully suspended, but it was at this point in my life I first began to realise it's a very elastic thing. Right now it moved like treacle oozing over a bench.

The Hillman finally appeared. It rounded the corner and came sliding sideways down the grass. Dad didn't even stick to the property's dirt roads—he just took the most direct route down the hill and across the field.

The car crunched to a halt on the gravel. Dad was up the stairs and barking instructions. He threw me a set of keys.

'Mate,' he said. 'It's your job to put all these snakes back in the snake house.'

I nodded. It was all that was necessary. He turned to Brother Connor.

'Can you give me a hand here, Brother?'

Dad took Roy under the arms. Brother Connor got the soggy end. I knew a Christian Brother would never complain about something like that. They struggled down the stairs and laid Roy in the back seat. Dad jumped into the driver's seat and took off without saying a word. We all stood and watched the car disappear in the dust. Me on the platform, feeling somehow separate.

All there was for a moment was the noise of the cicadas.

I looked down around me to the bags full of snakes, and the pungent dark stain that remained on the snake platform planks, like the photographic negative of a pair of legs.

'Is there anything we can do?' asked Brother O'Grady.

I forgot I was in charge. The Snake King. The Python Prince. He was talking to me.

'No,' I said. 'I think I'd better do this myself.'

He stood there nodding. I bent and gathered a few bags. When I stood up they were all still there looking at me—the cripples and their minders in their circle of solace, my seventy peers and their shepherds. I met Brother O'Grady's eyes.

'Do you think he'll be all right?' he asked.

I thought it was a strange question coming from someone who was closer to God than I was.

'I hope so,' I muttered, slightly embarrassed.

He nodded wisely, as if pondering the deeper implications of my answer. It was at that moment that I realised that what everyone was in fact doing was awaiting my instructions.

I put down the snake bags from my left hand. I pointed to an open field across the other side of the creek.

'Um ... the minibikes and horses are over there. They brought them specially for us. Maybe you'd, er, like to, you know, go over there and have lunch and stuff ...'

'Yes. Yes.' Brother O'Grady turned to Brother Connor with a look of relief. 'An excellent idea. Right.'

That's when time slipped back into gear. The Brothers did the usual thing that teachers do, marshalling the little troops into forward formations. The cripple minders all started talking at once, about what had happened and what they did and how they had felt. One of them stroked the hair of the boy whose lap the snake had fallen into.

The boy sensed the easing of tension in the minders. His head lolled back and he grinned in a funny lopsided way and a long trail of spittle fell from his mouth and bounced like elastic from his chin.

Loaded down with my calico snake bags, I began the long walk up to the snake house. Everything was churning in my head. I could feel the urgent beating of my heart. I was thinking of Roy and how quickly he'd turned dark. I was thinking of the serene way the tiger snake had lunged at him, of how quickly its venom must have spread like a terrible heat up his arm and into his chest.

And I was thinking of the cold bottle of milk, how it had gone so quickly from white to transparent as Roy drank it down, gulp gulp gulp, like it would cool the venom and give him life.

José Borghino

BLOOD ORANGE

L ondon at dawn. Twenty-four hours flying from Melbourne and I hadn't slept—like every other form of human comfort, sleep is *verboten* in economy. I felt crumpled and shop-soiled.

Steve was there, waiting in the crowd when I wheeled my trolley out of customs. It was almost six months since I'd seen him. I wasn't expecting him, but I'd hoped. He said we were booked on the train for Spain later that night. To stave off jetlag I decided I wouldn't sleep: I'd stay up and synchronise my body clock with Big Ben.

This was my first mistake.

Back at Steve's flat, we toasted our reunion with swigs of duty-free Johnny Walker. After a stodgy pub lunch and too many pints of Guinness we still had hours to kill before the train left, so we went to drinks with some of Steve's toffy English friends, people he'd skied with in Val d'Isère in France the previous season.

This was my second mistake.

They were rude, thick and privileged—never an attractive combination. The chaps baited us with gibes about beer-swilling colonials and our erotic preference for belching sheep. Haw! Haw! Haw! They did this while sucking tubes of Fosters and while their girlfriends huddled together in the corner of the room, nervous and annoyed, like a flock of newly-drenched ewes. Such ironies passed the boys by, however, without so much as wrinkling their collective cortex. They reminded me too clearly of their Melbourne clones: lawyers, doctors, politicians. I sank into a corner, muttering darkly about Gibraltar, and drank their Chivas Regal like there was no tomorrow.

This was my third mistake.

Just before midnight, the train pulled out of London towards sunny weather, good food, affordable wine and friends who cheered when police baton-charged British soccer hooligans. I was feeling better already.

The train soon filled with crewcut soldiers and unshaven guest-workers heading south for the holidays. Cramped into our rigid seats, unbroken sleep was too much to hope for. By the time we reached the Mediterranean two days later, my internal time zone was somewhere off the coast of Madagascar and I was not showing a lot of judgement.

My cousin, Alejo, was waiting to collect us at Alicante station. 'Great timing,' he said in Spanish, as I translated for Steve, 'tonight's the Feast of San Rafael at the village. Get your stuff in the boot and we'll be there in an hour.' La Nucia is the village down the coast where I and most of my mother's family were born. I had planned to visit it in a few weeks' time. I don't understand why I said yes. Maybe it was days of sleep deprivation on planes and trains. There was something automatic and involuntary about it—I felt like a turtle filled with leathery eggs, struggling up its original beach, hypnotised by the stars.

Two hours later we were leaning against a crumbling white-washed wall outside one of the garage bars which spring up in the alleyways of La Nucia every year at fiesta time. We were laughing and drinking Spanish coñac from plastic cups. There were five of us, dressed in black, like escapees from a funeral. Apart from Alejo, Steve and me, there were two of Alejo's musician friends: Agustín and Eusebio. Five crows swaying on a wire, looking for trouble.

It was eleven o'clock at night and the whole town was in the streets, weaving in and out of bars and cafés. Some of the older locals half-recognised me. They greeted my cousin by name but glanced suspiciously at me over their shoulders as they walked on. They saw my mother in my face but they couldn't be sure; it had been ten years since they'd seen either of us. Tomorrow I'd explain.

Alejo was the drummer and Agustín and Eusebio thrashed guitars in a punk band called Snot. It was 1980, Franco had been dead five years and everyone in Spain felt free to talk, look and behave like a prat. Some would later achieve pratdom. We met some of Alejo's friends and he lied to them, saying that the two Gringos were from a hot new Australian band called Cabramatta and that we were in Spain to cut a new LP. For once it didn't embarrass me that I spoke Spanish with an accent redolent of the area around the Pelaco factory in Melbourne rather than the olive plantations of Andalusia.

The members of Snot were eager to practise their English but, as they had learned the language by listening to Black Sabbath and Led Zeppelin songs, I found myself doing a lot of translating. Steve was explaining to Agustín, the bass guitarist, how to pronounce his name. 'Estib,' said Agustín confidently.

'Not b. V. Steevvvv.' Steve's lips danced across his face enacting the difference between a bilabial plosive and a labiodental fricative.

'Estif.' Agustín winked at me when Steve turned away.

'No, no, no,' Steve moaned. Agustín managed to grin and look unutterably sad at the same time. The rest of us laughed into our cups.

I asked Alejo why none of his band looked particularly punky, nothing like the green-haired, safety-pinned lostboys back in Oz. 'Gigs are scarce,' he explained. 'When we play at punk bars we tear a few t-shirts, gel up our hair and we're more rotten than Rotten. When we play rock 'n' roll we're called China and you'd swear the ghost of Elvis cruises the

Costa Blanca in a shot-up, pink cadillac. Sometimes we play techno-pop for the tourists and we're called Eclipse. We don't change but the name does.'

'Next you'll tell me you do bossa novas and Julio Iglesias covers for menopausal German mothers.'

'There's a new Danish colony up the coast. We're doing the opening as a kind of country-jazz-cajun-flamenco fusion band called De Puta Madre. Cousin, we'll blow those Vikings to Elsinore and back.'

'It's good to be flexible,' I said and had another drink.

As the alcohol slid down my throat, I looked up at the sky, a black cape smeared with stars. The horns of a crescent moon pricked Orion's backside. La Nucia was decked out in party lights and a breeze slid off El León Dormido, the mountain that crouched behind the village, bringing with it the smell of the desert. Now and then the sound of a splutter of fireworks followed by cheers drifted across the rooftops mingling with 'Staying Alive' and 'Y Viva España'.

'No, no e at the beginning. Just s. Sssteeevvv.' Steve had shifted his attention to Eusebio, the band's lead guitarist. 'Estip,' said Eusebio triumphantly. Steve groaned and drained his cup.

We sloped down to the end of the alley where the edges of the village tumbled into dark, terraced orange groves. The light reached only the first few trees on the terraces. The frogs and crickets held their own here against the amplified music splashing down from the village. Further into the grove, owls and prowling cats watched and waited.

I smelled the trees and the water in the irrigation ditches and I remembered one day, years ago, walking through these terraces with my father. He stopped to pick an orange from a tree and peeled it with a pocket knife. I had never seen a blood orange before. The rind was yellow but the flesh was streaked with red. I remembered how sweet the orange tasted, how its sweetness was heightened by the knowledge that my father had stolen it. I remembered how happy I had been, sharing that secret with him.

Agustín sat on a rock at the edge of the orange grove. He produced a joint from his pocket, ceremoniously blessed it and lit up. 'Substance abuse is an important but little-discussed subtext in *El Quijote*,' he said, smiling to himself, pleased with this, his latest theory, as he passed around the sweet-smelling hash joint. He held the smoke in his lungs for a while and then blew it out with a cackle like a demonic parrot. His hooked gipsy nose and the flaming red t-shirt under his black denim jacket adding to the effect.

'You're talking through your alto clef again,' Eusebio laughed. 'Didn't the Jesuits teach you anything? Quijote's an abstemious old fart. He hardly has a sip in the whole book.'

'I can read between the lines, Mr Finger-Picking-Good. The old codger's as high as a kite most of the time. Where's the first place Quijote goes?' Agustín continued. 'A pub. He gets sloshed and asks the barman to dub him "Sir Knight" in the morning. And the barman does it to get rid of him, because Quijote's drinking the place dry and can't pay the bill. It's obvious.'

'What's obvious,' Alejo piped in, 'is that you've been standing too close to the woofers. Your brains are loose.'

The joint had come back around to Agustín. He took it and dabbed spittle on the paper just below the glowing ash. 'Miguel de Cervantes Saavedra was the Timothy Leary of the 16th Century. Tune in, turn on, smoke the windmills!' We laughed as he held the joint to his mouth and inhaled.

'To Don Pisspot de la Mancha,' proclaimed Eusebio, holding up his coñac. 'To Don Pisspot,' we chimed.

I smoked and drank and the stars danced above me as I sat in this circle of friends. I imagined my father in 1955 beneath the same stars, a Frenchman in shorts. A tourist in La Nucia. I wondered if he'd come to the Feast of San Rafael and got drunk, if he'd gone dancing with my mother in one of the bars up the hill. The fireworks were louder and more frequent. A signal rocket spiralled up over the rooftops and exploded. Within an hour, the family groups that filled the village would all go home and the streets would be left to gangs from each of La Nucia's four districts. They would hunt for stragglers from opposing gangs and hurl buckets of firecrackers and rockets at them. We moved back up the hill towards the centre of town, while Agustín delivered his Theory of Levity as it related to drink, 'Everything that goes down must come up.'

Steve wanted to stay to see the firecracker fight, but if you weren't in a gang you were everyone's target, with no protection. Each year, tourists stopped off innocently in La Nucia on San Rafael's night and scuttled home with stories of crazed Spaniards rampaging after them, armed with dynamite. The best option was to make our way home and prepare for the inevitable hangovers. I was so stoned and drunk and tired I had to keep walking. I was sure that if I sat down I wouldn't get up again, and these boys were in no state to carry me. I'd be found the next morning, a small smouldering pile of ashes, the victim of a rocket attack, a sacrifice to San Rafael. I laughed as I staggered.

The end of the street we were walking up was blocked by a temporary wooden barricade. On the other side of the barricade, drenched by a number of powerful spotlights, was La Nucia's central square. I could hear the sounds of a crowd and there was the high smell of dung and urine-soaked hay in the air. I should have twigged.

Alejo was the first to reach the barricade and clambered up. None of us thought twice as we swung up and over. We landed in the sand on the other side and stopped dead. There, five metres away, as surprised to see us as we were to see it, was a very angry, very black Spanish bull. 'Fucking Jesus,' Steve said under his breath. I remember thinking at the time that he'd summed up the situation pretty well. The adrenalin kicked in. I suddenly felt very sober.

The bull was not fully grown. More of a calf, really. Probably a heifer. I didn't feel inclined to check. Its horns were enough to ponder. The lights and fireworks made the animal jumpy and the local trainee toreros had been running it around the arena for an hour, taunting it and flicking its hindquarters with ropes and sticks. Was the right word for it a 'novillo'? I remember regretting that I hadn't taken more notice of Hemingway.

At the opposite end of the square, instead of the wooden barricade which made up the three other sides of the stockade, a double palisade of steel poles had been built to support a viewing platform. The poles were set wide enough apart to allow people in and out of the arena but close enough to keep the bull inside.

The bull snorted. A second signal rocket burst directly above us. We ran. The bull charged. Alejo, Agustín, Eusebio and I made it to the palisade with steamy breath and a pair of horns tickling our behinds. But Steve had doubled back and was trying to climb over the wooden barricade. Furious at having missed us, the bull wheeled around and set Steve in its sights. Agustín ran into the ring straight at the bull and shouted in perfect English, 'Steve! Jump!' The bull stopped, Agustín stopped, everything stopped.

A third signal rocket arched slowly across the Milky Way above us and shattered in slow motion.

Steve scrambled over to safety. The bull turned on Agustín, who was now stranded in the middle of the ring. All he could do was run at an angle across the bull's path and keep turning. He watched the bull over his shoulder as he ran. The bull closed in but had to pivot to follow Agustín as he swerved around its horns, his right hand fending the animal's muzzle. A horn caught Agustín under the arm and, as the bull's head reared, Agustín was suddenly off the ground, being shaken like a rag and thudding into the bull's crown. I saw a flash of red across his chest as he slid off the bull's horn onto the ground.

Before Agustín hit the ground, the local toreros had run into the ring and drawn the bull's attention. Eusebio and Alejo dragged his body through the steel poles. We stood around him, wild-eyed and panting. Alejo examined his friend. The bull's horns had slid up along Agustín's side, ripping his red t-shirt and catching his denim jacket under the armpit. The force of the bull's charge had thrown Agustín in the air, but apart from some scratches, he was unharmed.

Agustín looked at Steve and said, 'No e at the beginning and a v at the end, eh amigo?'

Barbara Wels

ALCOHOL – the Plain FacTs

N ow I see him. He's sitting by the window of the newly refurbished Sceptre Bar, formerly the Sceptre and Crown Hotel. He is sitting with me, frowning. We were on our way to my sister's exhibition opening up on Panaroma Street, but the majestic gold letters on the roof of the hotel have pulled us in. Drawn us through the enlarged picture windows which open on to the street, for me to drink one mineral water to Paul's three Coronas. Amid the light, the especially good light, and the smell of newly polished floorboards, we are almost alone. Men with blurred tattoos and thinning cardigans balance on stools along the safety rail of the bar. Every few minutes their heads rotate, like laughing clowns in sideshow alley.

—I always thought, I say, this place had room for improvement.

—It's those old men I feel sorry for, says Paul.

I shake my head. He is drinking too much beer, too fast.

—Don't tell me, I sigh.

Pick a scene, any scene, and my lover will zoom into the part where sadness or injustice lurk.

—Ruthie, look at them, he says. They've probably been coming here every day for years, for decades. But none of these changes are for their benefit, to thank them for their patronage, to keep *them* coming back.

Paul, Champion of the Underdog. I know not to pick a fight with a champion whose arguments get faster and sharper when there's beer on the sidelines.

FACT: SPEECH AND WALKING ARE AMONG THE MOTOR SKILLS AFFECTED BY ALCOHOL. UNDER THE INFLUENCE, LOWERED LEVELS OF INHIBITION MAY CAUSE INTROVERTS TO BECOME EXTRAOR-DINARILY TALKATIVE, IF NOT AGGRESSIVE.

Now I don't. I don't see him at all. It's over. It's for the best. I cut my hair. I concentrate on details, such as money, more than my day job makes. One Saturday morning I put on my black job interview suit, adding a brooch of the Eiffel tower to the lapel, a stripey t-shirt, shoes that suggest I'm Capable of Anything. I catch a train down to Panaroma Street and sit in an Italian coffee bar to drink espresso and then, because it is offered, grappa. First burning and then installing bravado at the back of my throat, the grappa propels me down the street to put my best face forward. Towards a job interview mumbling Sceptre, Sceptre, September, scepticism, exceptional.

Now I see myself, in T.'s eyes. T., the manager of Sceptre, looks like he's swallowed a fly.

—Oh no, no, no, he says. We can't call you *Ruthie* . . .

T.'s exquisite diction and manner of speaking royally make his suggestion sound like a stage name, or a foreign landmark. I've always felt self-conscious in make-up and high heels, but the grappa forces me to ask.

—Are you telling me I look like RuPaul?

T. laughs.

—We're thinking of the streets of Paris, he says. We're thinking that haircut, Jean Seburg in Capri pants and a stripey t-shirt, the location, a version of her look, but not her name; Jean is definitely not you. So, Rue, when can you start?

I'm doing this for the money, and the decor. Rue. Rue de Rivoli. I can live with it.

—Tonight, I say. I can start tonight.

Case study 1
Paul, aged 27, would spend money on beer before rent or

new saucepans, if given half a chance. His collection of (allegedly) exotic beer bottles has grown to unmanageable proportions. At night he drinks Remy Martin, and then refuses to brush his teeth because it will ruin the cognac aftertaste. At times charming, generous and imaginative when drunk, he is equally prone to ruminate on the darker aspects of Life, casting aspersions on the insight, values and ethics of those around him. As his hangovers become more frequent, his girlfriend refuses to compensate for his behaviour by making him poached eggs for breakfast, as she used to. She is evasive. She decides she can't change him. Claims he is becoming what she feared, but won't elaborate.

I don't see him, now that it's over. I see others, in his place, in my place, across the bar. Customers supported by the interior features of the Sceptre, juggling their poisons, their medicines, in glasses and bottles. Patrons laughing, moving closer to one another, kissing, waving their arms with generous and dubious offers, leaning, arguing, falling, rearranging, reacquainting, rushing in and out of doors and dancing because today hasn't really happened and there's no official tomorrow. I work in a fog of other people's movements, work for cash, work for a plane fare, work to eventually forget I ever did this. The people I serve are coming here to forget too, and what I serve them dulls and rearranges the links between one experience and another. It is my job to remember what it is that makes each of them forget. If I make a mistake they will start remembering and this is not what they are paying me for. I must remember; I am here so they can forget. So I can pack my bags and get myself overseas, to forget the Sceptre, these people, and the circumstances that brought me here.

The roll call of staff at Sceptre is like an alphabet, amended by T. Apart from Fifi, everyone has a one syllable name. These people are professionals. These are no second jobs. Everyone is pale, everyone wears make-up. Apart from me, everyone sleeps by day and lives by night. T. alternately coddles and bosses us. His sense of style goes all the way down to the design on the promotional matches. He likes everything to be a certain way. He keeps seven white cats and is particular about our style of dress, and the tone we are to use with customers.

—Be friendly, he says, yet aloof, not too familiar.

If there was more money in it, T. would have worked in theatre.

FACT: PULSE RATE AND BLOOD PRESSURE INCREASE WITH EVERY DROP OF ALCOHOL. OVERINDULGENCE CAN OVERWHELM THE CIRCULATION LEADING TO A STATE OF SHOCK OR LOSS OF CONSCIOUSNESS.

I feel like crying, standing before the mirror in my black trousers and a *Coke Adds Life* t-shirt. I'm too tired. I don't want to go to work, my legs won't hold me up. I want to sleep for thirteen hours and wake up as I'm clearing customs at Bombay airport. To go to India, to Nepal, to Turkey, to France I must go to work these extra nights. (Brace yourself, Ruthie. And fast, or you'll be late.) Because it is hot, because

I need something to send me on my way, I drink two Gordons and tonics. With lemon moons and cracked ice in a tumbler the colour of the night sky. Gin casts my mind to women carrying children they do not want. Women in another time sucking on bottles of it and immersing their bodies in boiling hot baths, and trying to get rid of babies.

Case study 2

Charles, aged 55, sits at the same table every evening. The hotel is not what it used to be, but he's standing his ground. One hand for his glass, one hand covering the hole in the head of the beige Guide Dog for the Blind which is chained to the wall. Until it's closing time or he's run out of money (whichever comes first) Charles gives the dog a gold coin for every drink he buys. He'll talk to me, to the dog, to the air about Avril for hours. I suppose Avril's his ex-wife. Everything was all right when she was there, he says. I see the two of them living in Surfers Paradise, in a block of flats with the sea beating their ears into sleep. Pouring Charles pot after pot of Victoria Bitter, I wonder; was it before or after that he realised he loved her?

Whether or not it's a wives' tale (it's always the old wives not the new ones who generate these approaches to life) it is not a good idea to drink gin before going to work. Dry those glasses and wipe down the bar and remember, girl, that juniper berries only make you perceive hidden wounds.

FACT: ALCOHOL IS A DEPRESSANT.

Just a lift, a little lift before my Saturday night shift at Sceptre starts. Here's an easy pick-me-up, passed on by Z., a former altar boy. Take a slice of lemon with the rind cut off, add a yin sprinkling of fresh coffee grounds, a yang touch of white sugar, rest the arrangement on your tongue like a communion wafer and hold fast while you take a shot of Smirnoff. Brrrr. Mmmmm. Wide awake, sucking on that sweet shivery hit of vodka, citrus and caffeine. One is ample. As the books say, all things in moderation.

Case study 3
Jade, aged 23, can always be found by the pool table, laughing, drinking Bacardi and Coke, wearing a blue t-shirt with two capital A's inside a golden triangle. A for Alcoholics. A for Anonymous. I have never seen her leave Sceptre with the same boy.

I watch legions of customers not thinking or caring who sees what they do, playing as if they're invisible. There's posing, that's meant to be observed, responded to, but it's the details I watch, when it's slow at Sceptre, which is not often. I'm amazed by what I see, and relieved and sometimes worn down by what people do. By what they need and how they try to obtain it. I watch strangers, familiar faces, acquaintances, friends. We all do, Z. and E. and the others and me. Don't look now, we say, but the guy with the tattooed head is ... We exchange snippets of character, plot and dialogue from one episode to the next. The girl in the AA t-shirt stars in our soap opera. It's not malicious, it's delicious. I don't talk about karma. I am beginning to understand the secret of alcohol. As the books say, I live for today.

FACT: PROLONGED USE OF ALCOHOL CAUSES SHRINKING OF THE CEREBRAL CORTEX, AFFECT-ING THOUGHT PROCESSES AND KNOWLEDGE CENTRES. TOO MUCH KNOWLEDGE IS A DANGER-OUS THING. A DECLINE INTO MUDDY IGNORANCE HAS ITS BENEFITS.

Drink, drunk. As a skunk, as a strunkey, as a monkey, as drunk as a monk. As the night wears on, my customers' hearts move up to their sleeves. I can see everything in them straining for a good fight, or a half-decent fuck, or a shot of freedom. As the night wears on, I have to close myself down in case they want it from me. Sobriety depletes my generosity, my interest in the varieties of the human condi-tion, my compassion, my tolerance. I give nothing out that's not paid for and count the hours until I'm finished, the months until I'll be gone.

Case study 4
Elouisa, aged 27, demonstrates her capacity for tequila slammers. Sceptre is so busy, it takes this customer two drinks and a few glances before we recognise each other.
—Omigod! You look exactly the same!
Elouisa is out on a hen's night. Now she is a dentist and her older sister just had her fifth baby and she has just found out that she may be a diabetic. But she's not thinking about that tonight. Then some of the other hens come over

and in an expedition of little black dresses they are leaving now, heading off to a club in the city.

Jed is asking Do you know her? and I escape into the walk-in fridge for a shot of Wild Turkey. Brrrmph. That's better. So my old school friend spends her days examining people's mouths. Elouisa the Fang Carpenter. Who was next? Are you right? At the bar serving people drinks I'm suddenly noticing teeth. Pointy and brown and white and uneven varieties, and a sexy boy with a gap between his two front ones. I remember something Elouisa and I shared. How on Saturday afternoons we used to go to Miss Brompton's house to study for the Temperance Exam and Certificate. How Miss Brompton gave us all the facts about alcohol, and tested our knowledge. How at three-thirty old Mrs Brompton would emerge from her bungalow in the garden, and we'd have strawberry Tina wafer biscuits, and milk from crystal goblets. Did I ever sit that exam?

FACT: A QUALITY WINE IS THE IDEAL ACCOMPANIMENT TO ALL SOCIAL OCCASIONS.

Elouisa is sober, the next time she comes into Sceptre, but I'm still frantically busy.

—We could go out for dinner, she suggests, catch up.

Will she remind me to floss? Stop it, Ruthie, stop feeling inadequate. Okay, so here we are eating Thai with a bottle of 1994 Plantagenet Omrah Vineyard Chardonnay. Elouisa talks about her plans to build a mud-brick house and how the reception centre caught fire during her cousin's wedding celebrations. I describe the Sceptre, and my other life; where I wear a suit, where people are restrained and outbursts of emotion are reserved for the photocopier. We work our way on to men, living arrangements and people we once knew. We laugh a lot, drink more, collude in eating dessert.

—Do you remember, asks Elouisa, Mrs Brompton's teeth?

—Pardon?

—Mrs Brompton had the most beautiful teeth I ever saw. Miss Brompton told me it was because her mother had never in her whole life touched liquor.

—I remember the glasses she served milk in, I say. And the facts. I liked the facts about alcohol. I liked learning them, and reeling them off. I liked words like cortex and medulla and cerebellum.

—The only thing I can really remember is Mrs Brompton's teeth, smiles Elouisa. And from what I know now, I'm sure they were dentures.

Case study 5

Yukio, aged 35, uses Johnnie Walker Black Label to improve his English. He has an import business, works twelve to fifteen hours a day, but reveals that his shyness gets in the way of his fluency, in the way of business. At Sceptre he becomes infinitely more sociable per glass. I watch him make friends for the night. I watch his laugh make others laugh. I watch him with his head down, in intimate conversation with strangers, especially red-haired women. They are not talking about the spirulina and green tea he imports.

If I drink champagne, pardon me, sparkling wine, the bubbles take away my sense of gravity, make me six centimetres taller by inserting air pockets between my shoes and the carpet. The space between my shoes and the carpet leaves roaming room for T.'s seven cats. The cats think I am a tree and they clamber up my arms purring with a few ouches on the way. But it all ends up in stroking and the bringing out of soft and loving sides from customer to cat to me, which spills over into the general atmosphere. I'm already tall, with sparkling wine I'm larger than life, but quick and I make people laugh. Also, when I am six centimetres taller, I can look over and into my customers' heads and see what makes them tick. Such knowledge gives me an accurate ability to flirt and flatter. The softness of cats plus accurate flattery increases generosity. For me, generosity spills over to increase the incidence of tips per hour. This brings me closer to the price of my air ticket. Closer and closer.

FACT: TRUE FRENCH CHAMPAGNE IS THE MOST DELIGHTFUL DRINK OF ALL. ON AN EMPTY STOMACH ITS EFFECTS ARE RAPID. DILATION OF THE BLOOD VESSELS MAKES THE SKIN FEEL HOT AND FLUSHED, AND THE DRINKER IS FLOODED WITH FEELINGS OF CONFIDENCE AND WELL-BEING.

Yukio is in the shower and I am lying in his bed, dangling my arms into a bedside drawer, looking for protection. I find a Japanese / English phrase book. I feel like I'm ten years old and looking in the dictionary for the word screw. Yukio's phrase book includes translations for *More, baby* and *I think I am falling in love with you.* I'm trying to make sense of the Japanese pronunciations when Yukio lies down beside me. My customer's skin is smooth, almost hairless, and he still tastes of the drinks I have measured out for him. Sweet Yukio, sweet sex. But I can't stay all night, I have to go home to get up for my day job. For business, nods Yukio, massaging my neck until the taxi comes, folding the fare into my hand.

Case study 6

Antonio, aged 62, drinks Campari and soda every day after work. He is a barber. Someone offered him an apprentice-ship when he was fifteen and needing something to do, that's what he did. In his day, he says, you did not have the choice. Maybe he could have been a carpenter, that's what he would have liked. The beautiful furniture he could have made. He does not really listen to his customers, he says, the things they tell him. But it is nice at the end of the day to have a drink and say that is the end of that. And he loves his wife and his children and his grandchildren and next year he will go back to Italy, for the first time since he was a boy.

For business, at Sceptre, I remember to remember what everyone drinks. My customers spend their days trimming hair, importing Japanese health foods, selling plane tickets, making films, dressing shop windows, keeping the world as we know it going. At the end of the day, they come to Sceptre to feel better about it all. I keep my job by selling them something that might make them forget. And then, at some time when I need to make myself feel better, I'll go to them (or someone like them) for a trim, for an escape route, for a story, for a t-shirt with a different slogan.

FACT: WE MAKE EACH OTHER FEEL BETTER, WE MAKE EACH OTHER FEEL WORSE.

Antonio comes to me, and I go to him. At Antonio's there is no hairdresser talk, nothing personal about either of us, and nothing about hair or hair care products. Just the basic information, the vibration of the shears, the last details with the scissors adding up to a standard $10 boy haircut. Antonio does not do appointments. Every second Friday I turn up and flick through *Australasian Post* until it is my turn. I follow my horoscope and Captain Cash, who *helps the needy and belts the greedy*. Paul is an avid Captain Cash fan. I wonder if he still writes to Captain Cash, from time to time, to test his powers of judgement. Darryl of Victoria sounds suspiciously like Paul.

I will never forget you. Yukio's pronunciation is perfect, when he tells me he is returning to Kyoto. I have clearly sidestepped the law that guarantees falling madly in love just before an indefinite overseas trip. I go clubbing with E. and Z. and Jed. Irregular boyfriends to go cruising with, while they look for boyfriends. After preening and drinking and dancing and amyl and more dancing we feel so much better. They call me Goddess Rue because they know I'm saving up to go to India and find myself. They all want to go to San Francisco and lose themselves. But they are hopeless at saving, Darling, hopeless.

Case study 7

Ruthie, 26, develops a fondness for vibrant red wines spiced with pungent oak, particularly when taken before bed, no matter how early, no matter how late. Drink, drunk, may as well finish the bottle. Her father worked and drank hard, drinks still, works no longer, perhaps it's been in her blood all along, and these days she works hard. Fifty-five or sixty hours a week sometimes; in need of a perfect, oaky bridge between a long day at the office and a frantic night behind the bar at Sceptre and a ticket to somewhere else. Perhaps it's the most satisfying, available way to end the day and say that is that. Serenity, courage and an antidote for feeling better and worse at the same time.

Tomorrow I will stop drinking. Or the day after that. At least, stop drinking this much. Well, sometime in the future, as the books say, this too will pass. I will stop, or cut down. My increasing pleasure in celebrating and preparing and compensating for events with toasts and aperitifs and night-caps, really, it's just a phase. Like the satisfaction I once gleaned from Mrs Brompton's plain facts and her Tina wafer biscuits, and later from Bavarian dancing, and from collecting broken kitchen appliances, and from being with Paul. Pick a scene, any scene, Paul zooming into the part where sadness or injustice lurks, drinking to feel better or worse about it. I didn't see that before, couldn't see the truth for the facts. The plain truth that everyone needs some kind of antidote, to replace the last one.

FACT: NOW I DON'T SEE HIM. I LIFT MY GLASS AND DRINK FOR MOOD, NOT TASTE. FAR BETTER, I HAVE LEARNED, TO CHOOSE MY EMOTION, THAN HAVE ONE CHOOSE ME.

Terry Serio

THE PASSENGER

'**F**ucking pollution,' the Passenger thought, as he sat
in a cab stuck on Crown Street surrounded by
thousands of equally impeded vehicles silently
farting idling gas into the early evening air.

'Smash on the Bridge,' mumbled the driver.

'What?'

The cabbie glanced into the rear-view mirror, revealing
a bored eye. 'Smash on the Bridge,' he mumbled again.

'Fuck!' The Passenger threw the cabbie the fare and stepped out into a steady Sydney drizzle. A businessman holding a briefcase over his head scuttled through the maze of softly vibrating metal and leapt into the cab. 'Expensive place to sit, mate!'

The Passenger walked between the cars. The drivers stared blankly ahead. 'Who the fuck is running this country,' he grumbled to himself as the cars idled and the radios played. The Bridge loomed in the distance. Ahead the lights changed and a motorcyclist threaded his way through the traffic.

'Lucky prick! I'd get one of those if I weren't so dangerous,' thought the Passenger, topping up his blood alcohol level from a flask out of his jacket. He felt good walking. In fact, for the first time in ages he felt powerful. He'd taken control—sort of. Then he felt embarrassed by his indulgence, doubly so when he realised someone was staring at him. A bloated wino. 'Reeagh!' said the wino, giving him a blast with both red eyes. Was it recognition?

The Passenger, less powerful now, edged his way around the man with the chilled bottle of metho and slowly backed away. He had a sudden yearning for his punk days when that kind of intimidation was an effective tool against the disco crowd. He glanced back at his abandoned cab still idling in the traffic and felt a sad affinity with it, as though it were a lamb slowly being shunted onto the killing floor.

He hurled the empty flask into a bin and walked into the nearest bar. Dance music throbbed around the walls. A small white Mazda coupe with a roll-cage and wide tyres floated past outside ... the same beat, throbbing ... the driver unmoved ... staring.

The Passenger felt everything was floating. He faced the bar. Saliva filled his mouth in anticipation. The room was dark and strange, and looked as though the owner had secured the licence halfway through demolition and in a fit of budget-driven brilliance had said, 'Leave it—that's enough. I love it!' then gone and bought a welder, some large truck springs, a heap of crappy furniture from Tempe tip and ventured fearlessly into interior design.

Fuck it. He needed a drink. He sat on what he hoped was a bar stool, took out a twenty and looked expectantly at the barman. Extremely tight T-shirt, bead choker, hint of goatee and moustache, hair cut very short with a fringe like Richard Burton in a Roman epic. He thought he looked gay but had long ago given up having opinions about such things after many a dinner-party-mauling over what he thought was innocent observation. The barman came over, raised his eyebrows and pointed at him.

The Passenger raised his voice above the music. 'VB please, mate!' Mate. Would that be considered a homosexual overture? Should he apologise? Retract? He didn't know how to behave anymore.

'Three-fifty thanks, mate.'

He breathed a sigh of relief. Just a can. No glass and only three-fifty. The Passenger felt good. A good old VB. In the up-market bars where he usually drank, he could never bring himself to order anything less than a five dollar Peroni. He smiled wistfully to himself. As a pogo-ing intellectual superior, marching to the beat of the Sex Pistols and the

Clash, you wouldn't be caught dead drinking anything but a VB.

His hand went to his waist. There it was. The roll. How often did he inadvertantly check it? What did he think—that it would suddenly leave him? He should probably drink less beer. He looked around. The place was filling up.

He signalled the barman. 'Same again ... and a vodka no ice.' He downed his beer and undid his top button. (He always did up his top button these days—no tie, just the button.) He slid off his perch and casually glanced around again. No one was watching ... the barman was flat-out. So he tried it. A quick pogo. Him and his roll. He knew what he was doing but the roll had no fucking idea. It started way too late, immediately grabbing for the hips it knew so well then joining in on the landing in an appallingly brave but belated effort. The Passenger caught his own miserable expression in the broken-tiled mirror behind the bar. His once-full, sensuous mouth looked ridiculous below his wide-set eyes which made him look like a rabbit in headlights.

'What was that?' A female voice. He heard it above the music, then thought he'd imagined it. Caught in headlights. A tap on his arm. He turned and saw the most startling creature. 'Were you pogo-ing?' Her eyebrow rings glinted in the dull light. Long braids sprouted from her head. He noticed her face and neck were lightly perspiring and a strong floral smell seemed to steam out of her colourful, wispy attire. 'I'm talking to you!'

The Passenger looked into the first open face he had seen in about fourteen years and felt like running screaming into the traffic. Sadly it was still moving far too slowly to do him any harm and the thought of a mere bruising seemed pointless, so he said, 'Yes. I was.'

Her eyes were laughing. 'Just the one, was it?'

The last frayed guy-rope holding aloft the languidly fluttering flag of his youth gave way ... the barman delivered another round of drinks and somewhere Sid made another futile 'gob' for his generation.

Still observing him, she took a slow mean slug from her plastic bottle of water. 'Nice face,' she said.

His head was already turning before his brain realised she was talking about him. He looked at her and another thing happened that hadn't happened in a long time. His dick moved. No nudity. No stroking. No thoughts of erotica ... it had moved of its own accord.

'Let's have a bong,' she said and walked out the door.

In one smooth unforgotten action he took a giant sip of his VB, slipped it into his coat pocket ... gulped the vodka, and followed her past the doorman into the rain. He marvelled at the 'second nature' of this concealment and carrying of unfinished beer—a leftover from his student days when beer conservation was an imperative. Again he felt he was floating and at the same time being dragged—towards what? Should he turn away? No. He was always turning away, turning the other cheek, turning the handle that drove the generator that lit up other people's lives. Fuck it.

She went into an alleyway and stood outside what looked to be a derelict three-story building. She tugged on a long piece of nylon cord. He looked up, a face appeared and then a set of keys dropped down.

'Don't you have keys?' he said.

'That's Lacy. She never goes out.'

He followed her up a set of stairs with no railings, wide stairs, ruined cornices and damp walls ... *Bladerunner*! Maybe she and her 'Lacy' were freaks who were intent on kicking the living shit out of him. Suddenly he was nervous. He noticed as she climbed that she looked very athletic.

'Come on,' she beckoned as she walked onto the landing on the top floor. She smiled at him as he turned lagging and faced her up the last level of stairs. 'Do you live here?' The Passenger tried to disguise his rising panic.

She just laughed and took his hand. 'Enter the vortex,' she said and pushed him through a heavy wooden door.

'Jesus.' Dark. Heavy techno music, purple floor lights, a couple of computers with psychedelic screen-savers, a tinsel-covered trapeze hanging from a rafter. In the corner, a kitchen. A wave of relief. There's sanity in a kitchen. A stove, a sink, a fridge. Yes. 'You've got a kitchen,' he said.

Smiling, she took his beer, poured it down the sink and filled two tumblers with vodka from the freezer. She moved right into his personal space, slid her hands into his, put her lips about a centimetre from his mouth and said quietly, 'Relax, mister.' She kissed him on the lips. The Passenger thought he'd been hit by lightning. She pulled back slightly and drank. Then made a cat like sound in the back of her throat and kissed him again. He was floating high above the ground like a lit-up zeppelin and this time someone else was turning the handle. The vodka tasted good. She started to push him gently backwards and with each push she would take a step to catch up and again plant her soft lips on his, then pull back.

'What about the bong?' he asked.

'Broken,' she said and started to undo his belt. His loins reacted in a way they hadn't since Bruna del'Orto put her hand down his pants out the back at his first school dance. He could hardly breathe.

She pushed the Passenger down onto a velvet covered mattress, threw back her drink and fell on him.

'What about Lacy?' he gasped.

She sat up, smiling wickedly. 'Surfing the net,' she said and slipped out of her top. Pierced nipples. His dick went limp. He wanted out. His dick was gone and he felt stupid.

With the tiniest smile she took his soft white hand and held it to her face. She nuzzled it and kissed it and guided it over her body to those rings. She moved his fingers gently over her nipples and she began to mewl quietly. Her lower body started moving softly, rhythmically—she was arousing herself. She was using him to arouse herself. She found him attractive? He couldn't believe it.

She began to undo his shirt. He stiffened. He'd always felt self-conscious about his hairy body. His wife was always saying 'Why don't you get a wax?' and leaving her glossy magazines open at selected pages showing perfectly formed hairless men. He'd taken to not removing his shirt in public. He even felt his doctor looking at him in disgust. Hirsute. Simian.

He tried to stop the undoing but she looked at him and shook her head and continued her work. 'Mmmm,' she moaned and placed her hands on his chest. She leant forward and rubbed her cheeks on his chest hair, then caught the hair around his nipples in her teeth and tugged gently.

Incredibly, silent tears ran down the Passenger's cheeks and onto the velvet throwover. Somehow this strange girl knew and raised her head and licked them from his eyes.

He pulled her to him and kissed her. And at that moment he loved her. His dick was hard. He felt powerful. So this was empowerment.

They wrestled him out of his clothes and she lowered herself onto him, moving firmly and purposefully against him until, out of nowhere, she orgasmed. She seemed to swoon, her head on his chest . . . nibbling his neck . . . licking him . . . moving her hips again . . .

'My God.' The Passenger was in ecstacy. She enjoyed sex so completely. His own wife seemed to enjoy it about as much as trying on dresses (which was quite a lot) and used the same facial expression.

'Don't come in me,' she breathed. Her metal-enhanced nipples rubbed deliciously against his chest. His dick was as hard as rock. Her strange perfume transported him. ' . . . Aaagh!' he yelped as his chest hair became caught, tangled tight on a nipple ring. She shrieked. 'Oh my god, I've hurt her,' he thought. She shrieked again and her body started convulsing. His chest hair pain completely disappeared in the depth of her ecstacy and suddenly he was on the verge of orgasm. He pulled out and she massaged him to ejaculation. And what ejaculation! He felt delirious as she lay spent on top of him giggling softly and holding his dick. She didn't mind his semen at all. If his wife got it on her hand or stomach she would waft into the bathroom wearing that 'I don't think so' look she also reserved for those shop assistants whose 'Try on?' suggestions were inappropriate.

They lay together for an hour. He had been aware of someone moving around the warehouse, had heard floor-boards creaking. He thought of the flats and warehouses of his student days. The pits. Lucky to have milk, empty VB cartons everywhere. Middle-class boys doing it hard ... mothers coming over to pick up the washing. Pathetic.

Something bumped the bed. 'Oh, thanks, Lace.' A skinny girl in a wheelchair handed her the vodka. 'Can you get me some scissors? We're stuck.' Lacy smiled and wheeled herself away. They struggled onto their sides and passed the bottle. They didn't talk and he felt no pressure to. Lacy returned with the scissors, handed them to her, and rolled away again. The Passenger went to take them. 'Not yet,' she said and hid them playfully behind her back. She made him feel like a child. Open. Happy. No pressure.

The coming week had plenty in store. Dinner tonight at a Woollahra terrace, dinner tomorrow night in a brasserie with bentwood chairs, the night after that was ... dinner at his wife's best friend's Whale Beach getaway with all the gang—the husbands all going on about their new BMWs and property investments, the wives smiling proudly. He'd once had a pair of Doc Martens ten-holers. He drifted into sleep.

'We're going to be late!' He blinked his eyes open. His wife stood over him frowning. 'Honestly!' she said in that exasperated tone. He just lay there staring at her, clawing his way up out of the grey folds of sleep.

'We-are-going-to-be-late.' She spun on her beautifully turned ankles and huffed out of the room. The Passenger sat up on the edge of the bed, bewildered. He looked around—familiar same clothes, his house, but a strange scent in his nostrils—and stood up and wandered around the room, trembling slightly. Had he gone mad? Outside he heard his wife's car. He was overcome with sadness. Now she was leaning on the horn. He picked up his jacket, grabbed a fresh flask from the liquor cupboard and walked like a zombie out to her car.

'Your top button's undone!' She glared at him angrily as she accelerated away. 'What on earth's the matter with you? You've been in the most ridiculous mood since you got home!'

He couldn't speak. He floated. He was a Woody Allen character with no dialogue. It had seemed so tangible.

They arrived. He followed her up the quarry-tile steps. No. He was sucked into her slipstream as she stormed—heels clattering irritably—up those perfectly laid quarry-tile steps. More and more he felt he existed in that dangerous yet sheltered area just behind the lethal tearing wheels of her semitrailer personality.

After the doorbell, a strange ritual of repeated pecking kisses and false compliments—then a race for the champagne. All the men were drinking beer. He opted for red wine. The women sat with their lipstick smears like brand names on their champagne flutes.

Suddenly he was singled out. 'Someone said they saw you in a gay bar last night.' The Passenger spilt his wine all over his shirt. Everyone laughed. 'Go and rinse that under the tap or it will stain. Much as I'd be amused at his turning gay he was at home at six last night. As always.'

He looked at his wife across the table and felt, as always, that her life was lived behind some tinted protective glass. Sure, the tint changed and with it her aura—and often in that light she appeared quite beautiful—but fourteen years of knocking before entering? He stood up and edged self-consciously around his chair. He needn't have. The conversation had moved on—so had the headlights.

The bathroom was beautifully appointed. A little pile of folded fluffy dark green hand towels, miniature glycerine soaps, bottles of expensive perfumes and body sprays impeccably placed. The Passenger felt tired and looked at his expression in the mirror. Dead face. A big blot of red wine on the front of his shirt. He removed his jacket, pulled the shirt off and stretched the area around the stain into a tight flat square and ran it under the tap. He watched the stain disappear into the sink. He took the heavy black and chrome hair dryer off a hook next to the mirror and began drying the shirt.

His eyes drifted to his roll. It seemed to be smaller. Drifting. A lot smaller. With a jolt like grabbing for forgotten keys or sunglasses he felt his left breast. He closed his eyes. He felt the heat flow out of his body, to be replaced by just one sense—a sickening ache in his gut—in his loins—in the place some people call their heart. He felt the flesh where there should have been thick hair. He took chest hair between two fingers, threaded it through and felt the edge of the cut.

How long did he stand there? God knows. Like

watching the Clash live in London, time stood still—he could remember nothing. Caught in some soundless slow-motion. Hundreds of black leather jackets moving as one.

He became aware of an incessant knocking on the door. Distant. Annoying. Now a voice. As he turned he caught one last expression in the mirror. He looked younger. Happier. He took the beautiful brass door handle and twisted it. The door swung open.

His wife stood there, silently weeping. Leaking from the eyes was a more apt expression, he thought. 'My poor Darling!' she sobbed.

He put on his jacket and looked down the dark hallway into the well-lit dining room at all the sad expressions. My God. When she was upset, they were upset.

He decided to go for a walk. The atmosphere in there was stifling. He fingered his chest hair and edged around his wife, then took the quarry-tiles two at a time. He glanced back and saw his wife waving at him and trying to speak— but he was moving too fast now and the air was rushing into his ears. He felt a real urge to go to the Bridge.

It appeared to him as some extra-terrestrial craft that had clamped itself onto the two small headlands on either side of the harbour. Sometimes it would hold the whole city to ransom. As an engineering feat it was a marvel, although they didn't make it easy to climb. Getting around the 'spike' gate and hanging your arse out over the traffic four metres below could be nerve-wracking. The Passenger loved it at the top—the first time he did it was with Nick, Neil and Sean after a Sunnyboys gig at the Zoo in William Street, it was raining and slippery and they were all pissed and stoned. The red light was like a warm fire. He drank from his flask, stood right on the edge of the eastern arch and looked out past the Opera House and beyond to the coast, a faint glow of orange was beginning to appear.

'Hey, mister!' He turned, smiling. It was her. She looked demure. Her facial rings glowed red under the light of the Bridge and she smiled that knowing smile. Their secret tryst. He smiled across at her, kissed his finger and placed it carefully against his left breast. She looked back at him with indulgent love and blew a kiss.

The Passenger smiled and leapt off the bridge. As he floated down to the water he was annoyed to find that Rod Stewart's 'Sailing' had suddenly appeared in his head. Below him an old harbour tug floated by, powerful engines pounding, smoke spewing from its funnel into the early morning air. Just before he blacked out and less than twenty metres from the water, the Passenger thought, 'Fucking pollution'.

Margaret McClusky

Sex, Lies and Psychiatry

Elizabeth liked Jeremy. He was a pretty boy, with the sort of smile orthodontists would give their eye teeth to take credit for.

'If you really, sincerely want to give up,' said Jeremy, 'really, sincerely want to, I'll keep on seeing you.'

Elizabeth stared at the triffid-like plastic potplant in the corner of the office, and wondered why all psychiatrists seemed to have such bad taste. But at least there wasn't a couch. She'd been on enough of them and none of them had done any good.

'I can be your companion—your professional companion,' Jeremy quickly corrected himself as Elizabeth felt the rush of blood up her cheeks, 'on that journey.'

Elizabeth saw the base camp at Mount Everest. Hand-in-hand they made their way across the snow. When she slipped, he helped her up again. When he slipped, she got him to his feet again. She had always liked Jewish men. One of the nicest things about them was that they never talked about football. Only about second generation survival guilt. And their mothers.

'If you fall off the wagon, don't beat up on yourself,' Jeremy went on, smiling his perfect smile. 'Just start again the next day, and keep on coming back here.'

Elizabeth considered. The suicidal fantasies had been getting worse and worse. And she liked the permissiveness of the deal. She didn't have to be perfect, a good girl, a tedious god-botherer. Or a wowser. Like her mother. She was still a bad girl, could still be a bad girl, and recover.

'And if you start feeling really bad between appointments, really bad, all bets are off,' Jeremy continued, opening his palms. Though she would have liked to correct the cliché, she could still see that his hands were perfect too. 'You should phone me. Page me and I'll phone you back.'

Elizabeth phoned at five o'clock in panic. Ten days off the bottle and she knew she was crashing. The hospital switchboard played muzak for five minutes. She was finally permitted to leave a message. She waited half an hour, her heart lurching around in her chest, then ran around the corner and bought a bottle of Scotch. She left another message at the hospital. Another half-hour passed. She was sweating. Another message. Another half-hour. Then she opened the Scotch.

She drank half a glass and began to relax. She drank another half-glass and began to think all the bad things she'd ever thought about the medical profession in general and shrinks in particular. Obviously the pretty boy with the perfect teeth and the perfect hands hadn't meant a word he'd said. She began her plans for suicide.

She woke at seven, poured a Scotch and phoned the hospital.

'This is Dr McKenzie,' she said. 'I paged Dr Gold three times last night and he hasn't returned my call. Would you phone him at home and have him call me *at once?*'

'Oh yes doctor,' the switchboard said, flustered. 'I can't think why . . .'

'Thank you *so* much,' Elizabeth said in the voice she had perfected for dealing with idiots, and hung up.

The bottle of Scotch was three-quarters empty. Pretty boys full of promises and no intentions had always been her downfall. She picked up her suicide plan and began to write down who got what. She would leave the Peter Caddy pastels to Alice, and Kate Ryan's nude to her latest ex, who had always liked it, lying on top of her and stroking away. The books would take a bit of sorting out, and then there were the letters. She had almost finished the list of letters to write and had finished the bottle when the phone rang.

'Thank you so much for calling back,' Elizabeth said in the voice she reserved for professional idiots.

'I'm sorry about last night. The batteries in my pager were flat. I didn't realise ...'

'You complete moron. You call yourself a professional and you can't even work a fucking pager!'

A child was having a temper tantrum in Jeremy's background. 'You are a complete joke. I suppose you only got into medicine on your third try and your lecturers thought that, in the unlikely event of you scraping through, you might *just* be good enough to do psychiatry.'

'Yes, Elizabeth ...'

'You *are* a joke. Like that Cook and Moore thing, "*Yes, Elizabeth, you think that I'm a joke.*"'

'Elizabeth ...'

'You can't work a pager, you employ a secretary who's about as efficient as Daffy Duck, you ... you ... you're so fucking stupid I'm surprised you can find your way out of the house, let alone treat ...'

'You're obviously very angry, Elizabeth. I'm sorry that ...'

'"You're obviously very angry, Elizabeth",' she said, draining the dregs of the Scotch. 'Of all the therapists I've been to, you are the worst. A joke. A complete waste of time.'

'Yes, yes, yes ...' She heard the irritation in his usually monotonic voice. She smiled. She was finally getting at him.

'Let me give you a piece of advice.' The toddler from hell was still wailing in the background. 'Go and get voice lessons. You have the most boring voice I've ever heard. I can recommend a good speech therapist, although even she'd find you pretty heavy going.'

'Elizabeth, why did you want me to phone you?'

'Because I'm going to kill myself.'

'Look, come in this morning and we'll talk about it . . .'

'I'm not coming in this morning. I *told* you. I'm going to kill myself.'

'You've got an appointment tomorrow. I'll expect to see you then.'

'When I don't show up, you'll know I jumped. Now say goodbye nicely. *Doctor.*'

'I'm not saying goodbye.' The agitation in his voice was growing stronger. 'I'm not going to say "Bye Bye, Elizabeth. Have a nice death." I won't . . .'

'Goodbye,' Elizabeth said pleasantly, and hung up.

She bought another bottle of Scotch. She sat comfortably on the couch and gazed out the window. It was a beautiful day. A lovely day to die. She was looking forward to it. She started planning her funeral.

She felt a pang of guilt about the flowers. She wanted loads and loads of flowers. On the other hand, she should ask for donations in lieu to the Cat Protection Society. She chewed her pen, then wrote:

FUNERAL ARRANGEMENTS
1. Lots of flowers.
2. White Ladies Funeral Directors.
3. St Stephen's Church, Macquarie St.

Elizabeth liked St Stephen's. She'd only been there once but it had been a lovely funeral.

4. *Music*
 a. Piped in: Scots College Band (Something lachrymose and haunting).
 b. *The March of the Hebrew Slaves* (Nabucco).
It was her favourite piece of music. And it would certainly activate her mourners' tear ducts.
 c. Alice and James to choose other suitable music.
 d. *Under no circumstances is 'Amazing Grace' to be played!*
 e. Piped out: *Colonel Bogey*

Elizabeth allowed herself to give in to the luxury of tears. Nobody loved her. Nobody cared about her. It wasn't as if she hadn't tried. She'd been seeing shrinks, naturopaths, gurus, rebirthers, herbalists and a dozen faithless lovers for two decades and nothing had worked. But at least now she'd worked it out: she wasn't made for this world. The phone never rang unless she phoned first; no-one visited her. All Jeremy saw when she walked through his door was another $130. She'd been seduced, as usual. His promise of unconditional care had been meaningless.

'Could I speak to Dr Gloucester, please?'

'She's with a patient, Lizzie. Could you phone back in, say, half an hour.'

'It's urgent.' A sob escaped her deliberately controlled voice. 'It *can't* wait. *Please*, Jean, put me through now.'

'Hello Lizzie, what is it?' Elizabeth could imagine Katie sitting at her cluttered GP's desk, her pretty clothes and pretty hair, her pretty shoes and pretty, perfect life.

'I'm going to kill myself.'

'Lizzie, you'd better come in here.'

'No.'

'I can't help you if I can't see you.'

'I really just phoned to invite you to my funeral. It's going to be a nice one, probably next Tuesday or Wednesday, at St ...'

'Have you been drinking today?' Elizabeth thought Katie would have made a good hockey mistress: strict but fair, with absolutely no imagination.

'*Of course* I've been drinking. What else is there to do? My life's finished.' Tears escaped.

'Lizzie, it's the booze making you feel like this. You *have* to stop,' said Katie, strictly but fairly. Elizabeth was silently sobbing. 'Are you still there? Lizzie, I'll come and see you during my break. OK?'

'No.'

'Then go and see Jeremy.'

'No.'

'Lizzie, I've got a patient with me. I'll phone you back when I've finished. Just sit tight.'

The phone call didn't come, Elizabeth noted with satisfaction, as the minutes and half-hours ticked by. She gazed at the beautiful blue sky. Soon she would be up there, laughing with the angels. The only problem she had to work out now was which building to jump from. There was nothing high

465

enough nearby, but the housing commission flats in Glebe were only a short taxi ride away. The UTS building wasn't a bad idea either. But it was universally acknowledged as the ugliest monument to man's erection complex in the entire CBD. She wanted to jump from somewhere beautiful. The Gap was the obvious place, except for the hordes of Japanese tourists.

The phone rang.

'Elizabeth McKenzie and Associates.'

'You sound much better.'

'Yes, Katie, I am,' Elizabeth drawled. 'All I've got to do is decide on the right place. I'd prefer the Gap, but I'm not *quite* sure I want my last moments captured on video and shown to strangers in Okinawa as the highlight of a honeymoon visit to Oz.'

'Lizzie, why do you want to kill yourself?'

'Because nobody cares about me. I've been doing everything right and I still feel like this. Why won't you *help* me?' Elizabeth wailed.

'I *do* care about you. So does Jeremy. And all your friends . . .'

'There is *no*-one. *No-one*. What do I have to do to make someone realise I'm in such pain?'

'Look, if you won't come in here, and you won't see Jeremy, I'll come and see you after work.'

'No. I think, on reflection, it'll be the Gap. If you want to see me, make a booking for the next flight. Qantas's got a good package deal going. You get Tokyo, Osaka, Hiroshima or Okinawa.'

'If you keep talking like this Lizzie, I'm going to have to take some action,' said Katie the hockey mistress.

'OK, Katie. Have a nice life.' She slammed down the phone with satisfaction, unwound her sarong, pulled on jeans and a T-shirt and went round the corner for another bottle of Scotch. She needed a clearer head to make the final arrangements.

At 7.30 she opened the door to two boys. One was pretty and one was dark, Mephistophelian handsome.

'Elizabeth?'

'No. I'm Angie Grimm,' she smiled.

'You fit the description,' the pretty one said, looking uneasy.

Elizabeth beamed at the boy. 'Yeah, we're always being mistaken for sisters. What's up?'

'You have been scheduled and we're from Community Care. We're here to take you to hospital,' said Mephisto.

'I'm *Angie*,' Elizabeth corrected him pleasantly. 'I'm just cat-sitting for Lizzie. She didn't think she'd be back tonight,' she added cunningly.

'At nine o'clock it becomes a police matter,' Mephisto said sepulchrally.

Elizabeth frowned. 'Sounds serious. But all I can do is give her a message when she gets back. Should she go to the police station or what?'

The pretty boy handed her a card. 'She should phone that number. Before nine o'clock.' He seemed to be pleading with her.

'Well, I can only give her the message when she turns

up and I don't know when that'll be.' She tucked the card into her jeans' pocket. 'Thanks, guys. Bye.'

She poured herself another drink and turned on the TV. She felt too sleepy to phone for a taxi and go to the Gap. Besides, she needed to clean up a bit. The place looked like a tip: the sink piled with dishes and Scotch bottles all over the place. When she was dead she didn't want everyone going round saying she was a slattern. Or an alcoholic. Anyway, she was out of the mood for suicide. She turned up the sound as the late news came on. The latest poll showed Labor and the Coalition neck and neck on the eve of the election.

She drank some more Scotch, lit a cigarette and yawned. Then she remembered the police. She'd give them till 9.15 then go to bed. There was nothing they could do unless they could identify her. She tucked her licence in the sugar jar and poured herself another drink. She didn't feel drunk at all. She'd heard that you could drink yourself sober. Maybe that's what she'd done.

She flicked over to SBS. It was showing a gloomy Czech documentary. She liked gloomy eastern European documentaries. They always cheered her up. Just as the children were being loaded into the cattle trucks bound for Auschwitz, the doorbell rang. Elizabeth smiled ironically as she padded down the hall. It was a pity the cops hadn't been so prompt when she'd phoned them about the noisy party on Australia Day.

'Hi guys. I'm Angie Grimm,' she said, putting her hand out to shake the nearest cop's. There was another cop beside him, with Mephisto and the pretty boy hovering behind them. 'You're ... ?'

'Constable Ray Warren.' He didn't shake her hand. She'd been to school with a Ray Warren. But this wasn't him. He was young, smooth-faced, unsmiling. He reminded her of the Czech guards who'd pulled her off the train to Warsaw because she didn't have a transit visa.

'Elizabeth, you have been scheduled under the Mental Health Act and we're taking you to hospital.'

'Listen, guys, why don't you come in and we can sort this out.'

She led them down the hall. 'Take a seat.'

The Care Bear boys sat and she sat, picked up her Scotch and lit a cigarette. Her hands were shaking. Constable Ray Warren stood over her.

'There's nothing to sort out. We're taking you to hospital. Here is the schedule.'

Her hands were shaking so much that the paper flapped. The only thing she could read was Jeremy Gold's signature on the bottom. She handed the sheet back, put her cigarette down and tapped the phone.

'I have absolutely no intention of going *any*where with you,' she said, looking up at the cop and down her nose at the same time. It was a look that had quelled even the Year 9 boys at Blacktown High. 'If you don't leave my house *immediately*, I'll phone the police.'

'We are the police.'

'Oh really? The usual stumblebums who get the wrong house and the wrong person and blast their face off? And don't stand so close. You're trying to intimidate me.'

The cop stood his ground. Elizabeth picked up the receiver and raised her knee towards his groin, in one flowing movement.

The response was swift. PC Warren neatly avoided the knee, PC Speechless pulled the phone plug from its socket and together they marched her down the hall and then the stairs with all the enthusiasm that they might apply to the arrest of a known associate of Neddie Smith. Elizabeth started screaming. The cops' fingers dug into the soft, white flesh of her upper arms. Barefoot, bra-less, knickerless, she was dragged out of her home.

A crowd had gathered. A paddy wagon in a driveway was a novelty in the quiet, respectable neighbourhood.

'We know this is humiliating for a lady like you,' said PC Warren with satisfaction. 'But you've got no choice.'

'I am not humiliated, I am not a lady and I do have a choice, you fucking moron. Let me go. *Let me go!*'

They pushed her into the back of the paddy wagon, slammed the door, and the van backed out.

To calm herself she chanted her mantra, as she had in the border patrol hut at Breslav, among Poles suspected of smuggling in contraband like Colgate and Tampax. This could not be happening to her.

When the van stopped, PCs Warren and Speechless opened the door, ready to grab her. She gave them a look of contempt.

'I can walk by myself. Thank you.'

A brave boy in blue on either side of her, Elizabeth strode down the maze of brown corridors. Shoulders back, she watched for a door that would lead her to freedom.

There was none. They came out into the open again. Speechless and Warren conferred in worried whispers.

'Lost perhaps, PC Plod and PC Plod?'

'Did they say the locked ward was on the left or the right?'

Speechless spoke for the first time. 'Fucked if I know.'

Warren's words finally penetrated. Locked ward. Visions of padded cells, straightjackets and ECT danced in her head. She bolted. They grabbed her and she slumped in their arms. She screamed and screamed. If they wanted a raving loony, she'd give them a raving loony. They dragged her up a ramp, her heels scraping on the pebble concrete.

'Grab her ankles, mate,' said PC Plod to PC Plod. 'Stupid bitch.'

'Bloody heavy,' PC Plod laughed. A door opened and she was deposited on the carpet. The door slammed shut behind her. She could hear a TV close by, turned up full volume. But even that didn't drown out the moaning, the chattering, the manic laughter.

A man as colourless as the vinyl-clad, mock-timber windowless room suggested she sit down. Elizabeth perched on the edge of the desk, folded her arms and swung her leg.

'And who are you?'

'Dr Heffner, the psychiatric registrar.'

'Tell me, *Doctor*—if that's the correct expression—does the name James Barclay mean anything to you?'

'He's the Deputy Health Commissioner,' said Dr Colourless in a predictably colourless voice.

'And a very close friend of mine.' It was true. But

despite herself she could hear the bullied child's final, desperate defiance '*I'm gunna get my big brother to bash you up!*'

'You have no reason for complaint. You have been admitted to the acute ward for your own protection and welfare.' He tapped the schedule.

'Acute ward! Let's speak English, Doctor. I'm in the *locked* ward. The headbangers ward ...'

'We'd prefer you didn't use that expression,' Dr Colourless said repressively, making a note on his yellow legal pad.

'You have no right to keep me here. Phone Jeremy at once.' Dr Colourless pressed his greyish lips together, then dialled a number.

She could imagine Jeremy sitting in a soft chair, listening to music, his long legs stretched out complacently, in the safety of his own home.

'Jeremy? *Get me out of here!*'

'No.' He was sipping something. Camomile tea no doubt. Calmly. Measuredly. Soon he would be brushing and flossing his fine teeth. Calmly, measuredly, his life orderly, clean, disciplined, serene and complacent.

'Get me out of here!' She began to gabble. 'I've been dragged out of my house, bashed up by the cops ...' Dr C. made another note, but she was losing control. 'I'm covered in bruises, I'm in a room with a half-wit'—Dr C. made another note—'and surrounded by dribblers and chanters and mumblers and ... and ... and ...' Dr C. made another note. 'I want to go home!' she wailed.

'No. If you ...'

'You cunt, Jeremy!' She slammed the phone down. She was determined not to cry. She leant over, grabbed the schedule and tore it across and across and across, then threw the small squares on the floor. 'You can't keep me here now!'

'Jane!' called Dr C. A nurse appeared, collected all the bits of paper, and went away again.

'That was a very stupid thing to do,' Dr C. said in a toneless voice, the same toneless voice that Jeremy used. Perhaps they had voice lessons at shrink school after all. He picked up the phone while she paced the room. He was talking to Jeremy. The nurse came back with the schedule sticky-taped back together.

'You've got an origami expert on staff, have you?' said Elizabeth.

Jane said nothing. The registrar was still talking to Jeremy. '... And she tore up the schedule.'

Elizabeth laughed. She laughed because she did think it was funny. She laughed her normal laugh. She laughed loud enough for Jeremy to hear.

'You'll be staying here tonight and you'll see another psychiatrist in the morning. Jane, take Ms McKenzie to the small room.'

'You can lock the door,' said Jane. 'But we can open it from outside. And there's a copy of your rights. As a mental patient.' She pointed to a sheet of paper on the white cot and left.

Elizabeth hammered on the thick yellow perspex window until her hands hurt. She stared around the room for a ventilation grate, anything that would smash the perspex. There was nothing. Finally she sat down on her cot. There *had* to be a way out. She strolled down the corridor to the nurses' station. Dr Colourless was still there, writing up his notes. He took no notice of her.

'Jane,' Elizabeth said in a calm, soft voice. 'I need to make a couple of phone calls. I mean, people will be worried about where I am ...'

Without looking up Dr C. said, 'She can make them in the interview room. Tony?'

A large nurse with biceps that bespoke long hours at the gym and a head that spoke of little between the ears escorted her down the corridor. He unlocked the interview room. She tried to close the door behind her.

'Uhuh,' said Tony, shaking his bonehead. 'You have to be under obsevation. Apparently,' he said smugly, 'you laughed inappropriately before.'

Elizabeth did not deal with the Tonies of the world, much less listen to them. She was already dialling. 'Doctor's put it in his notes.'

James sounded tired when he picked up the phone. No doubt he had spent a wearying day dealing with psychiatrists who had sex with their patients, gynaecologists who raped and GPs who put Australia on the map by chalking up a world first: patient-to-patient transmission of HIV.

'I'm sorry you're in there, Lizzie,' James said. 'But there's nothing I can do about it.'

'But surely *you* of all people can get me out?'

'I can't intervene. Look, just try to get some sleep tonight. And be as cooperative as possible.'

Elizabeth started to shake again. James was an expert on mental health. He had written his thesis on it. Once upon a time in Australia there had been a Minister for Lunacy. They'd laughed over that, once upon a time, when Elizabeth was proof-reading the typescript and correcting some awkward grammar.

'I'll try,' she said weakly. Cooperative! She'd already torn up the schedule, sworn at her shrink, called the registrar a half-wit, never mind the fracas with the police and pretending to the Care Bears that she was someone else.

She began to dial Alice's number. Then remembered. The election was on Saturday. Alice would still be campaigning. The election. Were mad people allowed to vote? Bonehead was doing ape impersonations just outside the door, pursing up his lips, grinning at her, scratching his tiny head with one huge paw and flexing his bicep, scratching under his arms with the other.

Elizabeth pushed past the ape and ran back to the nurses' station. The registrar ignored her. Jane ignored her. When her torrent of invective failed to impress them with her sanity, she started throwing potplants. But after two, she was trying not to laugh. It was all too silly. Any normal person would have laughed, at their own silliness and the silliness of the situation. Here, laughter was dangerous. When she scored a near-miss with an African violet, Dr C., picking the soil out of his hair, finally looked up.

'Get out.'

'I won't.'

When Tony came towards her she stood her ground. He pushed her. She pushed him back. He pushed her.

'Get your hands off me!' But she was already out in the bleak corridor. The door was shut in her face.

Elizabeth slept in her clothes. She slept fitfully. She slept fitfully because every hour she was woken by a light shone through the peephole in the door. She slept fitfully because the depressive, at the peak of his dribbling, muttering mania started to grope at her.

'Sex? Sex! You want sex?' he gibbered. Fortunately the torch-wielding Jane turned up and drove him out, but not before he'd squeezed her breast.

'Weren't you *told* you could lock the door?' Jane asked, as if it was all her fault.

Elizabeth considered a number of cutting replies—when was the last time she'd needed to lock her bedroom door?—but Jane had gone off to harass some other loony. The manic man leered through the peephole as she shut and locked the door.

She woke at seven, wondering where she was. Then she remembered. Fear rose like bile. But surely any reasonable person would, now that she was sober, realise that all she'd suffered from was an acute panic attack? But she didn't know anymore. She picked up the piece of paper she'd thrown on the floor the night before:

YOUR RIGHTS

She skimmed it. Surely there must be a clause that would get her out.

'If you are found to be a mentally disordered person

you can only be kept in hospital for up to 3 days ...' Three days! Another three hours and she'd be a raving loony. *'If you are found to be a mentally ill person, you will be kept in hospital until you see a Magistrate who will hold an inquiry to decide what will happen to you ... The Magistrate may order that you be kept in hospital ... (not more than 3 months) ...'*

'Jane,' said Elizabeth, smiling, knocking on the open nurses' station door. 'Hi.'

'What do you want?'

'I'd like to see my schedule.'

She felt she'd pitched her request just right: not servile, not aggressive, just one ordinary person asking something reasonable of another.

'You were very impulsive last night,' Jane said. 'No.'

Elizabeth took a deep breath and said as normally as she could. 'Yeah, I was a bit upset, but ...'

'The visiting registrar will see you this morning and you can see it then—if he thinks it's appropriate.'

'What time will that be?'

Jane had gone back to writing something on a chart.

'About nine. Now if there's nothing else?'

Elizabeth opened her mouth to ask the vital question. *'Am I a mentally disordered person or a mentally ill person?'* But if she didn't know, had to ask, it would be written down somewhere: *'Appears confused as to her identity.'* It was *Catch 22.* It was *Cuckoo's Nest.*

In the bathroom that stank of cheap disinfectant and even

cheaper psychiatry, she threw up, then retched and retched, the yellow bile burning her throat. Sweat poured down her face. Her reflection wavered back at her yellow, in the mirror made of some strange, no doubt suicide-proof metal. She could see that her hair looked like a birch broom in a fit. Her face looked pinched and frightened. Her breasts bobbed low on her chest, underneath the thin, crumpled T-shirt. She was freezing. Why had she worn clothes that were so—inappropriate? '*You laughed* inappropriately. *It's in your report.*' '*That was a* stupid *thing to do.*' '*You were very* impulsive *last night.*' She would have to be very, very careful now. She was very, very, very frightened.

She sat on her bed and picked up YOUR RIGHTS again: '*The hospital staff may give you appropriate medical treatment even if you don't want it ...*' On her way to the nurses' station, she had seen a young Asian woman, glazed, somnambulistic, wandering in the corridor. And then the manic man being forced to drink a little cup of something green. '*Can I be given ECT against my will?*'

Elizabeth began pacing the corridor. She passed a beautiful young man, a hospital jacket tucked into track pants, pacing too. She smiled. Then regretted it. There might be something called *inappropriate smiling* as well, especially as the recipient of the smile didn't smile back. Instead, he deliberately bumped into her: she saw the dark, malevolent madness in his eyes. After six laps of the crooked corridor, she realised that everyone was pacing. She could not afford to be seen doing what real loonies did. She detoured into the common room and picked up an orange from a bowl.

Surely nothing loony could be construed from that. Surely. But Jane and a henchwoman were watching her from the courtyard just the same.

At last breakfast arrived, on a trolley, pushed by two nurses. Neither was Tony but both had biceps like footballs and looked as boneheaded. No, she mustn't even *think* such words. It was too dangerous.

'Beaut breakfast today, mate,' said the big one.

'Excellent, mate,' said the even bigger one. 'They've put a real treat on for us today.'

Elizabeth was very hungry: a well-cooked breakfast might ease the gnawing anxiety in her belly. She watched to see the routine, then took a tray from the trolley and sat down at a round plastic table by herself. She lifted the cover off the plate and saw a slice of greasy bacon and an omelette that would have soled shoes. Perhaps she was mentally ill after all. No-one in their right mind would have believed, even for a second, that a hospital would provide well-cooked food.

On the other hand ... if she didn't eat the omelette ... *Anorexia nervosa*? Some hospitals locked anorexic teenage girls in cells until they agreed to eat. At the very least, if she refused to eat, they might think she was being *uncooperative*.

She cooperated. After all, hadn't the big boys said it was a beaut breakfast? Despite years of vegetarianism, she got the bacon down. Then she bolted half the omelette to get rid of the taste. She saw that Jane's henchwoman was pretending not to watch her. *Bulimia*? *Eating disorder observed*? She was drinking the little plastic cup of orange juice when a middle-aged woman sat down at her table.

'You've just arrived, haven't you?' The woman was perfectly groomed—hair, face, nails—and was wearing a smart
dress and high heels.

'That's right.' Elizabeth gave her a small smile. She
seemed normal enough: not drooling, dribbling or chanting
anyway.

'Did you sleep well?' the woman asked kindly.

'Yes. Like a baby,' said Elizabeth.

'No you dint! No you dint!' A skinny, haggard woman
with a bad perm and even worse speech impediment jumped
up and down beside her, dribbling. 'Mad Marco tryda hoo-
hoo-hoot ya, dint he? Dint he?'

'It was my own fault,' said Elizabeth, loud enough for
Jane to hear. 'I forgot to lock my door.'

'He hoo-hoo-hooted me,' the woman boasted, 'and he'll
hoo-hoo-hoot you too. He'll get you in the end, yes he will,'
she sang as she danced off.

'I had a terrible night,' said the normal woman.

'I'm sorry to hear that.'

'If it wasn't last night, it'll be tonight. We'll all be butch-
ered in our beds.'

The woman cried quietly into her omelette. One of the
big boys came around with the toast. He deposited a slice
of white on Elizabeth's tray. She'd seen there was brown,
too. Had she or hadn't she been observed as the sort of
woman who would normally eat brown bread? If she didn't
ask for brown ... *Personality change? Erratic, uncharacter-
istic behaviour?* On the other hand, if she asked for brown
instead ... *Uncooperative? Unnecessarily assertive?* The big

boy seemed to be hovering over her, muscles quivering.

'Thanks,' said Elizabeth, smiling up at the nurse.

'You've changed,' he said and, unsmiling, did the rounds with the toast.

Elizabeth buttered her toast and made her choice from the three small silver packets on the tray. There was honey, jam and Vegemite. After some thought she chose Vegemite—surely there couldn't be anything more castiron sane than Vegemite?—and took her toast out into the courtyard. Jane followed her. Elizabeth sat down on a plastic chaise longue. An old woman in black was crouched on a plastic chair.

'Come on, Jessie,' Jane urged. 'Come in and have your breakfast.'

'You know I can't walk without me stick. Give me back my stick.'

'You know you can't have your stick. And you know why.'

'You tell her!' Jessie shouted at Elizabeth through clattering false teeth. 'A lady like you, she'll listen to you.'

Elizabeth's heart thumped painfully: she had made the wrong decision about the toast. *Variable, unpredictable behaviour?* She averted her eyes as Jessie, bent almost double under osteoporosis, shuffled into the common room, lurching and crying.

The rest were coming out. She had to make a quick decision. If she talked to them, Jane might see this as confirmation that she was used to fraternising with loonies and therefore one herself. On the other hand ... *Appears to be withdrawn? Lacks normal social skills?* After the debacle with the toast, she couldn't work out which way to jump.

A tall, skinny red-headed boy came and sat at the foot of her chaise longue. He sounded excited.

'Heard the cops brought you in last night.'

'That's right,' said Elizabeth warily.

'Bloody mongrel cops. Brought me in a coupla times. They don't usually bring the ladies in, but. Ladies usually cooperate before it gets to that stage. Husbands usually bring 'em in.'

Refused to cooperate with the police? Abnormal female behaviour?

'Bloody mongrels gave me a hard time. Handcuffs, the lot. I got put in the special room for that.' He seemed to be boasting. '"Uncontrollable and liable to cause harm to himself and others." That's what the Doc wrote in me file. Cops give you a hard time?'

Dr Colourless ... Dr *Heffner* had made a note when she complained about the way she had been treated by the big brave boys in blue. *Paranoia? Persecution complex?*

'No,' Elizabeth said, loud enough for Jane to hear. The boy seemed to lose interest and wandered away.

Elizabeth stared up at the sky. The sun was bronze, burning through the morning mist. It would be a hot day. It was a day for the beach, lunch, a long walk. James would already be at work. How long ago was the dinner party? Tuesday? It seemed a century ago and away. Then she recalled the conversation that she had somehow blocked out of her head.

James had talked about a recent study from America. To test the efficacy of diagnosis in psychiatric wards, three senior psychiatrists had volunteered to go into three different hospitals under assumed names and professions. They were to complain about a ringing in their ears. The next day they were to say that the ringing had stopped.

One of them was discharged the same day. Another was released after two weeks. The third was still there three years later.

Frank Moorhouse

DRiNK

Because of loss of energy—reaching for a book was an effort—sweating, horrendous neausea, inflammation of the oesophagus, pale shit, he went to have tests done by a GP in the city he was visiting.

The GP was grave. 'You have cirrhosis,' she said. She was appalled at how much he drank.

'You must never drink again,' she said, studying the liver function tests.

He'd told her that at the end of the day he had about four or five drinks before dinner—beers, martinis, bloody marys, or bourbons—followed by a half to full bottle of wine with dinner, followed maybe by a glass of beer to 'refresh the palate', followed by probably two ports or liqueurs or cognacs with coffee and then some after-dinner drinking, say a few beers or bourbons—about twelve to fifteen drinks of alcohol a day, each drink containing about half an ounce of alcohol. He drank about six days a week and within a month there would be a number of heavy drinking 'sessions' lasting over eight hours when, apart from dinner or lunch drinks, there would be another eight or so, bringing a session to about twenty drinks.

Not only did he find it hard to be honest about the amount he drank, sensing that it was a little gross, he also had never in his life *counted it up*.

He told his friend and drinking companion Richard that he had cirrhosis and would never drink again but Richard vehemently disputed this (after all, if one of them had cirrhosis, then all of them might!). Richard insisted that he have further tests done by a 'friendly doctor' who would give him a clean bill of health.

'But Richard,' he said, 'I *am* sick.'

The friendly doctor, himself a drinker, did liver function tests and interpreted them as 'the result of a heavy binge' and said that he'd be OK after a week off the booze.

His own GP said that if he were worried he'd refer him to a specialist.

'Yes, I'm worried,' he said.

When he told the liver disease specialist how much he

drank, the specialist said, 'Hell, I drink that much.'

The specialist diagnosed viral hepatitis—a mild case—and recommended abstaining from alcohol for six months to allow any damage to the liver to repair itself.

He decided to follow this course. It was his first extended abstinence from alcohol in twenty-five years—since he'd left school.

In the first week he worried that he did not have 'friends', only drinking companions, and that he would now be unacceptable company, that he would be socially deserted.

Drinking was a ritualised bonding, mutual intoxication was an act of helpless solidarity in the face of the human condition. How was he going to face the human condition without drink?

When he was younger he had sometimes wanted to 'drink himself to death'. In literature it had seemed a romantic and pleasant way to go, imagined as a slipping into intoxication and then into death, but he realised that he wilfully misunderstood the expression 'drinking yourself to death' and that it would be both painful and miserable.

Alcohol was like a camp fire they huddled around.

He tried the non-alcoholic drinks, noting for the first time that supermarkets carried something called non-alcoholic 'wine'. He finally settled on drinking a mix of non-alcoholic cider and soda water about fifty-fifty and became fond of it. He also drank virgin marys (bloody marys without alcohol).

Drinking companions were a special sort of friend—'he's good to drink with'—who would go willingly with you into the zones of intoxication and anything that might follow from that.

How static he now found his personality. The weather of his days seemed mild. Alcohol, he thought, introduced an exaggerated mental turbulence and strong winds into the personality.

He observed that now sober he was more absent-minded; he'd expected the opposite. But he did find that he no longer needed to keep notes of information given to him the night before.

After a month he had his first yearning for a drink—he yearned for a cold, flavoursome American beer—a Coors in a heavy glass beer mug—with salted popcorn in a dim American country and western bar with a stool-girl to chat with.

A form of intimacy, a description of a relationship, 'We did a lot of drinking together.'

He realised that alcohol was a relatively benign drug and that after twenty-five years of consistent drinking he suffered no distressing withdrawal symptoms.

He'd always known that uneasiness with people was behind some of his drinking. This was confirmed after his first public lunch with strangers when he developed neck tension.

He dreamed that he'd forgotten he should not drink and had accepted a drink and wiped out the progress of repair that his liver had achieved.

He observed a dinner party, his first sober dinner for years. He noticed the conversational risks that drinking encouraged, the making of puns, the wise-cracking, quipping, the saying of things which might fail. Other drinkers gave a generous reception to everything—at least in the early part of the dinner. Drinking permitted free association, emboldened a quickfire tempo, which he found beyond his non-drinking mind. He found his mind too self-critical, full of stray material, cluttered with marginal connections, too qualified by caution. Later intoxication, he observed, was not so generous. It could become querulous, dogmatic, obsessive, and attention to what others were saying became erratic.

He decided that as a non-drinker he should leave drinkers at midnight.

He had his second craving. He craved spaghetti bolognese, plenty of cheese, plenty of black pepper, with a bottle of Valpolicella. The craving came to him while reading *Her Privates We*—First World War soldiers eating spaghetti and drinking wine behind the lines. It was not a ravenous craving.

He realised that he'd sometimes had a drink to make himself 'feel like drinking'.

When he told Louise at a restaurant dinner that he was not drinking, Louise said, 'What a bore,' and at first found it disconcerting. Maybe she felt she was being denied the security of complicity.

He was reminded of the play *The Iceman Cometh* where Hickey returns to his former drinking buddies after having found 'peace of mind' and given up drinking.

Hickey tells his former drinking mates in the saloon that he isn't against drinking though.

> Just because I'm through with the stuff don't mean I'm going Prohibition. Hell, I'm not that ungrateful! It's given me too many good times ... If anyone wanted to get drunk, if that's the only way they can be happy and feel at peace with themselves, why the hell shouldn't they? ... I know all about that game from soup to nuts. I'm the guy that wrote the book ...

But they find that having a sober Hickey about affects their drinking. One of them, Rocky, says, 'But it don't do no good. I can't get drunk right.'

And then Harry Hope who owns the bar, says, 'When are you going to do something about this booze, Hickey? Bejees, we all know you did something to take the life out of it! It's like drinking dishwater! We can't pass out! ... there's no life or kick in it ...'

In the mornings he tended still to have a slight thickness of the mind, a pain from awakening back to life which he had always attributed to slight hangover.

But whatever slight pain there was in the morning it was not as horrendous as hangover and every morning he had a dream again that he had accidentally drunk alcohol and would have to start his six months over again.

In his period of sobriety he was for the first time able to examine the nature of his drinking. He saw it as maybe six drinking *sets* or separate waves of intoxication.

The first set of drinks, say the first three or so, achieved a perceptible change of mental weather—a change to a conscious mellowness, reasonably anxiety-free, although it had to be noted that the first drinks also usually punctuated the day and the end-of-work stress. The drinks celebrated a productive day or took the sting out of 'one hell of a day'.

The second set of drinks (say, the drinks with dinner) gave a free play to the mind, and stimulated some rush of ideas and words, a pleasing (or self-pleasing at least) rush of verbalisation.

The third set of drinks (equivalent to, say, the first of the after-dinner drinks) was simply a fuelling or maintaining of the first two waves of intoxication, the heightened animation and mellowness.

The fourth set of drinks—if embarked upon—represented for him the beginning of a pursuit of deeper relaxation or intoxication, some unspecified state of pleasure (through chance encounter, confessional conversation, uncontrolled hilarity, revelry or whatever). In recent years of drinking he'd found alcohol unreliable in achieving this effect.

The fifth set of drinks was pursuit of loss of self, a seeking of a high level of intoxication without real expectation and with no concern for the aftermath. Again, he'd found alcohol increasingly unreliable as a means of reaching this stage.

There was perhaps a sixth wave of intoxication—drinking to oblivion, passing out—which was something he had not done since his teens or early twenties.

He'd found that waves four and five could fail to occur and, instead, become sodden intoxication leading to irritability. When drinking he was now able to perceive that the potential of reaching these states was lost and that there would be no pay-off from further drinking. But with good drinking companions it was always tempting to try for the fourth and fifth state.

After three months of non-drinking he found that he still had the feeling after dinner parties that he had been 'intoxicated'. He could now observe the adrenalin effect as distinct from alcoholic stimulation. He now saw that his non-drinking personality too was *not* particularly different from his drinking personality. He still said dumb things, and, if relaxed, could still be reasonably spontaneous, outrageous, playful. His earlier observations of himself soon after he'd stopped drinking had been of a tense and self-conscious, fearful, non-drinker.

He listed the drinking experiences which he missed:

• for some reason he missed again the drinking of cold cans of beer with a friend in a car at a drive-in cinema, eating hot dogs with mustard and sauce (something he hadn't done for years).

• drinking Jack Daniel's 'old No. 7 Tennessee sour mash whiskey' and eating salted nuts on an international flight at 10 000 metres looking down on the world's terrain—say, the delta of the Ganges or the Russian steppes—or looking at the sun setting across a cloud bank, disoriented in time, ideally listening to Indian classical music in the headphones.

• champagne at intervals at the Sydney Opera House looking out onto the harbour.

• Jack Daniel's bourbon alone in a motel room in a strange city after a long journey, watching foreign television.

• a very cold Heineken beer and a Mexican meal arranged in a garden courtyard in the sun.

• Jack Daniel's beside the campfire in the bush, after a day of heavy going, on a cold night, with macadamia nuts.

• cans of West End beer off the ice while driving across the outback in a Volvo wagon on a hunting trip.

• a good cognac or a pernod and ice alone in his reading chair, with a book, in a dim room, reading for the night, with an occasional telephone call to or from a close friend.

• a correctly made, not too dry, but very very cold martini in a dim piano bar, with the pianist playing the blues.

Another dream that he had been drinking and had set back his recovery.

He'd lost the habitual urge for a drink at about six or seven at night.

He found himself searching interviews and biographies for references to drinking, how much successful people had drunk, drink and its effect on work.

He remembered how he'd felt when he'd been drinking that if he did not drink for a day or so he'd earned the right to a heavy drinking session. What would six months off the drink earn him?

The drinking 'session'.   He realised that really much of his drinking in the past had been in the form of the 'session', if not the 'spree'. Spree drinking was taking the drink wherever it might lead you in the night, unrestrained drinking as a launching pad into unrestrained behaviour. But a 'drinking session' was simply open-ended extended drinking.

He could remember the time when he'd felt that there was no point to 'a couple of drinks', that the drinking session was the only meaningful use of alcohol, 'serious drinking'.

But measured drinking, a consciously shaped intoxication, had its own hedonism, its own enchantments, especially when integrated with, say, sex.

This old lesson was nicely articulated by the eithteenth-century lawyer and bon vivant William Hickey (another Hickey) that alcohol was generally best when it was subservient to other activities and not the activity itself. Hickey said, 'I certainly have at different periods drunk very freely, sometimes to excess, but it never arose from the sheer love of wine; society—cheerful companions, and lively seducing women—always delighted and frequently proved my bane; but intoxication for itself I detested, and invariably suffered grievously from.'

But it was a damned hard lesson to remember at midnight, and it was a lesson which for him wouldn't stay learned—even after two hundred years.

He again dreamed he'd forgotten that beer was as dangerous to his recovery as any other alcohol and that he'd drunk it, setting himself back again.

He had his first sensation of agoraphobia. At an airport he'd found the concourse full of faces from plays, from films, from his past, from his own scripts and stories—the smell of the food at the tables, the rattle of dishes, machinery noises, all recalled in an overwhelming jumble other people and other places and other airports, other journeys.

A jamming of his mind with recollection. They'd all crushed in on him and he felt badly like a drink, like drinking heavily, but he resisted.

He recalled the search, in the later stages of intoxication, for the accelerating drink, the hit which would bring deep relaxation or wild loss of self. He would change drinks or order a stronger drink in the pursuit of the last grand wave of intoxication. It didn't always come.

Strangely, he sensed that his co-ordination had grown worse during the months of not drinking. He seemed to bump into things, stumbled more. He feared he had multiple sclerosis.

Maybe he'd done this when drunk too and just not noticed it.

He felt the gratification of a sense of health—loss of weight—a consciousness of fitness of being able to run further, cut more wood, walk further when backpacking. But it was by no means a dramatic increase in fitness, he had always been reasonably fit. He'd always wanted to be a 'healthy drunk'.

It was a bit like being an adolescent again.

Now when he did irrational things or said dumb things he would say to himself, 'But Jesus, I was sober!'

He feared every now and then that the non-alcoholic cider he was drinking was actually alcoholic and would re-check the label on the bottle.

He was now clearly aware of the chemicals which operated naturally in his body—he guessed they were things like adrenalin and hormonal activity—which caused excitation, agitation, senses of well-being. He could also clearly feel the effects of caffeine, MSG, sugar.

He observed that sometimes sexual attraction for that which was beyond possibility—say, seeing a sexually desirable woman in the street—or lost love—could transform itself almost immediately into a desire for alcohol. He had not observed the sexual desire–alcohol link so clearly before.

The martini mystique   Louise, his first adultery, had introduced him to the martini. He missed the cold chilling seep of intoxication which came from a strong, correctly made martini, with the taste of gin distinguishable from the taste of vermouth but with the exquisite blending of both tastes in the mouth to make the martini taste, blending then again with the olive. He liked to be able to detect the vermouth in the martini, which went against the fashion for the very dry, almost 100 per cent gin martini. He also enjoyed the 'third' martini—the watery cold one left in the jug, the leftovers, which was mostly iced water with a martini flavour.

   He wondered how his young wife Robyn had known about the origin of the martini. Had she had a lover back then too, who drank martinis?

The six months ended and he passed his liver function tests. His first cautious drink was a beer—a can of Carlton draught. He feared the nausea which was his last remembered reaction to alcohol. The Carlton did not taste as he wanted it to taste and he had no inclination to drink more that night but the taste did recall his first beer, drunk from a bottle at the back of a dance hall when he was a seventeen-year-old school captain—twenty-five years before.

Of all the drinking experiences he'd yearned for during his non-drinking period only the cans of beer with hot dogs in the drive-in cinema failed to live up to his expectation.

During his forced abstinence he discovered that alcohol was

not needed for him to enjoy uninhibited and spontaneous sex. He found he was marginally more active in what he described as affectionate, low-key sex. But upon returning to drinking he enjoyed again the extended sexual experiences with slow drinking—any drink—over a few hours, especially with Belle.

Robert Drewe

AfTeRWoRD

Whisky hangovers have their good points. A rum hangover marinates the brain in syrup and overlays all next day, next week, with a sticky aftertaste. With a gin hangover it's shoosh the kids and hide the guns and mother's knives and draw the blinds and roll up in cotton sheets till the season changes. (Joe says a gin hangover is like looking at life through a black snake's bum. Inwards *or* outwards. Things are bleak and won't get any better.) Draw a pistol with a brandy hangover and you'll shoot something important off you. But a whisky hangover is like peering through a steamed-up window: it cuts out unnecessaries. Even the worst ones, where the bright world quivers behind clouds of leaves and feathers, can slowly set certain trains of thought in motion.

The thoughts of Ned Kelly from
Our Sunshine

List of Contributors

Venero **Armanno** is the writer of short stories, novels and one day a screenplay that might even get produced. He enjoys red wine and hasn't touched Minchinbury since 1985. Or so he says. His latest novel is *Strange Rain*.

Tim **Baker** was born in Sydney in 1957 and has lived in Paris for many years. He is working on a multi-volume imaginative history of the 20th century, and a series of plays on the theme of racism.

Jean Bedford was born in England and grew up in the country in Victoria. She was educated at Monash University and the University of PNG. She has worked as a journalist and in creative writing courses at secondary and tertiary level. Her first novel, *Sister Kate*, was a best seller of more than 40,000 copies and was set on educational syllabuses. She is the author of ten works of fiction, including novels and short stories, and is currently working on a new novel. She is married to the writer Peter Corris and lives on the Illawarra coast south of Sydney.

Carmel Bird's recent collection of stories and essays is *Automatic Teller*. Her novels include *The White Garden* and *The Bluebird Cafe*, and she has written two books of inspiration for writers, *Dear Writer* and *Not Now Jack—I'm Writing a Novel*.

John Birmingham is on the run from some mistakes he made in Queensland. He is the author of *He Died With a Felafel in His Hand*, *The Search for Savage Henry* and *How to Be a White Man*. He has written for a number of pornographic magazines including *Playboy*, *Penthouse* and *Inside Sport*. Sometimes he writes for less pornographic magazines, such as *Juice* and *Rolling Stone*. He is working on a new book.

José Borghino is a freelance Spaniard, lives in Sydney and writes.

Matthew **Condon** lives in Sydney. His books include *The Motorcycle Cafe, Usher, The Ancient Guild of Tycoons, A Night at the Pink Poodle,* and *The Lulu Magnet.* His drink of choice is a chilled whisky sour served in a martini glass.

Rosemary **Creswell** is a Sydney writer and literary agent.

Max **Cullen,** well known as an actor, began as a copy-boy on the *Sydney Morning Herald.* He subsequently worked for nearly every newspaper and magazine publisher in Sydney as a lay-out artist, illustrator and cartoonist. He attended Julian Ashton's Art School and also studied sculpture under Lyndon Dadswell. He continues to do illustration for books and magazines as well as exhibiting his paintings and sculpture. Since 1990 he has worked on the Channel Nine 'Sunday' program as arts reporter. He is a published poet and short story writer and is constantly writing *the* novel.

Christopher **Cyrill** was born in 1970 and his first novel *The Ganges and its Tributaries* was published in 1993. In 1994 he won the Marten Bequest Scholarship. He is currently working full time on his second novel and a book of short stories entitled *Breathe a Word.*

Luke **Davies** was born in Sydney in 1962. He has published two books of poetry; *Four plots for four magnets,* and *Absolute Event Horizon,* which was shortlisted for the 1995

National Book Council Banjo Awards. He is currently travelling and working on a third book of poetry and a collection of short stories. He has just completed his first novel.

Barry Dickins was educated at The Albion Hotel in Lygon Street, Carlton. It housed failed fiction critics and former interesting drunkards. Dickins learnt to read there, mostly the agonies and comedies in men's and women's eyes—and even now, scrubbed-up and forty-seven, living in extreme ease in Melbourne's least leafy suburb, he rises like stout-vapour at dawn to stumble down the past to be with his wry ghost companions again at The Albion. Some hope. They're dead. He writes interviews with the rich and famous for the *Age* and is nearly always good for a quid. Dickins won the 1995 Victorian Premier's Award for Drama with a manuscript upon the life that briefly belonged to Ronald Joseph Ryan. He is married to Sarah Mogridge and they laugh with their sixteen-month-old son Louis till it gets dark.

Robert Drewe, the author of internationally acclaimed novels and short stories and, more recently, of plays, was born in Victoria in 1943 but grew up on the coast of Western Australia. His prize-winning books include *Fortune* and *The Bay of Contented Men*. His book *The Bodysurfers* has made Australian literary history, a short story collection which not only became a best seller but has been adapted for television, radio and film, and performed on the stage. His most recently produced play is *South American Barbecue*. Drewe edited *The Picador Book of the Beach*, and his new novel, *The Drowner*, was published in 1996.

Nick Earls' collection of short stories, *Passion*, was equal runner-up in the 1993 Steele Rudd Award. His young adult novel, *After January*, and adult novel, *Zigzag Street*, were both published in 1996. His work has appeared in a number of recent anthologies, including *Blur: stories by young Australian writers*.

Susan Errington was born at midnight, during a thunderstorm and total power blackout, in Adelaide, South Australia. After such an auspicious beginning, a literary career seemed the only logical choice. She studied Australian Literature at university where she was awarded the Brian Elliot prize and has travelled widely in Europe and Asia with Kym. Her first novel, *Olive Street*, was published in 1995 and was shortlisted for the Victorian Premier's Literary Award for first fiction. She is currently working on her second novel.

David Ireland is one of Australia's most respected and prominent novelists. Born in 1927, he is three times winner of the Miles Franklin Award for *The Unknown Industrial Prisoner* (1971), *The Glass Canoe* (1976) and *A Woman of the Future* (1979). 'Liz the Large', his story contained herein is extracted from his novel, *The Glass Canoe*, arguably Australia's most important literary work on the nation's most obsessive pastime: drinking. David's new novel *The Chosen* will be published in 1997.

Gretel Killeen started writing comedy accidentally when she stood up to perform a serious navel-gazing poem, and everybody laughed. From here she moved to writing and performing stand-up comedy. Gretel has worked in radio and television, including 'The Midday Show', 'The Big Gig', 'Andrew Denton and the Party Machine', 'TVTV' and 'Coast to Coast'. In the past six years Gretel has written six books, several of which have become best sellers, and contributed to four anthologies. She is currently working on her seventh book and her first feature film script, a romantic comedy that'll 'make you laugh, make you cry, make you want to redecorate'.

R D Lappan grew up in Melbourne and now lives in Brisbane. She is the author of several short stories and has just completed a novel.

Henry Lawson was born on the goldfields at Grenfell, NSW, in 1867. He endured a 'miserably unhappy' childhood, suffering from poverty and deafness. After his parents separated in 1883 he joined his mother in Sydney and worked as a carriage painter before becoming interested in writing. His compassionate and comical short stories, such as 'The Drover's Wife' and 'Water Them Geraniums', poignantly captured the rough lives of the rural poor. Supporting the ideals of mateship, trade unionism and socialism even if 'blood should stain the wattle', Lawson's writing was the dominant voice in the nationalist literary movement of the 1890s. He died on 2 September 1922 and was given a State funeral.

Richard **Lawson** was born in Brisbane in 1960 and learned to drink from a very tender age. At one time or another he has been a salesman, teacher, house-husband, roadie, song-writer, musician, video sound-recordist, phone TAB operator and book editor. All he has found to encourage lapses into over-indulgence. He is currently working to complete his first collection of short stories, *The Causeway Fables*. He is married and lives in Sydney with his wife and two kids.

Margaret **McClusky** is a writer and teacher. She has written numerous short stories and books, including *Wedlock*, a novel, attracting wide critical and public acclaim.

Tim **Moltmann** was born in Brisbane in 1959. He has lived in London and Sydney and now resides in Hobart with his son. 'Fibonacci Sequence' is his first published story.

Frank **Moorhouse** was born in Nowra, New South Wales, in 1938. His first book of stories, *Futility and Other Animals*, was published in 1969 while he was working as a reporter in Sydney. His other 'discontinuous narratives', in which characters, and often stories themselves, overlap, include *The Americans, Baby, The Electrical Experience, Tales of Mystery and Romance, The Everlasting Secret Family* and *Room Service*. He won the *Age* Book of the Year Award and the Australian Literature Society's Gold Medal for *Forty-Seventeen*. His most recent novel is *Grand Days*.

Mandy Sayer was born in Sydney in 1963. She is the author of three novels, *The Cross* (1995), *Blind Luck* (1993) and *Mood Indigo* (1990), winner of the 1989 *Australian/Vogel Literary Award*. Mandy has studied and performed tap-dance in Australia and the US and has taught at numerous dance schools and studios. She is currently completing her memoir, *Dreamtime Alice*, with the assistance of a 1996 Literature Board Fellowship from the Australia Council. She drinks vodka tonics.

Rosie Scott is a novelist who has also written a play, *Say Thanks to the Lady*, which won the Bruce Mason National Award (and inspired the Australian feature film, *Redheads*, winner of five international awards) a collection of poetry, *Flesh and Blood*, and a short story collection, *Queen of Love*. Her novels, *Glory Days*, shortlisted for the New Zealand National Awards, *Nights with Grace*, *Feral City*, shortlisted for the Banjo Award, *Lives on Fire* and *Movie Dreams*, shortlisted for the Christina Stead Award and the National Fiction Award and recently optioned for a feature film, have been variously published in the UK, USA, Germany, New Zealand and Australia. Her short stories and essays have also been published in all these countries and in France. After working in numerous occupations from actor to social worker she is now a fulltime writer living in Sydney.

Terry Serio grew up on the loose edge of a gravel road in the wheat belt of Western Australia. He was very soon packed off to school in Perth. At Curtin Uni he studied acting and literature and very soon put all his new found skills to work playing in bands, which eventually led to a somewhat interesting relationship with the Victorian police, and lead role in *Running on Empty*, the 1981 Australian classic cult road film. Terry's voice scored him the lead role in the smash hit *Hair*, and the role of Johnny O'Keefe in *Shout*. His boyish dial gets him invited to just about anybody's party and occasionally into trouble. Having avoided countless opportunities to get a proper job and settle down, Terry continues to slide around in the gravel, and is currently investigating the possibility of becoming rich and famous by writing and directing film. His great grandfather was a Finnish deep sea diver, but in spite of this hereditary shiftlessness, he is a curiously happy man.

Peta Spear was born in Rockhampton, Central Queensland. After living in Townsville and Brisbane and dropping out of university in both cities, she came to Sydney in search of a literary style. Peta began her writing career as a poet, her collection *My Sweet Sex* appearing in 1994. A collection of short stories first appeared in the Sydney Women's Writers Workshop's anthology *No Regrets* in 1982. Her collection of stories *Sex Crimes* was published in 1996 and she is currently working on her first novel, *Libertine*.

Leonie Stevens is the author of *Nature Strip* (1994) and *Big Man's Barbie* (1996), as well as numerous short stories. She is currently working on her third novel, *Glue*. She loves Scorcese films and day-time soaps, and drinks G & T (no ice).

Candace Sutton was born in Brisbane and has lived in Sydney for 13 years. She has worked as a journalist in Britain, the US and Africa. She is now a feature writer for the *Sun-Herald*. In her many years of experience writing and drinking, she was always encouraged to leave out the tales of intoxication and get on with the story. It is a relief to come clean. Her favourite drink is a lime margharita.

Emma Tom was born in Fairfield and grew up in the Western Suburbs of Sydney and the Far North Coast of New South Wales. She writes for the *Sydney Morning Herald* and her first novel, *Dead Set*, will be published by Random House next year.

Christos Tsiolkas was born in 1965. Educated through the State school system, he eventually completed an under-graduate degree at Melbourne University. Since then he has been writing fiction, scripts, essays and polemic while working a range of poorly paid jobs. His fiction has appeared in the anthologies *Blur, Picador New Writing 3*, and *Fruit* (Blackwattle Press), and his first novel, *Loaded*, was published in 1995. His most recent work, *Jump Cuts*, is a collaboration with Sasha Soldatow. Christos lives with his lover Wayne van der Stelt, and they share their home with two cats, Stanley and Stella.

Barbara Wels lives in inner city Melbourne. Her first novel for young readers, *Finwood and Lisa*, was published in 1993. *The Lifestyles of Previous Tenants*, a collection of stories for the adult market, was published in 1995. Barbara's work also appears in the anthology of young Australian writers, *Blur*, which was released in January 1996. Barbara has just completed a professional writing course at RMIT and actively works to promote the writing of young Australians.

Ben Widdicombe could use a ride home if you're going that way.

AcknowLEdgEMents

W e gratefully acknowledge the following authors
and publishers for permission to include the pro-
ceeding stories and vignettes:

'Drink' and 'Martini' © Frank Moorhouse, from *Forty-
Seventeen*, Pan Macmillan, 1988.

'Raging with Ralph' © Rosie Scott, from *Lives on Fire*,
UQP, 1993.

'Liz the Large' © David Ireland, from *The Glass Canoe*, Penguin, 1976.

'The Night They Planned Iris' Wedding' © Jean Bedford and 'Epithalamium' © Rose Creswell, from *Colouring In*, Penguin, 1986.

The Foreword is taken from 'A Fantasy of Man', being Volume II of the *Complete Works of Henry Lawson*, compiled and edited by Leonard Cronin, Lansdowne, 1984.

The Afterword is © Robert Drewe from his novel *Our Sunshine*, Pan Macmillan, 1991.

The editors wish to offer their thanks to Jane Palfreyman, Linda Funnell, and the rest of the team at Random House, for their enthusiasm.

Our gratitude goes especially to the writers who agreed to share their alcoholic tolerance and intolerance, favourite cocktail recipes, wines and ales, joys, nightmares and deeper secrets that are in evidence in *Smashed*. Thanks also to the barmen and women of Australia who unwittingly participated in the genesis of many stories in this collection.

HIC

Other Contributors
to MEN LOVE SEX

Venero Armanno	Damien Lovelock
Ian Beck	Roger McDonald
Tom Carment	Lex Marinos
James Cockington	Frank Moorhouse
Matthew Condon	Mark Mordue
Alan Close	David Owen
Christopher Cyrill	Eric Rolls
John Dale	John Stapleton
Julian Davies	Angus Strachan
Robert Drewe	Chad Taylor
Jonathan Griffiths	Clinton Walker
Mike Johnson	Archie Weller
Steven Lang	Tim Winton
Gerard Lee	William Yang

Other great anthologies from Random House/Vintage

MEN LOVE SEX
Edited by Alan Close

The thing is, most men labour under the delusion that they are basically good when in fact we are basically bad, programmed for mischief and evil from our very first days. When a man understands this he comes to freedom. I came to freedom on Christmas Eve at the foot of a rumpled bed in a huge, decaying old Queenslander. It was explosively hot in that dark little bedroom and a young woman just lay in front of me, close enough to reach out and touch had I felt like it—which I didn't. She had drawn herself up into a tight foetal ball and I stood back with my hands in my pockets, regarding her long, shuddering sobs and cries with a sort of wry, empowered detachment. I loved her desperately, you understand, and it felt good to see her this way.

John Birmingham, 'When a Man Realises He's Bad'

Our faces were very close together—he could see the tears start out in my eyes and he hit me again harder. I looked at him. Into his grey eys. He seemed to be staring right into me. He hit me harder still, but with a slow processional rhythm which allowed me to see he was not so much out of control as leasing out his power, suggesting what might await me if I continued on with this lunacy—the lunacy of love. He paused, drawing his hand back. 'You—don't— love—me,' he whispered in my ear, and his voice was curved

517

and carved with whatever had happened to him during his life.

Peter Wells, 'His Eternal Boy'

He had nightmares and cried in his sleep. He dreamed he had made a silver stake and driven it through her heart. He dreamed and she cried and begged him not to, that he wept too, but that he did it anyway driven by steel wings of fear. He shrieked aloud in his sleep and caused the subject of his dreams to lie in silent terror in bed, staring into the blackness with wide open eyes.

Peter Carey, 'He Found Her in late Summer'

WOMEN LOVE SEX
Edited by Susan Johnson

He's twenty years younger than me, at the age when he's sure he'll never be as old as I am now. I knew that in him, his arrogance, right from the start. I knew I should keep my distance. But because he spent his days in my shed, because he always came to the shed door and stood smoking while I hung my washing on the line, because he always came up the back steps when he heard my kettle whistle, and because I agreed to pose for him naked, he began to spend the autumn nights in my bed. He needed a lot of coddling. But he knew that with his full young lips, his eyelashes still black right down to their tips so you seemed to slip helplessly into the pulling tide of his eyes, his body gleaming like water— all this meant that he'd get his coddling from a woman old enough to be his mother.

Sue Woolfe, 'The Invention of the Computer'

My husband's lover is a tall young thing with a penchant for velvet and ankle-strapped shoes. Her handwriting unravels into bold characters across lined paper. She uses too many adverbs. She draws circles across her i's instead of dotting them. The notepaper always smells salty, as if she's annointed it with her love juice.

Mandy Sayer, 'My Husband's Lover'

Marlo and Kosta have managed to get out of bed by night-fall and as they come up from the Metro onto the Paris streets, the smell of chestnuts hits them both. 'You notice it, too?' he asks, laughing at her, knowing. 'I thought I was the only one who thinks Paris smells like semen.'

Gabrielle Lord, 'Paris Scorpion'

At night wrapped in blankets, in the back of the truck we slept under a multitude of stars. I have stopped bleeding. I am dying for Chris to make love to me again. Parked above the beach at Port Augusta I search frantically through my port for my diaphragm but it's disappeared.

Dorothy Hewett, 'Nullarbor Honeymoon'

Other Contributors

Candida Baker	Lyn Hughes
Robin Barker	Jane Hyde
Helen Barnes	Susan Johnson
Carmel Bird	Caro Llewellyn
Gabrielle Carey	Gillian Mears
Joanne Carrol	Maurilia Meehan
Arlene Chai	Jane Messer
Cathy Coote	Sally Morrison
Francesca da Rimini	Penelope Rowe
Ann Dombrowski	Rosie Scott
Justine Ettler	Peta Spear
Marion Halligan	Kathleen Stewart
Chloe Hooper	Amy Witting